Frederick Forsyth is the author of nine bestselling novels, including *The Day of the Jackal*, *The Odessa File*, *The Dogs of War*, *The Devil's Alternative*, *The Fourth Protocol* and *The Deceiver*.

an
t n

n

Check o
renew o

http://birm

Like us o

**Pleas**

# AVENGER

A young American aid volunteer, Ricky Colenso, is brutally murdered in the former Yugoslavia. His grandfather, the Canadian billionaire Steven Edmond, is bent on revenge. The quest to find Ricky's murderer leads Edmond to Cal Dexter, ex-Vietnam Special Forces, the one man who could bring the killer to justice. But what starts as a personal, domestic tragedy soon explodes into a terrifying drama on the centre stage of world terrorism.

*Books by Frederick Forsyth*
*Published by The House of Ulverscroft:*

THE DAY OF THE JACKAL
THE DEVIL'S ALTERNATIVE
THE ODESSA FILE
THE DOGS OF WAR
THE FOURTH PROTOCOL
THE DECEIVER

# FREDERICK FORSYTH

---

# AVENGER

*Complete and Unabridged*

# CHARNWOOD
*Leicester*

First published in Great Britain in 2003 by
Bantam Press, a division of
Transworld Publishers
London

First Charnwood Edition
published 2004
by arrangement with
Transworld Publishers
a division of
The Random House Group Limited
London

British Library CIP Data

Forsyth, Frederick, *1938 –*
  Avenger.—Large print ed.—
  Charnwood library series
  1. Suspense fiction
  2. Large type books
  I. Title
  823.9'14 [F]

  ISBN 1–84395–369–2

Published by
F. A. Thorpe (Publishing)
Anstey, Leicestershire

Set by Words & Graphics Ltd.
Anstey, Leicestershire
Printed and bound in Great Britain by
T. J. International Ltd., Padstow, Cornwall

This book is printed on acid-free paper

For the Tunnel Rats
You guys did something
I could never force myself to do.

# PREFACE

## The Murder

It was on the seventh time they had pushed the American boy down into the liquid excrement of the cesspit that he failed to fight back, and died down there, every orifice filled with unspeakable filth.

When they had done, the men put down their poles, sat on the grass, laughed and smoked. Then they finished off the other aid worker and the six orphans, took the relief agency off-road and drove back across the mountain.

It was 15 May 1995.

# PART ONE

# 1

## The Hardhat

The man who ran alone leaned into the gradient and once again fought the enemy of his own pain. It was a torture and a therapy. That was why he did it.

Those who know often say that of all the disciplines the triathlon is the most brutal and unforgiving. The decathlete has more skills to master, and with putting the shot needs more brute strength, but for fearsome stamina and the capacity to meet the pain and beat it there are few trials like the triathlon.

The runner in the New Jersey sunrise had risen as always on his training days well before dawn. He drove his pickup to the far lake, dropping off his racing bicycle on the way, chaining it to a tree for safety. At two minutes after five, he set the chronometer on his wrist, pulled the sleeve of the neoprene wetsuit down to cover it and entered the icy water.

It was the Olympic triathlon that he practised, with distances measured in metric lengths. A 1500-metre swim, as near as dammit one mile; out of the water, strip fast to singlet and shorts, mount the racing bike. Then forty kilometres crouched over the handlebars, all of it at the sprint. He had long ago measured the mile along the lake from end to end, and knew exactly which tree on the far bank marked the spot he had left the bike. He had marked out his forty kilometres along the country roads, always at that empty hour, and knew which tree was the point to abandon the bike and start the run. Ten kilometres was the run and there was a farm gatepost that marked the two-clicks-to-go point. That morning he had just passed it. The last two kilometres were uphill, the final heartbreaker, the no-mercy stretch.

The reason it hurt so much is that the muscles needed are all different. The powerful shoulders, chest and arms of a swimmer are not normally needed by a speed cyclist or marathon man. They are just extra poundage that has to be carried.

The speed-blurred driving of the legs and hips of a cyclist are different from the tendons and sinews that give the runner the rhythm and cadence to eat up the miles underfoot. The repetitiveness of the rhythms of one exercise does not match those of the other. The triathlete needs them all, then tries to match the performances of three specialist athletes one after the other.

At the age of twenty-five it is a cruel event. At the age of fifty-one it ought to be indictable under the Geneva Convention. The runner had passed his fifty-first the previous January. He dared a glance at his wrist and scowled. Not good; he was several minutes down on his best. He drove harder against his enemy.

The Olympians are looking at just under two

6

hours; the New Jersey runner had clipped two and a half hours. He was almost at that time now, and still two Ks to go.

The first houses of his hometown came into view round a curve in Highway 30. The old, pre-Revolution village of Pennington straddles the Thirty, just off Interstate 95 running down from New York, through the state and on to Delaware, Pennsylvania and Washington. Inside the village the Highway is called Main Street.

There is not much to Pennington, one of a million neat, clean, tidy, neighbourly small towns that make up the overlooked and underestimated heart of the USA. A single major crossroads at the centre where West Delaware Avenue crosses Main Street, several well-attended churches of the three denominations, a First National Bank, a handful of shops, and off-the-street residences scattered down the tree-clothed byroads.

The runner headed for the crossroads, half a K to go. He was too early for a coffee at the Cup of Joe café, or breakfast at Vito's Pizza, but even had they been open he would not have stopped.

South of the junction he passed the Civil War vintage, white clapboard house with the shingle of Mr Calvin Dexter, attorney-at-law, next to the door. It was his office, his shingle and his law practice, save for the occasions when he took time off and went away to attend to his other practice. Clients and neighbours accepted that he took fishing vacations now and then, knowing nothing of the small apartment under another name in New York City.

He drove his aching legs that last five hundred

yards to reach the turning into Chesapeake Drive at the south end of town. That was where he lived and the corner marked the end of his self-imposed Calvary. He slowed, stopped and hung his head, leaning against a tree, sucking in oxygen to heaving lungs. Two hours, thirty-six minutes. Far from his best. That there was probably no one within a hundred miles who, aged fifty-one, could come near it was not the point. The point, as he could never dare to explain to the neighbours who grinned and cheered him on, was to use the pain to combat the other pain, the always pain, the pain that never went away, the pain of lost child, lost love, lost everything.

The runner turned into his street and walked the last two hundred yards. Ahead of him he saw the newspaper lad hurl a heavy bundle onto his porch. The kid waved as he cycled past and Cal Dexter waved back.

Later he would take his motor scooter and go to retrieve his truck. With the scooter in the rear, he would drive home, picking up the racing bike along the road. First he needed a shower, some high-energy bars and the contents of several oranges.

On the stoop he picked up the bundle of newspapers, broke them open and looked. As he expected, there was the local paper, another from Washington, from New York the big Sunday *Times* and, in a wrapper, a technical magazine.

Calvin Dexter, the wiry, sandy-haired, friendly, smiling attorney of Pennington, New Jersey, had not been born to be any such thing, though he

8

was indeed born in the state.

He was created in a Newark slum, rife with roaches and rats, and came into the world in January 1950, the son of a construction worker and a waitress at the local diner. His parents, according to the morality of the age, had had no choice but to marry when a meeting in a neighbourhood dance hall and a few glasses too much of bad hooch had led to things getting out of hand and his own conception. Early on, he knew nothing of this. Babies never know how or by whom they got here. They have to find out, sometimes the hard way.

His father was not a bad man, by his lights. After Pearl Harbor he had volunteered for the armed forces, but as a skilled construction worker he had been deemed more useful at home, where the war effort involved the creation of thousands of new factories, dockyards and government offices in the New Jersey area.

He was a hard man, quick with his fists, the only law on many blue-collar jobs. But he tried to live on the straight and narrow, bringing his wage packet home unopened, trying to raise his toddler son to love Old Glory, the Constitution and Joe DiMaggio.

But later, after the Korean War, the job opportunities slipped away. Only the industrial blight remained and the unions were in the grip of the Mob.

Calvin was five when his mother left. He was too young to understand why. He knew nothing of the loveless union his parents had had, accepting with the philosophical endurance of the very young that people always shouted and quarrelled that way. He knew nothing of the travelling salesman who had promised her bright lights and better frocks. He was simply told she had 'gone away'.

He had accepted that his father was now home each evening, looking after him instead of having a few beers after work, staring glumly at a foggy television screen. It was not until his teens that he learned his mother, abandoned in her turn by the travelling salesman, had tried to return, but had been rebuffed by the angry and bitter father.

When he was seven his father hit upon the idea to solve the problem of a home and the need to search for work far and wide. They moved out of the walk-up tenement in Newark and acquired a second-hand trailer home. This became his home for ten years.

Father and son moved from job to job, living in the trailer, the scruffy boy attending whichever local school would take him. It was the age of Elvis Presley, Del Shannon, Roy Orbison, the Beatles over from a country Cal had never heard of. It was the age of Kennedy, the Cold War and Vietnam.

The jobs came and the jobs were completed. They moved through the northern cities of East Orange, Union and Elizabeth; then on to work outside New Brunswick and Trenton. For a time they lived in the Pine Barrens while Dexter Senior was foreman on a small project. Then they headed south to Atlantic City. Between the ages of eight and sixteen Cal attended nine grade schools in as many years. His formal education could fill an entire postage stamp.

But he became wise in other ways: street-wise, fight-wise. Like his departed mother, he did not grow tall, topping out at five feet nine inches. Nor was he heavy and muscular like his father, but his lean frame packed fearsome stamina and his fists a killer punch. Once he challenged the booth fighter in a fairground sideshow, knocked him flat and took the twenty-dollar prize.

A man who smelt of cheap pomade approached his father and suggested the boy attend his gym with a view to becoming a boxer, but they moved on to a new city and a new job.

There was no question of money for vacations, so when school was out, the kid just came to the construction site with his father. There he made coffee, ran errands, did odd jobs. One of the 'errands' involved a man with a green eyeshade who told him there was a vacation job taking envelopes to various addresses across Atlantic City and saying nothing to anyone. Thus for the summer vacation of 1965 he became a bookie's runner.

Even from the bottom of the social pile, a smart kid can still look. Cal Dexter could sneak unpaying into the local movie house and marvel at the glamour of Hollywood, the huge rolling vistas of the Wild West, the shimmering glitz of the screen musicals, the crazy antics of the Martin and Lewis comedies.

He could still see in the television adverts smart apartments with stainless-steel kitchens, smiling families in which the parents seemed to love each other. He could look at the gleaming

11

limousines and sports cars on the billboards above the highway.

He had nothing against the hardhats of the construction sites. They were gruff and crude, but they were kind to him, or most of them anyway. On site he too wore a hard hat and the general presumption was that once out of school he would follow his father into the building trade. But he had other ideas. Whatever life he had, he vowed, it would be far from the crash of the trip-hammer and the choking dust of cement mixers.

Then he realized that he had nothing to offer in exchange for that better, more moneyed, more comfortable life. He thought of the movies, but presumed all film stars were towering men, unaware that most are well under five feet nine. This thought only came to him because some barmaid said she thought he looked a bit like James Dean, but the building workers roared with laughter, so he dropped the idea.

Sport and athletics could get a kid out of the street and on the road to fame and fortune, but he had been through all his schools so fast he had never had a chance to make any of the school teams.

Anything involving a formal education, let alone qualifications, was out of the question. That left other kinds of working-class employment: table-waiter, bellhop, greasemonkey in a garage, delivery-van driver; the list was endless but for all the prospects most of them offered he might as well stay with construction. The sheer brutalism and danger of the work made it better paid than most.

Or there was crime. No one raised on the waterfronts or construction camps of New Jersey could possibly be unaware that organized crime, running with the gangs, could lead to a life of big apartments, fast cars and easy women. The word was, it hardly ever led to jail. He was not Italian-American, which would preclude full membership of the Mob aristocracy, but there were Wasps who had made good.

He quit school at seventeen and started the next day at his father's worksite, a public works housing project outside Camden. A month later the driver/operator of the earthmover fell ill. There was no substitute. It was a skilled job. Cal looked at the interior of the cab. It made sense.

'I could work this,' he said. The foreman was dubious. It would be against all the rules. Any inspector chancing along and his job would be history. On the other hand, the whole team was standing around needing mountains of earth shifted.

'There's an awful lot of levers in there.'

'Trust me,' said the kid.

It took about twenty minutes to work out what lever did which function. He began to shift dirt. It meant a bonus, but it was still not a career.

In January 1968 he turned eighteen and the Viet Cong launched the Tet offensive. He was watching television in a bar in Camden. After the newscast came several commercials and then a brief recruitment film made by the army. It mentioned that, if you shaped up, the army

13

would give you an education. The next day he walked into the US Army office in Camden and said:

'I want to join the army.'

Back then every American youth would, failing some pretty unusual circumstances or voluntary exile, become liable for compulsory draft just after the eighteenth birthday. The desire of just about every teenager and twice that number of parents was to get out of it. The Master Sergeant behind the desk held out his hand for the draft card.

'I don't have one,' said Cal Dexter. 'I'm volunteering.' That caught their attention.

The MS drew a form towards him, keeping eye contact like a ferret that does not want the rabbit to get away.

'Well, that's fine, kid. That's a very smart thing to do. Take a word of advice from an old sweat?'

'Sure.'

'Make it three years instead of the required two. Good chance of better postings, better career choices.' He leaned forward as one imparting a state secret. 'With three years, you could even avoid going to Vietnam.'

'But I want to go to Vietnam,' said the kid in the soiled denim. The MS thought this one over.

'Right,' he said very slowly. He might have said, 'There's no accounting for taste.' Instead he said:

'Hold up your right hand . . . '

★ ★ ★

14

Thirty-three years later the former hardhat pushed four oranges through the juicer, rubbed the towel over his wet head again, and took the pile of papers with the juice through to the sitting room.

He went to the technical magazine first. *Vintage Airplane* is not a big-circulation organ and in Pennington it could only be obtained by placing a special order. It caters for those with a passion for classic and World War II aeroplanes. The runner flicked to the small ads section and studied the wanted notices. He stopped, the juice halfway to his mouth, put down the glass and read the item again. It said:

'AVENGER. Wanted. Serious offer. No price ceiling. Please call.'

There was no Grumman Avenger Pacific-war torpedo dive bomber out there to be bought. They were in museums. Someone had uncovered the contact code. There was a number. It had to be a cellphone. The date was 13 May 2001.

# 2

# The Victim

Ricky Colenso was not born to die at the age of twenty in a Bosnian cesspit. It should never have ended that way. He was born to get a college degree and live out his life in the States, with a wife and children and a decent chance at life, liberty and the pursuit of happiness. It went wrong because he was too kind-hearted.

Back in 1970 a young and brilliant mathematician called Adrian Colenso secured tenure as a Professor of Math at Georgetown University, just outside Washington. He was twenty-five, remarkably young for the post.

Three years later, he gave a summer seminar in Toronto, Canada. Among those who attended, even though she understood little of what he was saying, was a stunningly pretty student called Annie Edmond. She was smitten and arranged a blind date through close friends.

Adrian Colenso had never heard of her father, which both puzzled and delighted her. She had already been urgently pursued by half a dozen fortune hunters. In the car back to the hotel she discovered that apart from an amazing grasp of quantum calculus, he also kissed rather well.

A week later he flew back to Washington. Miss Edmond was not a young lady to be gainsaid.

16

She left her job, obtained a sinecure at the Canadian consulate, rented an apartment just off Wisconsin Avenue and arrived with ten suitcases. Two months later they married. The wedding was a blue-chip affair in Windsor, Ontario; and the couple honeymooned in Caneel Bay, US Virgin Islands.

As a present, the bride's father bought the couple a large country house on Foxhall Road, off Nebraska Avenue, in one of the most rustic and therefore sought-after areas of Georgetown. It was set in its own forested one-acre plot, with pool and tennis court. The bride's allowance would cover its upkeep and the groom's salary would just about do the rest. They settled down into loving domesticity.

Baby Richard Eric Steven was born in April 1975 and soon nicknamed Ricky.

He grew up like millions of other American youngsters in a secure and loving parental home, doing all the things that boys do, spending time at summer camps, discovering and exploring the thrills of girls and sports cars, worrying over academic grades and looming examinations.

He was neither brilliant like his father nor dumb. He inherited his father's quirky grin and his mother's good looks. Everyone who knew him rated him a nice kid. If someone asked him for help, he would do all he could. But he should never have gone to Bosnia.

He graduated out of high school in 1994 and was accepted for Harvard the following autumn. That winter, watching on television the sadism of ethnic cleansing and the aftermath of the

17

refugees' misery and the relief programmes in a far-away place called Bosnia, he determined that he wanted to help in some way.

His mother pleaded that he should stay in the States; there were relief programmes right at home if he wanted to exercise his social conscience. But the images he had seen of gutted villages, wailing orphans and the blank-eyed despair of the refugees had affected him deeply, and Bosnia it had to be. Ricky begged that he be allowed to get involved.

A few calls from his father established that the world agency was the United Nations High Commission for Refugees, with a big office in New York.

By early spring of 1995 three years of civil war as the old federation of Yugoslavia tore itself apart had gutted the province of Bosnia. The UNHCR was there in strength, with a staff of about 400 'internationals' and several thousand locally recruited staffers. The outfit was headed up on the spot by a former British soldier, the full-bearded and restlessly energetic Larry Hollingworth, whom Ricky had seen on television. Ricky went to New York to inquire about procedures for enlistment.

The New York office was kind but less than enthusiastic. Amateur offers came in by the sackload, and the personal visits were several dozen a day. This was the United Nations; there were procedures, six months of bureaucracy, enough filled-out forms to break the springs of a pickup, and, as Ricky would have to be in Harvard by autumn, probably refusal at the end.

The dejected young man was heading down again in the elevator at the start of the lunch hour when a middle-aged secretary gave him a kindly smile.

'If you really want to help in there, you'll have to get over to the regional office in Zagreb,' she said. 'They take people on locally. It's much more relaxed right on the spot.'

Croatia had also once been part of the disintegrating Yugoslavia, but it had secured its separation, was now a new state, and many organizations were based in the safety of its capital, Zagreb. One of them was the UNHCR.

Ricky had a long call with his parents, got their grudging permission, and flew New York — Vienna — Zagreb. But the reply was still the same: forms to fill, only long-term commitments were really sought. Summertime amateurs were a lot of responsibility, precious little contribution.

'You really should try one of the NGOs,' suggested the regional controller, trying to be helpful. 'They meet right next door at the café.'

The UNHCR might be the world body but that was far from the end of it. Disaster relief is an entire industry and for many a profession. Outside United Nations and individual government efforts come the Non-Governmental Organizations. There were over three hundred NGOs involved in Bosnia.

The names of no more than a dozen would ring a bell with the general public: Save the Children (British), Feed the Children (American), Age Concern, War on Want, Médecins Sans

19

Frontières — they were all there. Some were faith-based, some secular, and many of the smaller ones had simply come into being for the Bosnian civil war, impelled by TV images beamed endlessly into the West. At the extreme bottom end were single trucks driven across Europe by a couple of beefy lads who had had a whip-round in their local bar. The jumping-off point for the drive on the last leg into the heart of Bosnia was either Zagreb or the Adriatic port of Split.

Ricky found the café, ordered a coffee and a slivovitz against the bitter March wind outside and looked around for a possible contact. Two hours later a burly, bearded man, built like a trucker, walked in. He wore a plaid mackinaw and ordered coffee and cognac in a voice Ricky placed as coming from North or South Carolina. He went up and introduced himself. He had struck lucky.

John Slack was a dispatcher and distributor of relief aid for a small American charity called Loaves 'n' Fishes, a recently formed offshoot of Salvation Road, which itself was the corporate manifestation in a sinful world of the Rev. Billy Jones, television evangelist and saver of souls (for the appropriate donation) of the fine city of Charleston, South Carolina. He listened to Ricky as one who had heard it all before.

'You drive a truck, kid?'

'Yes.' It was not quite true but he reckoned a big off-road was like a small truck.

'You read a map?'

'Of course.'

'And you want a fat salary?'

'No. I have an allowance from my grandpa.'

John Slack twinkled.

'You don't want anything? Just to help?'

'That's right.'

'OK, you're on. Mine's a small operation. I go and buy relief food, clothes, blankets, whatever, right here on the spot, mainly in Austria. I truck-drive it down to Zagreb, refuel and then head into Bosnia. We're based at Travnik. Thousands of refugees down there.'

'That suits me fine,' said Ricky. 'I'll pay all my own costs.'

Slack threw back what remained of his cognac.

'Let's go, kid,' he said.

The truck was a ten-ton German Hanomag and Ricky got the hang of it before the border. It took them ten hours to Travnik, spelling each other at the wheel. It was midnight when they arrived at the Loaves 'n' Fishes compound just outside the town. Slack threw him several blankets.

'Spend the night in the cab,' he said. 'We'll find you a billet in the morning.'

The Loaves 'n' Fishes operation was indeed small. It involved a second truck about to leave for the north to collect more supplies with a monosyllabic Swede at the wheel, one small, shared compound wired with chain-link fencing to keep out pilferers, a tiny office made out of a workman's portable cabin, a shed called a warehouse for unloaded but not yet distributed food aid, and three locally recruited Bosnian staffers. Plus two new black Toyota Landcruisers for small-cargo aid distribution. Slack introduced him all round and by afternoon Ricky had found lodging with a Bosnian widow in the town. To get to and from the compound he bought a ramshackle bicycle from the stash he kept in a money belt round his waist. John Slack noticed the belt.

'Mind telling me how much you keep in that pouch?' he asked.

'I brought a thousand dollars,' said Ricky trustingly. 'Just in case of emergencies.'

'Shit. Just don't wave it around or you'll create one. These guys can retire for life on that.'

Ricky promised to be discreet. Postal services, he soon discovered, were non-existent, inasmuch as no Bosnian state existed so no Bosnian Post Office had come into being and the old Yugoslav services had collapsed. John Slack told him any driver running up to Croatia or on to Austria would post letters and cards for everyone. Ricky wrote a quick card from the bundle he had bought in Vienna airport and thrown into his haversack. This the Swede took north. Mrs Colenso received it a week later.

Travnik had once been a thriving market town, inhabited by Serbs, Croats and Bosnian Muslims. Their presence could be discerned by the churches. There was a Catholic one for the departed Croats, an Orthodox one for the also departed Serbs, and a dozen mosques for the majority Muslims, the ones still called Bosnians.

With the coming of the civil war the tri-ethnic community which had lived in harmony for years was shattered. As pogrom after pogrom was reported across the land, all inter-ethnic trust evaporated.

The Serbs quit and retreated north of the Vlasic mountain range that dominates Travnik, across the Lasva river valley and into Banja Luka on the other side.

The Croats were also forced out and most went down the road ten miles to Vitez. Thus three single-ethnic strongholds were formed. Into each poured the refugees of that particular ethnic group.

In the world media the Serbs were portrayed as the perpetrators of all the pogroms, though they had also seen Serb communities butchered when isolated and in the minority. The reason was that in the old Yugoslavia the Serbs had had the dominant control of the army; when the country fell apart, they simply grabbed 90 per cent of the heavy weaponry, giving them an insuperable edge.

The Croats, also no slouches when it came to slaughtering non-Croat minorities in their midst, had been granted irresponsibly premature recognition by the German Chancellor Kohl; they could then buy weapons on the world market.

The Bosnians were largely unarmed, and kept that way on the advice of European politicians. As a result, they suffered most of the brutalities. In late spring 1995 it would be the Americans who, sick and tired of standing by and doing nothing, would use their military power to give the Serbs a bloody nose and force all parties to the conference table at Dayton, Ohio. The

Dayton Agreement would be implemented that coming November. Ricky Colenso would not see it.

By the time Ricky reached Travnik, it had stopped a lot of shells from Serb positions across the mountains. Most of the buildings were shrouded with planks leaning against the walls. If hit by an 'incomer' they would be splintered to matchwood, but save the house itself. Most windows were missing and were replaced by plastic sheeting. The brightly painted main mosque had somehow been spared a direct hit. The two largest buildings in town, the gymnasium (high school) and the once famous Music School, were stuffed with refugees.

With virtually no access to the surrounding countryside and thus no access to growing crops, the refugees, about three times the original population, were dependent on the aid agencies to survive. That was where Loaves 'n' Fishes came in, along with a dozen other smaller NGOs in the town.

But the two Landcruisers could be piled up with five hundred pounds of relief aid and still make it to various outlying villages and hamlets where the need was even greater than in Travnik centre. Ricky happily agreed to back-haul the sacks of food and drive the off-roads into the mountains to the south.

Four months after he had sat in Georgetown and seen on the television screen the images of human misery that had brought him here, he was happy. He was doing what he came to do. He was touched by the gratitude of the gnarled peasants and their brown, saucer-eyed children when he hauled sacks of wheat, maize, milk powder and soup concentrates into the centre of an isolated village that had not eaten for a week.

He believed he was paying back in some way for all the benefits and comforts that a benign God, in whom he firmly believed, had bestowed upon him at his birth simply by creating him an American.

He spoke not a word of Serbo-Croat, the common language of all Yugoslavia, nor the Bosnian patois. He had no idea of the local geography, where the mountain roads led, where was safe and where could be dangerous.

John Slack paired him with one of the local Bosnian staffers, a young man with reasonable, school-learned English, called Fadil Sulejman, who acted as his guide, interpreter and navigator.

Each week through April and the first fortnight of May he despatched either a letter or card to his parents, and with greater or lesser delays, depending on who was heading north for re-supplies, they arrived in Georgetown bearing Croatian or Austrian stamps.

It was in the second week of May that Ricky found himself alone and in charge of the entire depot. Lars, the Swede, had had a major engine breakdown on a lonely mountain road in Croatia, north of the border but short of Zagreb. John Slack had taken one of the Landcruisers to help him out and get the truck back into service.

Fadil Sulejman asked Ricky for a favour.

Like thousands in Travnik, Fadil had been

25

forced to flee his home when the tide of war swept towards it. He explained that his family home had been a farm or smallholding in an upland valley on the slopes of the Vlasic range. He was desperate to know if there was anything left of it. Had it been torched or spared? Was it still standing? When the war began, his father had buried family treasures under a barn. Were they still there? In a word, could he visit his parental home for the first time in three years?

Ricky happily gave him time off but that was not the real point. With the tracks up the mountain slick with spring rain, only an off-road would make it. That meant borrowing the Landcruiser.

Ricky was in a quandary. He wanted to help, and he would pay for the petrol. But was the mountain safe? Serbian patrols had once ranged over it, using their artillery to pound Travnik below.

That was a year ago, Fadil insisted. The southern slopes, where his parents' farmhouse was situated, were quite safe now. Ricky hesitated, and moved by Fadil's pleading, wondering what it must be like to lose your home, he agreed. With one proviso: he would come too.

In fact, in the spring sunshine, it was a very pleasant drive. They left the town behind and went up the main road towards Donji Vakuf for ten miles before turning off to the right.

The road climbed, degenerated into a track, and went on climbing. Beech, ash and oak in their spring leaf enveloped them. It was, thought

Ricky, almost like the Shenandoah where he had once gone camping with a school party. They began to skid on the corners and he admitted they would never have made it without four-wheel drive.

The oak gave way to conifers and at five thousand feet they emerged into an upland valley, invisible from the road far below, a sort of secret hideaway. In the heart of the valley, they found the farmhouse. Its stone smokestack survived, but the rest had been torched and gutted. Several sagging barns, unfired, still stood beyond the old cattle pens. Ricky glanced at Fadil's face and said:

'I am so sorry.'

They dismounted by the blackened firestack and Ricky waited as Fadil walked through the wet ashes, kicking here and there at what was left of the place he was raised in. Ricky followed him as he walked past the cattle pen and the cesspit, still brimming with its nauseous contents, swollen by the rains, to the barns where his father might have buried the family treasures to save them from marauders. That was when they heard the rustle and the whimper.

The two men found them under a wet and smelly tarpaulin. There were six of them, small, cringing, terrified, aged about ten down to four. Four little boys and two girls, the oldest apparently the surrogate mother and leader of the group. Seeing the two men staring at them, they were frozen with fear. Fadil began to talk softly. After a while the girl replied.

'They come from Gorica, a small hamlet

about four miles from here along the mountain. It means 'small hill'. I used to know it.'

'What happened?'

Fadil talked some more in the local lingo. The girl answered, then burst into tears.

'Men came, Serbs, paramilitaries.'

'When?'

'Last night.'

'What happened?'

Fadil sighed.

'It was a very small hamlet. Four families, twenty adults, maybe twelve children. Gone now, all dead. Their parents shouted that they should run away, when the firing started. They escaped in the darkness.'

'Orphans? All of them?'

'All of them.'

'Dear God, what a country. We must get them into the truck, down to the valley,' said the American.

They led the children, each clinging to the hand of the next eldest up the chain, out of the barn into the bright spring sunshine. Birds sang. It was a beautiful valley.

At the edge of the trees they saw the men. There were ten of them and two Russian GAZ jeeps in army camouflage. The men were also in camo. And heavily armed.

★ ★ ★

Three weeks later, scouring the mailbox but facing yet another day with no card, Mrs Annie Colenso rang a number in Windsor, Ontario. It

28

answered at the second ring. She recognized the voice of her father's private secretary.

'Hi, Jean. It's Annie. Is my dad there?'

'He surely is, Mrs Colenso. I'll put you right through.'

# 3

# The Magnate

There were ten young pilots in 'A' flight crew
hut and another eight next door in 'B' Flight.
Outside on the bright green grass of the airfield
two or three Hurricanes crouched with that
distinctive hunch-backed look caused by the
bulge behind the cockpit. They were not new
and fabric patches revealed where they had taken
combat wounds high above France over the
previous fortnight.

Inside the huts the mood could not have been
in greater contrast to the warm summer
sunshine of 25 June 1940 at Coltishall field,
Norfolk, England. The mood of the men of No.
242 Squadron, Royal Air Force, known simply as
the Canadian squadron, was about as low as it
had ever been, and with good cause.

Two Four Two had been in combat almost
since the first shot was fired on the Western
Front. They had fought the losing battle for
France from the eastern border back to the
Channel coast. As Hitler's great blitzkrieg
machine rolled on, flicking the French army to
one side, the pilots trying to stem the flood
would find their bases evacuated and moved
further back even while they were airborne. They
had to scavenge for food, lodgings, spare parts

30

and fuel. Anyone who has ever been part of a retreating army will know the overriding adjective is 'chaotic'.

Back across the Channel in England, they had fought the second battle above the sands of Dunkirk as beneath them the British army sought to save what it could from the rout, grabbing anything that would float to paddle back to England, whose white cliffs were enticingly visible across the flat calm sea.

By the time the last Tommy was evacuated from that awful beach and the last defenders of the perimeter passed into German captivity for five years, the Canadians were exhausted. They had taken a terrible beating: nine killed, three wounded, three shot down and taken prisoner.

Three weeks later they were still grounded at Coltishall, without spares or tools, all abandoned in France. Their CO, Squadron Leader 'Papa' Gobiel, was ill, had been for weeks, and would not return to command. Still, the Brits had promised them a new commander, who was expected any time.

A small open-topped sports car emerged from between the hangars and parked near the two timber crew huts. A man climbed out, with some difficulty. No one came out to greet him. He stumped awkwardly towards 'A' Flight. A few minutes later he was out of there and heading for 'B' hut. The Canadian pilots watched him through the windows, puzzled by the rolling walk with feet apart. The door opened and he appeared in the aperture. His shoulders revealed his rank of squadron leader. No one stood up.

'Who's in charge here?' he demanded angrily.

A chunky Canuck hauled himself upright, a few feet from where Steve Edmond sprawled in a chair and surveyed the newcomer through a blue haze.

'I guess I am,' said Stan Turner. It was early days. Stan Turner already had two confirmed kills to his credit but would go on to score a total of fourteen and a hatful of medals.

The British officer with the angry blue eyes turned on his heel and lurched away towards a parked Hurricane. The Canadians drifted out of their huts to observe.

'I do not believe what I am watching,' muttered Johnny Latta to Steve Edmond. 'The bastards have sent us a CO with no bloody legs.'

It was true. The newcomer was stumping around on two prosthetics. He hauled himself into the cockpit of the Hurricane, punched the Rolls Royce Merlin engine into life, turned into the wind and took off. For half an hour he threw the fighter into every known aerobatic manoeuvre in the text-book and a few that were not yet there.

He was good in part because he had been an aerobatic ace before losing both legs in a crash long before the war, and in part just because he had no legs. When a fighter pilot makes a tight turn or pulls out of a power dive, both ploys being vital in air combat, he pulls heavy G-forces on his own body. The effect is to drive blood from the upper body downwards, until blackout occurs. Because this pilot had no legs, the blood had to stay in the upper body, nearer the brain, and his squadron would learn that he could pull tighter turns than they could. Eventually he landed the Hurricane, climbed out and stumped towards the silent Canucks.

'My name is Douglas Bader,' he told them, 'and we are going to become the best bloody squadron in the whole bloody Air Force.'

He was as good as his word. With the Battle of France lost and the battle of the Dunkirk beaches a damn close-run thing, the big one was coming: Hitler had been promised by his air-force chief Goering mastery of the skies to enable the invasion of Britain to succeed. The Battle of Britain was the struggle for those skies. By the time it was over, the Canadians of 242, always led into combat by their legless CO, had established the best kill-to-loss ratio of all.

By late autumn, the German Luftwaffe had had enough and withdrew back into France. Hitler snapped his anger at Goering and turned his attention east to Russia.

In three battles, France, Dunkirk and Britain, spread over only six months of the summer of '40, the Canadians had racked up eighty-eight confirmed kills, sixty-seven in the Battle of Britain alone. But they had lost seventeen pilots, the KIAs (killed in action), and all but three were Canucks.

Fifty-five years later Steve Edmond rose from his office desk and crossed once again, as he had done so many times down the years, to the photo on the wall. It did not contain all the men he had flown with; some had been dead before others arrived. But it showed the seventeen Canadians

33

at Duxford one hot and cloudless day in late August at the height of the battle.

Almost all gone. Most of them KIA during the war. The faces of boys from nineteen to twenty-two stared out, vital, cheerful, expectant, on the threshold of life, yet mostly never destined to see it.

He peered closer. Benzie, flying on his wingtip, shot down and killed over the Thames estuary on 7 September, two weeks after the photo. Solanders, the boy from Newfoundland, dead the next day.

Johnny Latta and Willie McKnight, standing side by side, would die wingtip to wingtip somewhere over the Bay of Biscay in January 1941.

'You were the best of us all, Willie,' murmured the old man. McKnight was the first ace and double ace, the 'natural': nine confirmed kills in his first seventeen days of combat, twenty-one air victories when he died, ten months after his first mission, aged just twenty-one.

Steve Edmond had survived to become fairly old and extremely rich, certainly the biggest mining magnate in Ontario. But all through the years he had kept the photo on the wall, when he lived in a shack with a pick for company, when he made his first million dollars, when (especially when) *Forbes* magazine pronounced him a billionaire.

He kept it to remind him of the terrible fragility of that thing we call life. Often, looking back, he wondered how he survived. Shot down the first time, he had been in hospital when 242

34

Squadron left in December 1941 for the Far East. When he was fit again, he was posted to Training Command.

Chafing at the bit, bombarding higher authority with requests to fly combat again, he had finally been granted his wish in time for the Normandy landings, flying the new Typhoon ground-attack fighter-bomber, very fast and very powerful, a fearsome tank-killer.

The second time he was shot down was near Remagen as the Americans stormed across the Rhine. He was among a dozen British Typhoons giving them cover in the advance. A direct hit in the engine gave him a few seconds to gain height, lose the canopy and throw himself out of the doomed aeroplane before it blew up.

The jump was low and the landing hard, breaking both legs. He lay in a daze of pain in the snow, dimly aware of round steel helmets running towards him, more keenly aware that the Germans had a particular loathing of Typhoons and the people he had been blowing apart were an SS-Panzer division, not known for their tolerance.

A muffled figure stopped and stared down at him. A voice said, 'Well lookee here.' He let out his pent breath in relief. Few of Adolf's finest spoke with a Mississippi drawl.

The Americans got him back across the Rhine dazed with morphine and he was flown home to England. When the legs were properly set, he was judged to be blocking up a bed needed for fresh incomers from the front, so he was sent to a convalescent home on the South Coast, there to hobble around until repatriation to Canada.

He enjoyed Dilbury Manor, a rambling Tudor pile steeped in history, with lawns like the green baize of a pool table and some pretty nurses. He was twenty-five that spring and carried the rank of Wing Commander.

Rooms were allocated at one per two officers, but it was a week before his room-mate arrived. He was about the same age, American, and wore no uniform. His left arm and shoulder had been smashed up in a gunfight in Northern Italy. That meant covert ops, behind enemy lines. Special Forces.

'Hi,' said the newcomer, 'Peter Lucas. You play chess?'

Steve Edmond had come out of the harsh mining camps of Ontario, joining the Royal Canadian Airforce in 1938 to escape the unemployment of the mining industry when the world had no use for its nickel. Later that nickel would be part of every aero-engine that kept him aloft. Lucas had come from the New England top social drawer, endowed with everything from the day of his birth.

The two young men were sitting on the lawn with a chess table between them when the radio through the refectory hall window, speaking in the impossibly posh accent of the BBC newsreaders in those days, announced that Field Marshal von Rundstedt had just signed on Luneberg Heath the instruments of unconditional surrender. The 8th of May, 1945.

The war in Europe was over. The American and Canadian sat and remembered all the friends who would never go home, and each would later recall it was the last time he cried in public.

A week later they parted and returned to their respective countries. But they formed a friendship in that convalescent home by the English coast that would last for life.

It was a different Canada when Steve Edmond came home, and he was a different man, a decorated war hero returning to a booming economy. It was from the Sudbury Basin that he came. And to the Basin that he went back. His father had been a miner and his grandfather before that. The Canadians had been mining copper and nickel around Sudbury since 1885. And the Edmonds had been part of the action for most of that time.

Steve Edmond found he was owed a fat wedge of pay by the air force and used it to put himself through college, the first of his family to do so. Not unnaturally he took mineral engineering as his discipline and threw a course in metallurgy into the pot as well. He majored in both near the top of his class in 1948 and was snapped up by INCO, the International Nickel Company and principal employer in the Basin.

Formed in 1902, INCO had helped make Canada the primary supplier of nickel to the world, and the company's core was the huge deposit outside Sudbury, Ontario. Edmond joined as a trainee mine-manager.

Steve Edmond would have remained a mine-manager living in a comfortable but run-of-the-mill framehouse in a Sudbury suburb

37

but for the restless mind that was always telling him there must be a better way.

College had taught him that the basic ore of nickel, which is pentlandite, is also a host to other elements; platinum, palladium, iridium, ruthenium, rhodium, tellurium, selenium, cobalt, silver and gold also occur in pentlandite. Edmond began to study the rare earth metals, their uses and the possible market for them. No one else bothered. This was because the percentages were so small their extraction was uneconomical, so they ended up in the slagheaps. Very few knew what rare earth metals were.

Almost all great fortunes are based upon one cracking good idea and the guts to go with it. Hard work and luck also help. Steve Edmond's cracking idea was to go back to the laboratory when the other young mine-managers were helping with the barley harvest by drinking it. What he came up with was a process known now as 'pressure acid leaching'.

Basically, it involved dissolving the tiny deposits of rare metals out of the slag, then reconstituting them back to metal.

Had he taken this to INCO, he would have been given a pat on the back, maybe even a slap-up dinner. Instead, he resigned his post and took a third-class train seat to Toronto and the Bureau of Patents. He was thirty and on his way.

He borrowed, of course, but not too much, because what he had his eye on did not cost much. When every excavation of pentlandite ore became exhausted, or at least exploited until it became uneconomical to go on, the mining companies left behind huge slagheaps called 'tailing dams'. The tailings were the rubbish, no one wanted them. Steve Edmond did. He bought them for cents.

He founded Edmond Metals, known on the Toronto Exchange simply as Emmys, and the price went up. He never sold out, despite the blandishments, never took the gambles proposed to him by banks and financial advisors. That way he avoided the hypes, the bubbles and the crashes. By forty he was a multi-millionaire and by sixty-five, in 1985, he had the elusive mantle of billionaire.

He did not flaunt it, never forgot where he came from, gave much to charity, avoided politics while remaining affable to them all, and was known as a good family man.

Over the years there were indeed a few fools who, taking the mild-mannered exterior for the whole man, sought to cheat, lie or steal. They discovered, often too late from their point of view, that there was as much steel in Steve Edmond as in any aero-engine he had ever sat behind.

He married once, in 1949, just before his big discovery. He and Fay were a love match and it stayed that way until motor neuron disease took her away in 1994. There was one child, their daughter Annie, born in 1950.

In his old age, Steve Edmond doted on her as always, approved mightily of Professor Adrian Colenso, the Georgetown University academic she had married at twenty-two, and loved to bits his only grandson Ricky, then aged twenty, away somewhere in Europe before starting college.

Most of the time Steve Edmond was a contented man with every right to be so, but there were days when he felt tetchy, ill at ease. Then he would cross the floor of his penthouse office suite high above the city of Windsor, Ontario, and stare again at the young faces in the photo. Faces from far away and long ago.

The internal phone rang. He walked back to his desk.

'Yes, Jean.'

'It's Mrs Colenso on the line from Virginia.'

'Fine. Put her through.' He leaned back in the padded swivel chair as the connection was made. 'Hi, darling. How are you?'

The smile dropped from his face as he listened. He came forward in the chair until he was leaning on the desk.

'What do you mean 'missing'? . . . Have you tried phoning? . . . Bosnia? No lines . . . Annie, you know kids nowadays don't write . . . maybe it's stuck in the mail over there . . . yes, I accept he promised faithfully . . . all right, leave it to me. Who was he working for?'

He took a pen and pad and wrote what she dictated.

'Loaves 'n' Fishes. That's its name? It's a relief agency? Food for refugees. Fine, then it'll be listed. They have to be. Leave it to me, honey. Yes, as soon as I have anything.'

When he put the phone down he thought for a moment, then called his chief executive officer.

'Among all those young Turks you employ, do

40

you have anyone who understands researching on the internet?' he asked. The executive was stunned.

'Of course. Scores.'

'I want the name and private number of the chief of an American charity called Loaves 'n' Fishes. No, just that. And I need it fast.'

He had it in ten minutes. An hour later he came off a long call with a gleaming building in Charleston, South Carolina, headquarters of one of those television evangelists, the sort he despised, raking in huge donations from the gullible against guarantees of salvation.

Loaves 'n' Fishes was the pompadoured saviour's charity arm which appealed for funds for the pitiful refugees of Bosnia, then gripped by a vicious civil war. How much of the donated dollars went to the wretched and how much to the reverend's fleet of limousines was anyone's guess. But if Ricky Colenso had been working as a volunteer for Loaves 'n' Fishes in Bosnia, the voice from Charleston informed him, he would have been at their distribution centre at a place called Travnik.

'Jean, do you remember a couple of years back a man in Toronto lost a couple of old masters in a burglary at his country home? It was in the papers. Then they reappeared. Someone at the club said he used a very discreet agency to track them down and get them back. I need his name. Call me back.'

This was definitely not on the internet, but there were other nets. Jean Searle, his private secretary of many years, used the secretaries' net, and one of her friends was secretary to the Chief of Police.

'Rubinstein? Fine. Get me Mr Rubinstein in Toronto or wherever.'

That took half an hour. The art collector was found visiting the Rijksmuseum in Amsterdam to stare, once again, at Rembrandt's *Night Watch*. He was taken from his dinner table, given the six-hour time difference. But he was helpful.

'Jean,' said Steve Edmond when he had finished, 'call the airport. Get the Grumman ready. Now. I want to go to London. No, the English one. By sunrise.'

It was 10 June 1995.

# 4

# The Soldier

Cal Dexter had hardly finished taking the oath of allegiance when he was on his way to boot camp for basic training. He did not have far to go; Fort Dix is right there in New Jersey.

In the spring of 1968 tens of thousands of young Americans were pouring into the army, 95 per cent of them unwilling draftees. The drill sergeants could not have cared less. Their job was to turn this mass of shorn-to-the-skull young male humanity into something resembling soldiers before passing them on, just three months later, to their next posting.

Where they came from, who their fathers were, what their level of education was, were all of glorious irrelevance. Boot camp was the greatest leveller of them all, barring death. That would come later. For some.

Dexter was a natural rebel, but he was also more street-wise than most. The chow was basic but it was better than he had had on many construction sites, so he wolfed it down.

Unlike the rich boys, he had no problem with dormitory sleeping, open-doored ablutions or the requirement to keep all his kit very, very neatly in one small locker. Most useful of all, he had never had anyone clear up after him, so he expected nothing of the sort in camp. Some others, accustomed to being waited upon, spent a lot of time jogging around the parade square or doing press-ups under the eye of a displeased sergeant.

That said, Dexter could see no point in most of the rules and rituals, but was smart enough not to say so. And he absolutely could not see why sergeants were always right and he was always wrong.

The benefit of signing on voluntarily for three years became plain very quickly. The corporals and sergeants, who were the nearest thing to God in basic training camp, learned of his status without delay and eased up on him. He was, after all, close to being 'one of them'. Mama-spoiled rich boys had it worst.

Two weeks in, he had his first assessment panel. That involved appearing before one of those almost invisible creatures, an officer. In this case, a major. 'Any special skills?' asked the major for what was probably the ten thousandth time.

'I can drive bulldozers, sir,' said Dexter.

The major studied his forms and looked up.

'When was this?'

'Last year, sir. Between leaving school and signing on.'

'Your papers say you are just eighteen. That must have been when you were seventeen.'

'Yes, sir.'

'That's illegal.'

'Lordy, sir, I'm sorry about that. I had no idea.'

Beside him he could feel the ramrod-stiff corporal trying to keep a straight face. But the major's problem was solved.

'I guess it's engineering for you, soldier. Any objections?'

'No, sir.'

Very few said goodbye at Fort Dix with tears in their eyes. Boot camp is not a vacation. But they did come out, most of them, with a straight back, square shoulders, a buzzcut head, the uniform of a private soldier, a kitbag and a travel pass to their next posting. In Dexter's case it was Fort Leonard Wood, Missouri, for Advanced Individual Training.

That was basic engineering; not just driving a bulldozer, but driving anything with wheels or tracks, engine repair and vehicle maintenance and, had there been time, fifty other courses besides. Another three months later, he achieved his Military Operational Skill certificate and was posted to Fort Knox, Kentucky.

Most of the world only knows Fort Knox as the US Federal Reserve's gold depository, fantasy Mecca of every daydreaming bank robber and subject of numerous books and films.

But it is also a huge army base and home of the Armour school. On any base that size there is always some building going on, or tank pits to be dug, or a ditch to be filled in. Cal Dexter spent six months as one of the Post Engineers at Fort Knox before being summoned to the Command office.

He had just celebrated his nineteenth birthday; he carried the rank of Private First

45

Class. The commanding officer looked grim, as one about to impart bereavement. Cal thought something might have happened to his father.

'It's Vietnam,' said the major.

'Great,' said the PFC. The major, who would happily spend the rest of his career in his anonymous marital home on the base in Kentucky, blinked several times.

'Well, that's all right then,' he said.

A fortnight later Cal Dexter packed his kitbag, said goodbye to the mates he had made on the post and boarded the bus sent to pick up a dozen transferees. A week later he walked down the ramp of a C5 Galaxy and into the sweltering, sticky heat of Saigon Airport, military side.

Coming out of the airport, he was riding up front with the bus driver. 'What do you do?' asked the corporal as he swung the troop bus between the hangars.

'Drive bulldozers,' said Dexter.

'Well, I guess you'll be a REMF like the rest of us round here.'

'REMF?' queried Dexter. He had never heard the word before.

'Rear Echelon Mother F****r,' supplied the corporal.

Dexter was getting his first taste of the Vietnam status ladder. Nine-tenths of GIs who went to Vietnam never saw a Vietcong, never fired a shot in anger, and rarely even heard one fired. The 50,000 names of the dead on the Memorial Wall by the Reflecting Pool in Washington, with few exceptions, come from the other ten per cent. Even with a second army of Vietnamese cooks, launderers and bottle-washers, it still took nine GIs in the rear to keep one out in the jungle trying to win the war.

'Where's your posting?' asked the corporal.

'First Engineer Battalion, Big Red One.'

The driver gave a squeak like a disturbed fruit bat.

'Sorreee,' he said. 'Spoke too soon. That's Lai Khe. Edge of the Iron Triangle. Rather you than me, buddy.'

'It's bad?'

'Dante's vision of hell, pal.'

Dexter had never heard of Dante and presumed he was in a different unit. He shrugged.

There was indeed a road from Saigon to Lai Khe; it was Highway 13 via Phu Cuong, up the eastern edge of the Triangle to Ben Cat and then on another fifteen miles. But it was unwise to take it unless there was an armoured escort, and even then never at night. This was all heavily forested country and teemed with Vietcong ambushes. When Cal Dexter arrived inside the huge defended perimeter that housed the 1st Infantry Division, the Big Red One, it was by helicopter. Throwing his kitbag once again over his shoulder, he asked directions for the HQ of the 1st Engineer Battalion.

On the way he passed the vehicle park and saw something that took his breath away. Accosting a passing GI he asked:

'What the hell is that?'

'Hogjaw,' said the soldier laconically. 'For ground clearing.'

Along with the 25th 'Tropic Lightning' Infantry Division out of Hawaii, the Big Red One tried to cope with what purported to be the most dangerous area of the whole peninsula, the Iron Triangle. So thick was the vegetation, so impenetrable for the invader and such a protective labyrinth for the guerrilla, that the only way to try to level the playing field was to clear the jungle.

To do this, two awesome machines had been developed. One was the tankdozer, an M-48 medium tank with a bulldozer blade fitted up front. With the blade down, the tank did the pushing while the armoured turret protected the crew inside. But much bigger was the Rome Plow or hogjaw.

This was a terrible brute if you happened to be a shrub or a tree or a rock. A sixty-ton tracked vehicle, the D7E, it was fitted with a specially forged, curving blade whose protruding, hardened-steel lower edge could splinter a tree with a three-foot trunk.

The solitary driver/operator sat in his cabin way up top, protected by a 'headache bar' above him to stop falling debris from crushing him dead, and with an armoured cab to fend off sniper bullets or guerrilla attack.

The 'Rome' in the name had nothing to do with the capital of Italy, but with Rome, Georgia, where the brute was made. And the point of the Rome Plow was to make any piece of territory that had received its undivided attention unusable as a sanctuary for Vietcong ever again.

Dexter walked to the battalion office, threw up

48

a salute and introduced himself. 'Morning, sir. PFC Calvin Dexter reporting for duty, sir. I'm your new hogjaw operator. Sir.'

The lieutenant behind the desk sighed wearily. He was nearing the end of his one-year tour. He had flatly refused to extend. He loathed the country, the invisible but lethal Vietcong, the heat, the damp, the mosquitoes and the fact that once again he had a prickly heat rash enveloping his private parts and rear end. The last thing he needed with the temperature nudging ninety was a joker.

But Cal Dexter was a tenacious young man. He badgered and pestered. Two weeks after arriving on post he had his Rome Plow. The first time he took it out, a more experienced driver tried to offer him some advice. He listened, climbed high into the cab, and drove it on a combined operation with infantry support all day. He handled the towering machine his way, differently, and better.

He was watched with increasing frequency by a lieutenant, also an engineer, but one who seemed to have no duties to detain him; a quiet young man who said little but observed much.

'He's tough,' said the officer to himself a week later. 'He's cocky, he's a loner and he's talented. Let's see if he chickens out easily.'

There was no reason for the big machine-gunner to hassle the much smaller plow-driver, but he just did. The third time he messed with the PFC from New Jersey, it came to blows. But not out in the open. Against the rules. But there was a patch of open ground behind the mess hall. It was agreed they would sort out their differences, bare knuckles, after dark.

They met by the light of headlamps, with a hundred fellow soldiers in a circle, taking bets mostly against the smaller man. The general presumption was that they would witness a repeat of the slugging match between George Kennedy and Paul Newman in *Cool Hand Luke*. They were wrong.

No one mentioned Queensberry Rules so the smaller man walked straight up to the gunner, slipped beneath the first head-removing swing and kicked him hard under the kneecap. Circling his one-legged opponent, the 'dozer driver landed two kidney punches and a knee in the groin.

When the big man's head came down to his level he drove the middle knuckle of his right hand into the left temple, and for the gunner, the lights went out.

'You don't fight fair,' said the stakeholder when Dexter held out his hand for his winnings.

'No, and I don't lose either,' he said. Out beyond the ring of lights the officer nodded at the two MPs with him, and they moved in to make their arrest. Later the limping gunner got his promised twenty dollars.

Thirty days in the cooler was the penalty, the more so as he declined to name his opponent. He slept perfectly well on the unpadded slab in the cell and was still asleep when someone started running a metal spoon up and down the bars. It was dawn.

'On your feet, soldier,' said a voice. Dexter

came awake, slid off the slab and stood to attention. The man had a lieutenant's single silver bar on his collar. 'Thirty days in here is really boring,' said the officer.

'I'll survive, sir,' said the ex-PFC, now busted back to private.

'Or you could walk now.'

'I think there has to be a catch to that, sir.'

'Oh, there is. You leave behind the big, jerk-off toys and come and join my outfit. Then we find out if you're as tough as you think you are.'

'And your outfit, sir?'

'They call me Rat Six. Shall we go?'

The officer signed the prisoner out and they adjourned for breakfast to the smallest and most exclusive mess hall in the whole 1st Division. No one was allowed in without permission and there were at that time only fourteen members. Dexter made fifteen, but the number would go down to thirteen in a week when two more were killed.

There was a weird emblem on the door of the 'hootch', as they called their tiny club. It showed an upright rodent with snarling face, phallic tongue, a pistol in one hand and a bottle of liquor in the other. Dexter had joined the Tunnel Rats.

For six years, in a constantly shifting sequence of men, the Tunnel Rats did the dirtiest, deadliest and by far the scariest job in the Vietnam War, yet so secret were their doings and so few their number that most people today, even Americans, have hardly or never heard of them.

There were probably not more than 350 over

51

the period: a small unit among the engineers of the Big Red One, an equal unit drawn from the Tropic Lightning (25th) Division. A hundred never came home at all. About a further hundred were dragged, screaming, nerves gone, from their combat zone and consigned to trauma therapy, never to fight again. The rest went back to the States and, being by nature taciturn, laconic loners, seldom mentioned what they did.

Even the USA, not normally shy about its war heroes, cast no medal and raised no plaque. They came from nowhere, did what they did because it had to be done, and went back to oblivion. And their story all started because of a sergeant's sore bottom.

The USA was not the first invader of Vietnam, just the last. Before the Americans were the French, who colonized the three provinces of Tonkin (north), Annam (centre) and Cochinchina (south) into their empire, along with Laos and Cambodia.

But the invading Japanese ousted the French in 1942 and after Japan's defeat in 1945 the Vietnamese believed that at last they would be united and free of foreign domination. The French had other ideas, and came back. The leading independence fighter (there were others at first) was the Communist Ho Chi Minh. He formed the Vietminh resistance army and the Viets went back to the jungle to fight on. And on and on, for as long as it took.

A stronghold of resistance was the heavily forested farming zone northwest of Saigon, running up to the Cambodian border. The

French accorded it their special attention (as would later the Americans) with punitive expedition after expedition. To seek sanctuary the local farmers did not flee; they dug.

They had no technology, just their ant-like capacity for hard work, their patience, their local knowledge and their cunning. They also had mattocks, shovels and palm-weave baskets. How many million tons of dirt they shifted will never be calculated. But dig and shift they did. By the time the French left after their 1954 defeat the whole of the Iron Triangle was a warren of shafts and tunnels. And no one knew about them.

The Americans came, propping up a regime the Viets regarded as puppets of yet another colonial power. They went back to the jungle and back to guerrilla war. And they resumed digging. By 1964 they had two hundred miles of tunnels, chambers, passages and hideouts, and all underground.

The complexity of the tunnel system, when the Americans finally began to comprehend what was down there, took the breath away. The down-shafts were so disguised as to be invisible at a few inches range at the level of the jungle floor. Down below were up to five levels of galleries, the lowest at fifty feet, linked by narrow, twisting passages that only a Vietnamese or a small wiry Caucasian could crawl through.

The levels were linked by trap doors, some going up, others heading down. These too were camouflaged, to look like blank end-of-tunnel walls. There were stores, assembly caverns, dormitories, repair shops, eating halls and even hospitals. By 1966 a full combat brigade could hide down there, but until the Tet Offensive that number was never needed.

Penetration by an aggressor was discouraged. If a vertical shaft was discovered, there could well be a cunning booby trap at the bottom. Firing down the tunnels served no purpose; they changed direction every few yards so a bullet would go straight into the end-wall.

Dynamiting did not work; there were scores of alternate galleries within the pitch-black maze down there, but only a local would know them. Gas did not work; they fitted water seals, like the U-bend in a lavatory pipe.

The network ran under the jungle almost from the suburbs of Saigon nearly to the Cambodian border. There were various other networks elsewhere but nothing like the Tunnels of Cu Chi, named after the nearest town.

After the monsoon the laterite clay was pliable, easy to dig, scrape back and drag away in baskets. In the dry, it set like concrete.

After the passing of Kennedy, Americans arrived in really significant numbers and no longer as instructors, but for combat, starting spring 1964. They had the numbers, the weapons, the machines, the firepower — and they hit nothing. They hit nothing because they found nothing; just an occasional VC corpse if they got lucky. But they took casualties, and the body count began to mount.

At first it was convenient to presume the VC were peasants by day, lost among the black-pyjama-clad millions, switching to guerrillas at

54

night. But why so many casualties by day, and no one to fire back at? In January 1966 the Big Red One decided to raze the Iron Triangle once and for all. It was Operation Crimp.

They started at one end, fanned out and moved forward. They had enough ammunition to wipe out Indochina. They reached the other end and had found no one. From behind the moving line sniper fire started and the GIs took five fatalities. Whoever was firing had only old, bolt-action Soviet carbines, but a bullet through the heart is still a bullet through the heart.

The GIs turned back, went over the same ground. Nothing, no enemy. They took more fatalities, always in the back. They discovered a few foxholes, a brace of air-raid shelters. Empty, offering no cover. More sniper fire but no running figures in black to fire back at.

On Day Four, Sergeant Stewart Green, massively fed up, as were his mates around him, sat for a rest. In two seconds he was up, clutching his butt. Fire ants, scorpions, snakes, Vietnam had them all. He was convinced he had been stung or bitten. But it was a nail-head. The nail was part of a frame, and the frame was the hidden door to a shaft that went straight down into blackness. The US Army had discovered where the snipers went. They had been marching over their heads for two years.

There was no way of fighting the Vietcong living and hiding down there in the darkness by remote control. The society that in three years would send two men to walk on the moon had no technology for the Tunnels of Cu Chi. There was only one way to take the fight to the invisible enemy.

Someone had to strip down to thin cotton pants and, with pistol, knife and torch, go down into that pitch-black, stinking, airless, unknown, unmapped, booby-trapped, deadly, hideously claustrophobic labyrinth of narrow passages with no known exit and kill the waiting Vietcong in their own lair.

A few men were found, a special type of man. Big, burly men were of no use. The 95 per cent who feel claustrophobic were no use. Loud mouths, exhibitionists, look-at-mes were no use. The ones who did it were quiet, soft-spoken, self-effacing, self-contained personalities, often loners in their own units. They had to be very cool, even cold, possessed of icy nerves and almost immune to panic, the real enemy below ground.

Army bureaucracy, never afraid to use ten words where two will do, called them 'Tunnel Exploration Personnel'. They called themselves the Tunnel Rats.

By the time Cal Dexter reached Vietnam they had been in existence for three years, the only unit whose Purple Heart (wounded in action) ratio was 100 per cent.

The commanding officer of the moment was known as Rat Six. Everyone else had a different number. Once joined, they kept themselves to themselves and everyone regarded them with a kind of awe, as men will be awkward in the company of one sentenced to die.

Rat Six had been right in his gut guess. The

tough little kid from the construction sites of New Jersey, with his deadly fists and feet, Paul Newman eyes and no nerves, was a natural.

He took him down into the Tunnels of Cu Chi and within an hour realized that the recruit was the better fighter. They became partners underground where there were no ranks and no 'sirs' and for nearly two tours they fought and killed down in the darkness until Henry Kissinger met Le Duc Tho and agreed America would quit Vietnam. After that there was no point.

To the rest of Big Red One the pair became a legend, spoken of in whispers. The officer was 'The Badger' and the newly promoted sergeant was 'The Mole'.

# 5

# The Tunnel Rat

In the army, a mere six years in age difference between two young men can seem like a generation. The older man appears almost a father figure. Thus it was with the Badger and the Mole. At twenty-five, the officer was six years older. More, he came from a different social background with a far better education.

His parents were professional people. After high school he had spent a year touring Europe, seeing ancient Greece and Rome, historical Italy, Germany, France and Britain.

He had spent four years at college for his degree in civil and mechanical engineering, before facing the draft. He, too, had opted for the three-year commission and gone straight to officer school at Fort Belvoir, Virginia.

Fort Belvoir was then churning out junior officers at a hundred a month. Nine months after entering, the Badger had emerged as a Second Lieutenant, rising to First when he shipped to Vietnam to join the 1st Engineer Battalion of Big Red One. He, too, had been headhunted for the Tunnel Rats, and in view of his rank quickly became Rat Six when his predecessor left for home. He had nine months of his required one-year Vietnam posting to complete, two months less than Dexter did.

But within a month it was clear that once the two men went into the tunnels, the roles were reversed. The Badger deferred to the Mole, accepting that the young man, with years on the streets and building sites of New Jersey, had a kind of sense for danger, the silent menace round the next corner, the smell of a booby trap, that no college degree could match, and which might keep them alive.

Before either man had reached Vietnam the US High Command had realized that trying to blow the tunnel system to smithereens was a waste of time. The dried laterite was too hard, the complex too extensive. The continuous switching of tunnel direction meant explosive forces could only reach so far, and not far enough.

Attempts had been made to flood the tunnels but the water just soaked away through the tunnel floors. Due to the water-seals, gas failed as well. The decision was made that the only way to bring the enemy to battle was to go down there and try to find the headquarters network of the entire Vietcong War Zone C.

This, it was believed, was down there somewhere, between the southern tip of the Iron Triangle at the junction of the Saigon and Thi Tinh rivers and the Boi Loi woods at the Cambodian end. To find that HQ, to wipe out the senior cadres, to grab the huge harvest of intelligence that must be down there — that was the aim and, if it could be achieved, was a price beyond rubies.

In fact the HQ was under the Ho Bo woods, upcountry by the bank of the Saigon river, and was never found. But every time the tankdozers or the Rome Plows uncovered another tunnel entrance, the Rats went down into hell to keep looking.

The entrances were always vertical and that created the first danger. To go down feet first was to expose the lower half of the body to any VC waiting in the side tunnel. He would be happy to drive a needle-pointed bamboo spear deep into the groin or entrails of the dangling GI before scooting backwards into the darkness. By the time the dying American had been hauled back up, with the haft of the spear scraping the walls and the venom-poisoned tip ripping at the bowels, chances of survival were minimal.

To go down head first meant risking the spear, bayonet or point-blank bullet through the base of the throat.

The safest way seemed to be to descend slowly until the last five feet, then drop fast and fire at the slightest movement inside the tunnel. But the base of the shaft might be twigs and leaves, hiding a pit with punji sticks. These were embedded bamboo spears, also venom-tipped, that would drive straight through the sole of a combat boot, through the foot and out of the instep. Being fish-hook carved and barbed, they could hardly be withdrawn. Few survived them either.

Once inside the tunnel and crawling forward, the danger might be the VC waiting around the next corner, but more likely the booby traps.

These were various, of great cunning and had to be disarmed before progress could be made.

Some horrors needed no Vietcong at all. The nectar bat and black-bearded tomb bat were both cave dwellers and roosted through the daylight in the tunnels until disturbed. So did the giant crab-spider, so dense on the walls that the wall itself appeared to be shimmering with movement. Even more numerous were the fire-ants.

None of these was lethal; that honour went to the bamboo viper whose bite meant death in thirty minutes. The trap was usually a yard of bamboo embedded in the roof, jutting downwards at an angle and emerging by no more than an inch.

The snake was inside the tube, head downwards, trapped and enraged, its escape blocked by a plug of kapok at the lower end. Threaded through this was a length of fishing line, heading through a hole in a peg in the wall on one side, thence to a peg across the tunnel. If the crawling GI touched the line, it would jerk the plug out of the bamboo above him and the viper would tumble onto the back of his neck.

And there were the rats, real rats. In the tunnels they had discovered their private heaven and bred furiously. Just as the GIs would never leave a wounded man or even a corpse in the tunnels, the Vietcong hated to leave one of their casualties up above for the Americans to find and add to the cherished 'body count'. Dead VC were brought below and entombed in the walls in the foetus position, before being plastered over with wet clay.

But a skim of clay will not stop a rat. They had their endless food source and grew to the size of cats. Yet the Vietcong lived down there for weeks or even months on end, challenging the Americans to come into their domain, find them and fight them.

Those who did it and survived became as accustomed to the stench as to the hideous life forms. It was always hot, sticky, cramped and pitch dark. And it stank. The VC had to perform their body functions in earthenware jars; when full, these were buried in the floors and capped with a tampon of clay. But the rats scratched them open.

Coming from the most heavily armed country on earth, the GIs who became Tunnel Rats had to cast all technology aside and return to primal man. One commando knife, one handgun, one flashlight, a spare magazine and two spare batteries were all that would fit down there. Occasionally a hand grenade would be used, but these were dangerous, sometimes lethal, for the thrower. In tiny spaces, the boom could shatter eardrums but, worse, the explosion would suck out all the oxygen for hundreds of feet. A man could die before more could filter in from outside.

For a Tunnel Rat to use his pistol or flashlight was to give his position away, to announce his coming, never knowing who crouched in the darkness up ahead, silent and waiting. In this sense, the VC always had the edge. They only had to stay silent and await the man crawling towards them.

Most nerve tearing of all, and the source of most deaths, was the task of penetrating the trapdoors that led from level to level, usually downwards.

Often a tunnel would come to a dead end. Or was it a dead end? If so, why dig it in the first place? In the dark, with fingertips feeling nothing ahead but laterite wall, no side tunnel to left or right, the Tunnel Rat had to use the flashlight. This would usually reveal, skilfully camouflaged and easily missable, a trapdoor in the wall, floor or ceiling. Either the mission aborted, or the door had to be opened.

But who waited on the other side? If the GI's head went through first and there was a Vietcong waiting, the American's life would end with a throat cut from side to side or the lethal bite of a garrotting noose of thin wire. If he dropped downward feet first, it could be the spear through the belly. Then he would die in agony, his screaming torso in one level, ruined lower body in the next down.

Dexter had the armourers prepare him small, tangerine-sized grenades with reduced explosive charge from the standard issue but more ball bearings. Twice in his first six months he lifted a trap door, tossed in a grenade with a three-second fuse, and pulled the door back down. When he opened a second time and went up with his flashlight on, the next chamber was a charnel house of torn bodies.

The complexes were protected from gas attack

by water traps. The crawling Tunnel Rat would find a pool of rank water in front of him.

That meant the tunnel continued the other side of the water.

The only way through was to roll onto the back, slide in upside down and pull the body along with fingertips scrabbling at the roof. The hope was that the water ended before the breath in the lungs. Otherwise he could die drowned, upside down, in blackness, fifty feet down. The way to survive was to rely on the partner.

Before entering the water, the point man would tie a lanyard to his feet and pass it back to the partner. If he did not give a reassuring tug on it within ninety seconds of entering the water, confirming that he had found air on the other side of the trap, his mate had to pull him back without delay because he would be dying down there.

Through all this misery, discomfort and fear there occurred a moment now and again when the Tunnel Rats hit the mother lode. This would be a cavern, sometimes recently vacated in a hurry, which had clearly been an important sub-Headquarters. Then boxes of papers, evidence, clues, maps and other mementoes would be ferried back to the waiting intelligence experts from G2.

Twice the Badger and the Mole came across such Aladdin's caves. Senior brass, unsure how to cope with such strange young men, handed out medals and warm words. But the Public Affairs people, normally avid to tell the world how well the war was going, were warned off. No one mentioned a word. One facility trip was arranged but the 'guest' from PA got fifteen yards down a 'safe' tunnel and had hysterics. After that, silence reigned.

But there were long periods of no combat, for the Rats as for all the other GIs in Vietnam. Some slept the hours away, or wrote letters, longing for the end of tour and the journey home. Some drank the time away, or played cards or craps. Many smoked, and not always Marlboro. Some became addicts. Others read.

Cal Dexter was one of those. Talking with his officer-partner he realized how blighted was his formal education, and started again from square one. He found he was fascinated by history. The base librarian was delighted and impressed, and prepared a long list of must-read books which he then obtained from Saigon.

Dexter worked his way through Attic Greece and Ancient Rome, learned of Alexander who had wept that, at thirty-one, he had defeated the known world and there were no more worlds to conquer.

He learned of Rome's decline and fall, of the Dark Ages and medieval Europe, the Renaissance and the Enlightenment, the Age of Elegance and the Age of Reason. He was particularly fascinated by the early years of the birth of the American Colonies, the Revolution and why his own country had had a vicious civil war just ninety years before he was born.

He did one other thing in those long periods when monsoon or orders kept him confined to base. With the help of the elderly Vietnamese who swept and cleaned the hootch for them all, he learned workaday Vietnamese until he could speak enough to make himself understood and understand more than that.

Nine months into his first tour two things happened. He took his first combat wound and the Badger ended his twelve-month stint.

The bullet came from a VC who had been hiding in one of the tunnels as Dexter came down the entrance shaft. To confuse such a waiting enemy, Dexter had developed a technique. He threw a grenade down the shaft, then went in fast, hand over fist. If the grenade did not blow away the false floor of the shaft, then there was no punji-stick trap down there. If it did, he had time to stop before he hit the spikes.

The same grenade ought to shred any VC waiting out of sight. On this occasion the VC was there, but standing well down the passage with a Kalashnikov AK47. He survived the blast, but injured, and fired one shot at the fast-falling Tunnel Rat. Dexter hit the deck with pistol out and fired back three times. The VC went down, crawled away, but was found later, dead. Dexter was nicked in the upper left arm, a flesh wound that healed well but kept him upstairs for a month. The Badger problem was more serious.

Soldiers will admit it, policemen will confirm it; there is no substitute for a partner you can utterly rely on. Since they formed their partnership in the early days, the Badger and the Mole did not really want to go into the tunnels with anyone else. In nine months, Dexter had seen four Rats killed down there. In one case, the surviving Tunnel Rat had come back to the surface screaming and crying. He would never go down a tunnel again, even after weeks with the psychiatrists.

But the body of the one who never made it was still down there. The Badger and the Mole went in with ropes to find the man and drag him out for repatriation and a Christian burial. His throat had been cut. No open casket for him.

Of the original thirteen, four more had quit at the end of their time. Eight down. Six recruits had joined. They were back to eleven in the whole unit.

'I don't want to go down there with anyone else,' Dexter told his partner when the Badger came to visit him in the base clinic.

'Nor me if it were the other way round,' said the Badger. They settled it by agreeing that if the Badger extended for a second one-year tour, the Mole would do the same in three months. So it was done. Both accepted a second tour and went back to the tunnels. The Division's Commanding General, embarrassed by his own gratitude, handed out two more medals.

There were certain rules down in those tunnels that were never broken. One was: never go down alone. Because of his remarkable hazard antennae the Mole was usually up at point with the Badger several yards behind. Another rule was: never fire off all six shots at once. It tells the VC you are now out of ammo, and a sitting duck. Two months into his second tour, in May 1970, Cal Dexter nearly broke them both, and was lucky to survive.

The pair had entered a newly discovered shaft up in the Ho Bo woods. The Mole was up front and had crawled three hundred yards along a tunnel that changed direction four times. He had fingertip-felt two booby traps and disconnected them. He failed to notice that the Badger had confronted his own personal pet hatred, two tomb bats that had fallen into his hair, and had stopped, unable to speak or go on.

The Mole was crawling alone, when he saw or thought he saw the dimmest of glows coming from round the next corner. It was so dim he thought his retina might be playing tricks. He slithered silently to the corner and stopped, pistol in right hand. The glow also stayed motionless, just round the corner. He waited like that for ten minutes, unaware his frozen partner was out of sight behind him. Then he decided to break the stand-off. He lunged his torso round the corner.

Ten feet away was a Vietcong, on hands and knees. Between them was the source of light, a shallow lamp of coconut oil with a tiny wick floating in it. The VC had evidently been pushing it along the floor to accomplish his mission, checking out the booby traps. For half a second the two enemies stared at each other, then both reacted.

With the back of his fingers the Vietnamese flicked the dish of hot nut-oil straight at the American's face. The light was snuffed out at once. Dexter raised his left hand to protect his eyes and felt the searing oil splash across the back of his knuckles. With his right hand he fired three times as he heard a frantic scuffling sound retreating down the tunnel. He was sorely tempted to use the other three rounds, but he did not know how many more were down there.

Had the Badger and the Mole but known it, they were crawling towards the headquarters complex of the Vietcong's entire Zone Command. Guarding it were fifty diehards.

Back in the States there was, all this while, a covert little unit called the Limited War Laboratory. Throughout the Vietnam War they dreamed up splendid ideas to help the Tunnel Rats, though none of the scientists ever went down a tunnel. They shipped their ideas over to Vietnam where the Rats, who did go down tunnels, tried them out, found them gloriously impractical and shipped them back again.

In the summer of 1970 the Limited War Laboratory came up with a new kind of gun for close-quarter work in a confined space. And at last they had a winner. It was a .44 Magnum handgun modified down to a three-inch barrel so as not to get in the way, but with special ammunition.

The very heavy slug of this .44 was divided into four segments. They were held together as one by the cartridge, but on emerging from the barrel separated to make four slugs instead of one. The Tunnel Rats found it very good for close-quarter work and likely to be deadly in the tunnels because if fired twice it would fill the tunnel ahead with eight projectiles instead of two. A far greater chance of hitting the Vietcong.

Only seventy-five of these guns were ever

made. The Tunnel Rats used them for six months, then they were withdrawn. Someone had discovered that they probably contravened the Geneva Convention. So the seventy-four traceable Smith and Wesson revolvers were sent back to the States and never seen again.

The Tunnel Rats had a short and simple prayer. 'If I have to take a bullet, so be it. If I have to take a knife, tough luck. But please, Lord, don't ever bury me alive down there.'

It was in the summer of 1970 that the Badger was buried alive.

Either the GIs should not have been down there or the B-52 bombers out of Guam should not have been bombing from 30,000 feet. But someone had ordered the bombers and that someone forgot to tell the Tunnel Rats.

It happens. Not a lot, but no one who has ever been in the armed forces will fail to spot a FUBAR: fouled up beyond all recognition.

It was the new thinking: to destroy the tunnel complexes by caving them in with massive explosions dropped by B-52s. Partly this had been caused by the change in psychology.

Back in the States the tide of opinion was now comprehensively against the Vietnam War.

Parents were now joining their children in the anti-war demonstrations.

In the war zone, the Tet Offensive of thirty months earlier had not been forgotten. The morale was simply dribbling away into the jungle floor. It was still unspoken among the High Command, but the mood was spreading that this war could not be won. It would be three more

70

years before the last GI would board the last plane out of there, but by the summer of 1970 the decision was made to destroy the tunnels in the 'free strike zones' with bombs. The Iron Triangle was a free strike zone.

Because the entire 25th Infantry Division was based there, the bombers had instructions that no bomb should fall less than three kilometres from the nearest US unit. But that day High Command forgot about the Badger and the Mole, who were in a different division.

They were in a complex outside Ben Suc, in the second level down, when they felt rather than heard the first 'crump' of bombs above them. Forgetting the VC, they crawled frantically towards the shaft going up to level one.

The Mole made it and was ten yards towards the final shaft up to daylight when the roof fall came. It was behind him. He yelled, 'Badger.' There was no reply. He knew there was a small alcove twenty yards ahead because they had passed it coming down. Drenched in sweat he dragged himself into it and used the extra width to turn around and head back.

He met the dirt pile with his fingertips. Then he felt a hand, then a second, but nothing beyond that except fallen earth. He began to dig, hurling the slag behind him but blocking his exit as he did so.

It took him five minutes to liberate his partner's head, five more to free the torso. The bombs had ceased, but up top the falling debris had blocked the air flues. They began to run out of oxygen.

71

'Get out of here, Cal,' hissed the Badger in the darkness. 'Come back with help later. I'll be OK.'

Dexter continued scrabbling at the dirt with his fingertips. He had lost two nails entirely. It would take over an hour to get help. His partner would not survive half that time with the air flues blocked. He put on his flashlight and shoved the lamp in his partner's hand.

'Hold that. Direct the beam back over your shoulder.'

By the yellow light he could see the mass covering the Badger's legs. It took another half hour. Then the crawl back to daylight, squeezing past the rubble he had cast behind him as he dug. His lungs were heaving, his head spinning; his partner was semi-conscious. He crawled round the last corner and felt the air.

In January 1971 the Badger reached the end of his second tour. Extension for a third year was forbidden, but he had had enough anyway. The night before he flew back to the States, the Mole secured permission to accompany his partner into Saigon to say farewell. They went into the capital with an armoured convoy. Dexter was confident he could hitch a lift back in a helicopter the next day.

The two young men had a slap-up meal then toured the bars. They avoided the hordes of prostitutes but concentrated on some serious drinking. At two in the morning they found themselves, feeling no pain, somewhere in Cholon, the Chinese quarter of Saigon across the river.

There was a tattoo parlour, still open and still available for business, especially in dollars. The Chinaman was wisely contemplating a future outside Vietnam.

Before they left him and took the ferry back across the river the young Americans had a tattoo created, one for each. On the left forearm. It showed a rat, not the aggressive rat on the door of the hootch at Lai Khe, but a saucy rat. Facing away from the viewer but looking back over his shoulder. A broad wink, trousers down, a mooning rat. They were still giggling until they sobered up. Then it was too late.

The Badger flew back to the States the next morning. The Mole followed ten weeks later, in mid-March. On 7 April 1971 the Tunnel Rats formally ceased to exist.

That was the day Cal Dexter, despite the urging of several senior officers, mustered out of the army and returned to civilian life.

# 6

# The Tracker

There are very few military outfits more secretive than the British Special Air Service regiment, but if there is one that makes the tight-lipped SAS look like the Jerry Springer show, it is the Det.

The 14th Independent Intelligence Company, also called the 14th Int, or the Detachment, or the Det, is an army unit drawing its recruits from right across the board, with (and unlike the all-male SAS) quite a proportion of women soldiers.

Although it can if need be fight with lethal efficiency, the main tasks of the Det are to locate, track to lair, survey and eavesdrop the bad people. They are never seen and their planted listening devices are so advanced that they are rarely found.

A successful Det operation would involve tailing a terrorist to the main hive, entering secretly at night, planting a 'bug' and listening to the bad people for days or weeks on end. In this manner the terrorists would be likely to reveal their next operation.

Tipped off, the slightly noisier SAS could then mount a sweet little ambush and, as soon as the first terrorist fired a weapon, wipe them out.

Legally. Self-defence.

Most of the Det operations up to 1995 had been in Northern Ireland where their covertly obtained information had led to some of the IRA's worst defeats. It was the Det who hit on the idea of slipping into a mortician's parlour where a terrorist, of either Republican or Unionist persuasion, was lying in a casket, and inserting a bug into the timber of the coffin.

This was because the terrorist godfathers, knowing they were 'under suss', would rarely meet to discuss planning. But at a funeral they would congregate, lean over the coffin and, covering their mouths from lip-readers behind the telescopes on the hillside above the cemetery, hold a planning conference. The bugs in the coffin would pick up the lot. It worked for years.

In years to come, it would be the Det who carried out the 'Close Target Reconnaissance' on Bosnia's mass-killers, allowing the SAS snatch squads to haul them off to trial in The Hague.

The company whose name Steve Edmond had learned from Mr Rubinstein, the Toronto art collector who had mysteriously recovered his paintings, was called Hazard Management, a very discreet agency based in the Victoria district of London.

Hazard Management specialized in three things and extensively used former Special Forces personnel among its staff. The biggest income-earner was Asset Protection, as its name implies the protection of extremely expensive property on behalf of very rich people who did not want to be parted from it. This was only carried out for limited-term special occasions, not on a permanent basis.

Next came Personnel Protection, PP as opposed to AP. This also was for limited time-span, although there was a small school in Wiltshire where a rich man's own personal bodyguards could be trained, for a substantial fee.

Smallest of the divisions in Hazard Management was known as L&R, Location and Recovery. This was what Mr Rubinstein had needed: someone to trace his missing masterpieces and negotiate their return.

Two days after taking the call from his frantic daughter, Steve Edmond had his meeting with the chief executive of Hazard Management and explained what he wanted.

'Find my grandson. This is not a commission with a budget ceiling,' he said.

The former Director of Special Forces, now retired, beamed. Even soldiers have children to educate. The man he called in from his country home the next day was Phil Gracey, former captain in the Parachute Regiment and ten years a veteran of the Det. Inside the company, he was simply known as 'The Tracker'.

Gracey had his own meeting with the Canadian and his interrogation was extremely detailed. If the boy was still alive, he wanted to know everything about his personal habits, tastes, preferences, even vices. He took possession of two good photographs of Ricky Colenso and the grandfather's personal cell-phone number. Then he nodded and left.

The Tracker spent two days almost continuously on the phone. He had no intention of moving until he knew exactly where he was going, how, why and whom he sought. He spent hours reading written material about the Bosnian civil war, the aid programmes and the non-Bosnian military presence on the ground. He struck lucky on the last.

The United Nations had created a military 'peace-keeping' force, the usual lunacy of sending a force to keep the peace where there was no peace to keep, then forbidding them to create the peace, ordering them instead to watch the slaughter without interfering. The military were called UNPROFOR and the British government had supplied a large contingent. It was based at Vitez, just ten miles down the road from Travnik.

The regiment assigned there in June 1995 was recent; its predecessor had been relieved only two months earlier and the Tracker traced the colonel commanding the earlier regiment to a course at Guards depot, Pirbright. He was a mine of information. On the third day after his talk with the Canadian grandfather, the Tracker flew to the Balkans; not straight into Bosnia (impossible) but to the Adriatic resort of Split on the coast of Croatia. His cover story said he was a freelance journalist, which is a useful cover, being completely unprovable either way. But he also included a letter from a major Sunday newspaper asking for a series of articles on the effectiveness of relief aid. Just in case.

In twenty-four hours in Split, enjoying an

unexpected boom as the main jumping-off point for central Bosnia, he had acquired a second-hand but tough off-road and a pistol. Just in case. It was a long, rough drive through the mountains from the coast to Travnik, but he was confident his information was accurate; he would run into no combat zone, and he did not.

It was a strange combat, the Bosnian civil war. There were rarely any lines, as such, and never a pitched battle. Just a patchwork quilt of mono-ethnic communities living in fear, hundreds of fire-gutted, ethnically 'cleansed' villages and hamlets and, roaming between them, bands of soldiery, mostly belonging to one of the surrounding 'national' armies, but also including groups of mercenaries, freebooters and psychotic paramilitaries posing as patriots. These were the worst.

At Travnik, the Tracker met his first reverse. John Slack had left. A friendly soul with Age Concern said he believed the American had joined Feed the Children, a much bigger NGO, and was based in Zagreb. The Tracker spent the night in his sleeping bag in the rear of the 4x4 and left the next day for another gruelling drive north to Zagreb, the Croatian capital. There he found John Slack at the Feed the Children warehouse. He could not be much help.

'I have no idea what happened, where he went or why,' he protested. 'Look, man, the Loaves 'n' Fishes operation closed down last month, and he was part of that. He vanished with one of my two brand new Landcruisers; that is, fifty per cent of my transportation.

'Plus, he took one of my three local Bosnian helpers. Charleston was not best pleased. With peace moves finally in the offing they did not want to start over. I told them there was still a lot to do, but they closed me down. I was lucky to find a billet here.'

'What about the Bosnian?'

'Fadil? No chance he was behind it all. He was a nice guy. Spent a lot of time grieving for his lost family. If he hated anyone, it was the Serbs, not Americans.'

'Any sign of the money belt?'

'Now that was stupid. I warned him. It was too much either to leave behind or carry around. But I don't think Fadil would kill him for that.'

'Where were you, John?'

'That's the point. If I had been there it would never have happened. I'd have vetoed the idea, whatever it was. But I was on a mountain road in south Croatia trying to get a truck with a solid engine block towed to the nearest town. Dumb Swede. Can you imagine driving a truck with an empty oil sump and not noticing?'

'What did you discover?'

'When I got back? Well, he had arrived at the compound, let himself in, taken a Landcruiser and driven off. One of the other Bosnians, Ibrahim, saw them both, but they didn't speak. That was four days before I returned. I kept trying his mobile but there was no answer. I went apeshit. I figured they'd gone partying. At first I was more angry than worried.'

'Any idea which direction?'

'Uhuh. Ibrahim said they drove off north. That

is, straight into central Travnik town. From the town centre the roads lead all over. No one in town remembers a thing.'

'You got any ideas, John?'

'Yep. I reckon he took a call. Or more likely Fadil took a call and told Ricky. He was very compassion-driven. If he had taken a call about some medical emergency in one of the villages high in the backcountry, he'd have driven off to try and help. Too impulsive to leave a message.

'You seen that country, pal? You ever driven through it? Mountains and valleys and rivers. I figure they went over a precipice and crashed into a valley. Come the winter when the leaves fall, I think someone will spot the wreckage down below among the rocks. Look, I have to go. Good luck, eh? He was a nice kid.'

The Tracker went back to Travnik, set up a small office-cum-living quarters and recruited a happy-to-be-employed Ibrahim as his guide and interpreter.

He carried a satphone with several spare batteries and a scrambler device to keep communications covert. It was just for keeping in touch with head office in London. They had facilities he did not.

He believed there were four possibilities ranging from dumb via possible to likely. The dumbest of the four was that Ricky Colenso had decided to steal the Landcruiser, drive south to Belgrade in Serbia, sell it off, abandon all his previous life and live like a bum. He rejected it. It simply was not Ricky Colenso and why would he steal a Landcruiser if his grandpa could buy the factory?

Next up was that Sulejman had persuaded Ricky to take him for a drive, then murdered the young American for his money belt and the vehicle. Possible. But as a Bosnian Muslim without a passport, Fadil would not get far in Croatia or Serbia, both hostile territory for him, and a new Landcruiser on the market would be spotted.

Three, they had run into person or persons unknown and been murdered for the same trophies. Among the out-of-control freelance killers wandering the landscape were a few groups of Mujahedin, Muslim fanatics from the Middle East, come to 'help' their persecuted fellow Muslims in Bosnia. It was known they had already killed two European mercenaries, even though they were supposed to be on the same side, plus one relief worker and one Muslim garage owner who declined to donate petrol.

But way out top of the range of probabilities was John Slack's theory. The Tracker took Ibrahim and, day by day, followed every road out of Travnik for miles into the back-country. While the Bosnian drove slowly behind him, the Tracker scoured the road edges over every possible steep slope into the valleys below.

He was doing what he did best. Slowly, patiently, missing nothing, he looked for tyre marks, crumbled edges, skid lines, crushed vegetation, wheel-flattened grass. Three times, with a rope tied to the Lada off-road, he went down into ravines where a clump of vegetation

81

might hide a crushed Landcruiser. Nothing.

With binoculars he sat on road edges and scanned the valleys below for a glint of metal or glass down there. Nothing. By the end of an exhausting ten days he had become convinced Slack was wrong. If an off-road that size had swerved off the road and over the edge, it would have left a trace, however small, even forty days later. And he would have seen that trace. There was no crashed vehicle lying in those valleys around Travnik.

He offered a reward for information big enough to make the mouth water. Word about the prize spread in the refugee community and hopefuls came forward. But the best he got was that the car had been seen driving through town that day. Destination unknown. Route taken, unknown.

After two weeks he closed his operation down and moved to Vitez, headquarters of the newly resident British Army contingent.

He found a billet at the school which had been converted into a sort of hostel for the mainly British Press. It was on a street known as TV Alley, just outside the army compound but safe enough if things turned nasty.

Knowing what most army men think of the Press, he did not bother with his 'freelance journalist' cover story, but sought a meeting with the colonel commanding on the basis of what he was, ex-Special Services.

The colonel had a brother in the Paras. Common background, common interests. Not a problem, anything he could do to help?

Yes, he had heard about the missing American boy. Bad show. His patrols had kept a look out, but nothing. He listened to the Tracker's offer of a substantial donation to the Army Benevolent Fund. A reconnaissance exercise was mounted, a light aircraft from the Artillery people. The Tracker went with the pilot. They flew the mountains and ravines for over an hour. Not a sign.

'I think you're going to have to look at foul play,' said the colonel over dinner.

'Mujahedin?'

'Possibly. Weird swine, you know. They will kill you as soon as look at you if you're not a Muslim, or even if you are but not fundamentalist enough. May fifteenth? We'd only been here for two weeks. Still getting the hang of the terrain. But I've checked the Incident Log. There were none in the area. You could try the ECMM sitreps. Pretty useless stuff, but I've got a stack in the office. Should cover May fifteenth.'

The European Community Monitoring Mission was the attempt of the European Union based in Brussels to horn in on an act that they could influence in no way at all. Bosnia was a UN affair until finally, in exasperation, taken over and resolved by the USA. But Brussels wanted a role, so a team of observers was created to given them one. This was the ECMM. The Tracker went through the stack of reports the next day.

The EU monitors were mainly armed forces officers loaned by the EU defence ministries with nothing better to do. They were scattered

83

through Bosnia where they had an office, a flat, a car and a living allowance. Some of the situation reports, or sitreps, read more like a social diary. The Tracker concentrated on anything filed 15 May or the three days following. There was one from Banja Luka dated 16 May that caught his eye.

Banja Luka was a fiercely Serbian stronghold well to the north of Travnik and across the Vlasic mountain chain. The ECMM officer there was a Danish major, Lasse Bjerregaard. He said that the previous evening, i.e. 15 May, he had been taking a drink in the bar of the Bosna Hotel when he witnessed a blazing row between two Serbs in camouflage uniform. One had clearly been in a rage at the other and was screaming abuse at him in Serbian. He slapped the face of the junior man several times, but the offending party did not answer back, indicating the clear superiority of the slapper.

When it was over the major tried to seek an explanation from the barman, who spoke halting English which the Dane spoke fluently, but the barman shrugged and walked away in a very rude manner which was unlike him. The next morning the uniformed men were gone and the major never saw them again.

The Tracker thought it was the longest shot of his life but he called the ECMM office in Banja Luka. Another change of posting; a Greek came on the line. Yes, the Dane had returned home the previous week. The Tracker called London suggesting they ask the Danish Defence Ministry. London came back in three hours.

Fortunately the name was not so common. Jensen would have been a problem. Major Bjerregaard was on furlough and his number was in Odense.

The Tracker caught him that evening when he returned from a day on the water with his family in the summer heatwave. Major Bjerregaard was as helpful as he could be. He remembered the evening of 15 May quite clearly. There was, after all, precious little for a Dane to do in Banja Luka; it had been a very lonely and boring posting.

As each evening, he had gone to the bar around 7.30 for a pre-dinner beer. About half an hour later a small group of Serbs in camouflage uniform had entered the bar. He did not think they were Yugoslav Army because they did not have unit flashes on their shoulders.

They seemed very full of themselves and ordered drinks all round, slivovitz with beer chasers, a lethal combination. Several rounds of drinks later, the major was about to adjourn to the dining room because the noise was becoming deafening when another Serb entered the bar. He seemed to be the commander, because the rest subsided.

He spoke to them in Serbian and he must have ordered them to come with him. The men began to swig their beers back and put their packs of cigarettes and lighters in their uniform pockets. Then one of them offered to pay.

The commander went berserk. He started screaming at the subordinate. The rest went deathly quiet. So did the other customers. And

85

the barman. The tirade went on, accompanied by two slaps to the face. Still no one protested. Finally the leader stormed out. Crestfallen and subdued, the others followed. No one offered to pay for the drinks.

The major had tried to secure an explanation from the barman with whom, after several weeks of drinking, he was on good terms. The man was white-faced. The Dane thought it might be rage at the scene in the bar, but it looked more like fear. When asked what it was all about, he shrugged and stalked to the other end of the now empty bar, and pointedly faced the other way.

'Did the commander rage at anyone else?' asked the Tracker.

'No, just at the one who tried to pay,' said the voice from Denmark.

'Why him alone, major? There is no mention in your report as to possible reason.'

'Ah. Didn't I put that in? Sorry. I think it was because the man tried to pay with a hundred-dollar bill.'

# 7

## The Volunteer

The Tracker packed his gear and drove north from Travnik. He was passing from Bosnian (Muslim) territory into Serb-held country. But a British Union Jack fluttered from a pennant above the Lada, and with luck that ought to deter long-range pot-shots. If stopped, he intended to rely on his passport, letter-proof that he was just writing about relief aid, and generous presents of Virginia-tobacco cigarettes bought from the Vitez barracks shop.

If all that failed, his pistol was fully loaded, close to hand and he knew how to use it.

He was stopped twice, once by a Bosnian militia patrol as he left Bosnia-controlled country, and once by a Yugoslav Army patrol south of Banja Luka. Each time his explanation, documents and presents worked. He rolled into Banja Luka five hours later.

The Bosna Hotel was certainly never going to put the Ritz out of business, but it was about all the town had. He checked in. There was plenty of room. Apart from a French TV crew, he judged he was the only foreigner staying there. At seven that evening he entered the bar. There were three other drinkers, all Serbs and all seated at tables, and one barman. He straddled the stool at the bar.

'Hallo. You must be Dusko.'

He was open, friendly, charming. The barman shook the proffered hand.

'You been here before?'

'No, first time. Nice bar. Friendly bar.'

'How you know my name?'

'Friend of mine was posted here recently. Danish fellow. Lasse Bjerregaard. He asked me to say hi if I was passing through.'

The barman relaxed considerably. There was no threat here.

'You Danish?'

'No, British.'

'Army?'

'Heavens no. Journalist. Doing a series of articles about aid agencies. You'll take a drink with me?'

Dusko helped himself to his own best brandy.

'I would like to be journalist. One day. Travel. See the world.'

'Why not? Get some experience on the local paper, then go to the big city. That's what I did.'

The barman shrugged in resignation.

'Here? Banja Luka? No paper.'

'So try Sarajevo. Even Belgrade. You're a Serb. You can get out of here. The war won't last for ever.'

'To get out of here costs money. No job, no money. No money, no travel, no job.'

'Ah yes, money, always a problem. Or maybe not.'

The Englishman produced a wad of US dollars, all hundred bills, and counted them onto the bar.

88

'I am old-fashioned,' he said. 'I believe people should help each other. It makes life easier, more pleasant. Will you help me, Dusko?'

The barman was staring at the thousand dollars a few inches from his fingertips. He could not take his eyes off them. He dropped his voice to a whisper.

'What you want? What do you do here? You not reporter.'

'Well, I am in a way. I ask questions. But I am a rich asker of questions. Do you want to be rich like me, Dusko?'

'What you want?' repeated the barman. He flicked a glance towards the other drinkers, who were staring at the pair of them.

'You've seen a hundred-dollar bill before. Last May. The fifteenth, wasn't it? A young soldier tried to settle the bar bill with it. Started one hell of a row. My friend Lasse was here. He told me. Explain to me exactly what happened and why.'

'Not here. Not now,' hissed the frightened Serb. One of the men from the tables was up and walking towards the bar. A wiping cloth flicked expertly down over the money. 'Bar close at ten. You come back.'

At half past ten, with the bar closed and locked, the two men sat in a booth in half-darkness and talked.

'They were not the Yugoslav Army, not soldiers,' said the barman. 'Paramilitary people. Bad people. They stay three days. Best rooms, best food, much drink. They leave but not pay.'

'One of them tried to pay you.'

'True. Only one. He was good kid. Different

89

from others. I don't know what he was doing with them. He had education. The rest were gangsters. Gutter people.'

'You didn't object to them not paying for three days' stay?'

'Object? Object? What I say? These animals have guns. They kill, even fellow Serbs. They all killers.'

'So when the nice kid tried to pay you, who was the one who slapped him around?'

He could feel the Serb tense rigid in the gloom.

'No idea. He was boss man, group leader. But no name. They just call him Chief.'

'All these paramilitaries have names, Dusko. Arkan and his Tigers. Frankie's Boys. They like to be famous. They boast of their names.'

'Not this one. I swear.'

The Tracker knew it was a lie. Whoever he was, the freelance killer inspired a sweat-clammy measure of fear among his fellow Serbs.

'But the nice kid . . . he had a name?'

'I never heard it.'

'We are talking about a lot of money here, Dusko. You never see him again, you never see me again, you have enough to start up in Sarajevo after the war. The kid's name.'

'He paid the day he left. Like he was ashamed of the people he was with. He came back and paid by cheque.'

'It bounced? Came back? You have it?'

'No, it was honoured. Yugoslav dinars. From Belgrade. Settlement in full.'

'So, no cheque?'

'It will be in the Belgrade bank. Somewhere, but probably destroyed by now. But I wrote down his ID card number, in case it bounced.'

'Where? Where did you write it?'

'On the back of an order pad. In ballpoint.'

The Tracker traced it. The pad, for taking long and complicated drinks orders that could not be memorized, only had two sheets left. Another day and it would have been thrown away. In ballpoint on the cardboard back was a seven-figure number and two capital letters. Eight weeks old, still legible.

The Tracker donated a thousand of Mr Edmond's dollars and left. The shortest way out of there was north into Croatia and a plane from Zagreb airport.

The old seven-province federal republic of Yugoslavia had been disintegrating in blood, chaos and cruelty for five years. In the north, Slovenia was the first to go, luckily without bloodshed. In the south, Macedonia had escaped into separate independence. But at the centre, the Serbian dictator Slobodan Milosevic was trying to use every brutality in the book to cling on to Croatia, Bosnia, Kosovo and Montenegro and his own native Serbia. He had lost Croatia but his appetite for power and war remained undiminished.

The Belgrade into which the Tracker had arrived in 1995 was still untouched. Its desolation would be provoked in the Kosovo war, yet to come.

His London office had advised there was one private detective agency in Belgrade, headed up by a former senior police officer whom they had used before. He had endowed his agency with the not too original name of Chandler and it was easy to find.

'I need,' the Tracker told the investigator, Dragan Stojic, 'to trace a young guy for whom I have no name but only the number of his state ID card.'

Stojic grunted.

'What did he do?'

'Nothing, so far as I know. He saw something. Maybe. Maybe not.'

'That's it. A name?'

'Then I would like to talk to him. I have no car and no mastery of Serbo-Croat. He may speak English. Maybe not.'

Stojic grunted again. It appeared to be his speciality. He had apparently read every Philip Marlowe novel and seen every movie. He was trying to be Robert Mitchum in *The Big Sleep* but at five feet four inches and bald, he was not quite there.

'My terms . . . ' he began.

The Tracker eased another ten hundred-dollar bills across the desk. 'I need your undivided attention,' he murmured.

Stojic was entranced. The line could have come straight from *Farewell, My Lovely*.

'You got it,' he said.

To give credit where credit is due, the dumpy ex-inspector did not waste time. Belching black smoke, his Yugo saloon, with the Tracker in the passenger seat, took them across town to the district of Konjarnik where the corner of

92

Ljermontova Street is occupied by the police headquarters of Belgrade. It was, and remains, a big, ugly block in brown and yellow, like a huge angular hornet on its side.

'You better stay here,' said Stojic. He was gone half an hour and must have shared some conviviality with an old colleague, for there was the plummy odour of slivovitz on his breath. But he had a slip of paper.

'That card belongs to Milan Rajak. Aged twenty-four. Listed as a law student. Father a lawyer, successful, upper middle-class family. Are you sure you've got the right man?'

'Unless he has a doppelgänger, he and an ID card bearing his photograph were in Banja Luka two months ago.'

'What the hell would he be doing there?'

'He was in uniform. In a bar.'

Stojic thought back to the file he had been shown but not allowed to copy.

'He did his national military service. All young Yugoslavs have to do that. Aged eighteen through twenty-one.'

'Combat soldier?'

'No. Signals Corps. Radio operator.'

'Never saw combat. Might have wished he had. Might have joined a group going into Bosnia to fight for the Serbian cause. A deluded volunteer? Possible?'

Stojic shrugged.

'Possible. But these paramilitaries are scumbags. Gangsters all. What would this law student be doing with them?'

'Summer vacation?' said the Tracker.

'But which group? Shall we ask him?'
Stojic consulted his piece of paper.
'Address in Senjak, not half an hour away.'
'Then let's go.'
They found the address without trouble, a solid, middle-class villa on Istarska Street. Years serving Marshal Tito and now Slobodan Milosevic had done Mr Rajak senior no harm at all. A pale and nervous-looking woman probably in her forties but looking older answered the door.

There was an interchange in Serbo-Croat.

'Milan's mother,' said Stojic. 'Yes, he's in. What do you want, she asks.'

'To talk to him. An interview. For the British Press.'

Clearly bewildered, Mrs Rajak let them in and called to her son. Then she showed them into the sitting room. There were feet on the stairs and a young man appeared in the hall. He had a whispered conversation with his mother and came in. His air was perplexed, worried, almost fearful. The Tracker gave him his friendliest smile and shook hands. The door was still an inch open. Mrs Rajak was on the phone speaking rapidly. Stojic shot the Englishman a warning glance, as if to say, 'Whatever you want, keep it short. The artillery is on its way.'

The Englishman held out a notepad from a bar in the north. The two remaining sheets on it were headed Hotel Bosna. He flicked the cardboard over and showed Milan Rajak the seven numbers and two initials.

'It was very decent of you to settle the bill, Milan. The barman was grateful. Unfortunately the cheque bounced.'

'No. Not possible. It was cl — '

He stopped and went white as a sheet.

'No one is blaming you for anything, Milan. So just tell me: what were you doing in Banja Luka?'

'Visiting.'

'Friends?'

'Yes.'

'In camouflage? Milan, it's a war zone. What happened that day two months ago?'

'I don't know what you mean. Mama . . . '

Then he broke into Serbo-Croat and the Tracker lost him. He raised an eyebrow at Stojic.

'Dad's coming,' muttered the detective.

'You were with a group of ten others. All in uniform. All armed. Who were they?'

Milan Rajak was beaded with sweat and looked as if he was going to burst into tears. The Tracker judged this to be a young man with serious nerve problems.

'You are English? But you are not Press. What are you doing here? Why you persecute me? I know nothing.'

There was a screech of car tyres outside the house, running feet up the steps from the pavement. Mrs Rajak held the door open and her husband charged in. He appeared at the door of the sitting room, rattled and angry. A generation older than his son, he did not speak English. Instead, he shouted in Serbo-Croat.

'He asks what you are doing in his house, why

95

you harass his son,' said Stojic.

'I am not harassing,' said the Tracker calmly. 'I am simply asking. What was this young man doing eight weeks ago in Banja Luka and who were the men with him?'

Stojic translated. Rajak senior began shouting.

'He says,' explained Stojic, 'that his son knows nothing and was not there. He has been here all summer and if you do not leave his house he will call the police. Personally, I think we should leave. This is a powerful man.'

'OK,' said the Tracker. 'One last question.'

At his request, the former Director of Special Forces, who now ran Hazard Management, had had a very discreet lunch with a contact in the Secret Intelligence Service. The Head of the Balkans Desk had been as helpful as he was allowed.

'Were those men Zoran's Wolves? Was the man who slapped you around Zoran Zilic himself?'

Stojic had translated more than half before he could stop himself. Milan understood it all in English. The effect was in two parts. For several seconds there was a stunned, glacial silence. The second part was like an exploding grenade.

Mrs Rajak emitted a single scream and ran from the room. Her son slumped in a chair, put his head in his hands and started to shake. The father went from white to puce, pointed at the door and started shouting a single word which Gracey presumed to mean 'out'. Stojic headed for the door. The Tracker followed.

As he passed the shaking young man he

96

stooped and slipped a card into his top jacket pocket.

'If you ever change your mind,' he murmured. 'Call me. Or write. I'll come.'

There was a strained silence in the car back to the airport. Dragan Stojic clearly felt he had earned every dime of his thousand dollars. As they drew up at international departures he spoke across the car roof at the departing Englishman.

'If you ever come back to Belgrade, my friend, I advise you not to mention that name. Not even in jest. Especially not in jest. Today's events never took place.'

Within forty-eight hours the Tracker had completed and filed his report to Stephen Edmond, along with his list of expenses. The final paragraphs read:

I fear I have to admit that the events that led to your grandson's death, the manner of that death or the resting place of the body will probably never be illuminated. And I would be raising false hopes if I said I thought there was a chance that your grandson was still alive. For the present and the foreseeable future the only judgement has to be: missing presumed killed.

I do not believe that he and the Bosnian accompanying him crashed off some road in the area and into a ravine. Every possible such road has been personally searched. Nor do I believe the Bosnian murdered him for the truck or the money belt or both.

I believe they inadvertently drove into

harm's way and were murdered by person or persons unknown. There is a likelihood that these persons were a band of Serbian paramilitary criminals believed to have been in the general area. But without evidence, identification, a confession or court testimony, there is no possibility of charges being brought.

It is with deepest regret that I have to impart this news to you, but I believe it to be almost certainly the truth.

I have the honour to remain, Sir,

Your obedient servant,

Philip Gracey.

It was 22 July 1995.

# 8

# The Lawyer

The main reason Calvin Dexter decided to leave the army was one he did not explain because he did not want to be mocked. He had decided he wanted to go to college, get a degree and become a lawyer.

As for funds, he had saved several thousand dollars in Vietnam and he could seek further help under the terms of the GI Bill.

There are few 'ifs' and 'buts' about the GI Bill; if an American soldier leaving the army for reasons other than dishonourable discharge wishes to apply, then his government will pay to put him through university to degree level. The allowance paid, rising over the past thirty years, can be spent by the student any way he wants, so long as the college confirms he is in full-time studentship.

Dexter reckoned that a rural college would probably be cheaper but he wanted a university with its own law school as well, and if he was ever going to practise law, then there would be more opportunities in the far bigger New York State than in New Jersey. After scouring fifty brochures, he applied for Fordham University, New York City.

He sent in his papers in the late spring, along

with the vital Discharge Document, the DD214 with which every GI left the army. He was just in time.

In the spring of 1971, though the sentiment against the Vietnam war was already high, and nowhere higher than in academia, the GIs were not seen as being to blame; rather as victims.

After the chaotic and undignified pullout of 1973, sometimes referred to as a scuttle, the mood changed. Though Richard Nixon and Henry Kissinger sought to put the best spin on things that they could, and though a disengagement from the unwinnable disaster that Vietnam had become was almost universally welcomed, it was still seen as a defeat.

If there is one thing the average American does not want to be associated with too often, it is defeat. The very concept is un-American, even on the liberal Left. The GIs coming home post-1973 thought they would be welcomed, as they had done their best, they had suffered, they had lost good friends; they met a blank wall of indifference, even hostility. The Left was more concerned with My Lai.

That summer of 1971, Dexter's papers were considered, along with all other applicants, and he was accepted for a four-year degree course in political history. In the category of 'life experience' his three years in the Big Red One were considered a positive, which would not have happened twenty-four months later.

The young veteran found a cheap, one-room walk-up in the Bronx, not far from campus, for back then Fordham was housed in a cluster of unglamorous redbrick buildings in that borough. He calculated that if he walked or used public transport, ate frugally and used the long summer vacation to go back to the construction industry he could make enough to survive until graduation. Among the construction sites on which he worked over the next three years was the new wonder of the world, the slowly rising World Trade Center.

The year 1974 was marked by two events that were to change his life. He met and fell in love with Angela Marozzi, a beautiful, vital, life-loving Italian-American girl working in a flower shop on Bathgate Avenue. They married that summer and with their joint income moved to a larger apartment.

That autumn, still one year from graduation, he applied for admission to the Fordham Law School, a faculty within the university, but separate in its location and administration, across the river in Manhattan. It was far harder to get into, having few places and being much sought after.

Law School would mean three more years of study after graduation in 1975 to the law degree, then the Bar Exam and finally the right to practise as an attorney-at-law in the State of New York.

There was no personal interview involved, just a mass of papers to be submitted to the Admissions Committee for their perusal and judgement. These included school records right back to grade school, which were awful, more recent grades for political history, a self-written assessment and references from present advisors, which were excellent. Hidden in this mass of paperwork was his old DD214.

He made the shortlist and the Admissions Committee met to make the final selection. There were six of them, headed by Professor Howard Kell, at seventy-seven well past retirement age, bright as a button, an emeritus professor and the patriarch of them all.

It came to one of two for the last available place. The papers marked Dexter as one of those. There was a heated debate. Professor Kell rose from his chair at the head of the table and wandered to the window. He stared out at the blue summer sky. A colleague came over to join him at the window.

'Tough one, eh, Howard? Whom do you favour?'

The old man tapped a paper in his hand and showed it to the senior tutor. The tutor read the list of medals and gave a low whistle.

'He was awarded those before his twenty-first birthday.'

'What the hell did he do?'

'He earned the right to be given a chance in this faculty, that's what he did,' said the professor.

The two men returned to the table and voted. It would have been three against three but the chairman's vote counted double in such a contingency. He explained why. They all looked at the DD214.

'He could be violent,' objected the politically correct Dean of Studies.

'Oh, I hope so,' said Professor Kell. 'I'd hate to think we were giving these away for nothing nowadays.'

Cal Dexter received the news two days later. He and Angela lay on their bed; he stroked her growing belly and talked of the day he would be a wealthy lawyer and they would have a fine house out at Westchester or Fairfield County.

Their daughter Amanda Jane was born in the early spring of 1975 but there were complications. The surgeons did their best but the outcome was unanimous. The couple could adopt, of course, but there would be no more natural pregnancies. Angela's family priest told her it was the will of God and she must accept His will.

Cal Dexter graduated in the top five of his class that summer and in the autumn began the three year course in Law. It was tough, but the Marozzi family rallied around; Mama baby-sat Amanda Jane so that Angela could wait tables. Cal wanted to remain a day student rather than revert to night school, which would extend the law course by an extra year.

He laboured through the summer vacations in the first two years but in the third managed to find work with the highly respectable Manhattan law firm of Honeyman Fleischer.

Fordham has always had a vigorous alumni network and Honeyman Fleischer had three senior partners who had graduated at Fordham Law School. Through a personal intervention by his tutor, Dexter secured vacation work as a legal assistant.

That summer of 1978 his father died. They had not been close after his return from Vietnam, for the parent had never understood why his son could not return to the construction sites and be content with a hard hat for the rest of his life.

But he and Angela had visited, borrowing Mr Marozzi's car, and shown Dexter Senior his only grandchild. When the end came it was sudden. A massive heart attack felled the building labourer on a worksite. His son attended the humble funeral alone. He had hoped his dad could attend his graduation ceremony and be proud of his educated son, but it was not to be.

He graduated that summer and pending his Bar Exam secured a lowly but full-time position with Honeyman Fleischer, his first professional employment since the army seven years earlier.

Honeyman Fleischer prided itself on its impeccable liberal credentials, avoided Republicans, and to prove its lively social conscience, fielded a pro bono department to undertake legal representation for no reward for the poor and vulnerable.

That said, the senior partners saw no need to exaggerate and kept their pro bono team to a few of their lowest-paid newcomers. That autumn of 1978, Cal Dexter was as lowly in the legal pecking order at Honeyman Fleischer as one could get.

Dexter did not complain. He needed the money, he cherished the job, and covering the down-and-outs gave him a hugely wide spectrum of experience, rather than the narrow confines of one single speciality. He could defend on charges of petty crime, negligence claims and a variety of other disputes that eventually came to a court of appeal.

It was that winter that a secretary popped her head round the door of his cubby-hole office and waved a file at him.

'What's that?' he asked.

'Immigration appeal,' she said. 'Roger says he can't handle it.'

The head of the tiny pro bono department chose the cream, if ever any cream appeared, for himself. Immigration matters were definitely the skimmed milk.

Dexter sighed and buried himself in the details of the new file. The hearing was the next day.

It was 20 November 1978.

# 9

## The Refugee

There was a charity in New York in those years called Refugee Watch. 'Concerned citizens' was how it would have described its members; 'do-gooders' was the less admiring description.

Its self-appointed task was to keep a weather eye open for examples of the flotsam and jetsam of the human race who, washed up on the shores of the USA, wished to take literally the words written on the base of the Statue of Liberty and stay.

Most often, these were forlorn, bereft people, refugees from a hundred climes, usually with a most fragmentary grasp of the English language and who had spent their last savings in the struggle to survive.

Their immediate antagonist was the Immigration and Naturalization Service, the formidable INS, whose collective philosophy appeared to be that 99.9 per cent of applicants were frauds and mountebanks who should be sent back whence they came, or at any rate somewhere else.

The file tossed onto Cal Dexter's desk that early winter of 1978 concerned a couple fleeing from Cambodia, Mr and Mrs Hom Moung.

In a lengthy statement by Mr Moung who seemed to speak for them both, translated from

106

the French which was the French-educated Cambodian's language of choice, his story emerged.

Since 1975, a fact already well known in the USA and later to become better known through the film *The Killing Fields*, Cambodia had been in the grip of a mad and genocidal tyrant called Pol Pot and his fanatical army the Khmer Rouge.

Pot had some hare-brained dream of returning his country to a sort of agrarian Stone Age. Fulfilment of his vision involved a pathological hatred of the people of the cities and anyone with any education. These were for extermination.

Mr Moung claimed he had been headmaster of a leading lycée or high school in the capital, Phnom Penh, and his wife a staff nurse at a private clinic. Both fitted firmly into the Khmer Rouge category for execution.

When things became impossible, they went underground, moving from safe house to safe house among friends and fellow professionals, until the latter had all been arrested and taken away.

Mr Moung claimed he would never have been able to reach the Vietnamese or Thai borders because in the countryside, infested with Khmer Rouge and informers, he would not have been able to pass for a peasant. Nevertheless, he had been able to bribe a truck driver to smuggle them out of Phnom Penh and across to the port of Kampong Son. With his last remaining savings, he persuaded the captain of a South

Korean freighter to take them out of the hell that his homeland had become.

He did not care or know where the *Inchon Star* was headed. It turned out to be New York harbour, with a cargo of teak. On arrival, he had not sought to evade the authorities but had reported immediately and asked permission to stay.

Dexter spent the night before the hearing hunched over the kitchen table while his wife and daughter slept a few feet away through the wall. The hearing was his first appeal of any kind, and he wanted to give the refugee his best shot. After the statement, he turned to the response of the INS. It had been pretty harsh.

The local Almighty in any US city is the District Director, and his office is the first hurdle. The Director's colleague in charge of the file had rejected the request for asylum on the strange grounds that the Moungs should have applied to the local US Embassy or Consulate and waited in line, according to American tradition.

Dexter felt this was not too much of a problem; all US staff had fled the Cambodian capital years earlier when the Khmer Rouge stormed in.

The refusal at the first level had put the Moungs into deportation procedure. That was when Refugee Watch heard of their case and took up the cudgels.

According to procedure, a couple refused entry by the District Director's Office at the Exclusion Hearing could appeal to the next level up, an Administrative Hearing in front of an Asylum Hearing Officer.

Dexter noted that at the Exclusion Hearing, the INS's second ground for refusal had been that the Moungs did not qualify under the five necessary grounds for proving persecution: race, nationality, religion, political beliefs and/or social class. He felt he could now show that as a fervent anti-Communist — and he certainly intended to advise Mr Moung to become one immediately — and as head teacher, he qualified on the last two grounds at least.

His task at the hearing on the morrow would be to plead with the Hearing Officer for a relief known as Withholding of Deportation, under Section 243(h) of the Immigration and Nationality Act.

In tiny print at the bottom of one of the papers was a note from someone at Refugee Watch that the Asylum Hearing Officer would be a certain Norman Ross. What he learned was interesting.

Dexter showed up at the INS building at 26 Federal Plaza over an hour before the hearing to meet his clients. He was not a big man himself, but the Moungs were smaller, and Mrs Moung was like a tiny doll. She gazed at the world through lenses that seemed to have been cut from the bottoms of shot glass tumblers. His papers told him they were forty-eight and forty-five respectively.

Mr Moung seemed calm and resigned. Because Cal Dexter spoke no French, Refugee Watch had provided a lady interpreter.

Dexter spent the preparation hour going over

109

the original statement, but there was nothing to add or subtract.

The case would be heard not in a real court, but in a large office with imported chairs for the occasion. Five minutes before the hearing, they were shown in.

As he surmised, the representative of the District Director re-presented the arguments used at the Exclusion Hearing to refuse the asylum application. There was nothing to add or subtract. Behind his desk, Mr Ross followed the arguments already before him in the file, then raised an eyebrow at the novice sent down by Honeyman Fleischer.

Behind him, Cal Dexter heard Mr Moung mutter to his wife, 'We must hope this young man can succeed, or we will be sent back to die.' But he spoke in his own native language.

Dexter dealt with the DD's first point: there has been no US diplomatic or consular representation in Phnom Penh since the start of the killing fields. The nearest would have been in Bangkok, Thailand, an impossible target that the Moungs could never have realized. He noted a hint of a smile at the corner of Ross's mouth as the man from the INS went pink.

His main task was to show that faced with the lethal fanaticism of the Khmer Rouge any proven anti-Communist like his client would have been destined on capture to torture and death. Even the fact of being a head teacher with a college degree would have guaranteed execution.

What he had learned in the night was that Norman Ross had not always been Ross. His father had arrived around the turn of the century as Samuel Rosen, from a shtetl in modern Poland, fleeing the pogroms of the Tsar, then being carried out by the Cossacks.

'It is very easy, sir, to reject those who come with nothing, seeking not much but the chance of life. It is very easy to say no and walk away. It costs nothing to decree that these two Orientals have no place here and should go back to arrest, torture and the execution wall.

'But I ask you, supposing our fathers had done that, and their fathers before them, how many, back in the homeland-turned-bloodbath, would have said: 'I went to the land of the free, I asked for a chance of life, but they shut their doors and sent me back to die.' How many, Mr Ross? A million? Nearer ten. I ask you, not on a point of law, not as a triumph for clever lawyer semantics, but as a victory for what Shakespeare called the quality of mercy, to decree that in this huge country of ours there is room for one couple who have lost everything but life and ask only for a chance.'

Norman Ross eyed him speculatively for several minutes. Then he tapped his pencil down on his desk like a gavel and pronounced.

'Deportation withheld. Next case.'

The lady from Refugee Watch excitedly told the Moungs in French what had happened. She and her organization could handle procedures from that point. There would be administration. But no more need for advocacy. The Moungs could now remain in the United States under the protection of the government, and eventually a

111

work permit, asylum and, in due course, naturalization would come through.

Dexter smiled at her and said she could go. Then he turned to Mr Moung and said:

'Now, let us go to the cafeteria and you can tell me who you really are and what you are doing here.'

He spoke in Mr Moung's native language. Vietnamese.

At a corner table in the basement café Dexter examined the Cambodian passports and ID documents.

'These have already been examined by some of the best experts in the West, and pronounced genuine. How did you get them?'

The refugee glanced at his tiny wife.

'She made them. She is of the Nghi.'

There is a clan in Vietnam called Nghi, which for centuries supplied most of the scholars of the Hue region. Their particular skill, passed down the generations, was for exceptional calligraphy. They created court documents for their emperors.

With the coming of the modern age, and especially when the war against the French began in 1945, their absolute dedication to patience, detail and stunning draughtsmanship meant the Nghi could transmute to some of the finest forgers in the world.

The tiny woman with the bottle-glasses had ruined her eyesight because for the duration of the Vietnam war, she had crouched in an underground workshop creating passes and identifications so perfect that Vietcong agents

112

had passed effortlessly through every South Vietnamese city at will and had never been caught.

Cal Dexter handed the passports back.

'Like I said upstairs, who are you really, and why are you here?'

The wife quietly began to cry and her husband slid his hand over hers.

'My name,' he said, 'is Nguyen Van Tran. I am here because after three years in a concentration camp in Vietnam, I escaped. That part at least is true.'

'So why pretend to be Cambodian? America has accepted many South Vietnamese who fought with us in that war.'

'Because I was a major in the Vietcong.'

Dexter nodded slowly.

'That could be a problem,' he admitted. 'Tell me. Everything.'

'I was born in 1930, in the deep south, up against the Cambodian border. That is why I have a smattering of Khmer. My family was never communist, but my father was a dedicated nationalist. He wanted to see our country free of the colonial domination of the French. He raised me the same way.'

'I don't have a problem with that. Why turn communist?'

'That is my problem. That is why I have been in a camp. I didn't. I pretended to.'

'Go on.'

'As a boy before World War II, I was raised under the French lycée system, even as I longed to become old enough to join the struggle for independence. In 1942 the Japanese came, expelling the French even though Vichy France was technically on their side. So we fought the Japanese.

'Leading in that struggle were the communists under Ho Chi Minh. They were more efficient, more skilled, more ruthless than the nationalists. Many changed sides, but my father did not. When the Japanese departed in defeat in 1945, Ho Chi Minh was a national hero. I was fifteen, already part of the struggle. Then the French came back.

'Then came nine more years of war. Ho Chi Minh and the communist Vietminh resistance movement simply absorbed all other movements. Anyone who resisted was liquidated. I was in that war too. I was one of those human ants who carried the parts of the artillery to the mountain peaks around Dien Bien Phu where the French were crushed in 1954. Then came the Geneva Accords, and also a new disaster. My country was divided. North and South.'

'You went back to war?'

'Not immediately. There was a short window of peace. We waited for the referendum that was part of the Accords. When it was denied, because the Diem dynasty ruling the South knew they would lose it, we went back to war. The choice was the disgusting Diems and their corruption in the South or Ho and General Giap in the North. I had fought under Giap; I hero-worshipped him. I chose the communists.'

'You were still single?'

'No, I had married my first wife. We had three children.'

'They are still there?'

'No, all dead.'

'Disease?'

'B fifty-twos.'

'Go on.'

'Then the first Americans came. Under Kennedy. Supposedly as advisors. But to us, the Diem regime had simply become another puppet government like the ones imposed under the Japanese and the French. So again, half my country was occupied by foreigners. I went back to the jungle to fight.'

'When?'

'Nineteen sixty-three.'

'Ten more years?'

'Ten more years. By the time it was over, I was forty-two and I had spent half my life living like an animal, subject to hunger, disease, fear and the constant threat of death.'

'But after 1972, you should have been triumphant,' remarked Dexter. The Vietnamese shook his head.

'You do not understand what happened after Ho died in 1968. The party and the government fell into different hands. Many of us were still fighting for a country we hoped and expected would have some tolerance in it. The ones who took over from Ho had no such intention. Patriot after patriot was arrested and executed. Those in charge were Le Duan and Le Duc Tho. They had none of the inner strength of Ho, which could tolerate a humane approach. They had to destroy

115

to dominate. The power of the secret police was massively increased. You remember the Tet Offensive?'

'Too damn well.'

'You Americans seem to think it was a victory for us. Not true. It was devised in Hanoi, wrongly attributed to General Giap, who was in fact impotent under Le Duan. It was imposed on the Vietcong as a direct order. It destroyed us. That was the intent. Forty thousand of our best cadres died in suicide missions. Among them were all the natural leaders of the South. With them gone, Hanoi ruled supreme. After Tet, the North Vietnamese Army took control, just in time for the victory. I was one of the last survivors of the southern nationalists. I wanted a free and reunited country; yes, but also with cultural freedom, a private sector, farm-owning farmers. That turned out to be a mistake.'

'What happened?'

'Well, after the final conquest of the South in 1975 the real pogroms started. The Chinese. Two million were stripped of everything they possessed; either forced into slave labour or expelled, the Boat People. I objected and said so. Then the camps started, for dissident Vietnamese. Two hundred thousand are now in camps, mainly southerners. At the end of 1975, the Cong Ang, the secret police, came for me. I had written one too many letters of objection, saying that for me, everything I had fought for was being betrayed. They didn't like that.'

'What did you get?'

'Three years, the standard sentence for

116

're-education'. After that, three years of daily surveillance. I was sent to a camp in Hatay province, about sixty kilometres from Hanoi. They always send you miles from your home; it deters escape.'

'But you made it?'

'My wife made it. She really is a nurse, as well as being a forger. And I really was a schoolmaster in the few years of peace. We met in the camp. She was in the clinic. I had developed abscesses on both legs. We talked. We fell in love. Imagine, at our age. She smuggled me out of there; she had some gold trinkets, hidden, not confiscated. These bought a ticket on a freighter. So now you know.'

'And you think I might believe you?' asked Dexter.

'You speak our language. Were you there?'

'Yes, I was.'

'Did you fight?'

'I did.'

'Then I say as one soldier to another: you should know defeat when you see it. You are looking at complete and utter defeat. So, shall we go?'

'Where had you in mind?'

'Back to the Immigration people of course. You will have to report us.'

Cal Dexter finished his coffee and rose. Major Nguyen Van Tran tried to rise also but Dexter pressed him back into his seat.

'Two things, major. The war is over. It happened far away and long ago. Try to enjoy the rest of your life.'

The Vietnamese was like one in a state of shock. He nodded dumbly. Dexter turned and walked away.

As he went down the steps to the street, something was troubling him. Something about the Vietcong officer, his face, the expression of frozen astonishment.

At the end of the street passers-by turned to look at the young lawyer who threw back his head and laughed at the madness of Fate. Absently he rubbed his left hand where the one-time enemy's hot nut oil in the tunnel had scalded him.

It was 21 November 1978.

# 10

## The Geek

By 1985 Cal Dexter had left Honeyman Fleischer, but not for a job that would lead to that fine house at Westchester. He joined the office of the Public Defender, becoming what is called in New York a Legal Aid Lawyer. It was not glamorous and it was not lucrative, but it gave him something he could not have achieved in corporate or tax law, and he knew it. It was called job satisfaction.

Angela had taken it well, better than he had hoped. In fact, she did not really mind. The Marozzi family were close as grapes on the vine and they were Bronx people through and through. Amanda Jane was in a school she liked, surrounded by her friends. A bigger and better job and a move upmarket were not required.

The new job meant working an impossible amount of hours in a day and representing those who had slipped through a hole in the mesh of the American Dream. It meant defending in court those who could not begin to afford legal representation on their own account.

For Cal Dexter poor and inarticulate did not necessarily mean guilty. He never failed to get a buzz when some dazed and grateful 'client' who, whatever else his inadequacies, had not done

119

what he was charged with walked free. It was a hot summer night in 1988 when he met Washington Lee.

The island of Manhattan alone handles over 110,000 crime cases a year and that excludes civil suits. The court system appears permanently on the verge of overload and a circuit blow-out, but somehow seems to survive. In those years part of the reason was the 24-hours-a-day conveyor belt system of court hearings that ran endlessly through the great granite block at 100 Center Street.

Like a good vaudeville show the Criminal Courts Building could boast 'We never close'. It would probably be an exaggeration to say that 'all life is here' but certainly the lower parts of Manhattan life showed up.

That night in July 1988 Dexter was working the night shift as an on-call attorney who could be allocated a client on the say-so of an over-busy judge. It was and he was trying to slip away when a voice summoned him back to Court AR2A. He sighed; one did not argue with Judge Hasselblad.

He approached the bench to join an Assistant District Attorney already standing there clutching a file.

'You're tired, Mr Dexter.'

'I guess we all are, your honour.'

'No dispute, but there is one more case I'd like you to take on. Not tomorrow, now. Take the file. This young man seems to be in serious trouble.'

'Your wish is my command, judge.'

Hasselblad's face widened in a grin.

120

'I just love deference,' he rejoined.

Dexter took the file from the ADA and they left the court together. The file cover read: 'People of the State of New York versus Washington Lee'.

'Where is he?' asked Dexter.

'Right here in a holding cell,' said the ADA.

As he had thought from the mugshot staring at him from the file, his client was a skinny kid with the air of bewildered hopelessness worn by the uneducated who are sucked in, chewed up and spat out by any judicial system in the world. He seemed more bewildered than smart.

The accused was eighteen years old, a denizen of that charmfree district known as Bedford Stuyvesant, a part of Brooklyn that is virtually a black ghetto. That alone aroused Dexter's interest. Why was he being charged in Manhattan? He presumed the kid had crossed the river and stolen a car or mugged someone with a wallet worth stealing.

But no, the charge was bank fraud. So, passing a forged cheque, attempting to use a stolen credit card, even the old trick of simultaneous withdrawals at the opposite ends of the counter from a dummy account? No.

The charge was odd, unspecific. The District Attorney had laid a 'bare-boned' charge alleging fraud in excess of $10,000. The victim was the East River Bank, headquarters in midtown Manhattan, which explained why the charge was being pursued on the island, not in Brooklyn. The fraud had been detected by the bank security staff and the bank wished to pursue with maximum vigour according to corporate policy.

Dexter smiled encouragingly, introduced himself, sat down and offered cigarettes. He did not smoke but 99 per cent of his clients dragged happily on the white sticks. Washington Lee shook his head.

'They're bad for your health, man.'

Dexter was tempted to say that seven years in the state pen was not going to do great things for it either, but forbore. Mr Lee, he noted, was not just homely, he was downright ugly. So how had he charmed a bank into handing over so much money? The way he looked, shuffled, slumped, he would hardly have been allowed across the Italian marble lobby of the prestigious East River Bank.

Calvin Dexter needed more time than was available to give the case file full and proper attention. The immediate concern was to get through the formality of the arraignment and see if there was even a remote possibility of bail. He doubted it.

An hour later Dexter and the ADA were back in court. Washington Lee, looking completely bewildered, was duly arraigned.

'Are we ready to proceed?' asked Judge Hasselblad.

'May it please the court, I have to ask for a continuance,' said Dexter.

'Approach,' ordered the judge. When the two lawyers stood beneath the bench he asked: 'You have a problem, Mr Dexter?'

'This is a more complex case than at first appears, your honour. This is not hubcaps. The

122

charge refers to over ten thousand dollars, embezzled from a blue-chip bank. I need more study time.'

The judge glanced at the ADA who shrugged, meaning no objection.

'This day week,' said the judge.

'I'd like to ask for bail,' said Dexter.

'Opposed, your honour,' said the ADA.

'I'm setting the bail at the sum named in the charge, ten thousand dollars,' said Judge Hasselblad.

It was out of the question and they all knew it. Washington Lee did not have ten dollars, and no bail bondsman was likely to want to know. It was back to a cell. As they left the court, Dexter asked the ADA for a favour.

'Be a sport, keep him in the Tombs, not the Island.'

'Sure, not a problem. Try and grab some sleep, huh?'

There are two short-spell remand prisons used by the Manhattan court system. The Tombs may sound like something underground but it is in fact a high-rise remand centre right next to the court buildings and far more convenient for defence lawyers visiting their clients than Riker's Island, way up the East River. Despite the ADA's advice for a bit of sleep, the file probably precluded that. If he was to confer with Washington Lee the next morning he had some reading to do.

To the trained eye the wad of papers told the story of the detection and arrest of Washington Lee. The fraud had been detected internally and traced to Lee. The bank's Head of Security, one Dan Witkowski, was a former detective with the NYPD and he had prevailed on some of his former colleagues to go over to Brooklyn and arrest Washington Lee.

He had first been brought to, and lodged in, a precinct house in midtown. When a sufficient number of miscreants were gracing the cells of the precinct house, they were brought down to the Criminal Courts Building and relodged there on the timeless and unvarying diet of baloney and cheese sandwiches.

Then the wheels had ground their remorseless course. The rap sheet showed a short litany of minor street crime: hubcaps, vending machines, shoplifting. With that formality complete, Washington Lee was ready for arraignment. That was when Judge Hasselblad demanded that the youth be represented.

On the face of it, this was a youth born to nothing and with nothing, who would graduate from truancy to pilfering and thence a life of crime and frequent periods as a guest of the citizens of New York State somewhere 'up the river'. So how on earth had he sweet-talked the East River Bank, which did not even have a branch in Bedford Stuyvesant, out of $10,000? No answer. Not in the file. Just a bare-bones charge and an angry and vengeful Manhattan-based bank. Grand Larceny in the 3rd Degree. Seven years' hard time.

Dexter grabbed three hours' sleep, saw Amanda Jane off to school, kissed Angela goodbye and came back to Center Street. It was in an interview room in the Tombs that he was able to drag his story out of the black kid.

At school he had shone at nothing. His grades were a disaster. The future offered nothing but the road to dereliction, crime and jail. And then one of the school teachers, maybe smarter than the others or just kinder, had allowed the graceless boy access to his Hewlett Packard computer. (Here, Dexter was reading between the lines of the halting narrative.)

It was like offering the boy Yehudi Menuhin a chance to hold a violin. He stared at the keys, he stared at the screen, and he began to make music. The teacher, clearly a computer buff when personal machines were the exception rather than the norm, was intrigued. That was five years earlier.

Washington Lee began to study. He also began to save. When he opened and gutted vending machines, he did not smoke the proceeds, or drink them, or shoot them into his arm, or wear them as clothes. He saved them until he could buy a cheap bankrupt-stock computer in a closing-down sale.

'So how did you swindle the East River Bank?'

'I broke into their mainframe,' said the kid.

For a moment Cal Dexter thought a jemmy might have been involved so he asked his client to explain. For the first time the boy became animated. He was talking about the only thing he knew.

'Man, have you any idea how weak some of the defensive systems created to protect databases really are?'

125

Dexter conceded it was not a query that had ever detained him. Like most non-experts, he knew that computer-system designers created 'firewalls' to prevent unauthorized access to hyper-sensitive databases. How they did it, let alone how to outwit them, had never occurred to him. He teased the story out of Washington Lee.

The East River Bank had stored every detail of every account holder in a huge database. As clients' financial situations are regarded by most clients as very private, access to those details involved bank officers punching in an elaborate system of coded signals. Unless these were absolutely correct, the computer screen would simply flash the message 'Access Denied'. A third erroneous attempt to break in would start alarm signals flashing at head office.

Washington Lee had broken the codes without triggering the alarms, to the point where the main computer buried below the bank's HQ in Manhattan would obey his instructions. In short, he had performed coitus non-interruptus on a very expensive piece of technology.

His instructions were simple. He ordered the computer to identify every savings and deposit account held by clients of the bank and the monthly interest paid into those accounts. Then he ordered it to deduct one quarter from each interest payment and transfer that quarter into his own account.

As he did not have one, he opened one at the local Chase Manhattan. Had he known enough to transfer the money to the Bahamas, he would probably have got away with it.

It is quite a calculation to ascertain interest due on one's deposit account because it will depend on the ambient interest rate over the earning period, and that will fluctuate, and to get it to the nearest quarter takes time. Most people do not have that time. They trust the bank to do the maths and get it right.

Not Mr Tolstoy. He may have been eighty but his mind was still sharp as a pin. His problem was boredom, whiling away his hours in his tiny apartment on West 108th Street. Having spent his life as an actuary for a major insurance company, he was convinced that even nickels and dimes count, if multiplied enough times. He spent his time trying to catch the bank out in error. One day, he did.

He became convinced his interest due for the month of April was a quarter short. He checked the figures for March. Same thing. He went back two more months. Then he complained.

The local manager would have given him the missing dollar, but rules are rules. He filed the complaint. Head office thought it was a single glitch in a single account, but ran random checks on half a dozen other accounts. Same thing. Then the computer people were called in.

They established that the master computer had done this to every checking account in the bank and had been doing so for twenty months. They asked it why.

'Because you told me to,' said the computer.

'No, we didn't,' said the boffins.

'Well someone did,' said the computer.

That was when they called in Dan Witkowski.

127

It did not take very long. The transfers of all these nickels were to an account at the Chase Manhattan over in Brooklyn. Client name: Washington Lee.

'Tell me, how much did all this net you?' asked Dexter.

'Just shy of a million dollars.'

The lawyer bit the end off his pencil. No wonder the charge was so vague. 'In excess of ten thousand dollars' indeed. The very size of the theft gave him an idea.

Mr Lou Ackerman enjoyed his breakfast. For him it was the best meal of the day; never hurried like lunch, never over-rich like banquet dinners. He enjoyed the shock of the icy juice, the crunch of the cereal flakes, the fluffiness of well-scrambled eggs, the aroma of the freshly perked Blue Mountain coffee. On his balcony above Central Park West, in the cool of a summer morning before the real heat came upon the day, it was a joy. And it was a shame of Mr Calvin Dexter to spoil it.

When his Filipino manservant brought the pasteboard card to his terrace, he glanced at the words 'attorney-at-law', frowned and wondered who his visitor might be. The name rang a bell. He was about to tell his manservant to ask the visitor to come to the bank later in the morning, when a voice behind the Filipino said:

'I know it's impertinence, Mr Ackerman, and for that I apologize. But if you will give me ten minutes I suggest you will be glad we did not meet in the glare of attention at your office.'

128

He shrugged and gestured to a chair across the table.

'Tell Mrs Ackerman I'm in conference at the breakfast table,' he instructed the Filipino. Then to Dexter, 'Keep it short, Mr Dexter.'

'I will. You are pressing for the prosecution of my client, Mr Washington Lee, for having allegedly skimmed almost a million dollars from your clients' accounts. I think it would be wise to drop the charges.'

The CEO of the East River Bank could have kicked himself. You show a little kindness and what do you get? A ball-breaker ruining your breakfast.

'Forget it, Mr Dexter. Conversation over. No way. The boy goes down. There must be deterrence to this sort of thing. Company policy. Good day.'

'Pity. You see, the way he did it was fascinating. He broke into your computer mainframe. He waltzed through all your firewalls, your security guards. No one is supposed to be able to do that.'

'Your time is up, Mr Dexter.'

'A few seconds more. There will be other breakfasts. You have about a million clients, checking account and deposit account. They think their funds are safe with you. Later this week a skinny black kid from the ghetto is going to stand up in court and say that if he did it, any half-assed amateur could empty any of your clients' accounts after a few hours of electronic probing. How do you think your clients are going to like that?'

Ackerman put down his coffee and stared across the park.

'It's not true, and why should they believe it?'

'Because the Press benches will be packed and the TV and radio media will be outside. I think up to a quarter of your clients could decide to move bank.'

'We'll announce we are installing a whole new safeguard system. The best on the market.'

'But that's what you were supposed to have had before. And a Bedford Stuyvesant kid with no school grades broke it. You were lucky. You got the whole million dollars back. Supposing it happened again, for tens of millions in one awful weekend, and it went to the Caymans. The bank would have to reinstate. Would your board appreciate the humiliation?'

Lou Ackerman thought of his board. Some of the institutional shareholders were people like Pearson-Lehman, Morgan Stanley. The sort of people who hated to be humiliated. The sort who might have a man's job.

'It's that bad, uh?'

'I'm afraid so.'

'All right. I'll call the DA's office and say we have no further interest in proceeding, since we all have our money back. Mind you, the DA can still proceed if he wants to.'

'Then you'll be very persuasive, Mr Ackerman. All you have to say is: 'Scam, what scam?' After that, mum is the word, wouldn't you say?'

He rose and turned to leave. Ackerman was a good loser.

'We could always do with a good lawyer, Mr Dexter.'

'I've got a better idea. Take Washington Lee on the payroll. I'd have thought fifty thousand dollars a year is about right.'

Ackerman was on his feet, Blue Mountain brown-staining the napery.

'What the hell should I want that lowlife on the payroll for?'

'Because when it comes to computers, he's the best. He's proved it. He sliced through a security system that cost you a mint to install, and he did it with a fifty-dollar sardine can. He could install for you a totally impenetrable system. You could make a sales point out of it: the safest database west of the Atlantic. He's much safer inside the tent pissing out.'

Washington Lee was released twenty-four hours later. He was not quite sure why. Neither was the ADA. But the bank had had a bout of corporate amnesia and the District Attorney's office had its usual backlog. Why insist?

The bank sent a stretch limo to the Tombs to pick up their new staffer. He had never been in one before. He sat in the back and looked at the head of his lawyer poking in the window.

'Man, I don't know what you did or how you did it. One day maybe I can pay you back.'

'OK, Washington, maybe one day you will.'

It was 20 July 1988.

# 11

# The Killer

When Yugoslavia was ruled by Marshal Tito it was virtually a crime-free society. Molesting a tourist was unthinkable, women safely walked the streets and racketeering was non-existent.

This was odd, considering that the seven provinces that made up Yugoslavia, cobbled together by the Western Allies in 1918, had traditionally produced some of the most vicious and violent gangsters in Europe.

The reason was that post-1948 the Yugoslav government established a compact with the Yugoslav underworld. The deal was simple: you can do whatever you like and we will turn a blind eye under one condition — you do it abroad. Belgrade simply exported its entire crime world.

The speciality targets for the Yugoslav crime bosses were Italy, Austria, Germany and Sweden. The reason was simple. By the mid-1960s the Turks and the Yugoslavs had become the first wave of 'guest workers' in richer countries to the north, meaning that they were encouraged to come and do the mucky jobs that the overindulged indigenes no longer wanted to do.

Every large ethnic movement brings its own crime world with it. The Italian Mafia arrived in New York with the Italian immigrants; Turkish criminals soon joined the Turkish 'guest worker' communities across Europe. The Yugoslavs were the same, but here the agreement was more structured.

Belgrade got it both ways. Its thousands of Yugoslavs working abroad sent their hard currency home each week; as a communist state Yugoslavia was always an economic mess but the regular inflow of hard currency hid the fact.

So long as Tito repudiated Moscow, the USA and NATO remained pretty relaxed about what else he did. Indeed, he ranked as one of the leaders of the Non-Aligned countries right through the Cold War. The beautiful Dalmatian coast along the Adriatic became a tourist Mecca, bringing in even more foreign exchange, and the sun shone.

Internally, Tito ran a brutal regime where dissidents or opponents were concerned, but kept it quiet and discreet. The compact with the gangsters was run and supervised not so much by the civil police but by the secret police, known as State Security or DB.

It was the DB that laid down the terms. The gangsters preying on the Yugoslav communities abroad could return home for R and R with impunity, and did. They built themselves villas on the coast and mansions in the capital. They made their donations to the pension funds of the chiefs of the DB, and occasionally they were required to carry out a 'wet job' with no invoice and no trace-back. The mastermind of this cosy arrangement was the long-time intelligence boss, the fat and fearsome Slovenian Stane Dolanc.

Inside Yugoslavia there was a little prostitution, but well under local police control, and some lucrative smuggling which, again, helped official pension funds. But violence, other than the state kind, was forbidden. Young tearaways reached the level of running rival district street gangs, stealing cars (not belonging to tourists) and brawling. If they wanted to get more serious than that they had to leave. Those hard of hearing on this issue could find themselves in a remote prison camp with the cell key dropped down a deep well.

Marshal Tito was no fool, but he *was* mortal. He died in 1980 and things began to fall apart.

In the blue-collar Belgrade district of Zemun a garage mechanic called Zilic had a son in 1956 and named him Zoran. From an early age it became plain his nature was vicious and deeply violent. By the age of ten, his teachers shuddered at the mention of him.

But he had one thing that would later set him apart from other Belgrade gangsters like Zeljko Raznatovic, alias Arkan. He was smart.

Skipping school from fourteen onwards, he became leader of a teenage gang involved in the usual pleasures of stealing cars, brawling, drinking and ogling the local girls. After one particular 'rumble' between two gangs, three members of the opposing team had been so badly beaten with bicycle chains that they hovered between life and death for several days. The local police chief decided that enough was enough.

Zilic was hauled in, taken to the basement by

134

two stalwarts with lengths of rubber hose, and beaten till he could not stand. There was no ill-will involved; the police felt they needed him to concentrate on what they were saying.

The police chief then gave the youth a word of advice, or several. It was 1972, the boy was sixteen and a week later he left the country. But he already had an introduction to take up. In Germany, he joined the gang of Ljuba Zemunac — his surname was adopted, taken from the suburb of his birth. He also came from Zemun.

Zemunac was an impressively vicious mobster who would later be shot to death in the lobby of a German courthouse, but Zoran Zilic stayed with him for ten years, earning the older man's admiration as the most sadistic enforcer he had ever employed. In protection racketeering, the ability to inspire terror is vital. Zilic could do that and enjoy every moment.

In 1982 Zilic left and formed his own gang at the age of twenty-six. This might have caused a turf war with his old employer, but Zemunac shuffled off the mortal coil soon afterwards. Zilic remained at the head of his gang in Germany and Austria for the next five years. He had long mastered German and English. But back home, things were changing.

There was no one to replace Marshal Tito, whose war record as a partisan against the Germans and sheer force of personality had kept together this unnatural seven-province federation for so long.

The decade of the Eighties was marked by a series of coalition governments that rose and fell, but the spirit of secession and separate independence was raging through Slovenia and Croatia in the north, and Macedonia in the south.

In 1987, Zilic cast in his lot with a shabby little ex-communist party hack whom others had overlooked or underestimated. He sported two qualities he liked: an absolute ruthlessness in the pursuit of power, and a level of cunning and deviousness that would disarm rivals until it was too late. He had spotted the coming man. From 1987 he offered to 'take care' of the opponents of Slobodan Milosevic. There was no refusal and no charge.

By 1989 Milosevic had realized that communism was dead in the water; the horse to mount was that of extreme Serb nationalism. In fact, he brought not one but four horsemen to his country, those of the Apocalypse. Zilic served him almost to the end.

Yugoslavia was breaking up. Milosevic posed as the man to save the union, but made no mention that he intended to do this through genocide, known as ethnic cleansing. Inside Serbia, the province around Belgrade, his popularity stemmed from the belief that he would save Serbs everywhere from non-Serb persecution.

To do this, they had first to be persecuted. If the Croatians or Bosnians were slow on the uptake, this had to be arranged. A small local massacre would normally provoke the resident majority to turn on the Serbs among them. Then Milosevic could send in the army to save the

Serbs. It was the gangsters, turned paramilitary 'patriots', who acted as his agents provocateurs.

Where up until 1989 the Yugoslav state had kept its gangster underworld at arm's length and abroad, Milosevic took them into full partnership at home.

Like so many second-raters elevated to state power, Milosevic became fascinated by money. The sheer size of the sums involved acted on him like a snake-charmer's pipe to a cobra. It was not, for him, the luxury that money could buy. He remained personally frugal to the end. It was money as another form of power that hypnotized him. By the time he fell, it was estimated by the successor Yugoslavian government that he and his cronies had embezzled and diverted to their own foreign accounts about twenty billion dollars.

Others were not so frugal. These included his deeply ghastly wife and equally appalling son and daughter. The Milosevic household made *The Munsters* look like *Little House on the Prairie*.

Among those 'full partners' was Zoran Zilic, who became the dictator's personal enforcer, a killer for hire. Reward under Milosevic was never in cash. It came in the award of franchises for especially lucrative rackets, coupled with the assurance of absolute immunity. The tyrant's cronies could rob, torture, rape, kill, and there was absolutely nothing the regular police could do about it. He established a criminal-cum-embezzler regime, posed as a patriot and the

Serbs and West European politicians fell for it for years.

In all this brutality and bloodshed, he still did not save the Yugoslav federation or even his dream of a Greater Serbia. Slovenia left, then Macedonia and Croatia. By the Dayton Agreement of November 1995, Bosnia was gone, and by July 1999, he had not only effectively lost Kosovo, but also provoked the partial destruction by NATO bombs of Serbia itself.

Like Arkan, Zilic also formed a small squad of paramilitaries. There were others, like the sinister, shadowy and brutal Frankie's Boys, the group of Frankie Stamatovic — amazingly not even a Serb, but a renegade Croat from Istria. Unlike the florid and ostentatious Arkan, gunned down in the lobby of the Belgrade Holiday Inn, Zilic kept himself and his group so low-profile as to be invisible. But on three occasions during the Bosnia war he took his group north and raped, tortured and murdered his way across that miserable province until American intervention put a stop to it.

The third occasion was in April 1995. Where Arkan called his group his Tigers and had a couple of hundred of them, Zilic was content with Zoran's Wolves and he kept the numbers small. On the third sortie he had no more than a dozen. They were all thugs who had operated before, save one. He lacked a radio operator and one of his colleagues whose junior brother was in law school said his brother had a friend who had been an Army R/T operator.

Contacted via the fellow student, the new-comer agreed to forgo his Easter vacation and join the Wolves.

Zilic asked what he was like. Had he seen combat? No, he had done his military service in the Signals corps which was why he was ready for some 'action'.

'If he has never been shot at, then he surely has never killed anyone,' said Zilic. 'So this expedition should be quite a learning curve.'

The group set off for the north in the first week of May, delayed by technical problems to their Russian-made jeeps. They went through Pale, the tiny former ski resort now established as the capital of the self-styled Republika Serbska, the third of Bosnia now so 'cleansed' that it was uniquely Serb. They skirted Sarajevo, once the proud host of the winter Olympics, now a wreck, and went on into Bosnia proper, making their base at the stronghold of Banja Luka.

From there Zilic ranged outwards, avoiding the dangerous Mujahedin, looking for softer targets among any Bosnian Muslim communities who might lack armed protection.

On 14 May, they found a small hamlet in the Vlasic range, took it by surprise and wiped out the inhabitants, spent the night in the woods and were back at Banja Luka by the evening of the 15th.

The new recruit left them the next day, screaming that he wanted to get back to his studies after all. Zilic let him go, after warning him that if he ever opened his mouth he, Zilic, would personally cut off his dick with a broken wine glass and stuff both down his throat in that order. He did not like the boy anyway; he was stupid and squeamish.

The Dayton Agreement put an end to sport in Bosnia, but Kosovo was coming into season, and in 1998 he was operating there also, claiming to be suppressing the Kosovo Liberation Army, in fact concentrating on rural communities and some seriously interesting loot.

But he never neglected his real reason for allying with Slobodan Milosevic. His service to the despot had paid rich dividends. His 'business' dealings were a gangster's charter, the right to do what every Mafioso has to dodge the Law to achieve and yet to do it with presidential immunity.

Chief among the franchises that paid dividends of several hundred per cent were cigarettes and perfumes, fine brandies and whiskies and all forms of luxury goods. These franchises he shared with Raznatovic, the only other gangster of comparable importance, and a few others. Even with sweeteners to all the necessary police and political 'protection', he was a millionaire by the mid-Nineties.

Then he moved into prostitution, narcotics and arms dealing. With his fluent German and English he was better placed to deal with the international crime world than the others who were monolingual.

Narcotics and arms were especially lucrative. His dollar fortune entered eight figures. He also entered the files of the American Drug Enforcement Agency, the CIA, the Defence

Intelligence Agency (arms dealing) and the FBI.

Those around Milosevic, fat on embezzled money, power, corruption, ostentation, luxury and the endless sycophancy to which they were subjected, became lazy and complacent. They presumed the party would go on for ever. Zilic did not.

He avoided the obvious banks used by most of the cronies to store or export their fortunes. Almost every penny he made he stashed abroad, but via banks no one in the Serbian State knew anything about. And he watched for the first cracks in the plaster. Sooner or later, he reasoned acutely, even the awesomely weak politicians and diplomats of Britain and the European Union would see through Milosevic and call 'time out'. It happened over Kosovo.

A largely agricultural province, Kosovo ranked with Montenegro as all that was left of Serbia's fiefdoms within the Federation of Yugoslavia. It contained about 1,800,000 Kosovars, who are Muslims and hardly distinguishable from the neighbouring Albanians, and 200,000 Serbs.

Milosevic had been deliberately persecuting the Kosovars for a decade until the once moribund Kosovo Liberation Army was back in being. The strategy was to be the same as usual. Persecute beyond toleration; wait for the local outrage; denounce the 'terrorists'; enter in force to save the Serbs and 'restore order'. Then NATO said it would not stand by any more. Milosevic did not believe them. Mistake. This time they meant it.

In the spring of 1999 the ethnic cleansing

began, mainly accomplished by the occupying Third Army, assisted by the Security Police and the paramilitaries: Arkan's Tigers, Frankie's Boys and Zoran's Wolves. As foreseen, over a million Kosovars fled in terror over the borders into Albania and Macedonia. They were supposed to. The West was supposed to take them all in as refugees. But they did not. They started to bomb Serbia.

Belgrade stuck it out for seventy-eight days. Up front, the local reaction was anti-NATO. Behind their hands, the Serbs began to mutter that it was the mad Milosevic who had brought this ruin upon them. It is always educational to note how the war fever fades when the roof falls in. Zilic heard the muttering behind the hands.

On 3 June 1999 Milosevic agreed to terms. That was the way it was put. To Zilic it was unconditional surrender. He decided the moment had come to depart.

The fighting ended. The Third Army, having hardly taken a casualty to NATO's high-altitude bombing inside Kosovo, withdrew with all their equipment intact. The NATO allies occupied the province. The remaining Serbs began to flee into Serbia, bringing their rage with them. The direction of that rage began to move from NATO to Milosevic as the Serbs contemplated their shattered country.

Zilic began to slip any last vestiges of his fortune beyond reach, and to prepare his own departure. Through the autumn of 1999 the protests against Milosevic grew and grew.

In a personal interview in November 1999

142

Zilic begged the dictator to observe the writing on the wall, conduct his own coup d'état while he had a loyal army to do it, and do away with any further pretence at democracy or opposition parties. But Milosevic was by then in his own private world where his popularity was undiminished.

Zilic left his presence wondering yet again at the phenomenon that when men who have once held supreme power start to lose it, they go to pieces in every sense. Courage, willpower, perception, decisiveness, even the ability to recognize reality — all are washed away as the tide sweeps away a sandcastle. By December Milosevic was not exercising power; he was clinging to it. Zilic completed his preparations.

His fortune was no less than 500 million dollars; he had a place to go where he would be safe. Arkan was dead, executed for falling out with Milosevic. The principal ethnic cleansers of Bosnia, Karadzic and General Mladic of the Srebrenitsa massacre, were being hunted like animals through Republika Serbska where they had taken refuge. Others had already been snatched for the new war-crimes tribunal in The Hague. Milosevic was a broken reed.

As a matter of record, Milosevic declared on 27 July 2000 the coming presidential elections for 24 September. Despite copious rigging and a refusal to accept the outcome, he still lost. Crowds stormed the Parliament and installed his successor. Among the first acts of the new regime was to start investigating the Milosevic period: the murders, the twenty billion missing dollars.

The former tyrant holed himself up in his villa in the plush suburb of Dedinje. On 1 April 2001 President Kostunica was good and ready. The arrest moved in at last.

But Zoran Zilic was long gone. In January 2000 he just disappeared. He said no goodbyes and took no luggage. He went as one departing for a new life in a different world, where the old gewgaws would have no use. So he left them all behind.

He took nothing and no one with him, save his ultra-loyal personal bodyguard, a hulking giant called Kulac. Within a week he had settled in his new hideout, which he had spent over a year preparing to receive him.

No one in the intelligence community paid attention to his departure, save one. A quiet, secretive man in America noted the gangster's new abode with considerable interest.

# 12

# The Monk

It was the dream, always the dream. He could not be rid of it and it would not let him go. Night after night he would wake screaming, wet with sweat, and his mother would rush in to hold him and try to bring him comfort.

He was a puzzle and a worry to both his parents, for he could not or would not describe his nightmare, but his mother was convinced he never had such dreams until his return from Bosnia.

The dream was always the same. It was the face in the slime, a pale disc ringed with lumps of excrement, some bovine, some human, screaming for mercy, begging for life. He could understand the English, as could Zilic, and words like 'no, no, please, don't' are pretty international.

But the men with the poles laughed and pushed again. And the face came back, until Zilic rammed his pole into the open mouth and pushed downwards until the boy was dead under there somewhere. Then he would wake, shouting and crying, until his mother wrapped him in her arms, telling him it was all right, he was home in his own room at Senjak.

But he could not explain what he had done,

what he had been a part of, when he thought he was doing his patriotic duty to Serbia.

His father was less comforting, claiming he was a hardworking man who needed his sleep. By the autumn of 1995 Milan Rajak had his first session with a trained psychotherapist.

He attended twice a week at the grey-rendered five-storey psychiatric hospital on Palmoticeva Street, the best in Belgrade. But the experts at the Laza Lazarevic could not help either, because he dared not confess.

Relief, he was told, comes with purging, but catharsis requires confession. Milosevic was still in power, but far more frightening were the feral eyes of Zoran Zilic that morning in Banja Luka when he said he wanted to quit and go home to Belgrade. Much more terrifying were the whispered words of mutilation and death if he ever opened his mouth.

His father was a dedicated atheist, raised under the communist regime of Tito and a lifelong loyal servant of the Party. But his mother had kept her faith in the Serbian Orthodox church, part of the eastern communion with the Greek and Russian churches. Mocked by her husband and son, she had gone to her morning service down the years. By the end of 1995, Milan started to accompany her.

He began to find some comfort amid the ritual and the litany, the chants and the incense. The horror seemed to ebb in the church by the football ground, just three blocks from where they lived, and where his mother always went.

In 1996 he flunked his law exams to the

146

outrage and despair of his father who stormed up and down the house for two days. If the news from the academy was not to his taste, what his son had to say took his breath away.

'I do not want to be a lawyer, father. I want to enter the Church.'

It took time but Rajak Senior calmed down and tried to come to terms with his changed son. At least the priesthood was a profession of sorts. Not given to wealth, but respectable. A man could still hold his head up and say, 'My son is in the Church, you know.'

The priesthood itself, he discovered, would take years of study to achieve, most of that time in a seminary, but the son had other ideas. He wanted to live in seclusion and without delay. He wanted to become a monk, repudiating everything material in favour of the simple life.

Ten miles southeast of Belgrade he found what he wanted: the small monastery of Saint Stephen in the hamlet of Slanci. It contains no more than a dozen brothers under the authority of the abbot or Iguman. They work in the fields and barns of their own farm, grow their own food, accept donations from a few tourists and pilgrims, meditate and pray. There was a waiting list to join and no chance of jumping it.

Fate intervened in the meeting with the Iguman, Abbot Vasilije. He and Rajak Senior stared at each other in amazement. Despite the full black beard, flecked with grey, Rajak recognized the same Goran Tomic who had been at school with him forty years before. The abbot agreed to meet his son and discuss with him a possible career in the Church.

The abbot's shrewd intelligence divined that his former schoolmate's son was a young man torn by some inner turmoil that could not find peace in the outer world. He had seen it before. He could not create a vacancy for an instant monk, he pointed out, but men from the city occasionally joined the monks for the purpose of a religious 'retreat'.

In the summer of 1996, with the Bosnian war over, Milan Rajak came to Slanci on extended retreat to grow tomatoes and cucumbers, to meditate and to pray. The dream ebbed away.

After a month Abbot Vasilije gently suggested that he confess, and he did. In whispered tones, by the light of a candle by the altar, under the gaze of the man from Nazareth, he told the abbot what he had done.

The abbot crossed himself fervently and prayed: for the soul of the boy in the cesspit and for the penitent beside him. He urged Milan to go to the authorities and report against those responsible.

But the grip of Milosevic was absolute and the terror inspired by Zoran Zilic no less so. That the 'authorities' would have lifted a finger against Zilic was inconceivable. But the killer's promised vengeance would, when carried out, raise not a ripple on the water. So the silence went on.

The pain began in the winter of 2000. He noticed that it intensified with each body motion. After two months he consulted his father who presumed some passing 'bug'. Nevertheless, he arranged for tests at the Belgrade General

Hospital, the Klinicki Centre.

Belgrade has always boasted medical standards among the highest in Europe and the Belgrade General was up there with the best. There were three series of tests, and they were seen by specialists in proctology, urology and oncology. It was the professor heading the third department who finally asked Milan Rajak to visit his suite of rooms at the clinic.

'I believe you are a trainee monk?' he asked.

'Yes.'

'Then you believe in God?'

'Yes.'

'I sometimes wish I could also. Alas, I cannot. But you must now test your faith. The news is not good.'

'Tell me, please.'

'It is what we call colorectal cancer.'

'Operable?'

'I regret. No.'

'Reversible? Chemotherapy?'

'Too late. I am sorry, deeply sorry.'

The young man stared out of the window. He had been sentenced to death.

'How long, professor?'

'That is always asked, and always impossible to answer. With precautions, care, a special diet, some radiotherapy . . . a year. Possibly less, possibly more. Not much more.'

It was March 2001. Milan Rajak went back to Slanci and told the abbot. The older man wept for the one who was now like the son he had never had.

On 1 April the Belgrade police arrested

Slobodan Milosevic. Zoran Zilic had disappeared; at his son's request, Milan's puzzled father had used his contacts high in the police force to confirm that Yugoslavia's most successful and powerful gangster had simply disappeared more than a year earlier and was now living somewhere abroad, location unknown. His influence had disappeared with him.

On 2 April 2001, Milan Rajak sought out from his papers an old card. He took a sheet of paper and, writing in English, addressed a letter to London. The burden of the letter was in the first line.

'I have changed my mind. I am prepared to testify.'

Within twenty-four hours of receiving the letter three days later, and after a quick call to Stephen Edmond in Windsor, Ontario, the Tracker came back to Belgrade.

The statement was taken in English, in the presence of a certified interpreter and notary public. It was signed and witnessed:

★ ★ ★

Back then in 1995, young Serbian men were accustomed to believe what they were told, and I was no exception. It may be plain today what terrible things were done in Croatia and Bosnia, and later in Kosovo, but we were told the victims were isolated communities of Serbs in these former provinces, and I believed this. The idea that our own armed forces were carrying out mass murder of old people, women and children, was inconceivable. Only Croats and Bosnians did this sort of thing, we were told. Serbian forces were only concerned to protect and rescue Serbian minority communities.

When in April 1995 a fellow law student told me his brother and others were going to Bosnia to protect the Serbs up there, and needed a radio operator, I suspected nothing.

I had done my military service as a radio operator, but miles from any fighting. I agreed to give up my spring vacation to help my fellow Serbs in Bosnia.

When I joined the other twelve, I realized they were rough types, but I put this down to their being hardened combat soldiers, and blamed myself for being too spoiled and soft.

The column of four off-roads contained twelve men, including the leader, who joined us at the last minute. Only then did I learn he was Zoran Zilic, of whom I had vaguely heard, who had a fearsome but shadowy reputation. We drove for two days, north through Republika Serbska and into Central Bosnia. We arrived at Banja Luka and that became our base, notably the Bosna Hotel where we took rooms and ate and drank.

We made three patrols north, east and west of Banja Luka but found no enemy or threatened Serbian villages. On 14 May we drove south into the Vlasic range of mountains. We knew that beyond the range lay Travnik and Vitez, both enemy territory for us Serbs.

In the late afternoon we were driving along a track in the woods when we came across two little girls in front of us. Zilic got out and talked to them. He was smiling. I thought he was being nice to them. One told him her name was Laila. I did not understand. It was a Muslim name. She had signed her own death warrant and that of her village.

Zilic took the girls aboard the leading jeep and they pointed out where they lived. It was a hamlet in a valley in the woods: nothing much, about twenty adults and a dozen children, seven cottages, some barns and railed paddocks. When I saw the crescent above the tiny mosque I realized they were Muslims, but they clearly posed no threat.

The others poured out of the jeeps and rounded up everyone in the hamlet. I suspected nothing when they began to search the cottages. I had heard of Muslim fanatics, Mujahedin from the Middle East, Iran and Saudi Arabia, who also marauded through Bosnia and would kill any Serb on sight. Perhaps there were some hiding there, I thought.

When the search was over Zilic walked back to the lead vehicle and took position behind the machine gun mounted on a swivel behind the front seats. He shouted to his men to scatter and opened fire on the peasants huddled in the rail-fence cattle pen.

It happened almost before I could believe it had happened. The peasants began to jump and dance as the heavy bullets hit them. The other soldiers opened up with their sub-machine guns. Some of the peasants tried to save their children, throwing their bodies over them. A few of the smaller children got away in this manner, darting between the adults and reaching the trees before the bullets took them. Later I learned there were six who had escaped.

I felt violently sick. There was a stench of blood and entrails in the air — you never get the stench in films from Hollywood. I had never seen people die before, but these were not even soldiers or partisans. One old shotgun, perhaps for killing rabbits and crows, had been found.

When it was over, most of the shooters were disappointed. There had been no alcohol found, nor anything of value. So they torched the houses and the barns and we left them burning.

We spent the night in the forest. The men had brought their own slivovitz and most got drunk on it. I tried to drink, but brought it all back up. In my sleeping bag I realized I had made a terrible mistake. These were not patriots around me, but gangsters who killed because they enjoyed it.

The next morning, we began to drive down a series of mountain tracks, mainly along the face of the range, back towards the col that would lead us over the mountains to Banja Luka. That was when we found the farmhouse. It was alone in another small valley amid the woods. I saw Zilic in the first jeep rise from his seat and hold up his hand in a 'stop' signal. He gesticulated that we should cut our engines. The drivers did that, and there was silence. Then we heard voices.

Very quietly we got down from the jeeps, took guns and crept to the edge of the clearing. About a hundred yards away were two grown males leading six children out of a barn. The men were not armed and not in uniform. Behind them was a fire-gutted farmhouse, and to one side a new, black Toyota Landcruiser with the words 'Loaves 'n' Fishes' on the door panel. Both turned and stared when they saw us. The oldest of the children, a little girl of about ten, began to cry. I recognized her by her headscarf. It was Laila.

Zilic advanced towards the group with his gun raised, but neither made any attempt to fight. The rest of us fanned out and formed a horseshoe round the captives when we arrived close to them. The taller of the men spoke and I recognized American. So did Zilic. None of the others spoke a word of English. The American said, 'Who are you guys?'

Zilic did not answer. He strolled over to examine the brand new Landcruiser. At that moment the child Laila tried to make a run for it. One of the men grabbed but missed. Zilic turned from the off-road, drew his pistol, aimed, fired and blew the back of her head away. He was very proud of his marksmanship with a pistol.

The American was ten feet from Zilic. He took two strides, swung a fist with all his power and caught Zilic on the side of the mouth. If he had any chance of survival, that finished it. Zilic was caught by surprise, as he might have been, because no one in all Yugoslavia would have dared do that.

There were two seconds of complete disbelief as Zilic went down, blood pouring from his split lip. Then six of his men were on the American with boots, fists, gun butts. They beat him to a bloody pulp. I think they would have finished him off, but Zilic intervened. He was back up, dabbing the blood off his mouth. He told them to stop the beating.

The American was alive, shirt ripped open, torso red from kicking, face already swelling and cut. The open shirt revealed a broad money belt at his waist. Zilic gestured with one hand and one of his men ripped it off. It was stuffed with hundred-dollar bills, at least ten of them, it turned out. Zilic examined the man who had dared hit him.

'Dear me,' he said, 'so much blood. You need a cold bath, my friend, something to freshen you up.' He turned to his men. They were bewildered at his apparent concern for the American. But Zilic had seen something else in the clearing. The cesspit was brimming full, partly from animal slurry but also from human waste. It had once served both purposes. If the passing years had solidified the mixture, the recent rains had reliquefied it. On Zilic's orders the American was thrown into it.

The shock of the cold must have brought him to his senses. His feet found the bottom of the pit and he began to struggle. There was a cattle pen nearby with post and rail fencing. It was old and broken but some of the long poles were still whole. The men grabbed several and began to poke the American under the surface of the slime.

He began to scream for mercy each time his face appeared above the slime. He was begging

155

for his life. About the sixth time, maybe it was seven, Zilic grabbed a pole and rammed the end into the gaping mouth, smashing most of the teeth. Then he pushed downwards and kept pushing until the young man was dead.

I walked away to the trees and vomited up the sausage and black bread I had eaten for breakfast. I wanted to kill them all, but they were too many and I was too afraid. While I was being sick I heard several volleys. They had killed the other five children and the Bosnian aid worker who had brought the American to that spot. All the bodies were thrown into the slime pit. One of the men found that the words 'Loaves 'n' Fishes' on each front door of the Landcruiser were simply a decal with adhesive backing. They peeled off quite easily.

When we drove away there was no sign, except the startlingly bright splashes of red, the children's blood on the grass, and the twinkling of a few brass cartridges. That evening Zoran Zilic divided up the dollars. He gave a hundred dollars to each man. I refused to take them, but he insisted that I took a minimum of one note to remain 'one of the boys'.

I tried to get rid of it in the bar that evening, but he saw me and really lost his temper. The next day I told him I was going home, back to Belgrade. He threatened me that if I ever spoke one word of what I had seen, he would find me, mutilate and then kill me.

As I have long known, I am not a brave man and it was my fear of him that kept me silent all these years, even when the Englishman came

156

asking questions in the summer of 1995. But now I have made my peace, and am prepared to testify in any court in Holland or America, so long as God Almighty gives me the strength to stay alive.

I swear by Him that all I have said is the truth and nothing but the truth.

Given under my hand, Senjak District, Belgrade, this 7th day of April 2001.

Milan Rajak.

★ ★ ★

That night the Tracker sent a long message to Stephen Edmond in Windsor, Ontario, and the instructions that came back were unequivocal:

'Go wherever you must, do whatever it takes, find my grandson or whatever is left of him and bring him home to Georgetown, USA.'

# 13

## The Pit

Peace had come to Bosnia with the Dayton agreement of November 1995, but over five years later, the scars of war were not even disguised, let alone healed.

It had never been a rich province. No Dalmatian coast to attract the tourists; no mineral reserves; just low-tech agriculture in the farmlands between the mountains and the forests.

The economic damage would take years more to recover from, but the social damage was far worse. Few could imagine that in less than a generation or two Serb, Croat and Bosnian Muslim would accept living side by side with each other again, or even a few miles apart, save in armed watchful compounds.

The international bodies spouted the usual blather about reunification and restoring mutual trust, thus justifying the doomed attempts to put Humpty Dumpty back together again rather than facing the necessity of partition.

The task of governing the shattered entity went to the United Nations High Representative, a sort of pro-consul with near-absolute powers, backed by the soldiers of UNPROFOR. Of all the unglamorous tasks that fell to the people who had no time for posturing on the political stage but who actually made things happen, the least charming went to the ICMP — the International Commission on Missing Persons.

This was run with impressive and quiet efficiency by Gordon Bacon, a former British policeman. To the ICMP fell the task of listening to the tens of thousands of relatives of the 'disappeared ones' and taking their statements on the one hand, and tracing and exhuming the hundreds of mini-massacres that had taken place since 1992. The third job was to try to match statements with relics and restore the skull and bundle of bones to the right relatives, for final burial according to the religious creed or none.

The matching process would have been completely impossible without DNA, but the new technology meant that a swab of blood from the relative and a sliver of bone from the cadaver could provide proof of identity beyond doubt. By 2000 the fastest and most efficient DNA laboratory in Europe was not in some wealthy western capital but in Sarajevo, set up and run on tiny funds by Gordon Bacon. It was to see him that the Tracker drove into the Bosnian city two days after Milan Rajak had signed his name.

He did not need to bring the Serb with him. Rajak had revealed that before he died, the Bosnian aid worker Fadil Sulejman had told his murderers that the farm had once been his family home. Gordon Bacon read the Rajak statement with interest but no sense of novelty.

He had read hundreds before, but always from the few survivors, never from one of the perpetrators, and never involving an American. He realized the mystery of what he knew as the Colenso file might be solved at last. He contacted the ICMP commissioner for the Travnik zone and asked for the fullest cooperation with Mr Gracey when he arrived. The Tracker spent the night in his fellow countryman's spare bedroom and drove north again in the morning.

It is a mite over two hours into Travnik and he was there by midday. He had talked with Stephen Edmond, and a swab of the grandfather's blood was on its way from Ontario.

On 11 April the exhumation team left Travnik for the hills, aided by a local guide. Questions at the mosque had quickly discovered two men who had known Fadil Sulejman, and one of them said he knew the farm in the upland valley. He was in the leading off-road.

The digger team brought with them protective clothing, breathing aids, shovels, soft brushes, sieves and evidence bags, all the needs of their grisly trade.

The farm was much as it must have been six years earlier, but a bit more overgrown. No one had come to reclaim it; the Sulejman family appeared to have ceased to exist.

They found the sewage pit without difficulty. The spring rains had been less than in 1995 and the contents of the pit had hardened to malodorous clay. The diggers pulled on garments like a fly fisherman's waders, and over-jackets, but seemed immune to the smell.

Rajak had testified that on the day of the

murder, the pit was full to the brim, but if Ricky Colenso's feet had touched bottom, it must be about six feet deep. Without rain, the surface had receded two feet downwards.

After three feet of slime had been shovelled out, the ICMP commissioner ordered his men to throw out their shovels and resume with hand trowels. An hour later the first bones were visible and in a further hour of work with scraper and camel-hair brush, the massacre site was exposed.

No air had penetrated to the bottom of the pit, so there had been no maggots at work, since they depend on air. The decomposition was uniquely due to enzymes and bacilli.

Every fragment of soft tissue was gone, and when wiped with a damp cloth, the first skull to emerge gleamed clean and white. There were fragments of leather, from the boots and belts of the two men; an ornate belt buckle, surely American, plus metal studs from jeans and buttons from a denim jacket.

One of the men on his knees down below called out and passed up a watch. Seventy months had not affected the inscription on the back: 'Ricky, from Mom. Graduation. 1994'.

The children had all been thrown in dead and they had sunk on top of, or close to, each other. Time and decomposition had made a jumble of the bones of the six corpses, but the size of the skeletons proved who they had been.

Sulejman had also gone in dead; his skeleton lay on its back, spread-eagled, the way the body had sunk. His friend stood and looked down into the pit and prayed to Allah. He confirmed his former classmate had been around five feet eight inches tall.

The eighth body was the big one, over six feet. It was to one side, as if the dying boy had tried to crawl through the blackness to the side wall. The bones lay on their side, hunched in the foetal position. The watch came from that pile, and the belt buckle. When the skull was passed up, the front teeth were smashed, as Rajak had testified.

It was sundown when the last tiny bone was retrieved and bagged. The two grown men were in separate bags, the children shared their own; the reassembly of six small skeletons could be done in the mortuary down in the town.

The Tracker drove to Vitez for the night. The British army was long gone but he took a billet in a guesthouse he knew from before. In the morning he returned to the ICMP office in Travnik.

From Sarajevo, Gordon Bacon authorized the local commissioner to release the remains of Ricky Colenso to Major Gracey for transportation to the capital.

The swab from Ontario had arrived. In a remarkably fast two days the DNA tests were complete. The head of the ICMP in Sarajevo attested that the skeleton was indeed that of Richard 'Ricky' Colenso of Georgetown, USA. He needed formal authority from the next of kin to release the remains into the care of Philip Gracey of Andover, Hampshire, UK. That took two days to arrive.

162

In the interval, on instructions from Ontario, the Tracker bought a casket from Sarajevo's premier funeral parlour. The mortician arranged the skeleton with other materials to give heft and balance to the casket as if it contained a real cadaver. Then it was sealed for ever.

It was on 15 April that the Canadian magnate's Grumman IV arrived with a letter of authority to take over. The Tracker consigned the casket and the fat file of paperwork to the captain and went home to the green fields of England.

Stephen Edmond was at Washington Dulles to receive his own executive jet when it touched down on the evening of the 16th after a refuelling stop at Shannon. An ornate hearse took the casket to a funeral parlour for two days while final arrangements for interment were completed.

On the 18th the ceremony took place at the very exclusive Oak Hill Cemetery on R Street in Northwest Georgetown. It was small and private, in the Roman Catholic rite. The boy's mother, Mrs Annie Colenso, née Edmond, stood with her husband's arm around her, weeping quietly. Professor Colenso dabbed at his eyes and occasionally glanced over at his father-in-law as if he did not know what to do and sought some guidance.

Across the grave the 81-year-old Canadian stood in his dark suit like a pillar of his own pentlandite ore and looked unblinkingly down at the coffin of his grandson. He had not shown the report from the Tracker to his daughter or son-in-law and certainly not the testimony of Milan Rajak.

They knew only that a belated eyewitness had come forward who recalled seeing the black Landcruiser in a valley, and as a result, the two bodies had been found. But he had to concede that they had been murdered and buried. There was no other way of explaining the six-year gap.

The service ended, the mourners moved away to let the sextons work. Mrs Colenso ran to her father and hugged him, pressing her face against the fabric of his shirt. He looked down and gently stroked the top of her head, as he had when she was a small girl and something frightened her.

'Daddy, whoever did this to my baby, I want him caught. Not killed quickly and cleanly. I want him to wake in jail every morning for the rest of his life and know that he is there and will never come out again, and I want him to think back and know that it is all because he cold-bloodedly murdered my child.'

The old man had already made up his mind.

'I may have to move heaven,' he rumbled, 'and I may have to move hell. And if I must, I will.'

He let her go, nodded to the professor and strode away to his limousine. As the driver eased up the slope to the R Street gateway, he took his phone from the console and dialled a number. Somewhere on Capitol Hill a secretary answered.

'Put me through to Senator Peter Lucas,' he said.

The face of the senior senator for New

164

Hampshire lit up when he got the message. Friendships born in the heat of war may last an hour or a lifetime. With Stephen Edmond and Peter Lucas, it had been fifty-six years since they sat on an English lawn on a spring morning and wept for the young men of both their countries who would never come home. But the friendship had endured, as of brothers.

Each knew that, if asked, he would go to the wire for his friend. The Canadian was about to ask.

One of the aspects of the genius of Franklin Delano Roosevelt was that although a convinced Democrat he was quite prepared to use talent wherever he found it. It was just after Pearl Harbor that he summoned a conservative Republican who happened to be at a football game and asked him to form the Office of Strategic Services.

The man he summoned was General William 'Wild Bill' Donovan, the son of Irish immigrants, who had commanded the Fighting 69th Regiment on the Western Front in World War I. After that, as a trained lawyer, he had become Deputy Attorney General under Herbert Hoover, then spent years as a Wall Street legal eagle. It was not his law skills that Roosevelt wanted; it was his sheer combativeness, the quality he needed to create the USA's first foreign intelligence and Special Forces unit.

Without much hesitation the old warrior gathered around himself a corps of brilliant and well-connected young men as his gofers. They included Arthur Schlesinger, David Bruce and Henry Hyde, who would all go on to high office.

At that time Peter Lucas, raised to wealth and privilege between Manhattan and Long Island, was a sophomore at Princeton, and he decided on the day of Pearl Harbor that he too wanted to go to war. His father forbade any such thing.

In February 1942, the young man disobeyed his father and dropped out of college, all taste for study gone. He raced around trying to find something he really wanted to do; toyed with the idea of fighter pilot, took private flying lessons until he learned that he was constantly airsick.

In June 1942 the OSS was established. Peter Lucas offered himself at once and was accepted. He saw himself with blackened face, dropping by night far behind German lines. He attended a lot of cocktail parties instead. General Donovan wanted a first-class aide-de-camp, efficient and polished.

He saw at short range the preparations for the landings in Sicily and Salerno in which OSS agents were wholly involved, and begged for action. Be patient, he was told. It was like taking a boy to a sweet shop but leaving him inside a glass box. He could see but he could not touch.

Finally, he went to the general with a flat ultimatum. 'Either I fight under you, or I quit and join the Airborne.'

No one gave 'Wild Bill' Donovan ultimatums but he stared at the young man and maybe saw something of himself a quarter of a century earlier. 'Do both,' he said, 'in reverse order.'

With Donovan's backing all doors opened.

Peter Lucas shrugged off the hated civilian suit and went to Fort Benning to become a 'ninety-day wonder', a fast track commission to emerge as a Second Lieutenant in the Airborne.

He missed the D-Day Normandy landings, being still in parachute school. When he graduated, he returned to General Donovan. 'You promised,' he said.

Peter Lucas got his black-faced parachute drop, one cold autumn night, into the mountains behind the German lines in northern Italy. There he came across the Italian partisans who were dedicated communists, and the British Special Forces who seemed too laid-back to be dedicated to anything.

Within a couple of weeks he learned the 'laid-back' bit was an act. The Jedburgh group he had joined contained some of the war's most skilled and contented killers.

He survived the bitter winter of 1944 in the mountains, and almost made it to the end of the war intact. It was March 1945 when he and five others ran into a stay-behind squad of no-surrender SS men they did not know were still in the region. There was a firefight and he took two slugs from a Schmeisser sub-machine gun in the left arm and shoulder.

They were miles from anywhere, out of morphine, and it took a week of marching in agony to find a British forward unit. There was a patch-up operation on the spot, a morphine-dazed flight in a Liberator and a much better reconstruction in a London hospital.

When he was fit enough to leave, he was sent

to a convalescent home on the coast of Sussex. He shared a room with a Canadian fighter pilot nursing two broken legs. They played chess to while away the days.

Returning home, the world was his oyster. He joined his father's firm on Wall Street, took it over eventually, became a giant in the financial community and ran for public office when he was sixty. In April 2001, he was in his fourth and last term as a Republican senator for New Hampshire and he had just seen a Republican president elected.

When he heard who was on the line, he told his secretary to hold all calls and his voice filled the moving limousine ten miles away.

'Steve. Good to hear you again. Where are you?'

'Right here in Washington. Peter, I need to see you. It's serious.'

Catching his mood, the senator dropped the bonhomie. 'Sure, pal. Wanna tell me?'

'Over lunch. Can you make it?'

'I'll clear the diary. The Hay Adams. Ask for my usual corner table. It's quiet. One o'clock.'

They met when the senator strode into the lobby. The Canadian was waiting there.

'You sounded serious, Steve. You have a problem?'

'I just came from an interment up in Georgetown. I just buried my only grandson.'

The senator stared and his face creased with shared pain. 'Jesus, old friend, I am so sorry. I can't even imagine it. Illness? Accident?'

'Let's talk at the table. There's something I need you to read.'

When they were seated the Canadian answered his friend's question. 'He was murdered. In cold blood. No, not here, and not now. Six years ago. In Bosnia.'

He explained briefly about the boy's age, his desire back in 1995 to help alleviate the pain of the Bosnians, his odyssey through the capitals to the town of Travnik, his agreement to try to help his interpreter trace his family homestead. Then he passed over the Rajak confession.

Dry martinis came. The senator ordered smoked salmon platter, brown bread, chilled Meursault. Edmond nodded, meaning: the same.

Senator Lucas was accustomed to reading fast, but halfway through the report he gave a low whistle and slowed down.

While the senator toyed with the salmon and read the last pages, Steve Edmond glanced around. His friend had chosen well: a personal table just beyond the grand piano, secluded in a corner by a window through which part of the White House was visible. The Lafayette at the Hay Adams was unique, more like a house set at the heart of an eighteenth-century country estate than a restaurant in the middle of a bustling capital city.

Senator Lucas raised his head.

'I don't know what to say, Steve. This is perhaps the most awful document I have ever read. What do you want me to do?'

A waiter removed the plates and brought small black coffees and for each man a glass bowl of old Armagnac. They were silent while the young man was at the table.

169

Steve Edmond looked down at their four hands on the white cloth. Old men's hands, cord-veined, sausage-fingered, liver-spotted. Hands that had thrown a Hurricane fighter straight down into a formation of Dornier bombers; hands that had emptied an M-1 carbine into a trattoria full of SS-men outside Bolzano; hands that had fought fights, caressed women, held first-borns, signed cheques, created fortunes, altered politics, changed the world. Once.

Peter Lucas caught his friend's glance and understood his mood. 'Yes, we are old now. But not dead yet. What do you want me to do?'

'Maybe we could do one last good thing. My grandson was an American citizen. The USA has the right to require this monster's extradition from wherever he is. Back here. To stand trial for Murder One. That means the Justice Department. And State. Acting together on any government that harbours this swine. Will you take it to them?'

'My friend, if this government of Washington cannot give you justice, then no one can.'

He raised his glass.

'One last good thing.'

But he was wrong.

# 14

## The Father

It was only a family spat and it should have ended with a kiss-and-make-up. But it took place between a passionate Italian-blooded daughter and a doggedly tenacious father.

By the summer of 1991 Amanda Jane Dexter was sixteen and knockout attractive. The Naples-descended Marozzi genes had given her a figure to cause a bishop to kick a hole in a stained-glass window. The blond Anglo-Saxon lineage of Dexter endowed her with a face like the young Bardot. The local boys were over her like a rash and her father had to accept that. But he did not like Emilio.

He had nothing against Hispanics, but there was something sly and shallow about Emilio, even predatory and cruel behind matinée-idol looks. But Amanda Jane fell for him like a ton of bricks.

It came to a head during the long summer vacation. Emilio proposed he take her away for a holiday by the sea. He spun a good tale. There would be other young people, adults to supervise, beach sports, fresh air and the bracing tang of the Atlantic. But when Cal Dexter tried to eye-contact the young man, Emilio avoided his gaze. His gut instinct told him there was

171

something wrong. He said, 'No.'

A week later she ran away. There was a note to say they should not worry, everything would be fine, but she was a grown woman now and refused to be treated like a child. She never came back.

School holidays ended. She still did not appear. Too late, her mother, who had approved her request, listened to her husband. They had no address for the beach party, no knowledge of Emilio's background, parentage, or real home address. The Bronx address he had used turned out to be a lodging house. His car had Virginia numberplates but a check with Richmond told Dexter it had been sold for cash in July. Even the surname, Gonzalez, was as common as Smith.

Through his contacts Cal Dexter consulted with a senior sergeant in the Missing Persons Bureau of the NYPD. The officer was sympathetic but resigned.

'Sixteen is like grown-up nowadays, counsellor; they sleep together, vacation together, set up home together . . . '

The Department could only send out an all-points if there was evidence of threat, duress, forcible removal from the parental home, drug abuse, whatever.

Dexter had to concede there had been a single phone message. It had come at a time Amanda Jane would know her father would be at work and her mother out. The message was on the machine tape.

She was fine she said, very happy and they should not worry. She was living her own life and

172

enjoying it. She would be in touch when she was good and ready.

Cal Dexter traced the call. It came from a mobile phone, the sort that operates off a purchased SIM card and cannot be traced to the owner. He played the tape to the sergeant and the man shrugged. Like all Missing Person Bureaux in every force across the States he had a case overload. This was not an emergency.

Christmas came, but it was bleak. The first in the Dexter household in sixteen years without their baby.

★   ★   ★

It was a morning jogger who found the body. His name was Hugh Lamport, he ran a small IT consultancy company, he was an honest citizen trying to keep in shape. For him that meant a three-mile run every morning between six thirty and as near to seven o'clock as he could make it, and that even included cold bleak mornings like 18 February 1992.

He was running along the grass verge of Indian River Road, Virginia Beach, which was where he lived. The grass was easier on the ankles than tarmac or concrete. But when he came to a bridge over a narrow culvert, he had a choice. Cross via the concrete bridge or jump the culvert. He jumped.

He noticed something pass under him in the jump, something pale in the pre-dawn gloom. After landing, he turned and peered back into the ditch. She lay in the strange disjointed pose

173

of death, half in and half out the water.

Mr Lamport glanced frantically round and saw four hundred yards away through some trees a dim light; another early riser brewing the morning cup. No longer jogging but sprinting, he arrived at the door and hammered hard. The coffee brewer peered through the window, listened to the shouted explanation, and let him in.

The 911 call was taken by the night-duty dispatcher in the basement switchboard at Virginia City's police HQ on Princess Anne Road. She asked as a matter of urgency for the nearest patrol car and the response came from the First Precinct's sole cruiser, which was a mile from the culvert. It made that mile in a minute, to find a man in jogging kit and another in a dressing gown marking the spot.

It took the two patrol officers no more than two minutes to call in for homicide detectives and a full forensic team. The householder fetched coffee, which was gratefully received, and all four waited.

That whole sector of eastern Virginia is occupied by six cities with contiguous boundaries, a conurbation that extends for miles on both banks of the James River and Hampton Roads. It is a landscape studded with navy and air bases, for here the Roads run out into Chesapeake Bay and thence the Atlantic.

Of the six cities, Norfolk, Portsmouth, Hampton (with Newport News), James City, Chesapeake and Virginia Beach, the biggest by far is Virginia Beach. It covers 310 square miles and contains 430,000 citizens out of a total of 1.5 million.

Of its four precincts, Second, Third and Fourth cover the built-up areas, while First Precinct is large and mainly rural. Its 195 square miles run right down to the North Carolina border and are bisected by Indian River Road.

Forensics and Homicide arrived at the culvert around the same time, thirty minutes later. The Medical Examiner was five minutes after that. Dawn came, or what passed for dawn, and a drizzle set in.

Mr Lamport was driven home to shower off and make a full statement. The coffee brewer made a statement, which is to say he could only aver he had heard and seen nothing during the night.

The ME established quickly that life was extinct, that the victim was a young Caucasian female, that death had almost certainly occurred somewhere else and the body had been dumped, presumably from a car. He ordered the attendant ambulance to take the cadaver to the state morgue in Norfolk, a facility that serves all six cities.

The local homicide detectives took time out to muse that if the perpetrators, who seemed to have a moral code on the level of a snake's navel and an IQ to match, had driven three miles further on, they would have entered the swamp country at the head of Back Bay. Here, a weighted body could disappear for ever and none the wiser. But they had seemingly run out of patience and dumped their grisly cargo where it would be quickly found and start a manhunt.

At Norfolk, two things happened with respect to the corpse: an autopsy to establish cause, time and, if possible, location of death, and an attempt to secure identification.

The body itself yielded nothing to the second search: some skimpy but no longer provocative underwear, a badly torn and slinky dress. No medallions, bracelets, tattoos or purse.

Before the forensic pathologist began his task, the face, which bore lesions and contusions compatible with a savage beating, was restored as best possible with sutures and makeup, and photographed. The photo would be passed around the vice squads of all six cities, for the body's dress code seemed to indicate a possibility that she had been involved with what is hopefully called 'night life'.

The other two details the ID hunters needed and got were fingerprints and blood group. Then the pathologist started. It was the fingerprints they pinned their hopes on.

The six cities came up with a zero on the prints. Details went to the state capital at Richmond where prints covering the whole of Virginia were stored. Days went by. The answer came back. Sorry. The next step up is the FBI covering the entire USA. It uses IAFIS — the International Automated Fingerprints ID System.

The pathologist's report made even hardened homicide detectives queasy. The girl appeared not much more than eighteen, if that. She had once been pretty, but someone, plus her lifestyle, had put an end to that.

Vaginal and anal dilation was so exaggerated that she had clearly been penetrated, and repeatedly, by instruments far larger than a normal male organ. The terminal beating had not been the only one; there had been others before. And heroin abuse, probably dating back no more than six months.

To both homicide and vice detectives in Norfolk the report said 'prostitution'. It was no news to any of them that recruitment into vice was often accomplished by narcotic dependency, the pimp being the only source of the drug.

Any girl trying to escape the clutches of such a gang would certainly be punished; such 'lesson learning' could involve forced participation in exhibitions featuring brutal perversions and bestiality. There were creatures prepared to pay for this, and thus creatures prepared to supply it.

The post-autopsy body went into the cold room while the search for identity continued. She was still Jane Doe. Then a vice detective in Portsmouth thought he might recognize the circulated photograph, despite the damage and discoloration. He thought she might have been a hooker going under the name of Lorraine.

Enquiries revealed that 'Lorraine' had not been seen for several weeks. Prior to that she had worked for a notoriously vicious Hispanic gang who recruited by using good-looking gang members to pick up girls in the cities to the north and entice them south with promises of marriage, a lovely vacation, whatever it took.

The Portsmouth vice squad worked on the gang but with no result. The pimps claimed they had never known Lorraine's real name, that she had been a professional when she arrived, and that she had left voluntarily to return to the West Coast. The photograph was simply not clear enough to prove otherwise.

But Washington did. They came up with a firm ID based on the prints. Amanda Jane Dexter had tried to fool the security of a local supermarket and shoplift an item. The security camera won. The juvenile court judge accepted her story, backed by five classmates, and let her go with a caution. But her fingerprints were taken. They were with the NYPD, and had been passed to IAFIS.

'I think,' muttered Sgt Austin of the Portsmouth vice squad when he heard the news, 'that I might at last be able to get those bastards.'

It was another filthy winter morning when the phone rang in the apartment in the Bronx, but perhaps a good enough morning to ask a father to motor three hundred miles to identify his only child.

Cal Dexter sat on the edge of the bed and wished he had died in the Tunnels of Cu Chi rather than take this kind of pain. He finally told Angela, and held her while she sobbed. He rang his mother-in-law and she came over at once.

He could not wait for the aeroplane out of La Guardia for Norfolk International; he could not have sat and waited if there had been a flight delay due to fog, rain, hail, congestion. He took his car and drove. Out of New York, across the bridge to Newark, on through the country he knew so well as he had been hauled from one

178

construction site to another; out of New Jersey, through a chunk of Pennsylvania and another of Delaware, then south and ever more south past Baltimore and to the end of Virginia.

At the morgue in Norfolk he stared down at the once lovely and much-loved face, and nodded dumbly to the homicide detective with him. They went upstairs. Over coffee he ascertained the basic outlines. She had been beaten by person or persons unknown. She had died of severe internal haemorrhaging. The 'perps' had seemingly put the body in the trunk of a car, driven into the most rural part of First Precinct, Virginia Beach, and dumped it. Enquiries were proceeding, sir. He knew it was a fraction of the truth.

He made a long statement, told them all about 'Emilio', but it rang no bells with the detectives. He asked for his daughter's body. The police had no further objections but the decision was down to the Coroner's Office.

It took time. Formalities. Procedures. He took his car back to New York, returned by air and waited. Eventually he escorted his daughter's body, riding in the hearse, back home to the Bronx.

The casket was sealed. He did not want his wife or any of the Marozzis to see what was inside. The funeral was local. Amanda Jane was interred just three days short of her seventeenth birthday. A week later he returned to Virginia.

Sgt Austin was in his office in the Portsmouth police HQ at 711 Crawford Street when the front desk phoned to say there was a Mr Dexter

179

who wished to see him. The name did not ring a bell. He did not connect it with his recognition of a battered face in a photograph as the departed hooker, Lorraine.

He asked what Mr Dexter wanted and was told the visitor might have a contribution to make in an ongoing enquiry. On that basis, the visitor was shown up.

Portsmouth is the oldest of the six cities; it was founded by the British well before the revolution. Today it slumps on the southwest side of the Elizabeth River, mainly low-build red-brick, staring across the water at the high-rise modern glitz of Norfolk on the other side. But it is the place many of the servicemen go if they are looking for 'a good time' after dark. Sgt Austin's vice squad was not there for decoration.

The visitor did not look much compared to the muscular bulk of the former linebacker turned detective. He just stood in front of the desk and said:

'You remember the teenager, turned to heroin and prostitution, gang-raped and beaten to death, four weeks back? I'm her father.'

Alarm bells began to tinkle. The sergeant had risen and extended a hand. He withdrew it. Angry, vengeful citizens had his fullest sympathy and could expect nothing more. To any working cop they are tiresome and can be dangerous.

'I'm sorry about that, sir. I can assure you that every effort — '

'At ease, sergeant. I just want to know one thing. Then I'll leave you in peace.'

'Mr Dexter, I understand what you must be feeling, but I am not in a position — '

The visitor had put his right hand in his jacket pocket and was pulling something out. Had front desk security screwed up? Was the man armed? The sergeant's own piece was uncomfortably ten feet away in a desk drawer.

'What are you doing, sir?'

'I'm putting some bits of metal on your desk, Sergeant Austin.'

He went on until he was finished. Sgt Austin had been in the military, for they were of a similar age, but had never left the States.

He found himself staring down at two Silver Stars, three Bronze Stars, the Army Commendation Medal and four Purple Hearts. He had never seen anything like it.

'Far away and long ago, I paid for the right to know who killed my child. I bought that right with my blood. You owe me that name, Mr Austin.'

The vice detective walked to the window and looked across at Norfolk. It was irregular, completely irregular. Worth his job on the force.

'Madero. Benyamin 'Benny' Madero. Headed up a Latino vice gang. Very violent, very vicious.'

'Thank you,' said the man behind him. He collected his bits of metal.

'But in case you're thinking of paying him a private visit, you're too late. I'm too late. We're all too late. He's gone. He's back in his native Panama. I know he did it, but I don't have enough to apply through the courts.'

* ★ ★

A hand pushed open the door of the small emporium of Oriental art off Madison at 28th Street, Manhattan. Above the portal a bell jangled with the movement of the door.

The visitor looked around at the shelves stacked with jade and celadon, stone and porcelain, ivory and ceramic; at elephants and demi-gods, panels, wall hangings, parchments and innumerable Buddhas. At the rear of the shop a figure emerged.

'I need to be someone else,' said Calvin Dexter.

It had been fourteen years since he had given the gift of a new life to the former Vietcong jungle fighter and his wife. The Oriental did not hesitate for a second. He inclined his head.

'Of course,' he said. 'Please come with me.'

It was 15 March 1992.

# 15

## The Settlement

The fast fishing boat *Chiquita* slipped away from the quay in the resort port of Golfito just before dawn and headed down-channel for the open sea.

At her helm was owner and skipper Pedro Arias and if he had reservations about his American charter party he kept them to himself.

The man had turned up the previous day on a trail bike with local Costa Rican plates. In fact it had been bought, second hand but in excellent condition, further up the Panamerican Highway at Palmar Norte where the tourist had arrived by local flight from San José.

The man had strolled up and down the quay, checking out the various moored game-fishing boats before making his choice and his approach. With the trail bike chained to a nearby lamp-post and his haversack over his shoulder, the man looked like a mature backpacker.

But there was nothing 'backpacker' about the block of dollars he laid on the cabin table. This was the sort of money that caught a lot of fish.

But the man did not want to go fishing, which was why the rods were all racked along the cabin ceiling as the *Chiquita* cleared the headland at Punta Voladera and emerged into the Golfo

Dulce. Arias set her head due south to clear Punta Banco an hour away.

What the gringo actually wanted accounted for the two plastic drums of extra fuel strapped into the stern fishing deck. He wanted to be run out of Costa Rican waters, round the headland at Punta Burica and into Panama.

His explanation that his family was vacationing in Panama City and that the visitor wished to 'see some of the Panamanian countryside' by riding the length of the country struck Pedro Arias as being as substantial as the sea mist now dissolving in the rising sun.

Still, if a gringo wanted to enter Panama on a trail bike off a lonely beach without passing through certain formalities, Señor Arias was a man of wide tolerances, especially where neighbouring Panama was concerned.

At the breakfast hour the *Chiquita*, a thirty-one-foot Bertram Moppie, cruising happily at twelve knots over calm water, cleared Punta Banco and emerged into the swell of the real Pacific. Arias pulled her forty degrees to port to follow the coast two more hours to Burica Island and the unmarked border.

It was when they saw the first finger of Burica Island lighthouse jutting above the horizon and half past the hour as they turned the corner and veered back to the northeast.

Pedro Arias swept his arm towards the land to their left, the eastern coast of the Burica Peninsula.

'Now is all Panama,' he said. The American nodded his thanks and studied the map. He jabbed with a forefinger.

'Por aqui,' he said.

The area he indicated was a stretch of coast where no towns or resorts were marked, just a place that would have some abandoned empty beaches and some tracks back into the jungle. The skipper nodded and changed course to cut a straighter and shorter line across the Bay of Charco Azul. Forty kilometres, a tad over two hours.

They were there by one o'clock. The few fisherboats they had seen on the broad expanse of the bay had taken no notice of them.

The American wanted to cruise along the coast a hundred yards offshore. Five minutes later, east of Chiriqui Viejo, they saw a sandy beach with a brace of straw huts, the sort local fishermen use when they wish to overnight. That would mean a track leading inland. Not feasible for a vehicle, even an off-road, but manageable with a trail bike.

It took some grunting and pushing to get the bike down into the shallows; then the haversack was on the beach and they parted company. Fifty per cent at Golfito and fifty on delivery. The gringo paid up.

He was a strange one, thought Arias, but his dollars were as good as everyone else's when it came to feeding four hungry kids. He backed the *Chiquita* off the sand and headed out to sea. A mile offshore he emptied the two drums into his fuel tanks and gunned her south for the headland and home.

On the beach Cal Dexter took a screwdriver,

unscrewed the Costa Rica plates and hurled them far into the sea. From his haversack he took the plates a Panamanian motorcycle would carry and screwed them on.

His paperwork was perfect. Thanks to Mrs Nguyen he had an American passport, but not in the name of Dexter, which already bore an entry stamp apparently entered a few days earlier at Panama City airport. Plus a driving licence to match.

His halting Spanish, picked up around the courts and remand centres of New York where 20 per cent of his clients were Hispanic, was not good enough to pretend to be Panamanian. But a visiting American is allowed to ride upcountry to look for a fishing resort.

It was just over two years since, in December 1989, the USA had turned parts of Panama into an ashtray to topple and capture the dictator Noriega, and Dexter suspected most Panamanian cops had retained the basic message.

The narrow trail led back from the beach through dense rain forest to become, ten miles inland, a track. This became a dirt road with occasional farms, and there he knew he would find the Panamerican Highway, that feat of engineering that runs from Alaska to the tip of Patagonia.

At David City he filled the tank again and set off down the Highway for the 500-kilometre run to the capital. Darkness came. He ate at a wayside halt with truck drivers, tanked up again and rolled on. He crossed the toll bridge to Panama City, paid in pesos and cruised into the suburb of Balboa as the sun rose. Then he found a park bench, chained the bike and slept for three hours.

The afternoon was for the extended recce. The huge-scale city map he had purchased in New York gave him the layout of the city and the tough slum of Chorillo where Noriega and Madero had grown up a few blocks from each other.

But successful low-lifes prefer the high-life if they can get it, and Madero's reported watering holes were two he part-owned in upscale Paitilla, across the bay from the slums of Old Town.

It was two in the morning when the repatriated thug decided he was tired of the Papagayo Bar and Disco and wished to leave. The anonymous black door with discreet brass plaque, grille and eyehole opened and two men came out first: heavily built bodyguards, his personal gorillas.

One entered the Lincoln limousine by the kerb and started the engine. The other scanned the street. Sitting hunched on the kerb, feet in the gutter, the tramp turned and grinned a smile of rotting or missing teeth. Greasy grey locks fell to his shoulders; a fetid raincoat clothed his body.

Slowly he eased his right hand into a brown paper bag clutched to his chest. The gorilla slipped his hand beneath his left armpit and tensed. The hobo slowly pulled his hand from his bag clutching a bottle of cheap rum, took a swig and, with the generosity of the very drunk, held it out to the gorilla.

The man hawked, spat on the pavement, withdrew his own hand empty from beneath his jacket, relaxed and turned away. Apart from the wino, the pavement was empty and safe. He tapped on the black door.

Emilio, who had recruited Dexter's daughter, was the first out, followed by his boss. Dexter waited till the door closed and self-locked before he rose. The hand that came out of the paper bag a second time held a shortened barrel .44 magnum Smith and Wesson.

The gorilla who had spat never knew what hit him. The slug broke into four flying parts; all four penetrated at ten-feet range and performed considerable mischief inside his torso.

Drop-dead handsome Emilio did exactly that, mouth open to scream, when the second discharge took him in the face and neck, one shoulder and one lung simultaneously.

The second gorilla was halfway out of the car when he met his Maker in an unforeseen rendezvous with four spinning, tumbling metal fragments entering the side of his body exposed to the shooter.

Benyamin Madero was back at the black door, screaming for admission, when the fourth and fifth shots were fired. Some bold spirit inside had the door two inches open when a splinter went through his marcelled hair and the door shut in a hurry.

Madero fell, still hammering for admittance, sliding down the high-gloss panel work, leaving long red smears from his soaked guayabera tropical shirt.

The tramp walked over to him, showing no panic or particular hurry, stooped, turned him on his back and looked into his face. He was still alive but fading.

'Amanda Jane, mi hija,' said the gunman and used the sixth shot to shred the entrails.

Madero's last ninety seconds of life were no fun at all.

A housewife in an upper window across the street later told the police she saw the tramp jog away round a corner and heard the putt-putt of a scooter engine moving away. That was all.

Before sunrise the trail bike was propped against a wall two boroughs away, unchained, ignition key in place. It would survive no more than an hour before entering the food chain.

The wig, the prosthetic teeth and raincoat were bundled into a trashcan in a public park. The haversack, relieved of its remaining clothes, was folded and tossed into a builder's skip.

At seven an American business executive in loafers, chinos, polo shirt and lightweight sports jacket, clutching a soft Abercrombie and Fitch travel grip, hailed a cab outside the Miramar Hotel and asked for the airport. Three hours later the same American lifted off in Club Class on the regular Continental Airlines flight for Newark, NJ.

And the gun, the Smith and Wesson adapted to fire slugs that split in four lethal fragments for close-quarter work, that was down a storm drain somewhere in the city now dropping beneath the wingtip.

It might not have been allowed in the Tunnels of Cu Chi, but twenty years later it worked like a dream on the streets of Panama.

★ ★ ★

Dexter knew there was something wrong when he entered his latchkey in his own door in the Bronx. It opened to reveal the face of his mother-in-law, Mrs Marozzi, her cheeks streaked with tears.

Along with the grief, it was the guilt. Angela Dexter had approved of Emilio as a suitor for her daughter; she had agreed to the 'vacation' by the sea that the young Panamanian had proposed. When her husband said he had to leave for a week to take care of unfinished business, she presumed he meant some legal work.

He should have stayed. He should have told her. He should have understood what was in her mind. Leaving her parents' house where she had lodged since her daughter's funeral, Angela Dexter had returned to the apartment with an over-supply of barbiturates and ended her own life.

The ex-hardhat, soldier, student, lawyer and father went into a deep depression. Finally he came to two conclusions. The first was that he had no further life in the office of the Public Defender, scurrying from court to remand centre and back again. He handed in his papers, sold the apartment, bid a tearful farewell to the Marozzi family who had been good to him, and went back to New Jersey.

He found the small town of Pennington, content in its leafy landscape, but with no local lawyer. He bought a small one-man office and hung up his shingle. He bought a frame house on Chesapeake Drive and a pickup truck in lieu of the city sedan. He began to train in the brutal discipline of the triathlon to take away the pain.

His second decision was that Madero had died too easily. His just deserts should have been to stand in a US court and hear a judge sentence him to life without parole; to wake up each day and never see the sky; to know that he would pay until the end of his days for what he had done to a screaming girl.

Calvin Dexter knew that the US Army and two tours in the stinking hell under the jungle floor of Cu Chi had given him dangerous talents. Silence, patience, near-invisibility, the skill of a hunter, the relentlessness of a born tracker.

He heard via the media of a man who had lost his child to a murderer who had vanished abroad. He made covert contact, obtained the details, went out beyond the borders of his native land and brought the killer back. Then he vanished, becoming the genial and harmless lawyer of Pennington, NJ.

Three times in seven years he hung the 'Closed for Vacation' notice on his Pennington office and went out into the world to find a killer and claw him back into the range of 'due process'. Three times he alerted the Federal Marshals Service and slipped back into obscurity.

But each time it landed on his mat he checked the small ads column of *Vintage Airplane*, the only way the tiny few who knew of his existence could make contact.

He did it again that sunny morning of 13 May 2001. The advert read: 'AVENGER. Wanted. Serious offer. No price ceiling. Please call.'

# 16

## The File

Senator Peter Lucas was an old hand on capitol hill. He knew that if he were going to secure any official action as a result of the file on Ricky Colenso and the confession of Milan Rajak, he would have to take it high: right to the top.

Operating with section or department heads would not work. The entire mindset of civil servants at that level was to pass the buck to another department. It was always someone else's job. Only a flat instruction from the top floor would achieve a result.

As a Republican senator and friend over many years of George Bush Senior, Peter Lucas could get to the Secretary of State, Colin Powell, and the new Attorney General, John Ashcroft. That would cover State and Justice, the two departments likely to be able to do anything.

Even then, it was not that simple. Cabinet secretaries did not want to be brought problems and questions; they preferred problems and solutions.

Extradition was not his speciality. He needed to find out what the USA could do and ought to do in such a situation. That needed research, and he had a team of young graduates for precisely that purpose. He set them to work. His best ferret, a bright girl from Wisconsin, came back a week later.

'This animal, Zilic, is arrestable and transferable to the USA under the Comprehensive Crime Control Act of 1984,' she said.

The passage she had discovered came from the Congressional Hearing on Intelligence and Security of 1997. Specifically the speaker had been Robert M. Bryant, Assistant Director of the FBI, addressing the House Committee on Crime.

'I've highlighted the relevant passages, senator,' she said. He thanked her and looked at the text she laid before him.

'The FBI's extraterritorial responsibilities date back to the mid-1980s when Congress first passed laws authorizing the FBI to exercise federal jurisdiction overseas when a US national is murdered,' Mr Bryant had said four years earlier.

Behind the bland language was a staggering Act that the rest of the world had largely ignored, and most US citizens as well. Prior to the Comprehensive Crime Control Act of 1984, the global presumption was that if a murder was committed, whether in France or in Mongolia, only the French or Mongolian governments had jurisdiction to pursue, arrest and try the killer. That applied whether the victim was French, Mongolian or visiting American.

The USA had simply arrogated to itself the right to decide that if you kill an American citizen anywhere in the world, you might as well have killed him on Broadway. Meaning US jurisdiction covers the whole planet. No international conference conceded this; the USA simply said so. Then Mr Bryant went further.

' . . . and the Omnibus Diplomatic Security and Anti-terrorism Act of 1986 established a new extraterritorial statute pertaining to terrorist acts conducted abroad against US citizens.'

'Not a problem,' thought the senator. 'Zilic was not a Yugoslav Army serviceman, nor a policeman. He was freelance and the title of terrorist will stick. He is extraditable to the US under both statutes.'

He read on, 'Upon the approval of the host country, the FBI has the legal authority to deploy FBI personnel to conduct extraterritorial investigations in the host country where the criminal act was committed, enabling the United States to prosecute terrorists for crimes committed abroad against US citizens.'

The Senator's brow furrowed. This did not make sense. It was incomplete. The key phrase was 'Upon the approval of the host country'. But cooperation between police forces was nothing new. Of course the FBI could accept an invitation from a foreign police force to fly over and help them out. It had been going on for years. And why were two separate Acts needed, in 1984 and 1986?

The answer, which he did not have, was that the second Act went miles further than the first, and the phrase, 'Upon the approval of the host country', was just Mr Bryant being comforting to the committee. What he was hinting at but not daring to say (he was speaking during the

Clinton era) was the word 'rendition'.

In the 1986 Act the States awarded itself the right to ask politely for the murderer of an American to be extradited back to the States. If the answer was 'No', or seemingly endless delay amounting to a snub, that was the end of 'Mr Nice Guy'. The USA had entitled itself to send in a covert team of agents, snatch the 'perp' and bring him back for trial.

As FBI terrorist-hunter John O'Neill put it when the act was passed, 'From now on, host country approval has got jack shit to do with it.' A joint CIA/FBI snatch of an alleged murderer of an American is called a 'rendition'. There have been ten such very covert operations since the Act was passed under Ronald Reagan, and it all began because of an Italian cruise liner.

In October 1985 the *Achille Lauro*, out of Genoa, was cruising along the north coast of Egypt, with further stops on the Israeli coast in prospect, and carrying a mixed cargo of tourists, including some Americans.

She had been secretly boarded by four Palestinians from the Palestine Liberation Front, a terrorist group attached to Yasser Arafat's PLO, then in exile in Tunisia.

The terrorists' aim was not to capture the ship but to disembark at Ashdod, a stopping point in Israel, and take Israeli hostages there. But on 7 October, between Alexandria and Port Said, they were in one of their cabins, checking their weapons, when a steward walked in, saw the guns and started yelling. The four Palestinians panicked and hijacked the liner.

There followed four days of tense negotiations. In from Tunis flew Abu Abbas, claiming to be Arafat's negotiator. Tel Aviv would have none of it, pointing out that Abu Abbas was the boss of the PLF, not a benign mediator. Eventually a deal was struck: the terrorists would get passage off the ship and an Egyptian airliner back to Tunis. The Italian captain confirmed at gunpoint no one had been hurt. He was forced to lie.

Once the ship was free it became clear that on Day Three the Palestinians had murdered an old American tourist, 79-year-old, wheelchair-bound New Yorker Leon Klinghoffer. They had shot him in the face and thrown him and his chair into the sea.

For Ronald Reagan that was it; all deals were off. But the killers were airborne, on their way home, in an airliner of a sovereign state, friendly to America and in international airspace; that is, untouchable. Or maybe not.

The flat-top USS Saratoga happened to be steaming south down the Adriatic, carrying F-16 Tomcats. As darkness fell the Egyptian airliner was found off Crete, heading west for Tunis. Out of the gloom four Tomcats suddenly flanked the airliner. The terrified Egyptian skipper asked for an emergency landing at Athens. Permission denied. The Tomcats signalled he should accompany them or face the consequences. The same EC2 Hawkeye, also off the Saratoga, that had found the Egyptian plane passed the messages between the fighters and the airliner.

The diversion ended when the airliner, with the killers and Abu Abbas, their leader, on board, landed under escort at the US base at Sigonella, Sicily. Then it became complicated.

Sigonella was a shared base: US navy and Italian air force. Technically it is Italian sovereign territory; the USA only pays rent. The government in Rome, in a pretty high state of excitement, claimed the right to try the terrorists. The *Achille Lauro* was theirs, the air base theirs.

It took a personal call from President Reagan to the US Special Forces detachment at Sigonella to order them to back off and let the Italians have the Palestinians.

In due course, back in Genoa, home city of the liner, the small fry were sentenced. But their leader, Abu Abbas, flew out free as air on 12 October and is still at liberty.[1] The Italian Defence Minister resigned in disgust. The Premier at the time was Bettino Craxi. He later died in exile, also in Tunis, wanted for massive embezzlement while in office.

Reagan's response to this perfidy was the Omnibus Act, nicknamed the 'Never Again' Act. It was not finally the bright kid from Wisconsin but the veteran FBI terrorist hunter Oliver 'Buck' Revell, in retirement, who took a good dinner off the old senator and told him about 'renditions'.

Even then it was not thought that for Zilic a 'rendition' would ever be needed. Post-Milosevic,

---

[1] Abu Abbas was captured by US Special Forces in the desert west of Baghdad, Iraq, in April 2003 while this book was at the printers.

Yugoslavia was keen to return to the community of civilized nations. She needed large loans from the International Monetary Fund and elsewhere to rebuild her infrastructure after seventy-eight days of NATO bombing. Her new President Kostunica would surely regard it as a bagatelle to have Zilic arrested and extradited to the USA?

That certainly was the request Senator Lucas intended to proffer to Colin Powell and John Ashcroft. If worst came to worst, he would ask for a covert rendition to be authorized.

He had his writer-team prepare from the full 1995 report of the Tracker a one-page synopsis to explain everything from Ricky Colenso's departure to Bosnia to try to help pitiful refugees to his presence in a lonely valley on 15 May 1995.

What happened in the valley that morning, as described by Milan Rajak, was compressed into two pages, the most distressing passages heavily highlighted. Fronted by a personal letter from himself, the file was edged and bound for easy reading.

That was something else Capitol Hill had taught him. The higher the office, the shorter the brief should be. In late April he got his face-to-face with both Cabinet secretaries.

Each listened with grave visage, pledged to read the brief and pass it to the appropriate department within their departments. And they did.

The USA has thirteen major intelligence (information) gathering agencies. Between them they probably garner ninety per cent of all the intelligence, licit and illicit, gathered on the entire planet in any twenty-four-hour period.

The sheer volume makes absorption, analysis, filtration, collation, storage and retrieval a problem of industrial proportions. Another problem is that they will not talk to each other.

American intelligence chiefs have been heard to mutter in a late-night bar that they would give their pensions for something like the British Joint Intelligence Committee.

The JIC meets weekly in London under the chairmanship of a veteran and trusted mandarin to bring together the smaller country's four agencies: the Secret Intelligence Service (foreign); the Security Service (home); the Government Communications HQ (SIGINT, the listeners); and Scotland Yard's Special Branch.

Sharing intel and progress can prevent duplication and waste, but its main aim is to see if fragments of information learned in different places by different people could form the jigsaw puzzle that makes up the picture everyone is looking for.

Senator Lucas's report went to six of the agencies and each obediently scoured their archives to see what, if anything, they had learned and filed about a Yugoslav gangster called Zoran Zilic.

Alcohol, Tobacco and Firearms, known as ATF, had nothing. He had never operated in the USA and ATF rarely if ever goes abroad.

The other five were Defence Agency (DIA), who will have an interest in any arms dealer; National Security Agency (NSA), the biggest of them all, working out of their 'Black Chamber' in Annapolis Junction, Maryland, listening to trillions of words a day, spoken, emailed or faxed, with technology almost beyond science fiction; Drug Enforcement Agency (DEA), who will have an interest in anyone who has ever trafficked narcotics anywhere in the world; the FBI (of course), and the CIA. Both the latter spearhead the permanent search for knowledge about terrorists, killers, warlords, hostile regimes, whatever.

It took a week or more and April slipped into May. But because the order came right from the top, the searches were thorough.

The people at Defence, Drugs and Annapolis Junction all came up with fat files. In various capacities they had known about Zoran Zilic for years. Most of their entries concerned his activities since he became a major player on the Belgrade scene: as enforcer to Milosevic, racketeer in drugs and arms, profiteer and general low-life.

That he had murdered an American boy during the Bosnian war they had not known, and they took it seriously. They would have helped if they could. But their files all had one thing in common: they ran out sixteen months before the senator's enquiry.

He had vanished, vaporized, disappeared. Sorry.

At the CIA building, enveloped in summer foliage just off the Beltway, the Director passed the query to the Deputy Director Operations. He consulted downwards to five sub-divisions: Balkans, Terrorism, Special Ops and Arms dealings were four. He even asked, more as a formality than anything else, the small and obsessively secret office formed less than a year earlier after the massacre of the seventeen sailors on the *USS Cole* in Aden harbour, known as Peregrine.

But the answer was the same. Sure we have files, but nothing after sixteen months ago. We agree with all our colleagues. He is no longer in Yugoslavia, but where he is, we do not know. He has not come to our attention for two years, so there has been no reason to expend time and treasure.

The other major hope would have been the FBI. Surely, somewhere in the huge Hoover Building at Pennsylvania and 9th, there would be a recent file describing exactly where this cold-blooded killer could now be found, detained and brought to justice?

Director Robert Mueller, recently appointed successor to Louis Freeh, passed the file and request downwards with his 'Action Without Delay' tag, and it found the desk of Assistant Director Colin Fleming.

Fleming was a lifelong bureau man who could never remember the time, even as a boy, when he did not want to be a G-Man. He came from Scottish Presbyterian stock and his faith was as unflinching as his concept of law, order and justice.

On the work of the bureau he was a fundamentalist. Compromise, accommodation, concession — in the matter of crime these were mere excuses for appeasement. This he despised. What he may have lacked in subtlety he made up in tenacity and dedication.

He came from the granite hills of New Hampshire where the boast is that the rocks and the men vie for toughness. He was a staunch Republican and Peter Lucas was his senator. Indeed, he had campaigned locally for Lucas and had made his acquaintance.

After reading the skimpy report, he rang the senator's office to ask if he might read the full report by the Tracker and the complete confession of Milan Rajak. A copy was messengered over to him that same afternoon.

He read the files with growing anger. He too had a son to be proud of, a navy flier, and the thought of what had happened to Ricky Colenso filled him with a righteous wrath. The Bureau had got to be the instrument of bringing Zilic to justice either via an extradition or a rendition. As the man heading the desk covering all terrorism from overseas sources, he would personally authorize the rendition team to go and get the killer.

But the Bureau could not. Because the Bureau was in the same position as the rest. Even though his gangsterdom, drugs and arms dealing had brought him to the attention of the Bureau as a man to watch, Zilic had never been caught in an act of anti-American terrorism or support thereof; so when he had vanished, he had vanished and the Bureau had not pursued. Its file ran out sixteen months before.

It was with the deepest personal regret that Fleming had to join the others in the intelligence community in admitting they did not know where Zoran Zilic was.

Without a location, there could be no application to a foreign government for extradition. Even if Zilic were now sheltering in a 'failed' state where the writ of normal governmental authority did not run, a snatch operation could only be mounted if the Bureau knew where he was. In his personal letter to the senator, Assistant Director Fleming apologized that it did not.

Fleming's tenacity came with the Highland genes. Two days later he sought out and lunched with Fraser Gibbs. The FBI has two retired senior officers of almost iconic status, who can pack the student lecture halls at the Bureau's Quantico training facility when they go.

One is the towering ex-footballer, former Marine pilot Buck Revell; the other is Fraser Gibbs, who spent his early career penetrating organized crime as an undercover agent, about as dangerous work as you can get, and the second half crushing the Cosa Nostra down the eastern seaboard. When restored to Washington after a bullet in the leg left him with a limp, he was given the desk covering freelances, mercenaries, guns for hire. He considered Fleming's query with a furrowed brow.

'I did hear something once,' he conceded. 'A manhunter. Sort of bounty hunter. Had a code name.'

'A killer himself? You know government rules absolutely forbid that sort of thing.'

'No, that's the point,' said the old veteran. 'The rumour was, he doesn't kill. Kidnaps, snatches, brings them back. Now, what the hell was his name?'

'It could be important,' said Fleming.

'He was terribly secretive. My predecessor tried to identify him. Sent in an undercover man as a pretend client. But he smelt a trick somehow, made an excuse, left the meeting and disappeared.'

'Why didn't he just fess up and come clean?' asked Fleming. 'If he wasn't in the killing business . . .'

'I guess he figured that as he operated abroad, and as the Bureau doesn't like freelances operating on its own turf, we'd have sought top-level instruction and been ordered to close him down. And he'd probably have been right. So he stayed in the shadows and I never hunted him down.'

'The agent would have filed a report.'

'Oh, yes. Procedure. Probably under the man's code name. Never got any other name. Ah, that's it. Avenger. Punch in 'Avenger'. See what comes up.'

The file the computer disgorged was indeed slim. An advert had been entered in the personal small ads of a technical magazine for aeroplane buffs, seemingly the only way the man would communicate. A story had been spun, a rendezvous agreed.

The bounty hunter had insisted on sitting in deep shadow behind a bright lamp which shone forward away from him. The agent reported he was of medium height, slim build, probably no more than one hundred and sixty pounds. He never saw the face, and within three minutes the man suspected something. He reached out, killed the light, leaving the agent with no night-vision, and when the agent had quit blinking the man was gone.

All the agent could report was that as the bounty hunter's hand lay on the table between them, his left sleeve had ridden up to reveal a tattoo on the forearm. It appeared to be a rat grinning over its shoulder while showing the viewer its bottom.

None of this would have been the slightest interest to Senator Lucas or his friend in Canada. But the least Colin Fleming thought he could do was pass on the code name and the method of contact. It was a one-in-a-hundred chance, but it was all he had.

Three days later in his office in Ontario, Stephen Edmond opened the letter sent by his friend in Washington. He had already heard the news from the six agencies and had virtually given up hope.

He read the supplementary letter and frowned. He had been thinking of the mighty United States using its power to require a foreign government to bring forth its murderer, snap handcuffs on his wrists and send him back to the USA.

It had never occurred to him that he was too late; that Zilic had simply vanished; that all the billion-dollar agencies of Washington simply did not know where he was and therefore could do nothing.

He thought it over for ten minutes, shrugged

and pressed the intercom.

'Jean, I want to put a classified ad in the personal column 'wanted' section of an American technical magazine. You'll have to check it out. I've never heard of it. Called *Vintage Airplane*. Yeah, the text. Make it: 'AVENGER. Wanted. Serious offer. No price ceiling. Please call.' Then put my cellphone number and private line. OK, Jean?'

Twenty-six men in intelligence agencies in and around Washington had seen the request. All had responded that they did not know where Zoran Zilic was.

One of them had lied.

# PART TWO

PART TWO

# 17

## The Photo

Since the attempt by the FBI to unmask him six years earlier, Dexter had decided there was no need for face-to-face meetings. Instead, he built up several defensive lines to mask his location and his identity.

One of these was a small one-bedroom apartment in New York, but not the Bronx where he might be recognized. He rented it furnished, paid by the quarter, regular as clockwork, and always in cash. It attracted no official attention and neither did he when he was in residence.

He also used mobile phones only of the type using pay-as-you-talk SIM cards. These he bought in bulk out of state, used once or twice and consigned to the East River. Even the NSA, with the technology to listen to a phone call and trace the exact source, cannot identify the purchaser of these use-and-jettison SIM mobiles, nor direct police to the location of the call if the user is on the move, keeps the call short and gets rid of the technology afterwards.

Another ploy is the old-fashioned public phone booth. Numbers called from a booth can, of course, be traced; but there are so many millions of them that unless a specific booth or bank of them is suspected it is very hard to pick up the conversation, identify the caller as a wanted man, trace the location and get a police car there in time.

Finally he used the much-maligned US mails, with his letters being sent to a 'drop' in the form of an innocent Korean-run fruit and vegetable shop two blocks from his apartment in New York. This would be no protection if the mail or the shop was targeted and put under surveillance, but there was no reason why it should be.

He contacted the placer of the advert on the cellphone listed. He did so from a single-use mobile phone and he motored far into the New Jersey countryside to do it.

Stephen Edmond identified himself without demur and in five sentences described what had happened to his grandson. Avenger thanked him and hung up.

There are several giant newspaper-cuttings libraries in the USA and the best-known are those of the *New York Times*, *Washington Post* and Lexis Nexis. He used the third, visited its New York database and paid cash.

There was enough to confirm who Stephen Edmond was, and there had been two articles concerning the disappearance years ago of his grandson while a student aid worker in Bosnia, both from the *Toronto Star*. This caller seemed to be genuine.

Dexter called the Canadian back and dictated terms: considerable operating expenses, a fee on account and a bonus on delivery of Zilic to US jurisdiction, not payable in the event of failure.

'That's a lot of money for a man I have not

210

met and apparently will not meet. You could take it and vaporize,' said the Canadian.

'And you, sir, could go back to the US government, where I presume you have already been.'

There was a pause.

'All right, where should it be sent?'

Dexter gave him a Caymanian account number and a New York mailing address. 'The money order to the first, every line of research material already done to the second,' he said, and hung up.

The Caribbean bank would shift the credit through a dozen different accounts within its computer system but would also open a line of credit to a bank in New York. This would be in favour of a Dutch citizen who would identify himself with a perfect Dutch passport.

Three days later a file arrived in a stout envelope at a Korean fruit shop in Brooklyn. It was collected by the addressee, Mr Armitage. It contained a photocopy of the entire report from the Tracker, that of 1995 and of that same spring of 2001, including the confession of Milan Rajak. None of the files on Zoran Zilic in the archives of the various US intelligence agencies had ever been shown to the Canadian, so his knowledge of the man was sketchy. Worst of all, there was no picture.

Dexter went back to the media archives, which today are the primary source of any seeker after recent history. There is hardly an event or person who ever came to any notice at all whom some journalist did not write about, or some photographer did not photograph. But Zoran Zilic nearly made it.

Unlike the publicity-hungry Zeljko 'Arkan' Raznatovic, Zilic had an abhorrence of being photographed. He clearly went out of his way to avoid publicity of any kind. In this he resembled some of the Palestinian terrorists, like Sabri al-Banna, known as Abu Nidal.

Dexter came up with one major *Newsweek* feature going back to the Bosnian war; it was about all the Serbian so-called warlords but within it Zilic had only a few passing mentions, probably for lack of material.

There was one photograph of a man at a cocktail party of some sort, clearly cropped and blown up, which made it slightly hazy. The other was of a teenager; it came from Belgrade police files, and clearly went back to the days of the street gangs of Zemun. Either man could walk straight past him in the street and he would not recognize the Serbian.

The Englishman, the Tracker, mentioned a private investigation agency in Belgrade. It was now post-war, post-Milosevic. The Yugoslav capital, where Zilic had been born and raised, and from which he had vanished, seemed the place to start. Dexter flew New York to Vienna and on to Belgrade, and checked into the Hyatt. From his tenth-floor window the battered Balkan city stretched out beneath him. Half a mile away he could see the hotel where Raznatovic had been shot to death in the lobby despite his covey of bodyguards.

A taxi brought him to the agency called

Chandler, still run by Dragan Stojic, the Philip Marlowe wannabe. Dexter's cover was a publishing commission from the *New Yorker* asking for a 10,000-word biography of Raznatovic. Stojic nodded and grunted.

'Everyone knew him. Married a pop singer, glamorous girl. So what do you want from me?'

'The fact is, I have just about all I need for this piece,' said Dexter, whose American passport revealed him as Alfred Barnes. 'But there is a sort of afterthought I should give mention to. A one-time contemporary of Arkan in the Belgrade underworld. Name of Zoran Zilic.'

Stojic let out a long puff of air.

'Now that *was* a nasty piece of work,' he said. 'He never liked being written about, photographed or even talked about. People who uspet him in that area were . . . visited. There's not much on file about him.'

'I accept that. So what is Belgrade's premier cuttings agency for written material?'

'Not a problem, there's really only one. It's called VIP, it's got an office in Vracar and the editor-in-chief is Slavko Markovic.'

Dexter rose.

'That's it?' asked the Balkan Marlowe. 'Hardly worth an invoice.'

The American took a hundred-dollar bill and laid it on the desk. 'All information has a price, Mr Stojic. Even a name and address.'

Another cab took him to the VIP cuttings agency. Mr Markovic was at lunch so Dexter found a café and toyed with a light lunch and a glass of local red wine until he came back.

Markovic was as pessimistic as the private eye. But he punched up his in-house database to see what he had.

'One piece,' he said, 'and it happens to be in English.'

It was the Newsweek piece from the Bosnian war.

'That's it?' queried Dexter. 'This man was powerful, important, prominent. Surely there must be some trace of him?'

'That's the point,' said Markovic, 'he was all those things. And violent. Under Milosevic there was no argument. He seems to have cleaned out every record of himself before he quit. Police records, court records, state TV, media, the lot. Family, school contemporaries, former colleagues, no one wants to talk about him. Warned off. Mr No-face, that's him.'

'Do you recall when the last attempt was made to write anything about him?'

Markovic thought for a while.

'Now you mention it, I heard a rumour that someone tried. But it came to nothing. After Milosevic fell, and with Zilic vanished, someone tried to do a piece. I think it was cancelled.'

'Who was it?'

'My talking canary said it was a magazine here in Belgrade called Ogledalo. That means 'The Mirror'.'

The Mirror still existed and its editor was still Vuk Kobac. Even though it was print day, he agreed to give the American a few minutes of his time. He lost his enthusiasm when he heard the enquiry.

'That bloody man,' he said. 'I wish I had never heard of him.'

'What happened?'

'It was a young freelance. Nice kid. Keen, eager. Wanted a staff job. I hadn't got one vacant. But he pleaded for a chance. So I gave him a commission. Name of Petrovic. Srechko Petrovic. Only twenty-two, poor kid.'

'What happened to him?'

'He got run over, that's what happened to him. Parked his car opposite the apartment block where he lived with his mum, went to cross the road. A Mercedes came round the corner and ran him over.'

'Careless driver.'

'Very careless. Managed to run him over twice. Then drove off.'

'Discouraging.'

'And permanent. Even in exile, he can still order and pay for a hit to be done in Belgrade.'

'Any address for his mum?'

'Hold on. We sent a wreath. Must have sent it to the flat.'

He found it and bade his visitor goodbye.

'One last question,' said Dexter. 'When was this?'

'Six months ago. Just after New Year. A word of advice, Mr Barnes. Stick to writing about Arkan. He's safely dead. Leave Zilic alone. He'll kill you. Must rush, it's print day.'

The address said Blok 23, Novi Beograd. He recognized Novi Beograd, or New Belgrade, from the city map he had bought in the hotel bookshop. It was the rather bleak district in which the hotel itself stood, on a peninsula flanked by the rivers Sava and Dunav, the Danube itself, which was emphatically not blue. It stood across both rivers from central Belgrade.

In the communist years the taste had been for huge, high-rise apartment blocks for the workers. They had gone up on vacant lots in Novi Beograd, great poured-concrete beehives, each cavity a tiny flat with its door opening to a long open-sided passage, lashed by the elements.

Some had survived better than others. It depended on the level of prosperity of the inhabitants and thus the level of maintenance. Block 23 was a roach-infested horror. Mrs Petrovic lived on the ninth floor and the elevator was out of order. Dexter could take them at a run but he wondered how senior citizens would cope, the more so as they all seemed to be chain-smokers.

There was not much point in going up to see her alone. There was no chance she would speak English and he had no Serbo-Croat. It was one of the pretty and bright girls behind the reception desk at the Hyatt who accepted his offer to help him out. She was saving to get married and two hundred dollars for an hour's extra work at the end of her shift was quite acceptable.

They arrived at seven and just in time. Mrs Petrovic was an office cleaner and left each evening at eight to work through the night in the offices across the river.

She was one of those who have quite simply been defeated by life and the lined and

216

exhausted face told its own story. She was probably mid-forties going on seventy, her husband killed in an industrial accident with almost no compensation, her son murdered beneath her own window. As always with the very poor approached by the apparently rich, her first reaction was suspicion.

He had brought a large bunch of flowers. It had been a long, long time since she had had flowers. Anna, the girl from the hotel, arranged them in three displays around the tiny, shabby room.

'I want to write about what happened to Srechko. I know it cannot bring him back, but I can perhaps expose the man who did this to him. Will you help me?'

She shrugged.

'I know nothing,' she said. 'I never asked about his work.'

'The night that he died . . . was he carrying anything with him?'

'I don't know. The body was searched. They took everything.'

'They searched the body? Right there on the street?'

'Yes.'

'Did he have papers? Did he have notes that he left behind? Here in the flat?'

'Yes, he had bundles of papers. With his typewriter and his pencils. But I never read them.'

'Could I see them?'

'They are gone.'

'Gone?'

'They took them. Took them all. Even the ribbon from the typewriter.'

'The police?'

'No, the men.'

'Which men?'

'They came back. Two nights later. They made me sit in the corner, there. They searched everywhere. They took everything he had had.'

'There is nothing left at all of what he was working on for Mr Kobac?'

'Only the photo. I had forgotten about the photo.'

'Please tell me about the photo.'

It came out in small details, all via Anna, from language to language. Three days before he died, Srechko the cub reporter had attended a New Year party and red wine had been spilled on his denim jacket. His mother had put it in the laundry bag for washing later.

When he was dead there was no point. She too forgot about the laundry bag and the gangsters never thought to ask. When she was making a pile of her dead son's clothes the wine-stained denim jacket fell out. She felt the pockets quickly to see if her son had forgotten any money, but felt something semi-stiff. It was a photograph.

'Do you still have it? May I see it?' asked Dexter.

She nodded and crept away like a mouse to a sewing box in the corner. She came back with the photo.

It was of a man, caught unawares, who had seen the photographer at the last minute. He was trying to raise his outspread hand to cover his face, but the shutter had clicked just in time. He was full-face, upright, in a short-sleeved shirt and slacks.

The picture was in black and white, not of professional clarity, but with enlargement and enhancement was as good as he was ever likely to get. He recalled the teenage picture and the cocktail party photo he had found in New York and carried in the lining of his attaché case. They were all a bit grainy, but it was the same man. It was Zilic.

'I would like to buy this picture Mrs Petrovic,' he said. She shrugged and said something in Serbo-Croat.

'She says you may have it. It is of no interest to her. She does not know who he is,' said Anna.

'One last question. Just before he died, did Srechko go away for a while?'

'Yes, in December. He was away a week. He would not say where he had been, but he had a sunburn on his nose.'

She escorted them to her door and the landing exposed to the winds, which led to the non-functioning lift and the stairwell. Anna went first. When she was out of earshot Dexter turned to the Serbian mother who had also lost her child, and spoke gently in English.

'You can't understand a word I say, lady, but if I ever get this swine into a slammer in the States, it's partly for you. And it's on the house.'

Of course, she did not understand but she responded to the smile and said 'Hvala'. In a day in Belgrade he had learned that it means 'thank you'.

He had instructed the taxi to wait. He dropped Anna, clutching her two hundred dollars, at her home in the suburbs and on the way back to the centre studied the picture again.

Zilic was standing on what looked like an open expanse of concrete or tarmac. Behind him were big low buildings like warehouses. Over one of the buildings a flag floated, extended by the breeze, but part of it was off the picture.

There was something else sticking into vision out of frame, but he could not work it out. He tapped the taxi driver on the shoulder.

'Do you have a magnifying glass?' He did not understand, but elaborate pantomime cleared up the mystery. He nodded. He kept one in the glove compartment for studying his A-Z city road map if need be.

The long, flat object jutting into the picture from the left came clear. It was the wingtip of an aeroplane, but no more than six feet off the ground. So, not an airliner, but a smaller craft.

Then he recognized the buildings in the background. Not warehouses, hangars. Not the huge structures needed for sheltering airliners, but the sort needed for private planes, executive jets, whose tailfins rarely top more than thirty feet. The man was on a private airfield or the executive section of an airport.

They helped him at the hotel. Yes, there were several cybercafés in Belgrade, all open until late. He dined in the snack bar and took a taxi to the nearest. When he was logged on to his favourite search engine, he asked for all the flags of the world.

The flag fluttering above the hangars in the dead reporter's photo was only in monochrome, but it was clear the flag had three horizontal stripes of which the bottom one was so dark it looked like black. If not, then a very dark blue. He opted for black.

As he ran through the world's flags, he noted that a good half of them had some kind of logo, crest or device superimposed on the stripes. The one he sought had none. That cut the choice down to the other half.

Those who had horizontal stripes and no logo were no more than two dozen, and those with a black or near-black bottom stripe were five.

Gabon, Netherlands and Sierra Leone all had three horizontal stripes of which the lowest was deep blue, which could show up black in a monochrome photograph. Only two had a bottom stripe of three which was definitely black: Sudan and one other. But the Sudan had a green diamond up against the flagpole as well as three stripes. The remaining one had a vertical stripe nearest the flagpole. Peering at his photo, Dexter could just make out the fourth stripe; not clear, but it was there.

One vertical red stripe by the flagpole; green, white and black horizontals running out to the flapping edge. Zilic was standing on an airport somewhere in the United Arab Emirates.

Even in December a pale-skinned Slav could get a badly burned nose in the UAE.

# 18

## The Gulf

There are seven emirates in the UAE but only the three biggest and richest, Dubai, Abu Dhabi and Sharjah, spring readily to mind. The other four are much smaller and almost anonymous.

They all occupy the peninsula at the southeastern tip of the Saudi landmass, that tongue of desert that separates the Arabian Gulf to the north and the Gulf of Oman to the south.

Only one, Al Fujairah, faces south onto the Gulf of Oman and thence the Arabian Sea; the other six are strung in a line along the northern coast, staring at Iran across the water. Apart from the seven capitals, there is the desert oasis-town of Al Ain that also has an airport.

While still in Belgrade, Dexter found a portrait photographic studio with the technology to re-photograph the picture of Zoran Zilic, increase its clarity and then blow it up from playing-card to softback-book size.

While the photographer worked on one task, Dexter returned to the cybercafé, enquired after the United Arab Emirates and downloaded everything he could get. The following day he took the JAT regular service via Beirut to Dubai.

The wealthy Emirates derive their riches mainly from oil although they have all tried to broaden the base of their economies to include tourism and duty-free trade. Most of the oil deposits are offshore.

Rigs have to be resupplied constantly and although the vehicles used for heavy cargoes are seaborne lighters, personal transfers are faster and easier by helicopter.

The oil companies operating the rigs have their own helicopters but there is still ample room for charter firms, and the internet revealed three such, right in Dubai. The American Alfred Barnes had become a lawyer when he visited the first. He picked the smallest, on the grounds it was probably the least concerned with formalities and the most interested in wads of dollar bills. He was right on both counts.

The office was a Portakabin out at Port Rashid and the proprietor and chief pilot turned out to be a former British Army Air Corps flier trying to make a living. They do not come much more informal than that.

'Alfred Barnes, attorney-at-law,' said Dexter, extending his hand. 'I have a problem, a tight schedule and a large budget.'

The British ex-captain raised a polite eyebrow. Dexter pushed the photo across the cigarette-scorched desk.

'My client is, or rather was, a very wealthy man.'

'He lost it?' asked the pilot.

'In a way. He died. My law firm is the chief executor. And this man is the chief beneficiary. Only he doesn't know it and we cannot find him.'

'I'm a charter pilot, not Missing Persons. Anyway, I've never seen him.'

'No reason why you should. It's the background to the picture. Look carefully. An airport or airfield, right? The last I heard he was working in civil aviation here in UAE. If I could identify that airport, I could probably find him. What do you think?'

The charter pilot studied the background.

'Airports here have three sections: military, airlines and private flyers. That wing belongs to an executive jet. There are scores, maybe hundreds of them, in the Gulf. Most have company livery and most are owned by wealthy Arabs. What do you want to do?'

What Dexter wanted to buy was the charter captain's access to the flying side to all these airports. It came at a price and took two days. The cover was that he had to pick up a client. After sixty minutes inside the executive jet compound, when the fictional client failed to show up, the captain told the tower he was breaking off the charter and leaving the circuit.

The airports at Abu Dhabi, Dubai and Sharjah were huge and even the private aviation sector of each was far bigger than the background in the photograph.

The emirates of Ajman and Umm al-Qaiwain had no airport at all, being cheek by jowl with Sharjah airport. That left the desert city of Al Ain, Al Fujairah out on the far side of the peninsula facing the Gulf of Oman, and, right up in the north, the least known of them all, Ras al-Khaimah.

They found it on the morning of the second day. The Bell Jetranger swerved in across the desert to land at what the Britisher called Al K, and there were the hangars with the flag fluttering behind them.

Dexter had taken the charter for two full days, and brought his handgrip with him. He settled up with a fistful of hundred-dollar bills, stepped down and watched the Bell lift away. Looking around, he realized he was standing almost where Srechko Petrovic must have been when he snatched the photo that sealed his fate. An official stepped from an administration building and beckoned him to clear the area.

The arrival and departure building for both airline and private jet passengers was neat, clean and small, with the accent on small. Named after the emiral family, Al-Quassimi International Airport had clearly never disturbed those airlines whose names are world famous.

On the tarmac in front of the terminal building were Russian-built Antonovs and Tupolevs. There was an old Yakovlev single-prop bi-plane. One airliner bore the livery and logo of Tajikistan Airlines. Dexter went up one floor to the roof café and took a coffee.

The same floor contained the admin offices, including the supremely optimistic Public Relations department. The sole inhabitant was a nervous young lady robed from head to toe in a black chador, with only her hands and pale oval face visible. She had halting English.

Alfred Barnes had now become a development officer for tourism projects with a major US

225

company and wished to enquire about the facilities Ras al-Khaimah could offer to the executives seeking an exotic conference centre; especially he needed to know if they could be offered airport facilities for the executive jets in which they would arrive.

The lady was polite but adamant. All enquiries regarding tourism should be addressed to the Department of Tourism in the Commercial Centre, right next to the Old Town.

A taxi brought him there. It was a small cube of a building on a development site, about 500 yards from the Hilton and right on the edge of the brand-new deep-water harbour. It did not appear to be under siege from those seeking to develop tourism.

Mr Hussein al Khoury would have regarded himself, if asked, as a good man. That did not make him a contented man. To justify the first, he would have said he only had one wife but treated her well. He tried to raise his four children as a good father should. He attended mosque every Friday and gave alms to charity according to his ability and according to scripture.

He should have progressed far in life, inshallah. But it seemed Allah did not smile upon him. He remained stuck in the middle ranks of the Tourism Ministry; specifically, he remained stuck in a small brick cube on a development site next to the deep-water harbour, where no one ever called. Then one day the smiling American walked in.

He was delighted. An enquiry at last, and the

chance to practise the English over which he had spent so many hundreds of hours. After several minutes of courteous pleasantries — how charming of the American to realize that Arabs do not like to delve straight into business — they agreed that as the air conditioning had broken down and the outside temperature was nudging 100 degrees, they might use the American's taxi to adjourn to the coffee lounge of the Hilton.

Settled in the pleasant cool of the Hilton bar, Mr al Khoury was intrigued that the American seemed in no hurry to proceed to his business. Eventually the Arab said:

'Now, how can I help you?'

'You know, my friend,' said the American with seriousness, 'my whole life's philosophy is that we are put upon this earth by our mighty and merciful Creator to help one another. And I believe that it is I who am here to help you.'

Almost absentmindedly the American began to fumble in his jacket pockets for something. Out came his passport, several folded letters of introduction and a block of hundred-dollar bills that took Mr al Khoury's breath away.

'Let us see if we cannot help each other.'

The civil servant stared at the dollars.

'If there is anything I can do ... ' he murmured.

'I should be very honest with you, Mr al Khoury. My real job in life is debt collector. Not a very glamorous job, but necessary. When we buy things, we should pay for them. Not so?'

'Assuredly.'

'There is a man who flies into your airport

now and again. In his own executive jet. This man.'

Mr al Khoury stared at the photo for a few seconds, then shook his head. His gaze returned to the block of dollars. Four thousand? Five? To put Faisal through university . . .

'Alas, this man did not pay for his aeroplane. In a sense, therefore, he stole it. He paid the deposit, then flew away and was never seen again. Probably changed the registration number. Now, these are expensive things. Twenty million dollars each. So, the true owners would be grateful, in a very practical way, to anyone who could help them to find their aircraft.'

'But if he is here now, arrest him. Impound the aircraft. We have laws . . . '

'Alas, he has gone again. But every time he lands here, there is a record. Stored in the files at Ras al-Khaimah airport. Now, a man of your authority could require to see those archives.'

The civil servant dabbed his lips with a clean handkerchief.

'When was it here, this aeroplane?'

'Last December.'

Before leaving Block 23 Dexter had learned from Mrs Petrovic that her son had been away from 13 to 20 December. Calculating that Srechko had snatched his photograph, been seen, knew he had been seen, and had left immediately for home, he would have been in Ras al-Khaimah about the 18th. How he had known to come here, Dexter had no idea. He must have been a good, or very lucky, reporter. Kobac should have taken him on.

'There are many executive jets who come here,' said Mr al Khoury.

'All I need are the registration numbers and the types of every privately or corporately owned executive jet, specifically owned by Europeans, hopefully this one, parked here between 15 and 19 December last. Now, I would think, in those four days . . . what? . . . Ten?'

He prayed the Arab would not ask how he did not know the make of the jet if he represented the vendors. He began to peel off hundred-dollar bills.

'As a token of my good faith. And my complete trust in you, my friend. And the other four thousand later.'

The Arab still looked dubious, torn between desire for such a magnificent sum and fear of discovery and dismissal. The American pressed his case.

'If you were doing anything to harm your country, I would not dream of asking. But this man is a thief. Taking away from him what he has stolen can surely be only a good thing. Does not the Book praise justice against the wrongdoer?'

Mr al Khoury's hand covered the thousand dollars.

'I'll check in here, now,' said Dexter. 'Just ask for Mr Barnes when you are ready.'

The call came two days later. Mr al Khoury was taking his new role as secret agent rather seriously. He phoned from a booth in a public place.

'It is your friend,' said a breathless voice in the mid-morning.

'Hallo, my friend, do you wish to see me?' asked Dexter.

'Yes. I have the package.'

'Here or at the office?'

'Neither. Too public. The Al Hamra Fort. Lunch.'

His dialogue could not have been more suspicious, had anyone been eavesdropping, but Dexter doubted the Ras al-Khaimah secret service were on the case.

He checked out and ordered a taxi. The Al Hamra Fort Hotel was out of town, ten miles down the coast but in the right direction, heading back towards Dubai, a luxurious conversion from an old turreted Arab fortress into a five-star beachside resort.

He was there at midday, much too early for a Gulf lunch, but found a low-slung club chair in the vaulted lobby, ordered a beer and watched the entrance arch. Mr al Khoury appeared, hot and dripping even from the hundred-yard walk from his car in the parking lot, just after 1 p.m. Of the five restaurants they selected the Lebanese with its cold buffet.

'Any problems?' asked Dexter as they took their plates and moved down the groaning trestle tables.

'No,' said the civil servant. 'I explained my department was contacting all known visitors to send them a brochure describing the new and extra leisure facilities now available in Ras al-Khaimah.'

'That is brilliant,' beamed Dexter. 'No one thought it odd?'

'On the contrary, the officials in Air Traffic got out all the flight plans for December and insisted on giving me the whole month.'

'You mentioned the importance of the European owners?'

'Yes, but there are only about four or five who are not well-known oil companies. Let us sit.'

They took a corner table and ordered up two beers. Like many modern Arabs Mr al Khoury had no problem with alcoholic drinks.

He clearly enjoyed his Lebanese food. He had piled his plate with mezzah, houmous, moutabel, lightly grilled halloumi cheese, sambousek, kibbeh and stuffed vine leaves. He handed over a sheaf of paper and began to eat.

Dexter ran through the listings of filed flight plans for December, along with time of landing and duration of stay before departure, until he came to 15 December. With a red felt-tip pen he bracketed those appearing then and covering the period to 19 December. There were nine.

Two Grumman Threes and a Four belonged to internationally known US oil companies. A French Dassault Mystere and a Falcon were down to Elf-Aquitaine. That left four.

A smaller Lear jet was known to belong to a Saudi prince and a larger Cessna Citation to a multi-millionaire businessman from Bahrain. The last two were an Israeli-built Westwind that arrived from Bombay and a Hawker 1000 that came in from Cairo and departed back there. Someone had noted something in Arab script beside the Westwind.

231

'What does that mean?' asked Dexter.

'Ah, yes, that one is regular. It is owned by an Indian film producer. From Bombay. He stages through on his way to London or Cannes, or Berlin. All the film festivals. In the tower, they know him by sight.'

'You have the picture?'

Al Khoury handed back the borrowed photograph.

'That one, they think he comes from the Hawker.'

The Hawker 1000 had a registration number listed as P4-ZEM and was down as owned by the Zeta Corporation of Bermuda.

Dexter thanked his informant and paid over the promised balance of four thousand dollars. It was a lot for a sheaf of paper but Dexter thought it might be the lead he needed.

On his drive back to Dubai airport he mused on something he had once been told. That when a man changes his entire identity, he cannot always resist the temptation to keep back one tiny detail for old time's sake.

ZEM just happened to be the first three letters of Zemun, the district in Belgrade where Zoran Zilic was born and raised. And Zeta just happened to be the Greek and Spanish for the letter Z.

But Zilic would have hidden himself and his covering corporations, not to mention his aeroplane if indeed the Hawker was his, behind layers of protection.

The records would be out there somewhere, but they would be stored in databases of the type not available to the innocent seeker of knowledge.

Dexter could manage a computer as well as the next man, but there was no way he could hack into a protected database. But he remembered someone who could.

# 19

# The Confrontation

When it came to matters of right and wrong, of sin and righteousness, FBI Assistant Director Colin Fleming would brook no compromise. The concept of 'No Surrender' was in his bones and his genes, brought across the Atlantic a hundred years ago from the cobbled streets of Portadown. Two hundred years before that his ancestors had brought their Presbyterian code across to Ulster from the western coast of Scotland.

When it came to evil, to tolerate was to accommodate, to accommodate was to appease, and to appease was to concede defeat. That he could never do.

When he read the synthesis of the Tracker's report and the Serbian confession, and when he reached the details of the death of Ricky Colenso, he determined that the man responsible should, if at all possible, face due process in a court of law in the greatest country in the world, his own.

Of all those in the various agencies who read the circulated report and the joint request from Secretary Powell and Attorney General Ashcroft, he had taken it almost personally that his own department had no current knowledge of Zoran Zilic and could not help.

In a final bid to do something, he had circulated a full-face picture of the Serbian gangster to the thirty-eight 'legats' posted abroad.

It was a far better picture than had been contained in any Press archive, though not as recent as the one that a charlady in Block 23 had given to the Avenger. The reason for its quality was that it had been taken in Belgrade by a long-lens camera on the orders of the CIA Station Chief five years earlier when the elusive Zilic was a mover and shaker in the court of Milosevic.

The photographer had caught Zilic emerging from his car, in the act of straightening up, head raised, gaze towards the lens he could not see a quarter of a mile away. Inside the Belgrade embassy the FBI legat had obtained a copy from his CIA colleague, so both agencies possessed the same.

Broadly speaking, the CIA operates outside the USA and the FBI inside. But for all of that, in the ongoing fight against espionage, terrorism and crime, the Bureau has no choice but to collaborate intensively and extensively with foreign countries, especially allies, and to that end maintains its legal attachés abroad.

It may look as if the legal attaché is some kind of diplomatic appointment, answering to the Department of State. Not so. The 'legat' is the FBI representative inside the US embassy. Every one of them had received the photo of Zilic from Assistant Director Fleming with an instruction to display it in the hopes of a lucky break. It came in the unlikely form of Inspector Bin Zayeed.

Inspector Moussa bin Zayeed would also, if asked, have replied that he was a good man. He served his emir, Sheikh Maktoum of Dubai, with complete loyalty, took no bribes, honoured his god and paid his taxes. If he moonlighted by passing useful information to his friend at the American embassy, this was simply cooperation with his country's ally and not to be confused with anything else.

Thus it was he found himself, with the outside temperature in July over one hundred degrees, sheltering in the welcome cool of the air-conditioned embassy lobby and waiting for his friend to descend and take him out for lunch. His eye strayed to the bulletin board.

He rose and strolled over to it. There were the usual notices of coming events, functions, arrivals, departures and invitations to various club memberships. Among the clutter was a photograph and the printed question: 'Have you seen this man?'

'Well, have you?' asked a cheery voice behind him and a hand clapped him on the shoulder. It was Bill Brunton, his contact, lunch host and the legal attaché. They exchanged friendly greetings.

'Oh yes,' said the Special Branch officer. 'Two weeks ago.'

Brunton's bonhomie dropped away. The fish restaurant out at Jumeirah could wait a while.

'Let's step right back to my office,' he suggested.

'Do you remember where and when?' asked

236

the legat, back in his office.

'Of course. About a fortnight ago. I was visiting a relative in Ras al-Khaimah. I was on the Faisal Road; you know it? The seafront road out of town, between the Old Town and the Gulf.'

Brunton nodded.

'Well, a lorry was trying to manoeuvre backwards into a narrow worksite. I had to stop. To my left was a café terrace. There were three men at the table. One of them was this one.' He gestured to the photograph now face-up on the legat's desk.

'No question about it?'

'None. That was the man.'

'He was with two others?'

'Yes.'

'You recognized them?'

'One by name. The other only by sight. The one by name was Bout.'

Bill Brunton sucked in his breath. Vladimir Bout needed no introduction to virtually anyone in a Western or Eastern Block intelligence service. He was widely notorious, a former KGB major who had become one of the world's leading black-market arms dealers, a merchant of death of the first rank.

That he was not even born a Russian, but a half-Tajik from Dushanbe, attests to his skill in the nether arts. The Russians are nothing if not the most racist people on earth and back in the USSR referred to denizens of the non-Russian Republics collectively as 'chorny', meaning 'blacks'; and it was not meant as a compliment.

Only White Russians and Ukrainians could escape the term and rise through the ranks on equal par with an ethnic Russian. For a half-breed Tajik to graduate out of Moscow's prestigious Military Institute of Foreign Languages, a KGB-front training academy, and make it to the rank of major was unusual.

He was assigned to the Navigation and Air Transport Regiment of the Soviet Air Force, another covert 'front' for shipping arms consignments to anti-Western guerrillas and Third World regimes opposed to the West. Here he could use his mastery of Portuguese in the Angolan civil war. He also built up formidable contacts in the air force.

When the USSR collapsed in 1991, chaos reigned for several years and military inventories were simply abandoned as unit commanders sold off their equipment for almost any price they could get. Bout simply bought the sixteen Ilyushin 76s of his own unit for a song and went into the air charter and freight business.

By 1992 he was back in his native south; the Afghan civil war had started, just across the border from his native Tajikistan, and one of the prime contestants was his fellow Tajik, General Dostum. The only 'freight' the barbarous Dostum wanted was arms; Bout provided.

By 1993 he showed up in Ostend, Belgium, a jumping-off point to move into Africa via the Belgian ex-colony, the permanently war-torn Congo. His source of supply was limitless, the vast weapons pool of the old USSR, still operating on fictional inventories. Among his new clients were the Interahamwe, the genocidal butchers of Rwanda/Burundi.

This finally upset even the Belgians and he was hounded out of Ostend, appearing in 1995 in South Africa to sell to both the UNITA guerrillas in Angola and their enemies in the MPLA government. But with Nelson Mandela occupying the South African presidency, things went bad for him there too and he had to leave in a hurry.

In 1998 he showed up in the UAE and settled in Sharjah. The British and Americans put his dossier in front of the Emir and three weeks before Bill Brunton sat in his office with Inspector Bin Zayeed, Bout had been kicked out yet again.

But his recourse was simply to move ten miles up the coast and settle in Ajman, taking a suite of rooms in the Chamber of Commerce and Industry building. With only forty thousand people, Ajman has no oil and little industry and could not be as particular as Sharjah.

For Bill Brunton the sighting was important. He did not know why his superior, Colin Fleming, was interested in the missing Serb, but this report was certainly going to earn him a few Brownie points in the Hoover Building.

'And the third man?' he asked. 'You say you know him by sight? Any idea where?'

'Of course. Here. He is one of your colleagues?'

If Bill Brunton thought his surprises for the day were over, he was wrong. He felt his stomach perform some gentle aerobatics. Carefully, he withdrew a file from the bottom drawer of his desk. It was a compendium of embassy staff. Inspector Bin Zayeed was unhesitating in pointing to the face of the cultural attaché.

'This one,' he said. 'He was the third man at the table. You know him?'

Brunton knew him all right. Even though cultural exchanges were few and far between, the cultural attaché was a very busy man. This was because behind the façade of visiting orchestras, he was the Station Chief for the CIA.

★ ★ ★

The news from Dubai left Colin Fleming incandescent with rage. It was not that the secret agency out at Langley was conferring with a man like Vladimir Bout. That might be necessary in the course of information gathering. What had angered him was that someone high in the CIA had clearly lied to the Secretary of State, Colin Powell himself, and to his own superior, the Attorney General. A lot of rules had been broken here, and he was pretty sure he knew who had broken them. He called Langley and asked for a meeting as a matter of some urgency.

The two men had met before. They had clashed in front of the National Security Advisor, Condoleezza Rice, and there was little love lost between them. Occasionally, opposites attract, but not in this case.

Paul Devereaux III was the scion of a long line of those families who come as near to being aristocracy as the Commonwealth of Massachusetts has had for a long time. He was born a Boston Brahmin to his boot heels.

He was showing his intellectual brilliance way before school age and sailed through Boston College High School, the main feeder unit to one of the foremost Jesuit academies in America. His grades when he came out were summa cum laude.

At Boston College the tutors had him marked out as a highflyer, destined one day to join the Society of Jesus itself, if not to hold high office somewhere in academia.

He read for a BA in Humanities, with strong components being philosophy and theology. He read them all, devoured them; from Ignatius Loyola, of course, to Teilhard de Chardin. He wrangled late into the night with his senior tutor in theology over the concept of the doctrine of the lesser evil and the higher goal; that the end may justify the means and yet not damn the soul, providing the parameters of the impermissible are never breached.

In 1966 he was nineteen. It was the pinnacle of the Cold War when world communism still seemed capable of rolling up the Third World and leaving the West a beleaguered island. That was when Pope Paul VI appealed to the Jesuits and entreated them to spearhead the task of combating atheism.

For Paul Devereaux the two were synonymous: atheism was not always communism, but communism was atheism. He would serve his country not in the church or in academia but in

241

that other place quietly mentioned to him at the country club by a pipe-smoking man introduced by a colleague of his father.

A week after graduating from Boston College Paul Devereaux was sworn into the ranks of the Central Intelligence Agency. For him it was the poet's bright, confident morning. The great scandals were yet to come.

With his patrician's background and contacts he rose in the hierarchy, blunting the shafts of jealousy with a combination of easy charm and sheer cleverness. He also proved that he had a bucketful of the most prized currency of them all in the agency in those years: he was loyal. For that a man can be forgiven an awful lot, maybe sometimes a bit too much.

He spent time in the three major divisions: Operations (Ops), Intelligence (Analysis) and Counter-Intelligence (Internal Security). His career hit the buffers with the arrival as director of John Deutsch.

The two men simply did not like each other. It happens. Deutsch, with no background in intelligence gathering, was the latest in a long and, with hindsight, pretty disastrous line of political appointees. He believed Devereaux, with seven fluent languages, was quietly looking down on him, and he could have been right.

Devereaux regarded the new DCI as a politically correct nincompoop appointed by the Arkansan President whom, although a fellow Democrat, he despised, and that was before Paula Jones and Monica Lewinsky.

This was not a marriage made in heaven and it

almost became a divorce when Devereaux came to the defence of a division chief in South America accused of employing unsavoury contacts.

The entire agency had swallowed Presidential Executive Order 12333 with good grace, except for a few dinosaurs who went back to World War II. This was the EO brought in by President Ronald Reagan that forbade any more 'terminations'.

Devereaux had considerable reservations but was too junior to be sought out for his counsel. It seemed to him that in the thoroughly imperfect world occupied by covert intelligence gathering there would arise occasions where an enemy in the form of a betrayer might have to be 'terminated' as a preemption. Put another way, one life may have to be terminated to preserve a likely ten.

As to the final judgement in such a case, Devereaux believed that if the director himself was not a man of wholly sufficient moral integrity to be entrusted with such a decision, he should not be director at all.

But under Clinton, in the by now veteran agent's view, political correctness went quite lunatic with the instruction that disreputable sources were not to be used as informants. He felt it was like being asked to confine one's sources to monks and choirboys.

So when a man in South America was threatened with the wreckage of his career for using ex-terrorists to inform on functioning terrorists, Devereaux wrote a paper so sarcastic

243

that it circulated throughout the grinning staffers of Ops Division like illegal samizdat in the old Soviet Union.

Deutsch wanted to require the departure of Devereaux at that point but his deputy director, George Tenet, advised caution and eventually it was Deutsch who went, to be replaced by Tenet himself.

Something happened in Africa that summer of 1998 that caused the new director to need the mordant but effective intellectual, despite his views on their joint commander-in-chief. Two US embassies were blown up.

It was no secret to the lowliest cleaner that since the end of the Cold War in 1991 the new cold war had been against the steadily growing rise of terrorism, and the 'happening' unit within Ops Division was the Counter-Terrorism Center.

Paul Devereaux was not working in the CT Center. Because one of his languages was Arabic, and his career included three stints in Arabic countries, he was Number Two in Mid-East at the time.

The destruction of the embassies brought him out of there and into the headship of a small task force dedicated to one task and answering only to the director himself. The job in hand was called Operation Peregrine, after that falcon who hovers high and silent above his prey until he is certain of a lethal hit, and then descends with awesome speed and accuracy.

In the new office Devereaux had no-limits access to any information from any other source that he might want and a small but expert team.

For his Number Two he chose Kevin McBride, not an intellectual patch on himself, but experienced, willing and loyal. It was McBride who took the call and held his hand across the mouthpiece.

'Assistant Director Fleming at the bureau,' he said. 'Doesn't sound happy. Shall I leave?'

Devereaux signalled for him to stay.

'Colin . . . Paul Devereaux. What can I do for you?'

His brow furrowed as he listened.

'Why surely, I think a meeting would be a good idea.'

It was a safe house; always convenient for a row. Daily 'swept' for bugging security, every word recorded with the full knowledge of the conference participants, refreshments on immediate call.

Fleming thrust the report from Bill Brunton under Devereaux's nose and let him read it. The Arabist's face remained impassive.

'So?' he queried.

'Please don't tell me the Dubai inspector got it wrong,' said Fleming. 'Zilic was the biggest arms trafficker in Yugoslavia. He quit, disappeared. Now he is seen conferring with the biggest arms trafficker in the Gulf and Africa. Totally logical.'

'I wouldn't dream of trying to fault the logic,' said Devereaux.

'And in conference with your man covering the Arabian Gulf.'

'The Agency's man covering the Gulf,' said Devereaux mildly. 'Why me?'

'Because you virtually ran Mid-East, although

245

you were supposed to be second string. Because back then all company staff in the Gulf would have reported to you. Because even though you are now in some kind of Special Project, that situation has not changed. Because I very much doubt that two weeks ago was Zilic's first visit to that neck of the woods. My guess is you knew exactly where Zilic was when the request came through, or at least that he would be in the Gulf and available for a snatch on a certain day. And you said nothing.'

'So? Even in our business, suspicions are a long way from proof.'

'This is more serious than you seem to think, my friend. By any count you and your agents are consorting with known criminals and of the filthiest hue. Against the rules, flat against all the rules.'

'So. Some foolish rules have been breached. Ours is not a business for the squeamish. Even the bureau must have a comprehension of the smaller evil to obtain the greater good.'

'Don't patronize me,' snapped Colin Fleming.

'I'll try not,' drawled the Bostonian. 'All right, you're upset. What are you going to do about it?'

There was no need to be polite any more. The gloves were off and lying on the floor.

'I don't think I can let this ride,' said Fleming. 'This man Zilic is obscene. You must have read what he did to that boy from Georgetown. But you're consorting. By proxy, but consorting for all that. You know what Zilic can do, what he's already done. All on file and I know you must have read it. There's testimony that as a gangster he hung a non-paying shopkeeper from his heels six inches above a two-bar electric fire until his brains boiled. He's a raving sadist. What the hell are you using him for?'

'If indeed I am, then it's classified. Even from an assistant director of the bureau.'

'Give the swine up. Tell us where we can find them.'

'Even if I knew, which I do not admit, no.'

Colin trembled with rage and disgust.

'How can you be so bloody complacent?' he shouted. 'Back in 1945 the CIC in occupied Germany cut deals with Nazis who were supposed to help in the fight against communism. We should never have done that. We should not have touched those swine with a bargepole. It was wrong then, it's wrong now.'

Devereaux sighed. This was becoming tiresome and had long been pointless.

'Spare me the history lesson,' he said. 'I repeat, what are you going to do about it?'

'I'm taking what I know to your director,' said Fleming.

Paul Devereaux rose. It was time to go.

'Let me tell you something. Last December I'd have been toast. Today, I'm asbestos. Times change.'

What he meant was that in December 2000 the President had been Bill Clinton.

After a tiresome imbroglio in the vote-counting booths of Florida, the president sworn in January 2001 was one George W. Bush, whose most enthusiastic cheerleader was none other than CIA Director George Tenet.

And the brass-noses around George Dubya were not going to see Project Peregrine fail because someone just trashed the Clintonian rulebook. They were doing the same themselves anyway.

'This is not the end of it,' Fleming called at the departing back. 'He'll be found and brought back, if I have anything to do with it.'

Devereaux thought over the remark in his car on the way back to Langley. He had not survived the snakepit of the company for thirty years without developing formidable antennae. He had just made an enemy, maybe a bad one.

'He'll be found.' By whom? How? And what could the Hoover Building moralist 'have to do with it'? He sighed. An extra care in a stress-filled planet. He would have to watch Colin Fleming like a hawk . . . at any rate, like a peregrine falcon. The joke made him smile, but not for long.

# 20

## The Jet

When he saw the house, Cal Dexter had to appreciate the occasional irony of life. Instead of the GI-turned-lawyer getting the fine house in Westchester Country, it was the skinny kid from Bedford Stuyvesant. In thirteen years, Washington Lee had evidently done well.

When he opened the door that Sunday morning in late July, Dexter noted he had had the buck teeth fixed, the beaky nose sculpted back a bit and the wild mop of Afro hair was down to a neat trim. This was a thirty-two-year-old businessman with a wife and two small children, a nice house and a modest but prosperous computer consultancy.

All that Dexter once had he had lost; all that Washington Lee never hoped for he had earned. After tracing him, Dexter had called to announce his coming.

'Come on in, counsellor,' said the ex-hacker.

They took soda in canvas chairs on the back lawn. Dexter offered Lee a brochure. Its cover showed a twinjet executive aeroplane banking over a blue sea.

'That's public domain, of course. I need to find one of that model. A specific example. I need to know who bought it, when, who owns it now and most of all where that person resides.'

'And you think they don't want you to know?'

'If the proprietor is living openly and under his own name, I have it wrong. Bum steer. If I am right, he will be holed up out of sight under a false name, protected by armed guards and layers of computerized identity-protection.'

'And it's the layers you want pulled away.'

'Yep.'

'Things have got a lot tougher in thirteen years,' said Lee. 'Dammit, I'm one of the ones that made them tougher, from the technical standpoint. The legislators have done the same from the legal standpoint. What you are asking for is a break-in. Or three. Totally illegal.'

'I know.'

Washington Lee looked around him. Two little girls squealed as they splashed in a plastic paddling-pool at the far end of the lawn. His wife, Cora, was in the kitchen making lunch.

'Thirteen years ago I was staring at a long stretch in the pen,' he said. 'I'd have come out and gone back to sitting on tenement steps in the ghetto. Instead I got a break. Four years with a bank, nine years as my own boss, inventing the best security systems in the USA, even if I do say so. Now it's payback time. You got it, counsellor. What do you want?'

First they looked at the aeroplane. The name of Hawker went back in British aviation to the First World War. It was a Hawker Hurricane that Stephen Edmond had flown in 1940. The last frontline fighter was the ultra-versatile Harrier. By the Seventies smaller companies simply could

250

not afford the research and development costs of devising new warplanes in isolation. Only the American giants could do that, and even they amalgamated. Hawker moved increasingly into civil aircraft.

By the Nineties, just about all the UK aeroplane companies were under one roof, BAE or British Aerospace. When the board decided to downsize, the Hawker division was bought by the Raytheon Corporation of Wichita, Kansas. They kept on a small sales office in London and the servicing facility at Chester.

What Raytheon got for their dollars was the successful and popular HS 125 short-range twinjet executive runabout, the Hawker 800 and the top-of-the-range 3000-mile Hawker 1000 model.

But Dexter's own research in public domain showed the 1000 model had gone out of production in 1996, so if Zoran Zilic owned one, it would be second-hand. More, only fifty-two had ever been made and thirty of them were with an American-based charter fleet.

He was looking for one of the remaining twenty-two that had changed hands in the last two years, three at most. There was a handful of second-hand dealers who moved in the rarefied atmosphere of aeroplanes that expensive, but it was ten to one that during the owner-changeover it had undergone a full servicing, and that probably meant going back to Raytheon's Hawker division. Which made it likely they handled the sale.

'Anything else?' asked Lee.

251

'The registration. P4-ZEM. It's not with one of the main international civil aviation registers. The number refers to the tiny island of Aruba.'

'Never heard of it,' said Lee.

'Former Dutch Antilles, along with Curaçao and Bonaire. They stayed Dutch. Aruba broke away in 1986. Went solo. They all do secret bank accounts, company registrations, that sort of thing. It's a pain in the ass for international fraud regulations, but it's a cheap income for an otherwise no-resource island. Aruba has a tiny oil refinery. Otherwise its income is tourism based on some great coral; plus secret bank accounts, gaudy stamps and dodgy number plates. I would guess my target changed the old registration number to the new one.'

'So Raytheon would have no record of P4-ZEM?'

'Almost certainly not. That apart, they do not divulge client details. No way.'

'We'll see,' muttered Washington Lee.

In thirteen years the computer genius had learned a lot, in part because he had invented a lot. Most of America's real computer geeks are out in Silicon Valley, and for the eggheads of the valley to hold an East Coaster in some awe, he had to be good.

The first thing Lee had told himself a thousand times over: never get caught again. As he contemplated the first illegal task he had attempted in thirteen years, he determined there was no way anyone was ever going to trace a trail of cyber-clues back to a home in Westchester.

'How big is your budget?' he asked.

'Adequate. Why?'

'I want to rent a Winnebago motorhome. I need full domestic circuit power, but I need to transmit, close down and vanish. Two, I need the best personal computer I can get, and when this is over I have to deep-six it into a major river.'

'Not a problem. Which way are you going to attack?'

'All points. The tailfin register of the Aruba government. They have to cough up what that Hawker was called when Raytheon last saw it. Second, the Zeta Corporation in the Bermuda Companies' Register. Head office, destination of all communications, money transfers. The lot. Thirdly, those flight plans it filed. It must have come to that Emirate, what did you call it . . . ?'

'Ras al-Khaimah.'

'Right, Ras al Whatever. It must have reached there from somewhere.'

'Cairo. It came in from Cairo.'

'So its flight plan is logged in the Cairo Air Traffic Control archives. Computerized. I'll have to visit. The good news is I doubt if they will have too many defensive firewalls to protect them.'

'You need to go to Cairo?' asked Dexter.

Washington Lee looked at him as if he were mad.

'Go to Cairo? Why would I go to Cairo?'

'You said 'visit'.'

'I mean in cyberspace. I can visit the Cairo database from a picnic site in Vermont. Look, why don't you go home and wait, counsellor? This is not your world.'

Washington Lee rented his motorhome and bought his PC, plus the software he needed for what he had in mind. It was all with cash, despite the raised eyebrows, except the motorhome which needed a driver's licence, but renting a motorhome does not necessarily mean a hacker is at work. He also bought a power generator, petrol-driven, to give him standard domestic 'juice' whenever he needed to plug in and log on.

The first and easiest was to crack the Aruba tailfin registration bank, which operates out of an office in Miami. Rather than use a weekend, where an unauthorized visit would show up on Monday morning, he broke into the archive in a busy working day when the database was answering many questions and his would get lost in the clutter.

Hawker 1000 P4-ZEM had once been VP-BGG and that meant it had been registered somewhere in the British registration zone.

Washington Lee was using a system designed to hide its own identity and location called PGP, standing for 'Pretty Good Privacy', which is a system so secure that it is actually illegal. He had set up two keys, public and private. He had to send on the public key because that key can only encrypt; receiving answers would be on his private key, because that one can only decrypt. The advantage from his point of view was that the encryption system, worked out by some patriot who used pure theoretical maths as a hobby, was so impenetrable that it would be unlikely anyone could find out who he was or where he was located. If he kept time online

254

short and location mobile, he should get away with it.

His second line of defence was much more basic: he would communicate by email only through web cafés in the towns he passed through.

Cairo Air Traffic Control revealed that Hawker 1000 P4-ZEM, when it passed through with a refuelling stop in the land of the Pharaohs, came in from the Azores; every time.

The very fact that the line across the world ran from west to east via the mid-Atlantic Portuguese islands to Cairo thence to Ras al-Khaimah indicated P4-ZEM was starting its journey somewhere in the Caribbean basin or South America. It was not proof, but it made sense.

From a lay-by in North Carolina Washington Lee persuaded the Portuguese/Azores air traffic database to admit that P4-ZEM arrived from the west but was based at a private field owned by the Zeta Corporation. That made the line of pursuit via the filed flight plans into an impasse.

The island of Bermuda also operates a system of banking secrecy and corporate confidentiality for the benefit of clients who are prepared to pay top dollar for top security, and it prides itself on being very blue-chip indeed.

The database in Hamilton could not eventually resist the Trojan Horse decoy system fed into it by Washington Lee and conceded the Zeta Corporation was indeed registered and incorporated in the islands. But it could only yield three local nominees as directors, all of unimpeachable respectability. There was no mention of any

Zoran Zilic, no Serbian-sounding name.

Back in New York, Cal Dexter, armed with the suggestion from Washington Lee that the Hawker was based somewhere around the Caribbean, had contacted a charter pilot he had once defended when a passenger had become violently airsick and tried to sue on the grounds that the pilot should have picked better weather.

'Try the FIRs,' said the pilot. 'Flight Information Registers. They know who is based in their areas.'

The FIR for the southern Caribbean is in Caracas, Venezuela, and confirmed that Hawker 1000 P4-ZEM was based right there. For a moment Dexter thought he might have been wasting his time on all the other lines of enquiry. It seemed so simple. Ask the local FIR and they tell you.

'Mind you,' said his charter pilot friend, 'it doesn't have to live there. It's just registered as being there.'

'I don't follow.'

'Easy,' said the pilot. 'A yacht can have Wilmington, Delaware, all over its stern because it is registered there. But it can spend its whole life chartering in the Bahamas. The hangar this Hawker lives in could be miles from Caracas.'

So Washington Lee proposed the last resort and briefed Dexter. Two days of hard driving brought Lee to the city of Wichita, Kansas. He called Dexter when he was ready.

The vice-president sales took the New York call in his office on the fifth floor of the headquarters building.

'I am ringing on behalf of the Zeta Corporation of Bermuda,' said the voice. 'You recall you sold us a Hawker 1000 tailfin number VP-BGG, you know, the British-owned one, some months back? I'm the new pilot.'

'I surely do, sir. And who am I speaking with?'

'Only Mr Zilic is not happy with the internal cabin configuration and would like it made over. Can you offer that facility?'

'Why certainly we do cabin interiors right here at the works, Mr . . . er . . . '

'And it could have the necessary engine overhauls at the same time.'

The executive sat up bolt straight. He recalled the sale very well. Everything had been serviced to give a clear run of major items for a couple of years. Unless the new owner had been almost constantly airborne, the engines would not be due for overhaul for up to a year.

'May I enquire exactly who I am talking to? I do not think those engines are anywhere near to needing another overhaul,' he said.

The voice at the other end lost its self-confidence and began to stutter.

'Really? Aw, Jeez. Sorry about that. Must have the wrong airplane.'

The caller hung up. By now the vice-president sales was consumed with suspicion. To his recall he had never mentioned the sale of the registration of the British-sourced Hawker offered by the firm of Avtech of Biggin Hill, Kent. He resolved to ask security to trace that call and try to establish who had made it.

He would be too late, of course, because the

SIM-based mobile was heading into the East River. But in the meantime, he recalled the delivery pilot from the Zeta Corporation who had come up to Wichita to fly the Hawker to its new owner.

A very pleasant Yugoslav, a former colonel in that country's air force, with papers in perfect order including the full FAA records of the US flight school where he had converted to the Hawker. He checked his sales records: Captain Svetomir Stepanovic. And an email address.

He composed a brief email to alert the captain of the Hawker to the weird and troubling phone call and sent it. Across the landscaped grounds that surround the headquarters building, parked behind a clump of trees, Washington Lee scanned his electro-magnetic emanation monitor, thanked his stars the sales executive was not using the Tempest system to shield his computer from such monitors, and watched the EEM intercept the message. The text was immaterial to him. It was the destination he wanted.

Two days later in New York, the motorhome returned to the charter company, hard drive and software somewhere in the Missouri River, Washington Lee pored over a map and pointed with a pencil tip.

'It's here,' he said. 'Republic of San Martin. About fifty miles east of San Martin City. And the airplane captain is a Yugoslav. I think you have your man, counsellor. And now, if you'll forgive me, I have a home, a wife, two kids and a business to attend to.'

The Avenger got the biggest-definition maps

he could find and blew them up even larger. Right at the bottom of the lizard-shaped isthmus of land that links North and South America, the broad mass of the South begins with Colombia to the west and Venezuela dead centre.

East of Venezuela lie the four Guyanas. First is the former British Guyana, now called just Guyana. Next comes former Dutch Guyana, now Surinam. Farthest east is French Guyana, home of Devil's Island and the story of *Papillon*, now home to Kourou, the European space-launch complex. Sandwiched between Surinam and the French territory, Dexter found the triangle of jungle that was once Spanish Guyana, named, post-independence, San Martin.

Further research revealed it was regarded as the last of the true banana republics, ruled by a brutal military dictator, ostracized, poor, squalid and malarial. The sort of place where money could buy a bucket of protection.

At the beginning of August the Piper Cheyenne II flew along the coast at a sedate 1250 feet, high enough not to arouse too much suspicion as little more than an executive proceeding from Surinam to French Guyana, but just low enough to allow good photography.

Chartered out of the airport at Georgetown, Guyana, the Piper's 1200-mile range would take it just over the French border and back home again. The client, whose passport revealed him as US citizen Alfred Barnes, now purported to be a developer of vacation resorts looking for possible situations. The Guyanese pilot privately thought he would pay not to vacation in San Martin, but who was he to turn down a perfectly good charter, paid for in cash dollars?

As requested, he kept the Piper just offshore so that his passenger, sitting in the right-hand co-pilot seat, could keep his zoom lens ready for use out of the window if occasion arose.

After Surinam and its border, the Commini River, dropped away, there were no suitable sandy beaches for miles. The coast was a tangle of mangrove, creeping through brown, snake-infested water from the jungle to the sea. They passed over the capital, San Martin City, asleep in the blazing soggy heat.

The only beach was east of the city, at La Bahia, but that was the reserved resort of the rich and powerful of San Martin, basically the dictator and his friends. At the end of the republic, ten miles short of the banks of the Maroni River and the start of French Guyana, was El Punto.

A triangular peninsula, like a shark's tooth, jutting from the land into the sea; protected from the landward side by a sierra or cordillera of mountains from coast-to-coast, bisected by a single track over a single col. But it was inhabited.

The pilot had never been this far east, so the peninsula was, to him, simply a coastal triangle on his nav maps. He could see there was a kind of defended estate down there. His passenger began to take photographs.

Dexter was using a 35mm Nikon F5 with a motordrive that would give him five frames a second and get through his roll in seven seconds, but he absolutely could not afford to start circling in order to change film.

He was set for a very fast shutter speed, due to the aircraft vibration, which at any slower than 500 per second would cause blurring. With 400 ASA film and aperture set at f8, it was the best he could do.

On the first pass he got the mansion on the tip of the peninsula, with its protective wall and huge gate, plus the fields being tended by estate workers, rows of barns and farm buildings, and the chain-link fencing that separated the fields from the cluster of cuboid white cabanas that seemed to be the workers' village.

Several people looked up, and he saw two in uniform start to run. Then they were over the estate and heading for French territory. On the pass back, he had the pilot fly inland, so that from the right-hand seat he could see the estate from the landward angle. He was looking down from the peaks of the sierra at the estate running away to the mansion and the sea, but there was a guard in the col below the Piper who took its number.

He used up his second roll on the private airstrip running along the base of the hills, shooting the residences, workshops and the main hangar. There was a tractor pulling a twin-engined executive jet into the hangar and out of sight. The tailfin was almost gone. Dexter got one brief look at the fin before it was enveloped in the shadows. The number was P4-ZEM.

# 21

# The Jesuit

Paul Devereaux, for all that he was confident the FBI would not be allowed to dismantle his Project Peregrine, was perturbed by the acrimonious meeting with Colin Fleming. He underestimated neither the other man's intelligence, influence nor passion. What worried him was the threat of delay.

After two years at the helm of a project so secret that it was known only to CIA Director George Tenet and White House anti-terrorist expert Richard Clarke, he was close, enticingly close, to springing the trap he had moved heaven and earth to create.

The target was simply called UBL. This was because the whole intelligence community in Washington spelled the man's first name, Usama, using the letter 'U' rather than the 'O' favoured by the media.

By the summer of 2001 that entire community was obsessed by and convinced of a forthcoming act of war by UBL against the USA. Ninety per cent thought the onslaught would come against a major US interest outside America; only ten per cent could envisage a successful attack inside territorial USA.

The obsession ran through all the agencies,

but mostly through the anti-terrorist departments of the CIA and the FBI. Here the intention was to discover what UBL had in mind and then prevent it.

Regardless of presidential edict 12333 forbidding 'wet jobs', Paul Devereaux was not trying to prevent UBL; he was trying to kill him.

Early on in his career the scholar from Boston College had realized that advancement inside the Company would depend on some form of specialization. In his younger days, in the blaze of Vietnam and the Cold War, most debutantes had chosen the Soviet Division. The enemy was clearly the USSR; the language to be learned was Russian. The corridors became crowded. Devereaux chose the Arab world and the wider study of Islam. He was regarded as crazy.

He turned his formidable intellect to mastering Arabic until he could virtually pass for an Arab, and studied Islam to the level of a Koranic scholar. His vindication came on Christmas Day 1979; the USSR invaded a place called Afghanistan and most of the agents inside CIA headquarters at Langley were reaching for their maps.

Devereaux revealed that, apart from Arabic, he spoke reasonable Urdu, the language of Pakistan, and had a knowledge of Pashto, spoken by the tribesmen right through Pakistan's Northwest Frontier and into Afghanistan.

His career really took off. He was one of the first to argue that the USSR had bitten off far more than it knew; that Afghan tribes would not concede any foreign occupation; that Soviet

263

atheism offended their fanatical Islam; that with US material help a fierce mountain-based resistance could be fomented which would eventually bleed white General Boris Gromov's Fortieth Army.

Before it was over, quite a bit had changed. The Mujahedin had indeed sent fifteen thousand Russian recruits back home in caskets; the occupation army, despite the infliction of hideous atrocities on the Afghans, had seen their grip prised loose and their morale gutted.

It was a combination of Afghanistan and the arrival of Mikhail Gorbachev that between them put the USSR on the final skidpan to dissolution and ended the Cold War. Paul Devereaux had switched from Analysis to Ops and with Milt Bearden had helped distribute one billion dollars a year of US guerrilla hardware to the 'mountain fighters'.

While living rough, running, fighting through the Afghan mountains, he had observed the arrival of hundreds of young, idealistic, anti-Soviet volunteers from the Middle East, speaking neither Pashto nor Dari, yet prepared to fight and die far from home if need be.

Devereaux knew what he was doing there: he was fighting a superpower that threatened his own. But what were the young Saudis, Egyptians and Yemenis doing there? Washington ignored them and Devereaux's reports. But they fascinated him. Listening for hours to their conversations in Arabic, pretending he had no more than a dozen words of a language he spoke fluently, the CIA man came to appreciate that they were fighting not communism but atheism.

More, they also entertained an equally passionate hatred and contempt for Christianity, the West and most specifically the USA. Among them was the febrile, temperamental, spoilt off-spring of a hugely rich Saudi family, who distributed millions running training camps in the safety of Pakistan, funding refugee hostels, buying and distributing food, blankets and medicines to the other Mujahedin. His name was Usama.

He wanted to be taken as a great warrior, like Ahmad Shah Massoud, but in fact he was only in one scrap, in late spring 1987, and that was it. Milt Bearden called him a spoilt brat but Devereaux watched him carefully. Behind the younger man's endless references to Allah, there was a seething hatred that would one day find a target other than the Russians.

Paul Devereaux returned home to Langley and a cascade of laurels. He had chosen not to marry, preferring scholarship and his job to the distractions of wife and children. His deceased father had left him wealthy; his elegant townhouse in old Alexandria boasted a much-admired collection of Islamic art and Persian carpets.

He tried to warn against the foolishness of abandoning Afghanistan to its civil war after the defeat of Gromov, but the euphoria as the Berlin Wall came down led to a conviction that, with the USSR collapsing into chaos, the Soviet satellites breaking westwards for freedom and world communism dead in the water, the last and final threats to the world's only remaining superpower were evaporating like mist before the rising sun.

Devereaux was hardly home and settled in when in August 1990 Saddam Hussein invaded Kuwait. At Aspen President Bush and Margaret Thatcher, victors of the Cold War, agreed they could not tolerate such impudence. Within forty-eight hours the first F-15 Eagles were airborne for Thumrait in Oman, and Paul Devereaux was heading for the US embassy in Riyadh, Saudi Arabia.

The pace was furious and the schedule gruelling, or he might have noticed something. A young Saudi, also back from Afghanistan, claiming to be the leader of a group of guerrilla fighters and an organization called simply 'The Base', offered his services to King Fahd in the defence of Saudi Arabia from the belligerent neighbour to the north.

The Saudi monarch probably also did not notice the military mosquito or his offer; instead he permitted the arrival in his country of half a million foreign soldiers and airmen from a coalition of fifty nations to roll the Iraqi army out of Kuwait and protect the Saudi oilfields. Ninety per cent of those soldiers and airmen were infidels, meaning Christians, and their combat boots marched upon the same soil as contained the Holy Places of Mecca and Medina. Almost four hundred thousand were Americans.

For the zealot this was an insult to Allah and His prophet Muhammad that simply could not be tolerated. He declared his own private war, firstly against the ruling house that could do such a thing. More importantly, the seething rage that Devereaux had noticed in the mountains of the Hindu Kush had finally found its target. UBL declared war on America and began to plan.

If Paul Devereaux had been seconded to Counter-Terrorism the moment the Gulf War was over and won, the course of history might have been changed. But CT was a too-low priority in 1992; power passed to William Clinton; and both the CIA and the FBI entered the worst decade of their twin existences. In the CIA's case, that meant the shattering news that Aldrich Ames had been betraying his country for over eight years. Later it would be learned that the FBI's Robert Hanssen was still doing it.

At what ought to have been the hour of victory after four decades of struggle against the USSR, both agencies suffered crises of leadership, morale and incompetence.

The new masters worshipped a new god: political correctness. The lingering scandals of Irangate and the illicit aid to the Nicaraguan Contras caused the new masters a crisis of nerve. Good men left in droves; bureaucrats and bean-counters were elevated to chiefs of departments. Men with decades of front-line experience were disregarded.

At eclectic dinner parties Paul Devereaux smiled politely as congressmen and senators preened themselves to announce that at least the Arab world loved the USA. They meant the ten princes they had just visited. The Jesuit had moved for years like a shadow through the Muslim street. Inside him a small voice whispered: 'No, they hate our guts.'

On 26 February 1993, four Arab terrorists drove a rented van into the second level of the basement vehicle park below the World Trade Center. It contained between twelve and fifteen hundred pounds of home-made, fertilizer-based explosive called urea nitrate. Fortunately for New York, it is far from the most powerful explosive known.

For all that, it made a big bang. What no one knew for certain and no more than a dozen even suspected was that the blast constituted the salvo at Fort Sumter in a new war.

Devereaux was by then the deputy chief for the entire Middle East division, based at Langley but travelling constantly. It was partly what he saw in his travels and partly what came to him in the torrent of reports from the CIA stations throughout the world of Islam that caused his attention to wander away from the chancelleries and palaces of the Arab world that were his proper concern into another direction.

Almost as a sideline, he began to ask for supplementary reports from his stations; not about what the local prime minister was doing, but about the mood in the street, in the souks, in the medinas, in the mosques and in the teaching schools, the madrasas, that churn out the next generation of locally educated Muslim youths. The more he watched and listened, the more the alarm bells rang.

'They hate our guts,' his voice told him. 'They just need a talented coordinator.' Researching on his own time, he picked up the trail once again of the Saudi fanatic UBL. He learned the man had been expelled from Saudi Arabia for his impertinence in denouncing the monarch for permitting infidels onto the sacred sand.

He learned he was based in Sudan, another pure Islamist state where fundamentalist fanaticism was in power. Khartoum offered to hand the Saudi zealot over to the USA, but no one was interested. Then he was gone, back to the hills of Afghanistan where the civil war had ended in favour of the most fanatical faction, the ultra-religious Taliban party.

Devereaux noted that the Saudi arrived with huge largesse, endowing Taliban with millions of dollars in personal gifts and rapidly becoming a major figure in the land. He arrived with almost fifty personal bodyguards and found several hundred of his foreign (non-Afghan) Mujahedin still in place. Word spread in the bazaars of the Pakistani border towns of Quetta and Peshawar that the returnee had begun two frantic programmes: building elaborate cave complexes in a dozen places and constructing training camps. The camps were not for the Afghan military; they were for volunteer terrorists. The word came back to Paul Devereaux. Islamist hatred of his country had found its coordinator.

The misery of the Somali slaughter of the US Rangers came and went, caused by rotten intelligence. But there was more. Not only was the opposition of the warlord, Aideed, under-estimated, but there were others fighting there; not Somalis but more skilled Saudis. In 1996 a huge bomb destroyed the Al Khobar towers in Dhahran, Saudi Arabia, killing nineteen US servicemen and injuring many others.

Paul Devereaux went to see Director George Tenet.

'Let me go over to Counter-Terrorism,' he begged.

'CT is full and it's doing a good job,' said the DCI.

'Six dead in Manhattan, nineteen in Dhahran. It's Al Qaeda. It's UBL and his team who are behind it, even if they don't actually plant the bombs.'

'We know that, Paul. We're working on it. So is the bureau. This is not being allowed to lie fallow.'

'George, the bureau knows diddly about Al Qaeda. They don't have the Arabic, they don't know the psychology, they're good on gangsters but east of Suez might as well be the dark side of the moon. I could bring a new mind to this business.'

'Paul, I want you in the Middle East. I need you there more. The King of Jordan is dying. We don't know who his successor will be. His son Abdullah or his brother Hassan? The dictator in Syria is failing; who takes over? Saddam is making life more and more intolerable for the weapons inspectors. What if he throws them out? The whole Israel-Palestine thing is going south in a big way. I need you in the Middle East.'

270

It was 1998 that secured Devereaux his transfer. On 7 August two huge bombs were detonated outside two US embassies in Africa: at Nairobi and Dar es Salaam.

Two hundred and thirteen people died in Nairobi, with four thousand, seven hundred and twenty-two injured. Of the dead, twelve were Americans. The explosion in Tanzania was not as bad: eleven were killed, seventy-two injured. No Americans died, but two were crippled.

The organizing force behind both bombs was quickly identified as the Al Qaeda network. Paul Devereaux handed his Middle East duties to a rising young Arabist he had taken under his wing and moved to Counter-Terrorism.

He carried the rank of Assistant Director, but did not displace the existing incumbent. It was not an elegant arrangement. He hovered on the fringe of Analysis as a kind of consultant but quickly became convinced that the Clintonian rule of only employing sources of upright character as informants was complete madness.

It was the sort of madness that had led to the fiasco of the response to Africa. Cruise missiles destroyed a pharmaceutical factory on the outskirts of Khartoum, capital of Sudan, because it was thought the long departed UBL was manufacturing chemical weapons there. It turned out to be a genuine aspirin factory.

Seventy more Tomahawk Cruises were poured into Afghanistan to kill UBL. They turned a lot of big rocks into little rocks at several million dollars a pop, but UBL was at the other end of the country. It was out of this failure and the advocacy of Devereaux himself that Peregrine was created.

It was generally agreed around Langley that he must have called in a few markers to get his terms accepted. Project Peregrine was so secret that only Director Tenet knew what Devereaux intended. Outside the building the Jesuit had to confide in one other: White House Anti-Terrorist Chief Richard Clarke, who had started under George Bush Senior and continued under Clinton.

Clarke was loathed at Langley for his blunt and abrasive criticisms, but Devereaux wanted and needed Clarke for several reasons. The White House man would agree with the sheer ruthlessness of what Devereaux had in mind; he could keep his mouth shut when he wanted; more, he could secure Devereaux the tools he needed when he needed them.

But first, Devereaux was given permission to throw in the trash can all talk of not being allowed to kill the target, or use to that end 'assets' who might be utterly loathsome, if that is what it took. These permissions did not come from the Oval Office. From that moment Paul Devereaux was performing his own very private high-wire act, and no one was talking safety nets.

He secured his own office and picked his own team. He headhunted the best he could get and the DCI overruled the howls of protest. Having never been an empire-builder, he wanted a small, tight unit, and every one a specialist. He secured a suite of three offices on the sixth floor of the main building, facing over the birch and osier towards the Potomac, just out of sight save in winter when the trees were bare.

He needed a good, reliable, right-hand man: solid, trustworthy, loyal; one who would do as asked and not second-guess. He chose Kevin McBride.

Save in that both men were career 'lifers' who had joined the company in their mid-twenties and served thirty years, they were like chalk and cheese.

The Jesuit was lean and spare, working out daily in his private gym at home; McBride had thickened with the passing years, fond of his six-pack of beer on a weekend, most of the hair gone from the top and crown.

His annual 'vetting' records showed he had a rock-stable marriage to Molly, two youngsters who had just left home and a modest house in a residential development out beyond the Beltway. He had no private fortune and lived frugally off his salary.

Much of his career had been in foreign embassies, but never rising to chief of station. He was no threat, but a first-class Number Two. If you wanted something done, it would be done. You could rely. There would be no pseudo-intellectual philosophizing. McBride's values were traditional, down-home, American.

On 12 October 2000, twelve months into Project Peregrine, Al Qaeda struck again. This time the perpetrators were two Yemenis and they committed suicide to achieve their goal. It was the first time the concept of suicide bomber had been evoked since 1983 in Beirut against US

273

armed forces. At the Trade Towers, Mogadishu, Dhahran, Nairobi and Dar es Salaam, UBL had not demanded the supreme sacrifices. At Aden, he did. He was upping the stakes.

The *USS Cole*, a Burke-class destroyer, was moored in harbour at the old British coaling station and one-time garrison at the tip of the Saudi peninsula. Yemen was the birthplace of UBL's father. The US presence must have rankled.

Two terrorists in a fast inflatable packed with TNT roared through the flotilla of supply boats, rammed itself between the hull and the quay and blew itself up. Due to the compression between the hull and the concrete, a huge hole was torn. Inside the vessel, seventeen sailors died and thirty-nine were injured.

Devereaux had studied terror, its creation and infliction. He knew that whether imposed by the state or a non-governmental source, it always divides into five levels.

At the top are the plotters, the planners, the authorizers, the inspirers. Next come the enablers, the facilitators, without whom no plan can work. They are in charge of recruiting, training, funding, supply. Third come the doers: those deprived of normal moral thought, who push the Zyklon-B pellets into the gas chambers, plant the bomb, pull the triggers. At slot four are the active collaborators: those who guide the killers, denounce the neighbour, reveal the hiding place, betray the one-time school friend. At the bottom are the broad masses: bovine, stupid, saluting the tyrant, garlanding the murderers.

In the terror against the West in general, and the USA in particular, Al Qaeda fulfilled the first two functions. Neither UBL nor his ideological Number Two, the Egyptian Ayman Kawaheri, nor his Ops chief, Mohamed Atef, nor his international emissary, Abu Zubaydah, would ever need to plant a bomb or drive a truck.

The mosque-schools, the madrassas, would provide a stream of teenage fanatics, already impregnated with a deep hatred of the whole world that was not fundamentalist, plus a garbled version of a few distorted extracts of the Koran. To them could be added a few more mature converts, tricked into thinking that mass murder guaranteed Koranic paradise.

Al Qaeda would then simply devise, recruit, train, equip, direct, fund and watch.

On his way back in the limousine from his blazing row with Colin Fleming, Devereaux once again examined the morality of what he was doing. Yes, the disgusting Serb had killed one American. Somewhere out there was a man who had killed fifty, and more to come.

He recalled Father Dominic Xavier who had taxed him with a moral problem.

'A man is coming at you, with intent to kill you. He has a knife. His total reach is four feet. You have the right of self-defence. You have no shield, but you have a spear. Its reach is nine feet. Do you lunge, or wait?'

He would put pupil against pupil, each tasked to argue the opposite viewpoint. Devereaux never hesitated. The greater good against the lesser evil. Had the man with the spear sought the fight? No. Then he was entitled to lunge. Not counter-strike; that came after surviving the initial strike. But pre-emptive strike. In the case of UBL he had no qualms. To protect his country Devereaux would kill; and no matter how appalling the allies he had to call in aid. Fleming was wrong. He needed Zilic.

For Paul Devereaux there was an abiding enigma about his own country and its place in the world's affections, and he believed he had resolved it.

About 1945, just before he was born, and for the next decade through the Korean War and the start of the Cold War, the USA was not simply the richest and most militarily powerful country in the world; it was also the most loved, admired and respected.

After fifty years the first two qualities remained. The USA was stronger and richer than ever, the only remaining superpower, apparently mistress of all she surveyed.

And, through great swathes of the world, black Africa, Islam, left-wing Europe, loathed with a passion. What had gone wrong? It was a quandary that defied Capitol Hill and the media.

Devereaux knew his country was far from perfect; it made mistakes, often far too many. But it was in its heart as well-meaning as any and better than most. As a world traveller, he had seen a lot of that 'most' in near vision. Much of it was deeply ugly.

Most Americans could not comprehend the metamorphosis between 1951 and 2001, so they pretended it had not happened, accepting the Third World's polite mask for its inner feeling.

Had not Uncle Sam tried to preach democracy against tyranny? Had he not given away at least a trillion dollars in aid? Had he not picked up the hundred billion dollars a year defence tab for Western Europe for five decades? What justified the hate-you-hate-you demonstrations, the sacked embassies, the burnt flags, the vicious placards?

It was an old British spymaster who explained it to him in a London Club in the late Sixties as Vietnam became nastier and nastier and the riots erupted.

'My dear boy, if you were weak you would not be hated. If you were poor you would not be hated. You are not hated despite the trillion dollars; you are hated because of the trillion dollars.'

The old mandarin gestured towards Grosvenor Square, where left-wing politicians and bearded students were massing to stone the embassy.

'The hatred of your country is not because it attacks theirs; it is because it keeps theirs safe. Never seek popularity. You can have supremacy or be loved but never both. What is felt towards you is ten per cent genuine disagreement and ninety per cent envy.

'Never forget two things. No man can ever forgive his protector. There is no loathing that any man harbours more intense than that towards his benefactor.'

The old spy was long dead, but Devereaux

277

had seen the truth of his cynicism in half a hundred capitals. Like it or not, his country was the most powerful in the world. Once the Romans had that dubious honour. They had responded to the hatred with ruthless force of arms.

A hundred years ago the British Empire had been the rooster. They had responded to the hatred with languid contempt. Now the Americans had it, and they racked their consciences to ask where they had gone wrong. The Jesuit scholar and secret agent had long made up his mind. In defence of his country he would do what he believed had to be done, and one day go to his Maker and ask forgiveness. Until then the America-haters could take a long walk off a short jetty.

When he arrived at his office Kevin McBride was waiting for him and his face was gloomy.

'Our friend has been in touch,' he said. 'In a rage and a panic. He thinks he is being stalked.'

Devereaux thought, not of the complainant, but of Fleming at the FBI.

'Damn the man,' he said. 'Damn and blast him to hell. I never thought he'd do it, and certainly not that fast.'

# 22

# The Peninsula

There was a secure computer link between a guarded enclave on the shore of the Republic of San Martin and a machine in McBride's office. Like Washington Lee, it used the Pretty Good Privacy (PGP) system of unbreakable cyber codes to keep communications from prying eyes; the difference was that this one had authority.

Devereaux studied the full text of the message from the south. It had clearly been written by the estate's head of security, the South African van Rensberg. The English was over-formal, as of one using their second language.

The meaning was clear enough. It described the Piper Cheyenne of the previous morning; its double pass, heading eastwards towards French Guyana and then back again twenty minutes later. It reported the flash of sunlight off a camera lens in the right-hand window, and even the registration number when it passed too low over the col in the escarpment.

'Kevin, trace that aircraft. I need to know who owns it, who operates it, who flew it yesterday and who was the passenger. And hurry.'

★   ★   ★

In his anonymous apartment in Brooklyn, Cal Dexter had developed his seventy-two frames and blown them up to prints as large as he could before losing too much definition. From the same original negatives he had also made slides which he could project onto the wall-screen for closer study.

Of the prints he had created a single wall-map running the length of the sitting room, and from ceiling to floor. He sat for hours studying the wall, checking occasionally on a small detail with the appropriate slide. Each slide gave better and clearer detail, but only the wall gave the entire target. Whoever had been in charge of the project had spent millions and made of that once-empty peninsula a fearsome and ingenious fortress.

Nature had helped. The tongue of land was quite different from the hinterland of steamy jungle that made up much of the small republic. It jutted out from the main shore like a triangular dagger blade, guarded on its landward side by the chain of hills that some primeval force had thrown up millions of years ago.

The chain ran from the sea to the sea, and at each end dropped to the blue water in vertical cliffs. No one would ever walk round the ends to stroll from the jungle onto the peninsula.

On the landward side, the hills climbed gently from the littoral plain to about a thousand feet, with slopes covered in dense vegetation. Over the crests, on the seaward side, the slope was a vertiginous escarpment, denuded of any foliage, whether by nature or the hand of man. From the estate, anyone with binoculars looking up at the escarpment would easily see anything trying to descend onto the forbidden side.

There was one single cut, or col, in the chain. A narrow track ran up to it from the hinterland, then twisted and turned down the escarpment until it reached the estate below. In the col was a barrier and guardhouse, which Dexter had seen too late as it flashed below his window.

Dexter began to make a list of the equipment he would need. Getting in would not be a problem. It was getting out, bringing the target with him, and against a small army of estate guards, that would be close to impossible.

★　★　★

'It belongs to a one-plane, one-man charter firm based at Georgetown, Guyana,' said Kevin McBride that evening. 'Lawrence Aero Services, owned and run by George Lawrence, Guyanese citizen. It looks perfectly legitimate, the sort foreigners can charter to fly into the interior . . . or along the coast in this case.'

'Is there a number for this Mr Lawrence?' asked Devereaux.

'Sure. Here.'

'Did you try to contact him?'

'No. The line would have to be open. And why should he discuss a client with a complete stranger on the phone? He might just tip the client off.'

'You're right. You'll have to go. Use scheduled flights. Have Cassandra get you on the first flight. Trace Mr Lawrence. Pay him if you have to. Find out who our inquisitive friend with the camera was, and why he was there. Do we have a station in Georgetown?'

'No, next door. Caracas.'

'Use Caracas for secure communications. I'll clear it with the station chief.'

★ ★ ★

Studying his wall-sized photo montage, Cal Dexter's eye moved from the escarpment into the peninsula known simply as El Punto. Running along the base of the escarpment wall was a runway, taking up two-thirds of the fifteen hundred yards available. On the estate side of the runway was a chain-link fence that enclosed the entire airfield, hangar, workshops, fuel store, generator house and all.

Using a pair of compasses and estimating the hangar length at one hundred feet, Dexter was able to start calculating and marking distances between points. These put the cultivated farmland at around three thousand acres. It was clear that centuries of wind-borne dust and bird droppings had created a soil rich in goodness, for he could see grazing herds and a variety of lush crops. Whoever had created El Punto had gone for complete self-sufficiency behind the ramparts of escarpment and ocean.

The irrigation problem was solved by a glittering stream that erupted from the base of the hills and flowed through the estate before tumbling in a cataract into the sea. It could only originate in the high inland plateau and flow

282

through the protective wall in an underground flue. Dexter noted the words: 'Swim in?' Later he would line-dash them out. Without a rehearsal, it would be crazy to attempt a passage through an unknown underground tunnel. He recalled the terror inspired by crawling through the water traps of the tunnels of Cu Chi, and they were only a few yards long. This one could be miles, and he did not even know where it began.

At the base of the runway, beyond the wire, he could see a settlement of perhaps five hundred small white blocks, clearly dwelling units of some kind. There were dirt streets, some larger buildings for refectory halls and a small church. It was a village of sorts; but it was odd that, even with the men away in the fields and barns, there were no women or children on the streets. No gardens, no livestock. More like a penal colony. Perhaps those who served the man he sought had little choice in the matter.

He turned his attention to the main body of the agricultural estate. This contained all the cultivated fields, the flocks, barns, granaries, and a second settlement of low white buildings. But a uniformed man standing outside indicated these were barracks for the security staff, guards, overseers. By the look and the number and size of the quarters, and the likely occupancy rate, he put the guards alone at around one hundred. There were five more substantial villas, with gardens, apparently for the senior officers and flight personnel.

The photographs and the slides were serving their purpose, but he needed two things more.

One was a concept of three dimensions; the other was a knowledge of routines and procedures. The first would need a scale model of the whole peninsula; the second would require days of silent observation.

★　★　★

Kevin McBride flew the next morning from Washington Dulles direct to Georgetown, Guyana, with BWIA, landing at 2 p.m. Formalities at the airport were simple and with only a handgrip for a one-night stay, he was soon in a taxi.

Lawrence Aero Services was not hard to find. Its small office was in a back alley off Waterloo Street. The American knocked several times but there was no reply. The moist heat was beginning to drench his shirt. He peered through the dusty window and rapped again.

'Ain't no one there, man,' said a helpful voice behind him. The speaker was old and gnarled; he sat a few doors away in a patch of deep shade and fanned himself with a disc of palm leaves.

'I'm looking for George Lawrence,' said the American.

'You Briddish?'

'Uhuh. American.'

The old-timer considered this as if the availability of charter pilot Lawrence was entirely down to nationality.

'Friend of yours?'

'No. I was thinking of chartering his aeroplane for a flight, if I can find him.'

'Ain't been here since yesterday,' said the old

284

man. 'Not since they took him away.'

'Who took him away, my friend?'

The old man shrugged as if the abduction of neighbours was usual enough.

'The police?'

'No. Not them. They were white. Came in a rental car.'

'Tourists . . . clients?' said McBride.

'Maybe,' admitted the sage. Then he had an idea. 'You could try the airport. He keeps his plane there.'

Fifteen minutes later a sweat-drenched Kevin McBride was heading back to the airport. At the desk for private aviation he asked for George Lawrence. Instead he met Floyd Evans. Inspector Floyd Evans of the Georgetown Police Department.

He was taken back downtown yet again, this time in a prowl car, and was shown into an office where the air-conditioning was like a long-delayed cold bath and delicious. Inspector Evans toyed with his passport.

'What exactly are you doing in Guyana, Mr McBride?' he asked.

'I was hoping to pay a short visit with a view to bringing my wife on vacation later,' said the agent.

'In August? The salamanders shelter in August down here. Do you know Mr Lawrence?'

'Well, no. I have a pal in Washington. He gave me the name. Said I might like to fly into the interior. Said Mr Lawrence was about the best charter pilot. I just went to his office to see if he was available for charter. Is all. What did I do wrong?'

The inspector closed the passport and handed it back.

'You arrived from Washington today. That seems clear enough. Your tickets and entry stamp confirm. The Meridien Hotel confirms your one-night reservation for tonight.'

'Look, inspector, I still don't understand why I was brought here. Do you know where I can find Mr George Lawrence?'

'Oh yes. Yes, he's in the mortuary down at our general hospital. Apparently he was taken from his office yesterday by three men in a rented four-by-four. They checked it back in last night and flew out. Do those three names mean anything to you, Mr McBride?'

He passed a slip of paper over the desk. McBride glanced at the three names, all of which he knew to be false, because he had issued them.

'No, sorry, they mean nothing to me. Why is Mr Lawrence in the morgue?'

'Because he was found at dawn today by a vegetable seller coming to market. Dead in a ditch by the roadside just out of town. You, of course, were still in the air.'

'That's awful. I never met him, but I'm sorry.'

'Yes, it is. We have lost our charter pilot. Mr Lawrence lost his life and, as it happens, eight of his fingernails. His office has been gutted and all records of past clients removed. What do you think his captors wanted of him, Mr McBride?'

'I have no idea.'

'Of course, I forgot. You are just a travelling

salesman, are you not? Then I suggest you travel back home to the States, Mr McBride. You are free to go.'

'These people are animals,' protested McBride to Devereaux down the secure line from Caracas Station to Langley.

'Come on home, Kevin,' said his superior. 'I'll ask our friend in the south what, if anything, he discovered.'

Paul Devereaux had long cultivated a contact inside the FBI on the grounds that no man in his line of business could ever have too many sources of information and the bureau was not likely to share with him the very gems that would constitute true brotherly love.

He had asked his 'asset' to check in the archive database for files withdrawn by Assistant Director (Investigative Division) Colin Fleming since the request from on high had circulated regarding a murdered boy in Bosnia. Among the withdrawals was one marked simply 'Avenger'.

Kevin McBride, weary and travel-stained, arrived home the following morning. Paul Devereaux was in his office as early as usual and crisply laundered.

He handed a file to his subordinate.

'That's him,' he said. 'Our interloper. I spoke with our friend in the south. Of course, it was three of his thugs who brutalized the charter pilot. And you are right. They are animals. But right now they are vital animals. Pity, but unavoidable.'

He tapped the file.

'Code name Avenger. Age around fifty. Height, build . . . it's all there in the file. There is a brief description. Now masquerading as US citizen Alfred Barnes. That was the man who chartered the deeply unfortunate Mr Lawrence to fly him over our friend's hacienda. And there is no Alfred Barnes matching that description on State Department files as a US passport-holder. Find him, Kevin, and stop him. In his tracks.'

'I hope you don't mean terminate.'

'No, that is forbidden. I mean, identify. If he uses one false name, he may have others. Find the one he will try to use to enter San Martin. Then inform the appalling but efficient Colonel Moreno in San Martin. I am sure he can be relied on to do what has to be done.'

Kevin McBride retired to his own office to read the file. He already knew the chief of the secret police of the Republic of San Martin. Any opponent of the dictator falling into his hands would die, probably slowly. He read the Avenger file with his habitual great care.

★   ★   ★

Two states away, in New York City, the passport of Alfred Barnes was consigned to the flames. Dexter had not a clue or shred of proof that he had been seen, but as he and charter pilot Lawrence had flown over the col in the sierra, he had been jolted to see a face staring up at him; close enough to take the Piper's number. So, just in case, Alfred Barnes ceased to exist.

288

That done, he began to build his model of the fortress hacienda. Across the city, in downtown Manhattan, Mrs Nguyen Van Tran was myopically poring over three new passports.

It was 3 August 2001.

# 23

# The Voice

If it is not available in New York it probably doesn't exist. Cal Dexter used a sawn-timber shop to create a trestle table with a top of inch-ply that almost filled his sitting room.

Art shops furnished enough paints to create the sea and the land in ten different hues. Green baize from fabric shops made fields and meadows. Wooden building blocks were used for scores of houses and barns; model-makers' emporia provided balsa wood, fast glue and paste-on designs of brickwork, doors and windows.

The runaway's mansion at the tip of the peninsula was made of Lego from a children's store and the rest of the landscape was down to a magical warehouse providing for model railway enthusiasts.

Railway modellers want entire landscapes, with hills and valleys, cuttings and tunnels, farms and grazing animals. Within three days Dexter had fashioned the entire hacienda to scale. All he could not see was that which was out of sight to his airborne camera: booby traps, pitfalls, the workforce, security locks, gate chains, the full strength of the private army, their equipment and all interiors.

It was a long list and most of the queries on it could only be solved by days of patient observation. Still, he had decided his way in, his battle plan and his way out. He went on a buying spree.

Boots, jungle clothing, K-rations, cutters, the world's most powerful binoculars, a new cellphone . . . He filled a Bergen haversack that finally weighed close to eighty pounds. And then there was more; for some he had to go out of state to places in the USA with more lax laws, for others he had to dive into the underworld, and others were quite legal but raised eyebrows. By 10 August he was ready and so were his first ID papers.

★　★　★

'Spare a moment, Paul?'

Kevin McBride's yeoman face came round the edge of the door and Devereaux beckoned him in. His deputy brought with him a large-scale map of the northern coast of South America, from Venezuela east to French Guyana. He spread it out and tapped the triangle between the Commini and Maroni rivers, the Republic of San Martin.

'I figure he'll go in by the overland route,' said McBride. 'Take the air route. San Martin City has the only airport and it is small. Served only twice daily and then only by local airlines coming from Cayenne to the east or Paramaribo to the west.'

His finger stabbed at the capitals of French

Guyana and Surinam.

'It's such a God-awful place politically that hardly any businessmen go and no tourists. Our man is white, American, and we have his approximate height and build, both from the file and what that charter pilot described before he died. Colonel Moreno's goons would have him within minutes of debarkation. More to the point, he'd have to have a valid visa and that means visiting San Martin's only two consulates: Paramaribo and Caracas. I don't think he'll try the airport.'

'No dispute. But Moreno should still put it under night and day surveillance. He might try a private plane,' said Devereaux.

'I'll brief him on that. Next, the sea. There is just one port: San Martin City again. No tourist craft ever put in there, just freighters and not many of them. The crews are Lascars, Filipinos or Creoles; he'd stand out like a sore thumb if he tried to come in openly as a crewman or passenger.'

'He could come in off the sea in a fast inflatable.'

'Possible, but that would have to have been hired or bought in either French Guyana or Surinam. Or he is dropped from a freighter offshore, whose captain he has bribed for the job. He could motor in from twenty miles off the coast, dump the inflatable, puncture it, sink it. Then what?'

'What indeed?' murmured Devereaux.

'I figure he will need equipment, a heavy load of it. Where does he make landfall? There are no beaches along San Martin's coast, except here at the Bahia. But that's full of the villas of the rich, occupied in August, with bodyguards, night-watchmen and dogs.

'Apart from that, the coast is tangled mangrove, infested with snakes and crocs. How is he to march through all that? If he gets to the main east- west road, what then? I don't think it's on, even for a Green Beret.'

'Could he land off the sea right on our friend's peninsula?'

'No, Paul, he couldn't. It's girt on all seaward sides by cliffs and pounding surf. Even if he got up the cliffs with grapnel irons, the roaming dogs would hear the noise and have him.'

'So, he comes in by land. From which end?'

McBride used his forefinger again.

'I reckon from the west, from Surinam, on the passenger ferry across the River Commini, straight into the San Martin border post, on four wheels, with false papers.'

'He'd still need a San Martin visa, Kevin.'

'And where better to get it than right there in Surinam, one of the only two consulates they run? I reckon that's the logical place for him to acquire his car and his visa.'

'So what's your plan?'

'The Surinam embassy here in Washington and the consulate in Miami. He'll need a visa to get in there as well. I want to put them both on full alert to go back a week and from now on pass me details of every single applicant for a visitor visa. Then I check every one with the passport section at State.'

'You're putting all your eggs in one basket, Kevin.'

'Not really. Colonel Moreno and his Ojos Negros can cover the eastern border, the airport, docks and coast. I'd like to back my hunch our interloper will logically try to get all his kit into San Martin by car out of Surinam. It's far away the busiest crossing point.'

Devereaux smiled at McBride's attempt at Spanish. The San Martin secret police were known as 'black eyes' because they and their wraparound black sunglasses struck terror into the peons of San Martin.

He thought of all the US aid heading in that direction. There was no doubt the Surinam embassy would cooperate to the full.

'OK, I like it. Go for it. But hurry.'

McBride was puzzled.

'We have a deadline, boss?'

'Tighter than you know, my friend.'

★   ★   ★

The port of Wilmington, Delaware, is one of the largest and busiest on the east coast of the USA. High at the top of the long Delaware Bay that leads from the river to the Atlantic, it has miles of sheltered water, which, apart from taking the big ocean liners, also plays host to thousands of small coastal freighters.

The Carib Coast Ship and Freight Company was an agency handling cargoes for scores of such smaller ships and the visit of Mr Ronald Proctor caused no surprise. He was friendly,

294

charming, convincing, and his rented U-Haul pickup was right outside with the crate in the rear.

The freight clerk who handled his enquiry had no reason to doubt his veracity, all the more so when, in response to the query, 'Do you have documentation, sir?', he produced precisely that.

His passport was not only in perfect order, it was a diplomatic passport at that. Supporting letters and movement orders from the State Department proved that Ronald Proctor, a professional US diplomat, was being seconded to his country's embassy in Paramaribo, Surinam.

'We have a cost-free allowance, of course, but what with my wife's passion for collecting things on our travels, I fear we're one crate over the limit. I'm sure you know what wives are like? Boy, can they collect stuff.'

'Tell me about it,' agreed the clerk. Few things bond male strangers like commiserating about their wives. 'We have a freighter heading down to Miami, Caracas and Parbo in two days.'

He gave the capital of Surinam its shorter and more common name. The consignment was agreed and paid for. The crate would be seaborne within two days and in a bonded warehouse in Parbo docks by the twentieth. Being diplomatic cargo it would be customs-exempt when Mr Proctor called to collect it.

The Embassy of Surinam in Washington is at 4301 Connecticut Avenue and it was there that Kevin McBride flashed his identity as a senior officer of the Central Intelligence Agency and sat down with an impressed consular official in charge of the visa section. It was probably not the busiest diplomatic office in Washington and one man handled all visa applications.

'We believe he deals in drugs and consorts with terrorists,' said the CIA man. 'So far he remains very shady. His name is not important because he will certainly apply, if at all, under a false identity. But we do believe he may try to slip into Surinam as a way of cutting across to Guyana and thence to rejoin his cronies in Venezuela.'

'You have a photo of him?' asked the official.

'Alas, not yet,' said McBride. 'That is where we hope you might be able to help us if he comes here. We have a description of him.'

He slipped a sheet of paper across the desk with a short, two-line description of a man about fifty, five feet eight inches, compact, muscular build, blue eyes, sandy hair.

McBride left with photocopies of the nineteen applications for visas to Surinam that had been lodged and granted in the previous week. Within three days all had been checked out as legitimate US citizens whose details and passport photos lodged with the State Department fully matched those presented to the Surinam Consulate.

If the elusive Avenger of the file Devereaux had ordered him to memorize was going to show up, he had not done so yet.

In truth, McBride was in the wrong consulate. Surinam is not large and certainly not rich. It maintains consulates in Washington and Miami, plus Munich (but not in the German capital of Berlin), and two in the former colonial power,

The Netherlands. One is in The Hague but the bigger office is at 11 De Cuserstraat, Amsterdam.

It was in this office that Miss Amelie Dykstra, a locally recruited Dutch lady paid for by the Dutch Foreign Ministry, was being so helpful to the visa applicant before her.

'You are British, Mr Nash?'

The passport she had in her hand showed that Mr Henry Nash was indeed British and his profession was that of businessman.

'What is the purpose of your visit to Surinam?' asked Ms Dykstra.

'My company develops new tourist outlets, notably resort hotels in coastal situations,' said the Englishman. 'I am hoping to see if there are any openings in your country, well, Surinam, that is, before moving on to Venezuela.'

'You should see the Ministry of Tourism,' said the Dutch woman, who had never been to Surinam. From what Cal Dexter had researched about that malarial coast, such a ministry was likely to be an exercise in optimism over reality.

'Precisely my intention, as soon as I get there, dear lady.'

He pleaded a last flight waiting at Schiphol Airport, paid his thirty-five guilders, got his visa and left. In truth his plane was not for London but for New York.

★ ★ ★

McBride headed south again, to Miami and Surinam. A car from San Martin met him at

297

Parbo airport and he was driven east to the Commini River crossing point. The Ojos Negros who escorted him simply drove to the head of the queue, commandeered the ferry and paid no toll to cross to the San Martin side.

During the crossing McBride stepped out of the car to watch the sluggish brown liquid passing down to the aquamarine sea, but the haze of mosquitoes and the drenching heat drove him back to the interior of the Mercedes and its welcome cool air. The secret policemen sent by Colonel Moreno permitted themselves wintry smiles at such stupidity. But behind the black glasses the eyes were blank.

It was forty miles over bumpy, pot-holed, ex-colonial road from the river border to San Martin City. The road ran through jungle on both sides. Somewhere to the left of the road the jungle would give way to the swamps, the swamps to the mangrove tangle and eventually to the inaccessible sea. To the right the dense rainforest ran away inland, rising gently, to the confluence of the Commini and the Maroni, and thence into Brazil.

A man, thought McBride, could be lost in there within half a mile. Occasionally he saw a track running off the road and into the bush, no doubt to some small farm or plantation not far from the road.

Down the highway they passed a few vehicles, mostly pickup trucks or battered Land Rovers clearly used by better-off farmers, and occasionally a cyclist with a basket of produce above the rear wheel, his livelihood on its way to market.

There were a dozen small villages along the journey and the man from Washington was struck at the different ethnic type of the San Martin peasant from those one republic back. There was a reason.

All the other colonial powers, conquering and trying to settle virtually empty landscapes, planted their estates and then looked for a labour force. The local Indios took one peek at what was in store and vaporized into the jungle.

Most of the colonialists imported African slaves from the properties they already owned, or traded with, along the West African coast. The descendants of these, usually mixing the genes with the Indios and whites, had created the modern populations. But the Spanish Empire was almost totally New World, not African. They did not have an easy source of black slaves, but they did have millions of landless Mexican peons; and the distance from Yucatan to Spanish Guyana was much shorter.

The wayside peasants McBride was seeing through the windows of the Mercedes were walnut-hued from the sun; but they were not black, nor yet Creole. They were Hispanic. The whole labour force of San Martin was still genetically Hispanic. The few black slaves who had escaped the Dutch had gone into the jungle to become the Bushneger, who were very hard to find, and deadly when they were.

When Shakespeare's Caesar expressed the wish to have fat men around him, he presumed they would be jolly and amiable. He was not thinking of Colonel Hernan Moreno.

The man who was credited with keeping the gaudy and massively decorated President Muñoz in the palace on the hill behind the capital of this last banana republic was fat like a brooding toad, but he was not jolly.

The torments practised on those he suspected of sedition, or to be in possession of details of such people, were hinted at only in the lowest whispers and the darkest corners.

There was a place, up country it was rumoured, for such things, and no one ever came back. Dumping cadavers at sea like the secret police of Galtieri in Argentina was not necessary; it was not even required to break sweat with shovel and pick. A naked body pegged out in the jungle would attract fire ants, and fire ants can do to soft tissue in a night what normal nature needs months or years to achieve.

He knew the man from Langley was coming and chose to offer him lunch at the Yacht Club. It was the best restaurant in town, certainly the most exclusive, and it was located at the base of the harbour wall facing out over a glittering blue sea. More to the point, the sea winds at last triumphed over the stench of the back streets.

Unlike his employer the secret police chief avoided ostentation, uniforms, medals and glitz; his pinguid frame was encased in a black shirt and black suit. If there had been a hint of nobility of cast of feature, thought the CIA man, he might have resembled Orson Welles towards the end. But the face was more Hermann Goering.

Nevertheless, his grip on the small and

impoverished country was absolute and he listened without interruption. He knew exactly the relationship between the refugee from Yugoslavia who had sought sanctuary in San Martin, and now lived in an enviable mansion at the end of a piece of property Moreno himself hoped one day to acquire, and the president.

He knew of the huge wealth of the refugee and the annual fee he paid to President Muñoz for sanctuary and protection, even though that protection was really provided by himself.

What he did not know was why a very senior hierarch in Washington had chosen to bring together the refugee and the tyrant. It mattered not. The Serb had spent over five million dollars building his mansion, and another ten on his estate. Despite the inevitable imports to achieve such a feat, half that money had been spent inside San Martin, with tidy percentages going to Colonel Moreno on every contract.

More directly, Moreno took a fee for providing the slave labour force, and keeping the numbers topped up with fresh arrests and transportations. So long as no peon ever escaped or came back alive, it was a lucrative and safe arrangement. The CIA man did not need to beg for his cooperation.

'If he sets one foot inside San Martin,' he wheezed, 'I will have him. You will not see him again, but every piece of information he divulges will be passed to you. On that you have my word.'

On his way back to the river crossing and the waiting aeroplane at Parbo, McBride thought of the mission the unseen bounty-hunter had set himself; he thought of the defences, and the price of failure: death at the hands of Colonel Moreno and his black-eyed experts in pain. He shuddered, and it was not from the air-conditioning.

★　★　★

Thanks to the wonders of modern technology, Calvin Dexter did not need to return to Pennington to collect any messages left on the answering machine attached to his office telephone. He could make the collections from a public phone booth in Brooklyn. He did so on 15 August.

The cluster of messages was mainly from voices he knew before the speaker identified himself. Neighbours, law clients, local businessmen; mainly wishing him a happy fishing vacation and asking when he would be back at his desk.

It was the second-to-last message that almost caused him to drop the phone, to stare, unseeing, at the traffic rushing past the glass of the booth. When he had replaced the handset he walked for an hour trying to work out how it had happened, who had leaked his name and business and, most important of all, whether the anonymous voice was that of a friend or a betrayer.

The voice did not identify the speaker. It was flat, monotone, as if coming through several layers of paper tissue. It said simply: 'Avenger, be careful. They know you are coming.'

# 24

## The Plan

When professor Medvers Watson left, the Surinamese consul was feeling slightly breathless; so much so, the official very nearly excluded the academic from the list of visa applicants he was sending to Kevin McBride at a private address in the city.

'*Callicore maronensis*,' beamed the professor when asked for the reason he wished to visit Surinam. The consul looked blank. Seeing his perplexity, Dr Watson delved into his attaché case and produced Andrew Neild's masterwork: *The Butterflies of Venezuela*.

'It's been seen, you know. The type 'V'. Unbelievable.'

He whipped open the reference work at a page of coloured photographs of butterflies that, to the consul, looked pretty similar, barring slight variations of marking to the back wings.

'One of the *Limenitidinae*, you know. Subfamily, of course. Like the *Charaxinae*. Both derived from the *Nymphalidae*, as you probably know.'

The bewildered consul found himself being educated in the descending order of family, subfamily, genus, species and subspecies.

'But what do you want to do about them?'

303

asked the consul. Professor Medvers Watson closed his almanac with a snap.

'Photograph them, my dear sir. Find them and photograph them. Apparently there has been a sighting. Until now the *Agrias narcissus* was about as rare as it gets in the jungles of your hinterlands, but the *Callicore maronensis*? Now that would make history. That is why I must go without delay. The autumn monsoon, you know. Not far off.'

The consul stared at the US passport. Stamps for Venezuela were frequent. Others for Brazil, Guyana. He unfolded the letter on the headed paper of the Smithsonian Institute. Professor Watson was warmly endorsed by the head of the Department of Entomology, Division Lepidoptera. He nodded slowly. Science, environment, ecology, these were the things not to be gainsaid or denied in the modern world. He stamped the visa and handed back the passport.

Professor Watson did not ask for the letter, so it stayed on the desk.

'Well, good hunting,' he said weakly.

Two days later Kevin McBride walked into the office of Paul Devereaux with a broad smile on his face.

'I think we have him,' he said. He laid down a completed application form of the type issued by the Surinamese Consulate and filled out by the applicant for a visa. A passport-sized photo stared up from the page.

Devereaux read through the details.

'So?'

McBride laid a letter beside the form. Devereaux read that as well.

'And?'

'And he's a phoney. There is no US passport-holder in the name of Medvers Watson. State Department is adamant on that. He should have picked a more common name. This one sticks out like a sore thumb. The scholars at the Smithsonian have never heard of him. No one in the butterfly world has ever heard of Medvers Watson.'

Devereaux stared at the picture of the man who had tried to ruin his covert operation and thus had become, albeit unwittingly, his enemy. The eyes looked owlish behind the glasses, and the straggly goatee beard off the point of the chin weakened instead of strengthened the face.

'Well done, Kevin. Brilliant strategy. But then, it worked; and of course all that works becomes brilliant. Every detail immediately to Colonel Moreno in San Martin if you please. He may move quickly.'

'And the Surinam government in Parbo.'

'No, not them. No need to disturb their slumbers.'

'Paul, they could arrest him the moment he flies into Parbo airport. Our embassy boys could confirm the passport is a forgery. The Surinamese charge him with passport fraud and put him on the next plane back. Two of our marines as escort. We arrest him on touchdown and he's in the slammer, out of harm's way.'

'Kevin, listen to me. I know it's rough and I know the reputation of Moreno. But if our man has a big stack of dollars he could elude arrest in Surinam. Back here he could get bail within a day, then skip.'

'But, Paul, Moreno is an animal. You wouldn't send your worst enemy into his grip . . . '

'And you don't know how important the Serb is to all of us. Nor his paranoia. Nor how tight his schedule may be. He has to know the danger to himself is over, totally eliminated, or he will butt out of what I need him for.'

'And you still can't tell me?'

'Sorry, Kevin. No, not yet.'

His deputy shrugged, unhappy but obedient.

'OK, on your conscience, not mine.'

And that was the problem, thought Paul Devereaux when he was once again alone in his office, staring out at the thick green foliage between him and the Potomac. Could he square his conscience with what he was doing? He had to. The lesser evil, the greater good.

The unknown man with the false passport would not die easily, upon the midnight with no pain. But he had chosen to swim in hideously dangerous waters, and it had been his decision to do so.

That day, 18 August, America sweltered in the summer heat, and half the country sought relief in the seas, rivers, lakes and mountains. Down on the north coast of South America, 100 per cent humidity, sweeping in from the steaming jungles behind the coast, added ten more degrees to the hundred caused by the sun.

In Parbo docks, ten miles up the teak-brown Surinam River from the sea, the heat was like a tangible blanket, lying over the warehouses and quays. The pye-dogs tried to find the deepest shade to pant away the hours until sundown. Humans sat under slow-moving fans which merely moved the discomfort around a bit.

The foolish tossed down sugary drinks, sodas and colas, which merely made the thirst and dehydration worse. The experienced stayed with piping hot, sweet tea, which may sound crazy but was discovered by the British empire-builders two centuries earlier to be the best rehydrator of them all.

The fifteen-hundred-ton freighter, *Tobago Star*, crept up the river, docked at her assigned pier and waited for dark. In the cooler dusk she discharged her cargo, which included a bonded crate in the name of US diplomat Ronald Proctor. This went into a chain-link-fenced section of the warehouse to await collection.

★ ★ ★

Paul Devereaux had spent years studying terrorism in general, and the types that emanated from the Arab and Muslim world, not necessarily the same type, in particular.

He had long come to the conclusion that the conventional whine in the West, that terrorism stemmed from the poverty and destitution of those whom Fanon had called 'the wretched of the earth', was convenient and politically correct psychobabble.

From the Anarchists of Tsarist Russia to the IRA of 1916, from the Irgun and the Stern Gang

307

to EOKA in Cyprus, from the Baader-Meinhof group in Germany, CCC in Belgium, Action Directe in France, Red Brigades in Italy, Red Army Faction in Germany again, the Renko Sekkigun in Japan, through to the Shining Path in Peru, to the modern IRA in Ulster or the ETA in Spain, terrorism came from the minds of comfortably raised, well-educated, middle-class theorists with a truly staggering personal vanity and a developed taste for self-indulgence.

Having studied them all, Devereaux was finally convinced the same applied to all their leaders, the self-arrogated champions of the working classes. The same applied in the Middle East as in Western Europe, South America or Far East Asia. Imad Mugniyah, George Habash, Abu Awas, Abu Nidal and all the other Abus had never missed a meal in their lives. Most had college degrees.

In the Devereaux theory those who could order another to plant a bomb in a food hall and gloat over the resultant images all had one thing in common. They possessed a fearsome capacity for hatred. This was the genetic 'given'. The hatred came first; the target could come later and usually did.

The motive also came second to the capacity to hate. It might be Bolshevik revolution, national liberation or a thousand variants thereof, from amalgamation to secession; it might be anti-capitalist fervour; it might be religious exaltation.

But the hatred came first, then the cause, then the target, then the methods and finally the self-justification. And Lenin's 'useful dupes' always swallowed it.

Devereaux was utterly convinced that the leadership of Al Qaeda ran precisely true to form. Its co-founders were a construction millionaire from Saudi Arabia and a qualified doctor from Cairo. It mattered not whether their hatred of Americans and Jews was secular-based or religiously fuelled. There was nothing, absolutely nothing, that America or Israel could do, short of complete self-annihilation, that would even begin to appease or satisfy them.

None of them, for him, cared a damn for the Palestinians save as vehicles and justifications. They hated his country not for what it did but for what it was.

He recalled the old British spy chief in the window table at White's as the left-wing demonstrators went by. Apart from the usual snowy-haired British socialists who could never quite get over the death of Lenin, there were the British boys and girls who would one day get a mortgage and vote Conservative, and there were the torrents of students from the Third World.

'They'll never forgive you, dear boy,' said the old man. 'Never expect it and you'll never be disappointed. Your country is a constant reproach. It is rich to their poor, strong to their weak, vigorous to their idle, enterprising to their reactionary, ingenious to their bewildered, can-do to their sit-and-wait, thrusting to their stunted.

'It only needs one demagogue to arise to shout: 'Everything the Americans have they stole from you', and they'll believe it. Like Shakespeare's Caliban, their zealots stare in the mirror and roar in rage at what they see. That rage becomes hatred, the hatred needs a target. The working class of the Third World does not hate you; it is the pseudo-intellectuals. If they ever forgive you, they must indict themselves. So far their hatred lacks the weaponry. One day they will acquire that weaponry. Then you will have to fight or die. Not in tens but in tens of thousands.'

Thirty years down the line, Devereaux was sure the old Brit had got it right. After Somalia, Kenya, Tanzania, Aden, his country was in a new war and did not know it. The tragedy was made worse by the fact the establishment was steeped in ostriches as well.

The Jesuit had asked for the front line and got it. Now he had to do something with his command. His response was Project Peregrine. He did not intend to seek to negotiate with UBL, nor even to respond after the next strike. He intended to try to destroy his country's enemy before that strike. In Father Xavier's analogy, he intended to use his spear to lunge, before the knife-tip came in range. This problem was: where? Not more or less, not 'somewhere in Afghanistan', but 'where' to ten yards by ten yards, and 'when' to thirty minutes.

He knew a strike was coming. They all did; Dick Clarke at the White House, Tom Pickard at the Bureau headquarters in the Hoover Building, George Tenet one floor above his head at Langley. All the whispers out on the street said a 'big one' was in preparation. It was the where, when, what, how, they did not know, and thanks to the crazy rules forbidding them to ask nasty people, they were not likely to find out. That, plus the refusal to collate what they did have.

Paul Devereaux was so disenchanted with the whole lot of them that he had prepared his Peregrine plan and would tell no one what it was.

In his reading of tens of thousands of pages about terror in general and Al Qaeda in particular, one theme had come endlessly through the fog. The Islamist terrorists would not be satisfied with a few dead Americans from Mogadishu to Dar es Salaam. UBL would want hundreds of thousands. The prediction of the long-gone Britisher was coming true.

For those kind of figures the Al Qaeda leadership would need a technology they did not yet have but endlessly sought to acquire. Devereaux knew that in the cave complexes of Afghanistan, which were not simply holes in rocks but subterranean labyrinths including laboratories, experiments had been started with germs and gases. But they were still miles from the methods of mass-dissemination.

For Al Qaeda, as for all the terror groups in the world, there was one prize beyond rubies: fissionable material. Any one of at least a dozen killer groups would give their eye-teeth, take crazy risks, to acquire the basic element of a nuclear device.

It would never have to be an ultra-modern 'clean' warhead; indeed the more basic, the 'dirtier' in radiation terms, the better. Even at the level of their in-house scientists, the terrorists knew that enough fissionable element, jacketed within enough plastic explosive, would create enough lethal radiation over enough square miles to make a city the size of New York uninhabitable for a generation. And that would be apart from the half a million people irradiated into an early, cancerous grave.

It had been a decade and the underground war had been costly and intense. So far, the West, assisted by Moscow more recently, had won it and survived. Huge sums had been spent buying up any fragment of Uranium 235 or plutonium that came near to private sale. Entire countries, former Soviet Republics, had handed over every gram left behind by Moscow, and the local dictators, under the provisions of the Nunn-Lugar Act, had become very wealthy. But there was too much, far too much, quite simply missing.

Just after he founded his own tiny section in Counter-Terrorism at Langley, Paul Devereaux noticed two things. One was that a hundred pounds of pure, weapons-grade Uranium 235 was lodged at the secret Vinca Institute in the heart of Belgrade. As soon as Milosevic fell, the USA began to negotiate its purchase. Just a third of it, thirty-three pounds or fifteen kilograms, would be enough for one bomb.

The other thing was that a vicious Serbian gangster and intimate at the court of Milosevic wanted out, before the roof fell in. He needed 'cover', new papers, protection and a place to disappear to. Devereaux knew that place could never be the USA. But a banana republic . . . Devereaux cut him a deal and he cut him a price. The price was collaboration.

Before he quit Belgrade, a thumbnail-sized sample of Uranium 235 was stolen from the Vinca Institute, and the records were changed to show that a full fifteen kilograms had really gone missing.

Six months earlier, introduced by the arms dealer, Vladimir Bout, the runaway Serb had handed over his sample and documentary proof that he possessed the remaining fifteen kilos.

The sample had gone to Al Qaeda's chemist and physicist, Abu Khabab, another highly educated and fanatical Egyptian. It had necessitated his leaving Afghanistan and quietly travelling to Iraq to secure the equipment he needed to test the sample properly.

In Iraq another nuclear programme was underway. It also sought weapons-grade Uranium 235, but was making it the slow, old-fashioned way, with calutrons like the ones used in 1945 at Oak Ridge, Tennessee. The sample caused great excitement.

Just four weeks before the circulation of that damnable report compiled by a Canadian magnate concerning his long-dead grandson, word had come through that Al Qaeda would deal. Devereaux had to force himself to stay very calm.

For his killing machine, he had wanted to use an unmanned high-altitude drone called the Predator, but it had crashed just outside

Afghanistan. Its wreckage was now back in the USA but the hitherto unarmed UAV was being 'weaponized' by the fitting of a Hellfire missile so that it could in future not only see a target from the stratosphere but blow it to bits as well.

But the conversion would take too long. Paul Devereaux revamped his plan, but he had to delay it while different weaponry was put in place. Only when they were ready could the Serb accept the invitation to journey to Peshawar, Pakistan, there to meet with Kawaheri, Atef, Zubaydah and the physicist Abu Khabab. He would carry with him fifteen kilos of uranium; but not weapons-grade. Yellowcake would do, normal reactor fuel, isotope 238, 3 per cent refined, not the needed 88 per cent.

At the crucial meeting Zoran Zilic was going to pay for all the favours he had been accorded. If he did not, he would be destroyed by a single phone call to Pakistan's lethal and pro-Qaeda secret service, the ISI.

He would suddenly double the price and threaten to leave if his new price was not met. Devereaux was gambling there was only one man who could make that decision and he would have to be consulted.

Far away in Afghanistan, UBL would have to take that phone call. High above, rolling in space, a listener satellite linked to the National Security Agency would hear the call and pinpoint its destination to a place ten feet by ten feet.

Would the man at the Afghan end wait around? Could he contain his curiosity to learn whether he had just become the owner of enough uranium to fulfil his most deadly dreams?

Off the Baluchi coast the nuclear sub *USS Columbia* would open her hatches to emit a single Tomahawk cruise missile. Even as it flew it would be programmed by global positioning system (GPS) plus Terrain Contour Matching (TERCOM) and Digital Scene Matching Area Correlation (DISMAC).

Three navigational systems would guide it to that hundred-square-foot and blow the entire area containing the mobile phone to pieces, including the man waiting for his call-back from Peshawar. For Devereaux the problem was time. The moment when Zilic would have to leave for Peshawar, pausing at Ras al-Khaimah to pick up the Russian, was moving ever closer. He could not afford to let Zilic panic and withdraw on the ground that he was a hunted man and thus their deal was null and void. Avenger had to be stopped and probably destroyed. Lesser evil, greater good.

★　★　★

It was 20 August. A man descended from the Dutch KLM airliner straight in from Curaçao to Paramaribo airport. It was not Professor Medvers Watson, for whom a reception committee waited further down the coast.

It was not even the US diplomat, Ronald Proctor, for whom a crate waited at the docks.

It was the British resort-developer, Henry

315

Nash. With his Amsterdam-delivered visa he passed effortlessly through customs and immigration and took a taxi into town. It would have been tempting to book in at the Torarica, far and away the best in town. But he might have met real Britishers there, so he went to the Krasnopolsky on the Dominiestraat.

His room was top floor, with a balcony facing east. The sun was behind him when he went out for a look over the city. The extra height gave a hint of breeze to make the dusk bearable. Far to the east, seventy miles away and over the river, the jungles of San Martin were waiting.

# PART THREE

# 25

## The Jungle

It was the American diplomat, Ronald Proctor, who leased the car. It was not even from an established agency but from a private seller advertising in the local paper.

The Cherokee was second-hand but in good repair, and with a bit of work and a thorough service, which its US-army-trained new owner intended to give it, it would do what it had to.

The deal he made the vendor was simple and sweet. He would pay ten thousand dollars in cash. He would only need the vehicle for a month, until his own 4x4 came through from the States. If he returned it absolutely intact in thirty days, the vendor would take it back and reimburse five thousand dollars.

The seller was looking at an effort-free five thousand dollars in a month. Given that the man facing him was a charming American diplomat, and the Cherokee might come back in thirty days, it seemed foolish to go through all the trouble of changing the documents. Why alert the taxman?

Proctor also rented the lock-up garage and store shed behind the flower and produce market. Finally he went to the docks and signed for his single crate, which went into the garage to be carefully unpacked and repacked in two canvas kitbags. Then Ronald Proctor simply ceased to exist.

★　★　★

In Washington, Paul Devereaux was gnawed by anxiety and curiosity as the days dragged by. Where was this man? Had he used his visa and entered Surinam? Was he on his way?

The easy way to indulge the temptation would be to ask the Surinam authorities direct, via the US embassy on Redmondstraat. But that would trigger Surinamese curiosity. They would want to know why. They would pick him up themselves and start asking questions. The man called Avenger could arrange to be set free and start again. The Serb, already becoming paranoid at the thought of going to Peshawar, could panic and call the deal off. So Devereaux paced and prowled and waited.

★　★　★

Down in Paramaribo the tiny consulate of San Martin had been tipped off by Colonel Moreno that an American pretending to be a collector of butterflies might apply for a visa. It was to be granted immediately, and he was to be informed at once.

But no one called Medvers Watson appeared. The man they sought was sitting at a terrace café in the middle of Parbo with his last purchases in a sack beside him. It was 24 August.

What he had bought had come from the town's only camping and hunting shop, the Tackle Box on Zwarten Hovenbrug Street. As the London businessman Mr Henry Nash he had brought almost nothing that would be useful across the border. But with the contents of the diplomat's crate and what he had acquired that morning, he could think of nothing he might be missing. So he tilted back his Parbo beer and enjoyed the last he was going to have for some time.

Those who waited were rewarded on the morning of the 25th. The queue at the river crossing was, as ever, slow, and the mosquitoes, as ever, dense. Those crossing were almost entirely locals, with pedal bikes, motorcycles and rusty pick-ups, all loaded with produce.

There was only one smart car in the queue on the Surinam side, a black Cherokee, with a white man at the wheel. He wore a creased seersucker jacket in cream, off-white Panama hat and heavy-rimmed glasses. Like the others he sat and swatted, then moved a few yards forwards as the chain ferry took on a fresh cargo and cranked back across the Commini.

After an hour he was at last on the flat iron deck of the ferry, handbrake on, able to step down and watch the river. On the San Martin side he joined the queue of six cars awaiting clearance.

The San Martin checkpoint was tighter and there seemed to be a tension among the dozen guards who milled around. The road was blocked by a striped pole laid over two recently added oil drums weighted with concrete.

In the shed to one side, an immigration officer studied all papers, his head visible through the window. The Surinamese, here to visit relatives or buy produce to sell back in Parbo, must have wondered why, but patience has never been rationed in the Third World, nor information a glut. They sat and waited again. It was almost dusk when the Cherokee rolled to the barrier. A soldier flicked his fingers for the needed passport, took it from the American and handed it through the window.

The off-road driver seemed nervous. He sweated in rivers. He made no eye contact, but stared ahead. From time to time he glanced sideways through the booth window. It was during one of these glances that he saw the immigration officer start violently and grab his phone. That was when the traveller with the wispy goatee beard panicked.

The engine suddenly roared, the clutch was let in. The heavy black 4×4 threw itself forward, knocked a soldier flying with the wing-mirror, tossed the striped pole in the air and burst through, swerving crazily round the trucks ahead and charging off into the dusk.

Behind the Cherokee there was chaos. Part of the flying pole had whacked the army officer in the face. The immigration official came shouting out of his booth waving an American passport in the name of Professor Medvers Watson.

Two of Colonel Moreno's secret police goons, who had been standing behind the immigration officer in the shed, came running out with handguns drawn. One went back and began to gabble down the phone lines to the capital forty miles east.

Galvanized by the army officer clutching his broken nose, the dozen soldiers piled into the olive-drab truck and set off in pursuit. The secret policemen ran to their own blue Land Rover and did the same. But the Cherokee was round two corners and gone.

In Langley, Kevin McBride saw the flickering bulb flash on the desk phone that only linked him to the office of Colonel Moreno in San Martin City.

He took the call, listened carefully, noted what was said, asked a few questions and noted again. Then he went to see Paul Devereaux.

'They've got him,' he said.

'In custody?'

'Almost. He tried to come in as I thought, over the river from Surinam. He must have spotted the sudden interest in his passport, or the guards made too much of a fuss. Whatever, he smashed down the barrier and roared off. Colonel Moreno says there is nowhere for him to go. Jungle both sides, patrols on the roads. He says they'll have him by morning.'

'Poor man,' said Devereaux. 'He really should have stayed at home.'

Colonel Moreno was overly optimistic. It took two days. In fact, the news was brought by a bush farmer who lived two miles up a track running off the right-hand side of the highway into the jungle.

He said he recalled the noise of a heavy engine

323

growling past his homestead the previous evening and his wife had caught sight of a big and almost new off-road going up the track.

He naturally presumed it must be a government vehicle, since no farmer or trapper would dream of being able to afford such a vehicle. Only when it did not come back by the following night did he trudge down to the main road. There he found a patrol and told them.

The soldiers found the Cherokee. It had made one further mile beyond the farmer's shack when, trying to push onwards into the rain forest, it had nosed into a gully and stuck at forty-five degrees. Deep furrows showed where the fleeing driver had tried to force his way out of the gully, but his panic had merely made matters worse. It took a crane truck from the city to get the 4x4 out of the hole, turned around and heading for the road.

Colonel Moreno himself came. He surveyed the churned earth, the shattered saplings and torn vines.

'Trackers,' he said. 'Get the dogs. The Cherokee and everything in it to my office. Now.'

But darkness came down; the trackers were simple folk, not able to face the darkness when the spirits of the forest were abroad. They began next morning at dawn and found the quarry by noon.

One of Moreno's men was with them and had a cellphone. Moreno took the call in his office. Thirty minutes later Kevin McBride walked into Devereaux's office.

'They found him. He's dead.'

Devereaux glanced at his desk calendar. It revealed the date was 27 August.

'I think you should be there,' he said.

McBride groaned.

'It's a hell of a journey, Paul. All over the bloody Caribbean.'

'I'll sanction a company plane. You should be there by the breakfast hour tomorrow. It's not just I who have to be satisfied this damn business is over for good. Zilic has to believe it too. Go down there, Kevin. Convince us both.'

The man Langley knew only by his codename of Avenger had spotted the track off the main road when he flew over the region in the Piper. It was one of a dozen that left the highway between the river and the capital forty miles to the east. Each track serviced one or two small plantations or farms, then petered out into nothing.

He had not thought to photograph them at the time, saving all his film for the hacienda at El Punto. But he remembered them. And on the flight back with the doomed charter pilot Lawrence he had seen them again.

The one he chose to use was the third from the river. He had a start of half a mile over his pursuers when he slowed in order not to leave visible skid marks, and eased the Cherokee up the track. Round a bend, engine off, he heard the pursuers thunder past.

The drive to the farmstead was easy, first-gear, four-wheel work. After the farm it was all slog. He got the vehicle an extra mile through dense jungle, descended in the darkness, walked ahead, found a gully and crashed it.

He left what he intended the trackers to find and took the rest. It was heavy. The heat, even in the night, was oppressive. The notion that jungles at night are quiet places is a fallacy. They rustle, they croak, they roar. But they do not have spirits.

Using his compass and flashlight he marched west, then south, for about a mile, slashing with one of his machetes to create a kind of path.

After a mile he left the other part of what he intended the pursuers to find and, lightened at last to a small haversack, water bottle, flashlight and second machete, pressed on towards the river bank.

He reached the Commini at dawn, well upstream of the crossing point and ferry. The inflatable airbed would not have been his crossing of choice but it sufficed. Prone on the navyblue canvas, he paddled with both hands, withdrawing them from the water when a deadly cottonmouth glided past. The beady, lidless eye gazed at him from a few inches away, but the snake pressed on downstream.

An hour's paddling and drifting brought him to the Surinam bank. The trusty airbed was stabbed into oblivion and abandoned. It was mid-morning when the stained, streaked, wet figure, mottled with mosquito bites and hung with leeches, stumbled onto the road back to Parbo.

After five miles a friendly market trader allowed him to ride the cargo of watermelons the last fifty miles to the capital.

Even the kind souls at the Krasnopolsky would

have raised an eyebrow at their English businessman turning up in such a state, so he changed in the lock-up store, used a garage washroom and a gas lighter to burn off the leeches and returned to his hotel for a lunch of steak and fries. Plus several bottles of Parbo. Then he slept.

Thirty thousand feet up, the company Lear jet drifted down the eastern seaboard of the USA with Kevin McBride as its only passenger.

'This,' he mused, 'is the kind of transportation I really could force myself to get used to.'

They refuelled at the spook-heaven air base of Eglin, northern Florida, and again at Barbados. There was a car waiting at San Martin City airfield to bring the CIA man to Colonel Moreno's secret police headquarters in an oil-palm forest on the outskirts of town.

The fat colonel greeted his visitor in his office with a bottle of whisky.

'I guess a tad early for me, colonel,' said McBride.

'Nonsense, my friend, never too early for a toast. Come ... I propose. Death to our enemies.'

They drank. McBride, at that hour and in that heat, would have preferred a decent coffee.

'What have you got for me, colonel?'

'A little exposition. Better I show you.'

There was a conference room next to the office and it had clearly been arranged for the colonel's grisly 'exposition'. The central long table was covered with a white cloth which contained one exhibit. Round the walls were four other tables with collections of mixed items. It was one of the smaller tables that Colonel Moreno approached first.

'I told you our friend, Mr Watson, first panicked, drove down the main road, swerved up a track at the side and attempted to find escape by driving straight through the jungle? Yes? Impossible. He crashed his off-road into a gully and could not get out. Today, it stands in the yard beneath these windows. Here is part of what he abandoned in it.'

Table One contained mainly heavy-duty clothing, spare boots, water pannikins, mosquito netting, repellent, water-purification tablets.

Table Two had a tent, pegs, lantern, canvas basin on a tripod, miscellaneous toiletries.

'Nothing I wouldn't have on any normal camping trip,' remarked McBride.

'Quite right, my friend. He obviously thought he would be hiding in the jungle for some time, probably making an ambush for his target on the road out of El Punto. But that target hardly ever leaves by road at all, and when he does it is in an armoured limousine. This assassin was not very good. Still, when he abandoned his kit, he also abandoned this. Too heavy, perhaps.'

At Table Three the colonel whisked a sheet off the contents. It was a Remington Three-Double-O-Six, with a huge Rhino scope sight and a box of shells. Purchasable in American gun stores as a hunting rifle, it would also take a human head away with no problem at all.

'Now,' explained the fat man, enjoying his mastery of his list of discoveries, 'at this point your man leaves the car and eighty per cent of his equipment. He sets off on foot, probably aiming for the river. But he is not a jungle fighter. How do I know? No compass. Within three hundred metres he was lost, heading south into deeper jungle, not west to the river. When we found him, all this was scattered about.'

The last table contained a water can (empty), bush hat, machete, flashlight. There were tough-soled combat boots, shreds of camouflage trousers and shirt, bits of a completely inappropriate seersucker jacket, a leather belt with brass buckle and sheath knife, still looped onto the belt.

'That was all he was carrying when you found him?'

'That was all he was carrying when he died. In his panic he left behind what he should have taken. His rifle. He might have defended himself at the end.'

'So, your men caught up with him and shot him?'

Colonel Moreno threw up both hands, palms forward, in a gesture of surprised innocence.

'We? Shoot him? Unarmed? Of course not, we wanted him alive. No, no. He was dead by the midnight of the night he fled. Those who do not understand the jungle should not venture into it. Certainly not ill-equipped, at night, seized by panic. That is a deadly combination. Look.'

With self-adoring theatricality he whipped the sheet off the centre table. The skeleton had been brought from the jungle in a body bag, feet still in the boots, rags still around the bones. A hospital doctor had been summoned to rearrange the bones in the right order.

The dead man, or what was left of him, had been picked clean to the last tiny fragment of skin, flesh and marrow.

'The key to what happened is here,' said Colonel Moreno, tapping with his forefinger.

The right femur had been snapped cleanly through the middle.

'From this we can deduce what happened, my friend. He panicked, he ran. By flashlight only, blindly, without a compass. He made about a mile from the stranded car. Then he caught his foot in a root, a hidden tree stump, a tangled vine. Down he went. Snap. One broken leg.

'Now, he cannot run, he cannot walk, he cannot even crawl. With no gun he cannot even summon help. He can only shout, but to what end? You know we have jaguars in these jungles?

'Well, we do. Not many, but if one hundred and fifty pounds of fresh meat insists on shouting its head off, chances are a jaguar will find it. That's what happened here. The main limbs were scattered over a small clearing.

'It's a larder out there. The raccoon eats fresh meat. Also the puma and the coati. Up in the tree canopy the daylight will bring the forest vultures. Ever seen what they can do to a corpse? No? Not pretty, but thorough. At the end of them all, the fire ants.

'I know about fire ants. Nature's most fantastic cleaners. Fifty yards from the remains we found the ants' nest. They leave out scouts, you know. They cannot see, but their sense of smell is amazing, and of course within twenty hours he would have smelt to high heaven. Enough?'

'Enough,' said McBride. Early it might be; he fancied a second whisky.

Back in the colonel's office, the secret policemen laid out some smaller items. One steel watch, engraved MW on the back. A signet ring, no inscription.

'No wallet,' said the Colonel. 'One of the predators must have snatched it if it was made of leather. But maybe this is even better. He had to abandon it at the border-crossing point when he was recognized.'

It was a United States passport in the name of Medvers Watson. The profession was given as scientist. The same face McBride had seen before from the visa application form stared at him: eyeglasses, wispy goatee beard, slightly helpless expression.

The CIA man reckoned, quite rightly, that no one would ever see Medvers Watson again.

'May I contact my superior in Washington?'

'Please,' said Colonel Moreno, 'be my guest. I will leave you your privacy.'

McBride took his laptop from his attaché case and raised Paul Devereaux, tapping in a sequence of numbers that would keep the exchange from prying ears. With his cellphone plugged into the laptop, he waited until Devereaux came on line.

He told his superior the gist of what Colonel Moreno had told him, and what he had seen. There was silence for a while.

'I want you to come home,' said Devereaux.

'Not a problem,' said McBride.

'Moreno can keep all the toys, including the rifle. But I want that passport. Oh, and something else.'

McBride listened.

'You want . . . what?'

'Just do it, Kevin. Godspeed.'

McBride told the colonel what he had been ordered to do. The fat secret police chief shrugged.

'Such a short visit. You should stay. Lobster for lunch on my boat out at sea? Cold Soave? No? Oh well . . . the passport, of course. And the rest . . . '

He shrugged.

'If you wish. Take them all.'

'I'm told just one will do.'

# 26

## The Trick

McBride arrived back in Washington on 29 August. That same day, down in Paramaribo, Mr Henry Nash, with his passport issued by Her Majesty's Principal Secretary of State for Foreign and Commonwealth Affairs, to give him his full title, walked into the Consulate of the Republic of San Martin and asked for a visa.

There was no problem. The consul in the one-man office knew there had been a flap several days earlier when a refugee from justice had tried to enter his homeland, but the alarm had been stood down. The man was dead. He issued the entry visa.

★　★　★

That was the trouble with August. You could never get anything done in a hurry, not even in Washington, not even if your name was Paul Devereaux. The excuse was always the same: 'I'm sorry, sir, he's on vacation. He'll be back next week.' And thus it was as the month of August finally trickled away into September.

It was on the 3rd that Devereaux received the first of the two answers he sought.

'It's probably the best forgery we've ever seen,'

said the man from the State Department's passport division. 'Basically, it was once genuine and was printed by us. But two vital pages were removed by an expert and two fresh pages from another passport inserted. It is the fresh pages that bear the photo and name of Medvers Watson. To our knowledge there is no such person. This passport number has never been issued.'

'Could the holder of this passport fly into and out of the States?' asked Paul Devereaux. 'Is it that good?'

'Out of, yes,' said the expert. 'Flying out would mean it would only be checked by airline staff. No computer database involved. Flying in . . . that would be a problem if the INS officer chose to run the number through the database. The computer would reply: no such number.'

'Can I have the passport back?'

'Sorry, Mr Devereaux. We like to try and help you guys, but this masterpiece is going into our Black Museum. We'll have entire classes studying this beauty.'

And still there was no reply from the Forensic Pathology unit at Bethesda, the hospital where Devereaux had a few useful contacts.

It was on the 4th that Mr Henry Nash, at the wheel of a modest little rented compact, with a handgrip of summer clothes and wash kit, British passport in hand and San Martin visa stamped inside it, rolled onto the ferry at the Commini River border crossing.

His British accent might not have fooled

Oxford or Cambridge, but among the Dutch-speaking Surinamese and, he presumed, the Spanish-speaking San Martinos, there would be no problem. There was not.

Avenger watched the brown river flowing beneath his feet one last time and vowed he would be a happy man if he never saw the damned thing again.

On the San Martin side, the striped pole was gone, as were the secret police and soldiers. The border was back to its usual sleepy self. He descended, passed his passport through the side window of the booth, beamed an inane smile and fanned himself while he waited.

Running in a singlet in all weathers meant he habitually had a slight tan; two weeks in the tropics had deepened it to mahogany brown. His fair hair had received the attention of a barber in Paramaribo and was now so dark brown as to be almost black, but that simply matched the description of Mr Nash of London.

The glance through the trunk of his car and his valise of clothes was perfunctory, his passport went back into the top pocket of his shirt, and he rolled on down the road to the capital.

At the third track on the right, he checked no one was watching, and turned into the jungle again. Halfway to the farmstead he stopped and turned the car around. The giant baobab tree was not hard to locate and the tough black twine was still deep inside the cut he had sliced in the trunk a week earlier.

As he paid out the twine, the camouflaged Bergen rucksack came down from the branches where it had hung unseen. It contained all he hoped he would need for several days crouched on the crest of the cordillera above the hacienda of the runaway Serb, and for his descent into the fortress itself.

The customs officer at the border post had taken little notice of the ten-litre plastic jerrycan in the trunk. When the Englishman said 'Agua', he merely nodded and closed the lid. With the water added to the Bergen, the load would take even a triathlete to his limit for mountain climbing, but two litres a day would be vital.

The manhunter drove quietly through the capital, past the oil-palm forest where Colonel Moreno sat at his desk, and on to the east. He went into the resort village of La Bahia just after lunch, at the hour of siesta, and no one stirred.

The plates on the car were by now those of a San Martin national. He recalled the adage: where do you hide a tree? In the forest. Where do you hide a rock? In the quarry. He put the compact in the public car park, hefted the Bergen and marched eastwards out of town. Another backpacker.

Dusk descended. Ahead of him he saw the crest of the cordillera that separated the hacienda from the enveloping jungle. Where the road curved away inland, to loop around the hills and go on to the Maroni and the border to French Guyana, he left the road and began to climb.

He saw the narrow track snaking down from the col, and angled away from it towards a peak he had selected from the photographs taken from the aeroplane. When it became simply too black to move, he set down his Bergen, took a supper of high-value hard rations, a cup of the precious water, leaned against the haversack and slept.

In the camping stores of New York he had declined the US-Army derived MREs, Meals Ready to Eat, recalling that in the Gulf War they were so deeply awful that the GIs dubbed them Meals Rejected by Ethiopians. He made up his own concentrates to include beef, raisins, nuts and dextrose. He would be passing rabbit pellets, but he would keep his strength for when he needed it.

Before dawn he came awake, nibbled again, sipped again and climbed on. At one point, down the mountain and through a gap in the trees, he saw the roof of the guardhouse in the col far below.

Before the sun rose, he made the crest. He came out of the forest two hundred yards from where he wanted, so he crabbed sideways until he found the spot in the photograph.

His eye for terrain had not let him down. There was a slight dip in the line of the crest, screened by the last fuzz of vegetation. With camouflaged shirt and bush hat, daubed face and olive-coloured binoculars, motionless under leaves, he would be invisible from the estate below.

When he needed a break, he could slither backwards off the crest and stand up again. He made the small camp that would be home for up to four days, smeared his face and crawled into the hide. The sun pinked the jungles over French

Cayenne, and the first beam slipped across the peninsula below. El Punto lay spread out like the scale model that had once graced the sitting room of his apartment in Brooklyn, a shark tooth jabbing into the glittering sea. From below came a dull clang as someone smashed an iron bar into a hanging length of railway track. It was time for the forced labourers to rise.

★ ★ ★

It was not until the 4th that the friend Paul Devereaux had contacted in the Department of Forensic Pathology at Bethesda called back.

'What on earth are you up to, Paul?'

'Enlighten me. What am I up to?'

'Grave-robbing by the look of it.'

'Tell me all, Gary. What is it?'

'Well, it's a femur, all right. A thighbone, right leg. Clean break at the mid-section. No compound fracture, no splinters.'

'Sustained in a fall?'

'Not unless the fall involved a sharp edge and a hammer.'

'You're fulfilling my worst fear, Gary. Go on.'

'Well, the bone is clearly from an anatomical skeleton, purchasable in any medical store, used by students since the Middle Ages. About fifty years old. The bone was broken recently with a sharp blow, probably across a bench. Did I make your day?'

'No, you just ruined it. But I owe you, anyway.'

As with all his calls, Devereaux had recorded

it. When Kevin McBride listened to the playback his jaw dropped.

'Good God.'

'For the sake of your immortal soul, I hope he is, Kevin. You goofed. It's phoney. He never died. He choreographed the whole damn episode, duped Moreno and Moreno convinced you. He's alive. Which means he's coming back, or he's back already. Kevin, this is a major emergency. I want the company plane to take off in one hour and I want you on it.

'I will brief Colonel Moreno myself while you fly. When you get there Moreno will be checking every single possibility that this blasted Avenger came back or is on his way. Now, go.'

On the 5th, Kevin McBride faced Colonel Moreno again. Any veneer of amiability Moreno may have used before was gone. His toad-like face was mottled with anger.

'This is one clever man, mi amigo. You did not tell me this. Hokay, he fool me once. Not again. Look.'

Since the moment Professor. Medvers Watson had burst through the border controls, the secret police chief had checked every possible entrant into San Martin Republic.

Three game fishermen out of St Laurent du Maroni on the French side had suffered an engine breakdown at sea and been towed into San Martin marina. They were in detention and not happy. Four more non-Hispanics had entered from the Surinam direction. A party of French technicians from the Kourou space-launch facility in French Guyana had come over the River Maroni looking for cheap sex and were undergoing an even cheaper stay in jail.

Of the four from Surinam, one was Spanish and two Dutch. All their passports had been confiscated. Colonel Moreno slapped them onto his desk.

'Which one is false?' he asked.

Eight French, two Dutch, one Spanish. One missing.

'Who was the other visitor from the Surinam side?'

'An Englishman, we can't find him.'

'Details?'

The colonel studied a sheet with the records from the San Martin Consulate in Parbo and the crossing point on the Commini.

'Nash. Señor Henry Nash. Passport in order, visa in order. No luggage except a few summer clothes. Small compact car, rented. Unsuitable for jungle work. With this he gets nowhere off the main road or the capital city. Drove in on the fourth, two days ago.'

'Hotel?'

'He told our consulate in Parbo he would be staying in the city, the Camino Real Hotel. He had a reservation, faxed from the Krasnopolsky in Parbo. He never checked in.'

'Looks suspicious.'

'The car is also missing. No foreign car cannot be found in San Martin. But it has not been found. Yet it cannot drive off the main highway. So, I say to myself, a garage somewhere in the country. So, a helper; a friend, colleague, employee. The country is being scoured.'

340

McBride looked at the pile of foreign passports.

'Only their own embassies could verify these as forgeries or genuine. And the embassies are in Surinam. It means a visit for one of your men.'

Colonel Moreno nodded glumly. He prided himself on absolute control of the small dictatorship. Something had gone wrong.

'Have you Americans told our Serbian guest?'

'No,' said McBride. 'Have you?'

'Not yet.'

Both men had good reasons. For the dictator, President Muñoz, his asylum-seeker was extremely lucrative. Moreno did not want to be the one who caused him to quit and take his fortune with him.

For McBride it was a question of orders. He did not know it, but Devereaux feared Zoran Zilic might panic and refuse to fly to Peshawar to meet the Al Qaeda chiefs. Sooner or later someone was either going to have to find the manhunter or tell Zilic.

'Please keep me posted, colonel,' he said as he turned to leave. 'I'll stay at the Camino Real. It seems they have a spare room.'

'There is one thing that puzzles me, señor,' said Moreno as McBride reached the door. He turned.

'Yes?'

'This man, Medvers Watson. He tried to enter the country without a visa.'

'So?'

'He would have needed a visa to get in. He must have known that. He did not even bother.'

'You're right,' said McBride. 'Odd.'

'So, I ask myself, as a policeman, why? And you know what I answer, señor?'

'Tell me.'

'I answer: because he did not intend to enter legally; because he did not panic at all. Because he intended to do exactly what he did. To fake his own death, find his way back to Surinam. Then quietly return.'

'Makes sense,' admitted McBride.

'Then I say to myself: so he knew we were waiting for him. But how did he know?'

McBride's stomach turned over at the full implication of Moreno's reasoning.

Meanwhile, invisible in a patch of scrub on the flank of a mountain, the hunter watched, noted and waited. He waited for the hour that had not yet come.

# 27

## The Vigil

Dexter was impressed as he studied the triumph of security and self-sufficiency that a combination of nature, ingenuity and money had accomplished on the peninsula below the escarpment. Were it not dependent on slave labour, it would have been admirable.

The triangle jutting out to sea was larger than he had imagined in the scale model in his New York apartment.

The base, on which he now looked down from his mountain hideout, was about two miles from side to side. It ran, as his aerial photos had shown, from sea to sea and at each end the mountain range dropped to the water in vertical cliffs.

The sides of the isosceles triangle he estimated at about three miles, giving a total land area of almost three square miles. The area was divided into four parts, each with a different function.

Below him at the base of the escarpment was the private airstrip and the workers' village. Three hundred yards out from the cliff a twelve-foot-high chain-link fence topped with razor wire ran across the land from edge to edge. Where it met the sea, he could observe through his binoculars in the growing light, the fence

343

jutted over the cliff and ended in a tangle of rolls of razor wire. No way of slipping round the end of the fence; no way of going over the top.

Two-thirds of the strip created between the escarpment and the wire was dedicated to the airfield. Below him, flanking the runway, was a single large hangar, a marshalling apron and a range of smaller buildings that had to be workshops and fuel stores. Towards the far end, near the sea to catch the cooler breezes, were half a dozen small villas which he presumed to be the home of the aircrew and maintenance staff.

The only access and egress to and from the airfield was a single steel gate set in the chain-link fence. There was no guardhouse near the gate, but a pair of visible rods, and bogey wheels beneath the leading edge, indicated it was electrically powered and would open to the command of the appropriate bleeper. At half past five, nothing moved on the airfield.

The other third of the strip was consigned to the village. It was segregated from the airfield by another fence, running from the escarpment outwards and also topped with razor wire. The peasants were clearly not allowed on or near the airfield.

The clanging of the iron bar on the railway track stopped after a minute and the village stumbled into life. Dexter watched the first figures, clad in off-white trousers and shirts, with rope-soled espadrilles on their feet, emerge from the groups of tiny cabanas and head for the communal wash-houses. When they were all assembled, the watcher estimated about twelve hundred of them.

Clearly there were some staff who ran the village and would not go to work in the fields. He saw them working in open-fronted lean-to kitchens, preparing a breakfast of bread and gruel. Long trestle tables and benches formed the refectories under palm-thatch shelters, which would protect against occasional rain but more usually against the fierce sun.

At a second beating of the iron rail, the farm workers took bowls and a half-loaf and sat to eat. There were no gardens, no shops, no women, no children, no school. This was not a true village but a labour camp. The only remaining buildings were what appeared to be a food store, a general clothing and bedding store and the church with the priest's house attached. It was functional; a place to work, eat, sleep, pray for release and nothing else.

If the airfield was a rectangle trapped between the escarpment, the wire and the sea, so was the village. But there was one difference. A pitted and rutted track zig-zagged down from the single col in the whole mountain range, the only access by road to the rest of the republic. It was clearly not suitable for heavy-duty trucks; Dexter wondered how resupply of weighty essentials like gasoline, engine diesel and aviation fuel would take place. When the visibility lengthened he found out.

At the extremity of his vision hidden in the morning mist was the third portion of the estate, the walled five-acre compound at the end of the foreland. He knew from his aerial pictures it contained the magnificent white mansion in which the former Serbian gangster lived; half a dozen villas in the grounds for guests and senior staff; tonsured lawns, flowerbeds and shrubbery; and along the inner side of the fourteen-foot-high protecting wall, a series of lean-to cottages and stores for domestic staff, linen, food and drink.

In his pictures and on his scale model, the huge wall also went from cliff edge to cliff edge, and at this point the land was fifty feet above the sea which surged and thumped on the rocks below.

A lone but massive double-gate penetrated the wall at its centre with a road of pounded hardcore leading up to it. There was a guardhouse inside which controlled the gate-opening machinery, and a parapet ran along the inside of the wall to enable armed guards to patrol its entire length.

Everything between the chain-link fence below the watcher and the wall over two miles away was the food-producing farm. As the light rose, Dexter could confirm what his photos had told him: the farm produced almost everything the community within the fortress could need. There were grazing herds of beef and lamb. Sheds would certainly contain pigs and poultry.

There were fields of arable crops, grains, pulses, tubers. Orchards producing ten kinds of fruit. Acre after acre of salad-vegetable crops either in the open or under long domes of polythene. He surmised the farm would produce every conceivable kind of salad and fruit, along with meat, butter, eggs, cheese, oil, bread and rough red wine.

The fields and orchards were studded with barns and granaries, machine stores, and facilities to slaughter the beasts, mill the grain, bake the bread, press the grapes.

To his right, near the cliff edge but inside the farm, was a series of small barracks for the guard staff, with a dozen better-quality chalets for their officers and two or three company shops.

To his left, also at the cliff edge, also inside the farm, were three large warehouses and a gleaming aluminium fuel-storage farm. Right at the very edge of the cliff were two large cranes or derricks. That solved one problem: heavy cargoes came by sea and were hefted or pumped from the ship below to the storage facilities forty feet above the freighter's deck.

The peons finished their morning meal and again came the harsh clang as the iron bar smashed against the hanging length of rail. This time there were several reactions.

Uniformed guards spilled from their barracks further up the coast to the right. One put a silent whistle to his lips. Dexter heard nothing but out of the farmland a dozen loping Dobermanns emerged in obedience to the call and entered their fenced compound near the barracks. Clearly they had not eaten for twenty-four hours; they hurled themselves at the plates of raw offal set out and tore the meat to pieces.

That told Dexter what happened each sundown. When every staffer and slave was closed off in their respective compounds, the dogs would be released to hunt and prowl the three thousand acres of farmland. They must have been trained to leave the calves, sheep and pigs alone, but any wandering burglar would simply not survive. They were far too many for a single man to begin to combat. Entry by night was not feasible.

The watcher had buried himself so deeply in the undergrowth that anyone below, raising his or her eyes to the crest of the range, would see no glint of sun off lens-glass, nor would he catch a glimpse of the motionless camouflaged man.

At half past six, when the farming estate was ready to receive them, the iron clang summoned the labourers to work. They trooped towards the high gate that separated the village from the farm.

This gate was a far more complicated affair than the one from the airfield to the estate. It opened inwards to the farmland, in two halves. Beyond the gate, five tables had been set up and guards sat behind each. Others stood over them. The peons formed into five columns.

On a shouted command they shuffled forward. Each man at the head of the queue stooped at the table to offer a dog tag round his neck to the seated official. The number on the tag was checked and tapped into a database.

The workers must have lined up in the right column, according to their type of number, for after they were nodded through they reported to a charge-hand beyond the tables. In groups of about a hundred they were led away to their tasks, pausing at a number of tool sheds beside the main track to pick up what they needed.

Some were for the fields, some for the orchards, others were destined for animal husbandry, or the grain mill, the slaughter-house, the vineyard or the huge kitchen garden. As Dexter watched, the enormous farm came to life. But the security never slackened. When the village was finally empty, the double-gate closed and the men dispersed to their stations, Dexter concentrated on that security and looked for his opening.

It was in the mid-morning that Colonel Moreno heard back from the two emissaries he had sent out with foreign passports in their hands.

In Cayenne, capital of French Guyana to the east, the authorities had wasted no time. They were not best pleased that three innocent game fishermen had been detained for the crime of breaking down at sea, nor that five technicians had been picked up and detained without good cause. All eight French passports were pro-nounced one hundred per cent genuine and an urgent request was lodged that their owners be released and sent home.

To the west, in Paramaribo, the Dutch embassy said exactly the same about their two nationals; the passports were genuine, the visas in order, what was the problem?

The Spanish embassy was closed, but Colonel Moreno had been assured by the man from the CIA that the fugitive was about five feet eight inches tall, while the Spaniard was over six feet.

349

That just left the missing Mr Henry Nash of London.

The secret police chief ordered his man in Cayenne to come home, and the man in Parbo to hunt through every car rental agency to find what kind of car the Londoner had rented, and its registration number.

By mid-morning the heat on the hills was intense. A few inches from the unmoving watcher's face a lizard with red, erect ruff behind its head, walking on stones that would fry an egg, stared at the stranger, detected no threat and scuttled on its way. There was activity out by the cliff-top derricks.

Four muscular young men wheeled a thirty-foot aluminium patrol boat to the rear of a Land Rover and hitched up. The LR towed the vessel to a petrol pump where it was fuelled. It could almost have passed for a leisure craft except for the .30 Browning machine gun mounted in the waist.

When the boat was ready for sea, it was towed beneath one of the derricks. Four webbing bands suspended from a rectangular frame ended in four tough steel cleats. These were fixed into strong-points on the boat's hull. With the crew on board, the patrol boat was lifted off the hard pad, swung out to sea and lowered to the ocean. Dexter saw it go out of sight.

Minutes later he saw it again out at sea. The men on board hauled up and emptied two fish traps and five lobster pots, rebaited them, threw them back and resumed their patrol.

Dexter had noted that everything in front of

him would collapse into ruin without two life-giving elixirs. One was gasoline, which would power the generator plant situated behind the warehouse of the dock. This would provide the electricity which itself would power every device and motor on the whole estate, from gate opening to power-drill to bedside light.

The other elixir was water, fresh, clean, clear water in a limitless supply. It came from the mountain stream that he had first seen in the aerial photographs.

That stream was now below him and slightly to his left. It bubbled out of the mountainside, having made its way from somewhere deep in the rainforests of the interior.

It emerged twenty feet above the peninsula, tumbled down several rock falls and then entered a concrete-sided channel that had clearly been created for it. From that point, Man took over from Nature.

To reach the farmland it had to flow under the runway below the hunter. Clearly strong, square culverts had been inserted below the runway when it was built. Emerging from below the runway on the other side, the now-marshalled water flowed under the chain-link fence as well. Dexter had little doubt there was an impenetrable grille there. Without a grille anyone could have slipped into the stream within the airfield, gone under the wire and used the gully and the flowing water to elude the wandering dogs. Whoever designed the defences would not have allowed that.

In the mid-morning two things happened right

below his eyrie. The Hawker 1000 was towed out of the hangar into the sun. Dexter feared it might be needed to fly the Serb somewhere, but it was only pulled from the hangar to make space. What followed was a small helicopter of the sort traffic police use to monitor flow. It could hover barely inches away from the rock-face if required, and he would have to be invisible to avoid being spotted. But it remained below him with its rotors folded while the engine was serviced.

The other thing was that a quad-bike came from the farm to the electric gate. Using a bleeper to open the gate, the man on the quad motored in, waved a cheery greeting to the mechanics on the apron and went up the runway to where the stream passed under it.

He stopped the quad, took a wicker basket from the back and looked down at the flowing water. Then he tossed several chicken carcasses into the water. He did this on the upstream side of the runway. Then he crossed the tarmac and looked down into the water again. The carcasses must have been carried by the flow to press up against the grille at the departure side.

Whatever was in that water between the escarpment and the grille, it ate meat. Dexter could only think of one fresh-water denizen of those parts that ate meat: the piranha. If it could eat hens, it could eat swimmers. It mattered not if the water touched the roof longer than he could hold his breath, it was already a three-hundred-yard-long piranha pool.

After the chain-link fence the stream ran away

through the estate, feeding a glittering tracery of irrigation channels. Other taps underground would duct some of the flow to the workers' village, the villas, the barracks and the master mansion.

The rest, having served all parts of the estate, curved back towards the farm end of the runway, there to tumble over the edge and into the sea.

By early afternoon the heat lay on the land like a great, heavy, suffocating blanket. Out on the estate the workers had toiled from seven until twelve. They were then allowed to find shade and eat what they had brought in their small cotton totebags. Until four they were allowed to make siesta before the last three hours' labour, from four to seven.

Dexter lay and panted, envying the salamander basking on a rock a yard away, immune to the heat. It was tempting to throw pints of precious water down his throat to achieve relief, but he knew it must be rationed to prevent dehydration, rather than poured down for pleasure.

At four the clang of the iron rail told the workers to go back to the fields and barns. Dexter struggled to the edge of his escarpment and watched the tiny figures in rough cotton shirts and pants, nut-brown faces hidden under straw sombreros, take up the hoe and mattock again to keep the model farm weed-free.

To his left a battered-looking pickup rolled to the space between the derricks and stopped, after reversing its rear towards the sea. A peon in bloodstained overalls hauled a long steel chute from the back, fixed it to the tailgate and with a pitchfork began to hoist something onto the steel slide. Whatever it was slithered off and fell into the sea. Dexter adjusted his focus. The next forkful gave the game away. It was a black hide with the bullock's head still attached.

Back in New York, examining the photos, he had been struck that even with the cliffs there was nevertheless no attempt to make an access to the beautiful blue sea. No steps down, no diving platform, no moored raft, no lido, no jetty. Seeing the offal go in, he understood why. The water round the whole peninsula would be alive with hammerheads, tigers and great whites. Anything swimming, other than a fish, would last a few minutes.

About that hour Colonel Moreno took a call on a cellphone from his man across the border in Surinam. The Englishman, Nash, had rented his car from a small private and local company, which is why it had taken so long to trace. But he had it at last. It was a Ford Compact. He dictated the number.

The secret policeman issued his order for the morning. Every car park, every garage, every driveway, every track to be scoured for a Ford Compact of this Surinamese registration number. Then changed his orders. Any Ford with any registration number was to be traced. Searching to start at dawn.

Dusk and dark come in the tropics with bewildering speed. The sun had passed behind Dexter's back an hour earlier, bringing relief at last. He watched the estate workers come home, dragging weary feet. They handed in their tools; they were checked through the double-gate one by one, in their five columns, two hundred per column.

They came back to the village to join the two hundred who had not gone to the fields. In the villas and the barracks the first lights came on. At the far end of the triangle a white glow revealed where the Serb's mansion was floodlit.

The mechanics on the airfield closed up and took their mopeds to ride to the villas at the far end of the runway. When all was fenced and locked the Dobermanns were released, the world said farewell to 6 September, and the manhunter prepared to go down the escarpment.

# 28

## The Visitor

In a day of peering over the edge of the escarpment, the Avenger had realized two things about it that had not shown up on his photographs. One was that it was not steep all the way down. The slope was perfectly climbable until about a hundred feet from the level plain, at which point it dropped sheer. But he had brought more than that length of good climbing rope.

The other was that the nudity of all weeds and shrubs was down to an act of Man, not of Nature. Someone, preparing the defences, had had teams of men come over the edge of the drop in rope cradles to rip every twig and shrub out of the crevices in the slope, so as to give no leaf-cover at all.

Where the saplings were slim enough to be entirely ripped out, they had been. But some had had a stem that was simply resistant to the pull of a man on a rope's end. These had been sawn off short. But not short enough. The stumps formed hundreds of hand-and-toe holds for a climber going down or up.

In daylight such a climber would have been instantly visible, but not in darkness.

By 10 p.m. the moon was up, a sickle moon, just

356

enough to give dim light to the climber, not enough to make him visible against the shale face. Only delicacy would be needed not to cause a rock-fall. Moving from stump to stump, Dexter began to ease his way down to the airfield below.

When the slope became too steep even for climbing, Dexter used the coiled rope around his shoulders to abseil the rest.

He spent three hours on the airfield. Years earlier another of his 'clients' from the Tombs in New York had taught him the gentlemanly art of picking locks and the set of picks he carried with him had been made by a master.

The padlock on the doors of the hangar he left alone. The double doors would have rumbled if they were rolled back. There was a smaller door to one side with a single Yale-type locking mechanism and it cost him no more than thirty seconds.

It takes a good mechanic to repair a helicopter, and an even better one to sabotage it in such a manner that a good mechanic could not find the fault and mend it, or even notice the tampering.

The mechanic the Serb employed to look after his helicopter was good, but Dexter was better. Up close he recognized the bird as an EC 120 Eurocopter, the single-engine version of the twin EC 135. It had a big Perspex bubble at the front end with excellent all-round, up-and-down observation for the pilot and the man beside him, plus room for three more behind them.

Dexter concentrated not on the main rotor mechanism but on the smaller tail rotor. If that malfunctioned, the chopper would simply not be fit to fly. By the time he had finished, it was certainly going to malfunction and be very hard to repair.

The door of the Hawker 1000 was open, so he had a chance to inspect the interior and ensure that the executive jet had had no serious internal reconfiguration.

When he locked up the main hangar he broke into the mechanics' store, took what he wanted but left no trace. Finally he jogged gently to the far end of the runway, close to the backs of the residential villas, and spent his last hour there. In the morning one of the mechanics would notice with irritation that someone had borrowed his bicycle from where it leaned against the back fence.

When he had done all he came to do, Dexter found his hanging rope and climbed back to the stout stump where it was tied. Beyond that, he climbed, moving from root to root until he was back in his eyrie. He was soaked to the point where he could have wrung the sweat from his clothes. He consoled himself with the thought that body odour was one thing no one was going to notice in that part of the world. To replace the moisture, he allowed himself a full pint of water, checked the level of the remaining liquid, and slept. The tiny alarm in his watch woke him at six in the morning, just before the iron bar began to clang against the hanging rail far below.

At seven, Paul Devereaux raised McBride in his room at the Camino Real hotel.

'Any news?' asked the man from Washington.

'None,' said McBride. 'It seems pretty sure he came back masquerading as an Englishman, Henry Nash, resort developer. Then he vaporized. His car has been identified as a rented Ford Compact from Surinam. Moreno is starting a countrywide trawl for any Ford about now. Should have news sometime today.'

There was a long pause from the Counter-Terrorist Chief, still sitting in a robe in his breakfast room in Alexandria, Virginia, before leaving for Langley.

'Not good enough,' said Devereaux. 'I'm going to have to alert our friend. It will not be an easy call. I'll wait till ten. If there is any news of a capture or imminent capture before then, call me at once.'

'You got it,' said McBride.

There was no such news. At ten Devereaux made his call. It took ten minutes for the Serb to be summoned from the swimming pool to the radio shack, a small room in his basement which, despite its traditional name, was no shack and contained some highly modern and eavesdrop-free communications equipment.

At half past ten Avenger noticed a flurry of activity on the estate below him. Off-roads streamed from the mansion on the foreland, leaving trails of dust behind them. Below him the EC 120 was wheeled out of the hangar and its main rotors spread and locked into flying mode.

'Someone,' he mused, 'appears to have lit the blue touchpaper.'

The helicopter crew arrived from their homes

at the end of the runway on two motor scooters. Within minutes they were at the controls and the big rotors began slowly to turn. The engine kicked into life and the rotor rate rapidly increased to warm-up speed.

The tail rotor, vital to stop the whole machine from spinning round its own main axis, was also whirring round. Then something in its core bearings seemed to snag. There was a grinding of suffering metal and the spinning hub destroyed itself. A mechanic waved frantically to the two men inside the Perspex bubble and drew his hand across his throat.

The pilot and observer had been told by the instrument panel that they had a major bearing failure in the tail. They closed down. The main rotors ground to a halt and the crew climbed back out. A group formed round the tail, staring upwards at the damaged prop.

Uniformed guards poured into the village of the absent peons and began to search the cabanas, stores, even the church. Others, on quads, went off across the estate to spread the word to the gang-masters to keep an eye open for any signs of an intruder. There were none. Such signs as there had been eight hours earlier had been too well disguised.

Dexter put the uniformed guards at around one hundred. There was a community of about a dozen on the airfield, and the twelve hundred workers. Given more security personnel, plus domestic staff out of sight in the grounds of the mansion and twenty more technicians at the generating station and various repair shops,

Dexter now had an idea how many he was up against. And he still had not seen the mansion itself and its no doubt complex defences.

Just before midday Paul Devereaux called his man in the storm centre.

'Kevin, you have to go over and visit with our friend. I have spoken to him. He is in a high state of temper. I cannot stress enough how vital it is that this wretch plays his part in Project Peregrine. He must not butt out now. One day I'll be able to tell you how vital he is. For the moment, stand by him until the intruder is caught and neutralized. Apparently his helicopter is malfunctioning. Ask the colonel for a jeep to get you over the sierra. Call me when you get there.'

At midday Dexter watched a small coaster approach the cliffs. Holding station in the water just clear of the rocks, the freighter discharged crates from its deck and holds, which the derricks hoisted to the concrete apron where flat-back pickups awaited them. Clearly they were for those luxuries the hacienda could not produce.

The last item was a thousand-gallon fuel tank, an aluminium canister the size of a fuel tanker. An empty one was lowered to the boat's deck, and it steamed away across the blue ocean.

Just after one o'clock, below him and to his right, an off-road, having been checked through the guardhouse in the defile, grunted and coughed down the track to the village. It was in San Martin police markings, with a passenger beside the driver.

Traversing the village, the blue Land Rover came to the chain-link gates and stopped. The police driver descended to offer his ID to the guards manning it. They made a phone call, presumably to the mansion for clearance.

In the pause, the man in the passenger seat also descended and gazed around with curiosity. He turned to look back at the sierra he had just descended. High above, a pair of binoculars adjusted and settled on his face.

Like the unseen man above him on the crest, Kevin McBride was impressed. He had been with Paul Devereaux in the heart of Project Peregrine for two years, right through the first contact and recruitment of the Serbian. He had seen the files, knew, he thought, everything there was to know about him, yet they had never met. Devereaux had always reserved that dubious pleasure for himself.

The blue-liveried police jeep drove towards the high defending wall of the foreland compound, which towered over them as they approached the gate.

A small door in the gate opened and a burly man in slacks and sea island cotton shirt stepped out. The shirt flapped over the waistband, and for a reason. It obscured the Glock 9mm. McBride recognized him from the file: Kulac, the only one the Serb gangster had brought from Belgrade with him, his perpetual bodyguard.

The man approached the passenger door and beckoned. After two years away from home he still spoke not a word but Serbo-Croat.

'Muchas gracias. Adios,' said McBride to his

362

police driver. The man nodded, keen to get back to the capital.

Inside the giant timber gates, made of beams the size of rail sleepers and machine-operated, was a table. McBride was expertly frisked for concealed weapons, then his handgrip was searched on the table. A white-starched butler descended from an upper terrace and waited until the precautions were complete.

Kulac grunted that he was satisfied. With the butler in the lead, carrying the grip, the three went up the steps. McBride got his first real glimpse of the mansion.

It was three storeys tall, set in manicured lawns. Two peons in white tunics could be seen at a distance, intent on their gardening. The house was not unlike some of the more luxurious residences seen along the French, Italian and Croatian Rivieras, each upper room balconied but steel-shuttered against the heat.

The flagged patio on which they stood may have been several feet above the base of the gate they had entered, but it was still below the top of the protective wall. One could see over the wall to the cordillera through which McBride had come, but no sniper in the near ground was going to be able to fire over the wall to hit someone on the terrace.

Set into the patio was a gleaming blue swimming pool, and beside the pool a large table of white Carrara marble on stone supports was set for lunch. Silver and crystal glittered.

To one side a cluster of easy chairs surrounded a table on which an ice bucket played host to a bottle of Dom Perignon. The butler gestured that McBride should sit. The bodyguard remained upright and alert. From the deep shade of the villa a man emerged in white slacks and cream silk safari shirt.

McBride hardly recognized the man who had once been Zoran Zilic, gang enforcer from Zemun district, Belgrade, mobster of a dozen underworld rackets in Germany and Sweden, killer in the Bosnian war, runner of prostitutes, drugs and arms out of Belgrade, embezzler of the Yugoslav treasury and eventual fugitive from justice.

The new face bore little resemblance to the one in the CIA file. That spring the Swiss surgeons had done a good job. The Baltic pallor was replaced by a tropical tan, and only the fine white lines of scars refused to darken.

But McBride had once been told that ears, like fingerprints, were totally distinctive to each human being and, short of surgery, never change. Zilic's ears were the same, and his fingerprints, and when they shook hands McBride noticed the hazel, wild-animal eyes.

Zilic sat at the marble table and nodded to the only other vacant setting. McBride sat. There was a rapid exchange in Serbo-Croat between Zilic and the bodyguard. The muscular thug ambled away to eat somewhere else.

A very young and pretty Martino girl in a blue maid's uniform filled two flutes of champagne. Zilic proposed no toast; he studied the amber liquid, then downed it without pause.

'This man,' he said in good if not flawless

English, 'who is he?'

'We do not exactly know. He is a private contractor. Very secretive. Known only by his own chosen codename.'

'And what is that?'

'The Avenger.'

The Serb considered the word, then shrugged. Two more girls began to serve the meal. There were quail egg tartlets and asparagus in melted butter.

'All made on the estate?' asked McBride.

Zilic nodded.

'Bread, salads, eggs, milk, olive oil, grapes . . . I saw them all as we drove through.'

Another nod.

'Why does he come after me?' asked the Serb.

McBride thought. If he gave the real reason the Serb might decide there was no point in further cooperation with the USA or any part of its establishment on the grounds they would never forgive him anyway. His charge from Devereaux was to keep the loathsome creature inside the Peregrine team.

'We do not know,' he said. 'Contracted by somebody else. Perhaps an old enemy from Yugoslavia.'

Zilic thought it through then shook his head.

'Why did you leave it so late, Mr McBride?'

'We knew nothing of this man until you complained of the aeroplane flying over your estate and taking pictures. You took the registration number. Fine. Then you sent men to Guyana to intervene. Mr Devereaux thought we could find the interloper, identify him and stop him. He slipped through the net.'

The lobsters were cold in mayonnaise, also from local ingredients. To round off there were Muscat grapes and peaches, with strong black coffee. The butler offered Cohibas and waited until both were drawing well before leaving. The Serb seemed lost in thought.

The three pretty waitresses were lined up against the wall of the house. Zilic turned in his chair, pointed at one and snapped his fingers. The girl went pale but turned and entered the house, presumably to prepare herself for her master's arrival. 'I take a siesta at this hour. It is a local custom and quite a good one. Before I leave, let me tell you something. I designed this fortress with Major van Rensberg, whom you will meet. I regard it as probably the safest place on earth.

'I do not believe your mercenary will even be able to get in here. If he does, he will never leave alive. The security systems here have been tested. This man may have got past you; he will not get past my systems and near to me. While I enjoy my rest, Van Rensberg will show you round. Then you can tell Mr Devereaux his crisis is over. Until later.'

He rose and left the table. McBride stayed on. Below the terrace the door in the main gate opened and a man walked up the steps to the flagstones. McBride knew him from the files, but pretended not to.

Adriaan van Rensberg was another man with a history. During the period when the National Party and its apartheid policies ruled South

Africa, he had been an eager recruit to the Bureau of State Security, the dreaded BOSS, and had risen through the ranks due to his dedication to the extreme forms of that body's excesses.

After the arrival of Nelson Mandela, he had joined the extreme-right AWB party led by Eugene Terre-Blanche, and when that collapsed he thought it would be wiser to flee the country. After several years hiring his services as steward and security expert to a number of European fascist factions, he had caught the eye of Zoran Zilic and landed the plum job of devising, designing, building and commanding the fortress hacienda of El Punto.

Unlike Colonel Moreno, the South African's size was not down to fat but muscled bulk. Only the belly folding over the broad leather belt betrayed a taste for beer and plenty of it.

McBride noted that he had designed himself a uniform for the part: combat boots, jungle camouflage, leopardskin-ringed bush hat and flattering insignia.

'Mr McBride? The American gentleman?'

'That's me, pal.'

'Major van Rensberg, Head of Security. I am instructed to give you a tour of the estate. Shall we say tomorrow morning? Eight thirty?'

In the car park at the resort of La Bahia one of the policemen found the Ford. The plates were local, but forged and made up in a garage elsewhere. The manual in the glove compartment was in Dutch. As in Surinam.

Much later someone recalled seeing a

backpacker with a large camouflaged Bergen haversack, trekking away from the resort on foot. He was heading east. Colonel Moreno called back his entire police force and the army to their barracks. In the morning, he said, they would climb and sweep the cordillera from the landward side; from the road to the crest.

# 29

## The Tour

It was the second sunset and fall of darkness that Dexter had witnessed from his invisible lying-up position on the peak of the sierra, and it would be his last.

Still motionless, he watched the last lights snuff in the windows of the peninsula below him, then prepared to move. They rose early down there, and slept early. For him there would be, again, precious little sleep.

He feasted off the last of his field rations, packing down two days' supply of vitamins and minerals, fibre and sugar. He was able to finish off the last of his water, giving his body a reservoir for the next twenty-four hours. The big Bergen, the scrim netting and raincape could be abandoned. What he needed he had either brought with him or stolen the previous night. They all fitted into a smaller backpack. Only the coiled rope across his shoulders would remain bulky and would have to be hidden where it would not be found.

It was past midnight when he made what remained of his encampment as invisible as possible and left it.

Using a branch to brush out the tracks left by his own feet, he worked his way slowly to his right until he was over the labourers' village rather than the airfield. It took him half a mile and cost an hour. But he timed it right. The sickle moon rose. The sweat began to soak his clothes again.

He made his way slowly and carefully down the scarp, from handhold to handhold, stump to stump, root to root, until he needed the rope. This time he had to double it and hang the loop over a smooth root where it would not snag when he pulled from below.

He abseiled the rest, avoiding athletic leaps which might dislodge pebbles, but simply walking backwards, pace by pace, until he arrived in the cleft between the cliffs and the rear of the church. He hoped the priest was a good sleeper; he was only a few yards from his house.

He tugged gently on one strand of the double rope. The other slipped over the stump high up the face and at last cascaded down around him. He coiled it round his shoulder and left the shadows of the church.

Latrine facilities were communal and single-sex. There were no women in the labour camp. He had watched the men at their ablutions from above. The basis of the latrine was a long trench covered by boards to mask the inevitable stench, or at least the worst of it. In the boards were circular holes covered by circular lids. There was no concession to modesty. Taking a deep breath, Dexter lifted one of the lids and dropped his coiled rope into the black interior. With luck, it would simply disappear for ever, even if it were searched for, which was extremely unlikely.

The hutments in which the men lived and slept were small squares, little more than a police cell, but each worker had one to himself. They were in rows of fifty, facing another fifty and thus forming a street. Each group of one hundred ran outwards from a main highway, and that was the residential section.

The main road led to the square, flanked by the washing units, the kitchens and the thatch-topped refectory tables. Avoiding the moonlight of the main square, sticking to the shadows of the buildings, Dexter returned to the church. The lock on the main door detained him for no more than a few minutes.

There was not much to it, as churches go, but for those running the labour camp it was a wise precaution to provide a safety valve in this deeply Catholic country. Dexter wondered idly how the resident priest would square his job with his creed.

He found what he wanted at the far back, behind the altar and to one side, in the vestry. Leaving the main door unlocked, he went back to the rows of huts where the workers snored away their few hours of repose.

From above, he had memorized the location of the cabin he wanted. He had seen the man emerge for his breakfast. Fifth cabin down, left-hand side, third street off the main road after the plaza.

There was no lock; just a simple wooden latch. Dexter stepped inside and froze motionless to accustom his eyes to the almost complete darkness after the pale moonlight outside.

The hunched figure on the bunk snored on. Three minutes later, with complete night vision, Dexter could see the low hump under the coarse blanket. He crouched to remove something from his knapsack, then went towards the bed. The sweet odour of chloroform came up to him from the soaked pad in his hand.

The peon grunted once, tried to roll from side to side for a few seconds, then lapsed into deeper sleep. Dexter kept the pad in place to ensure hours of insensibility. When he was ready, he hefted the sleeping man over his shoulder in a fireman's lift and flitted silently back the way he had come, to the church.

In the doorway of the coral-stone building he stopped again and waited to hear if he had disturbed anyone, but the village slept on. When he found the vestry again he used stout masking tape to bind the peon's feet and ankles, and to cover the mouth, while leaving the nose free to breathe.

As he relocked the main door he glanced with satisfaction at the notice beside it on the blackboard. The notice was a lucky 'plus'.

Back in the empty shack he risked a pen light to examine the labourer's worldly possessions. They were not many. There was a portrait of the Virgin on one wall and stuck into the frame a faded photo of a smiling young woman. Fiancée, sister, daughter? Through powerful binoculars the man had looked about Dexter's age, but he might have been younger. Those caught up in Colonel Moreno's penal system and sent to El Punto would age fast. Certainly he was of the same height and build, which was why Dexter had picked him.

No other wall decorations; just pegs on which hung two sets of work clothes, both identical — coarse cotton trousers and a shirt of the same material. On the floor a pair of rope-soled espadrilles, stained and worn but tough and reliable. Other than that, a sombrero of plaited straw completed the work clothes. There was a canvas bag with drawstring for carrying lunch to the plantation. Dexter snapped off his torch and checked his watch. Five past four.

He stripped down to boxer shorts, selected the items he wanted to take with him, wrapped them in his sweaty T-shirt and bundled them into the lunch bag. The rest he would have to lose. This surplus was rolled into the knapsack, and disposed of during a second visit to the latrines. Then he waited for the clang of the iron bar on the hanging length of railway track.

It came as ever at half past six, still dark but with a hint of pink in the east. The duty guard, standing outside the village just beyond the chain-link double-gates of the farmland, was the source. All around Dexter the village began to come to life.

He avoided the run to the latrines and wash-troughs and hoped no one would notice. After twenty minutes, peering through a slit in the boards of the door, he saw that his alley was empty again. Chin down, sombrero tilted forward, he scurried to the latrines, one figure in sandals, pants and shirt among a thousand.

He crouched over an open hole while the

others took their breakfast. Only when the third clang summoned the workers to the access gate did he join the queue.

The five checkers sat at their tables, examined the dog tags, checked the work manifests, punched the number into the records of those admitted that morning, and to which labour gang assigned, and waved the labourer through, to join his gang-master and be led away to collect tools and start the allocated tasks.

Dexter reached the table attending to his queue, offered his dog tag between forefinger and thumb, like the others, leaned forward and coughed. The checker pulled his face away sharply to one side, noted the tag number and waved him away. The last thing the man wanted was a face full of chilli odour. The new recruit shuffled off to draw his hoe; the assigned task was weeding the avocado groves.

At half past seven Kevin McBride breakfasted alone on the terrace. The grapefruit, eggs, toast and plum jam would have done credit to any five-star hotel. At eight fifteen the Serb joined him.

'I think it would be wise for you to pack your grip,' he said. 'When you have seen what Major van Rensberg will show you, I hope you will agree this mercenary has a one per cent chance of getting here, even less of getting near me, and none of getting out again. There is no point in your staying. You may tell Mr Devereaux that I will complete my part of our arrangement, as agreed, at the end of the month.'

At eight thirty McBride threw his grip into the

rear of the South African's open jeep and climbed in beside the major.

'So, what do you want to see?' asked the Head of Security.

'I am told it is virtually impossible for an unwanted visitor to get in here at all. Can you tell me why?'

'Look, Mr McBride, when I designed all this I created two things. One, it is an almost completely self-sufficient farming paradise. Everything is here. Second, it is a fortress, a sanctuary, a refuge, safe from almost all outside invasion or threat.

'Now, of course, if you are talking about a full military operation, paratroopers, armour, of course it could be invaded. But one mercenary, acting alone? Never.'

'How about arrival by sea?'

'Let me show you.'

Van Rensberg let in the clutch and they set off, leaving a plume of rising dust behind them. The South African pulled over and stopped near a cliff edge.

'You can see from here,' he said as they climbed out. 'The whole estate is surrounded by sea, at no point less than twenty feet below the cliff top, in most areas fifty feet. Sea-scanning radar, disguised as TV dishes, warn us of anything approaching by sea.'

'Interception?'

'Two fast patrol boats, one at sea at all times. There is a one-mile limit of forbidden water round the whole peninsula. Only the occasional delivery freighter is allowed in.'

'Underwater entry? Amphibious special forces?' Van Rensberg snorted derisively.

'A special force of one? Let me show you what would happen.'

He took his walkie-talkie, called the radio basement and was patched through to the slaughterhouse. The rendezvous was across the estate, near the derricks. McBride watched a bucket of offal go down the slide and drop to the sea thirty feet below.

For several seconds there was no reaction. Then the first scimitar fin sliced the surface. Within sixty seconds there was a feeding frenzy. Van Rensberg laughed.

'We eat well here. Plenty of steak. My employer does not eat steak, but the guards do. Many of them, like me, are from the old country and we like our braai.'

'So?'

'When a beast is slaughtered, lamb, goat, pig, steer, about once a week, the fresh offal is thrown into the ocean. And the blood. That sea is alive with sharks. Blacktip, whitefin, tiger, giant hammerhead, they're all there. Last month one of my men fell overboard. The boat swerved back to pick him up. They were there in thirty seconds. Too late.'

'He didn't come out of the water?'

'Most of him did. But not his legs. He died two days later.'

'Burial?'

'Out there.'

'So the sharks got him after all.'

'No one makes mistakes around here. Not

with Adriaan van Rensberg in charge.'

'What about crossing the sierra, the way I came in yesterday?'

For answer van Rensberg handed McBride a pair of field glasses.

'Have a look at it. You cannot climb round the edges of it. It's sheer to the water. Come down the escarpment in daylight and you'll be seen in seconds.'

'But at night?'

'So, you reach the bottom. Your man is outside the razor wire, over two miles from the mansion and outside the wall. He is not a peon, not a guard; he is quickly spotted and . . . taken care of.'

'What about the stream I saw? Could one come in down the stream?'

'Good thinking, Mr McBride. Let me show you the stream.'

Van Rensberg drove to the airfield, entered with his own bleeper for the chain-link gate and motored to where the stream from the hills ran under the runway. They dismounted. There was a long patch of water open to the sky between the runway and the fence. The clear water ran gently over grasses and weeds on the bottom.

'See anything?'

'Nope,' said McBride.

'They're in the cool, in the shade, under the runway.'

It was clearly the South African's party piece. He kept a small supply of beef jerky in the jeep. When he tossed a piece in, the water seethed. McBride saw the piranha sweep out of the shadow and the cigarette-pack-sized piece of beef was shredded by a myriad needle teeth.

'Enough? I'll show you how we husband the water supply here and never lose security. Come.'

Back in the farmland, van Rensberg followed the stream for most of its meandering course through the estate. At a dozen points, spurs had been taken off the main current to irrigate various crops or top up different storage ponds, but they were always blind alleys.

The main stream curved hither and yon, but eventually came back to the cliff edge near the runway but beyond the wire. There it increased in speed and rushed over the cliff into the sea.

'Right near the edge I have a plate of spikes buried,' said van Rensberg. 'Anyone trying to swim through here will be taken by the current and swept along, out of control, between smooth walls of concrete, towards the sea. Passing over the spikes the helpless swimmer will enter the sea bleeding badly. Then what? Sharks, of course.'

'But at night?'

'Ah, you have not seen the dogs? A pack of twelve. Dobermanns and deadly. They are trained not to touch anyone in the uniform of the estate guards, and another dozen of the senior personnel no matter how dressed. It is a question of personal odour.

'They are released at sundown. After that every peon and every stranger has to remain outside the wire or survive for a few minutes until the roaming dogs find him. After that there is no chance for him. So, this mercenary of yours. What is he going to do?'

'I haven't the faintest idea. If he's got any sense, I guess he's gone by now.'

Van Rensberg laughed again.

'Very sensible of him. You know, back in the old country, up in the Caprivi Strip, we had a camp for mundts who were causing a lot of trouble in the townships. I was in charge of it. And you know what, Mr CIA-man? I never lost a single kaffir. Not one. By which I mean, no escapers. Never.'

'Impressive, I'm sure.'

'And you know what I used? Landmines? No. Searchlights? No. Two concentric rings of chain-link fencing, buried six feet deep, razor-topped, and between the rings wild animals. Crocs in the ponds, lions in the grassland. One covered tunnel in and out. I love Mother Nature.'

He checked his watch.

'Eleven o'clock. I'll drive you up the track to our guardhouse in the gap in the hills. The San Martin police will send a jeep to meet you there and take you back to your hotel.'

They were motoring back across the estate from the coast to the gate giving access to the village and the climbing track when the major's communicator crackled. He listened to the message from the duty telephone/radio operator in the cellar beneath the mansion. It pleased him. He switched off and pointed to the crest of the sierra.

'Colonel Moreno's men scoured the jungle

this morning, from the road to the crest. They've found the American's camp. Abandoned. You could be right. I think he's seen enough and chickened out.'

In the distance McBride could see the great double gate and beyond it the white of the buildings of the worker village.

'Tell me about the labourers, major.'

'What about them?'

'How many? How do you get them?'

'About twelve hundred. They are all offenders: within San Martin's penal system. Now, don't get holier-than-thou, Mr McBride. You Americans have prison farms. So this is a prison farm. Considering all things they live pretty well here.'

'And if they have served their sentences, when do they go back home?'

'They don't,' said van Rensberg.

A one-way ticket, thought the American, courtesy of Colonel Moreno and Major van Rensberg. A life sentence. For what offences? Jay-walking? Litter? Moreno would have to keep the numbers up. On demand.

'What about guards and mansion staff?'

'That's different. We are employed. Everyone needed inside the mansion wall lives there. Everybody stays inside when our employer is in residence. Only uniformed guards and a few senior staff like me can pass through the wall. Never a peon. Pool cleaners, gardeners, waiters, maids — all live inside the wall. The peons who labour on the estate, they live in their township. They are all single men.'

'No women, no children?'

'None. They are not here to breed. But there is a church. The priest preaches one text only — absolute obedience.'

He forbore to mention that for lack of obedience he retained the use of his rhino-hide sjambok whip as in the old days.

'Could a stranger come into the estate posing as part of the workforce, major?'

'No. Every evening the workforce for the next day is selected by the estate manager who goes to the village. Those selected walk to the main gate and report at sunrise, after breakfast. They are checked through one by one. So many desired, so many admitted. Not a single one more.'

'How many come through?'

'About a thousand a day. Two hundred with some technical skill for the repair shops, mill, bakery, slaughterhouse, tractor shed; eight hundred for hacking and weeding. About two hundred remain behind each day. The genuinely sick, garbage crews, cooks.'

'I think I believe you,' said McBride. 'This loner doesn't have a chance, does he?'

'Told you so, Mr CIA-man. He's chickened out.'

He had hardly finished when the communicator crackled again. His brow furrowed as he listened to the report.

'What kind of flap? Well, tell him to calm down. I'll be there in five minutes.'

He replaced the set.

'Father Vicente, at the church. In some kind of a panic. I'll have to drive by on our way to the mountains. A delay of a few minutes no doubt.'

On their left they passed a row of peons, aching backs bent over mattocks and hoes in the raging heat. Some heads lifted briefly to watch the passing vehicle bearing the man who had power of life and death over them. Gaunt, stubbled faces, coffee-brown eyes under straw brims. But one pair of eyes was blue.

# 30

## The Bluff

He was hopping up and down at the top of the church steps by the open door, a short tubby man with porcine eyes and a none-too-clean white soutane. Father Vicente, pastoral shepherd of the wretched forced labourers.

Van Rensberg's Spanish was extremely basic and habitually only expressed abrupt commands; that of the priest attempting English was not much better.

'Come queek, coronel,' he said and darted back inside. The two men dismounted, ran up the steps and followed him.

The soiled cassock swept down the aisle, past the altar and on to the vestry. It was a tiny room, its main feature a wall cupboard of basic carpentry, assembled and screwed to the wall to contain his vestments. With a theatrical gesture he threw the door open and cried: 'Mira.'

They looked. The peon was still exactly as Father Vicente had found him. No attempt had been made to release him. His wrists were firmly bound with tape in front of him; his ankles the same; a broad band of tape covered his mouth, from behind which came protesting mumbles. Seeing van Rensberg, his eyes indicated that he was terrified.

The South African leaned forward and tore away the gag without ceremony.

'What the hell is he doing here?'

There was a babble of terrified explanation from the man, and an expressive shrug from the priest.

'He says he not know. He says he go to sleep last night, he wake up in here. He has headache, he remember nothing more.'

The man was naked but for a pair of skimpy shorts. There was nothing for the South African to grab but the man's upper arms, so he seized these and brought the peon to his feet.

'Tell him he'd better start remembering,' he shouted at the priest, who translated.

'Major,' said McBride quietly, 'first things first. What about a name?'

Father Vicente caught the sense.

'He is called Ramon.'

'Ramon what?'

The priest shrugged. He had over a thousand parishioners; was he supposed to remember them all?

'Which cabin does he come from?' asked the American.

There was another rapid interchange of local Spanish. McBride could decipher written Spanish slowly, but the local San Martin patois was nothing like Castilian.

'It is three hundred metres from here,' said the priest.

'Shall we go and look?' said McBride. He produced a penknife and cut the tape from Ramon's wrists and ankles. The intimidated

384

worker led the major and the American across the plaza, down the main street and thence to his alley. He pointed to his door and stood back.

Van Rensberg went in, followed by McBride. There was nothing to find, save one small item which the American discovered under the bed. It was a pad of compressed cotton wool. He sniffed it and handed it to the major, who did the same.

'Chloroform,' said McBride. 'He was knocked out in his sleep. Probably never felt a thing. Woke up bound hand and foot, locked in a cupboard. He's not lying, just bewildered and terrified.'

'So what the hell was that for?'

'Didn't you mention dog tags on each man, checked when they went through the gate to work?'

'Yes. Why?'

'Ramon isn't wearing one. And it's not here on the floor. Somewhere in there I think you have a ringer.'

It sank in. Van Rensberg strode back to the Land Rover in the square and unhooked the walkie-talkie on the dash.

'This is an emergency,' he told the radio operator who answered. 'Sound the 'escaped prisoner' siren. Seal the gate of the mansion to everyone except me. Then use the PA to tell every guard on the estate, on or off duty, to report to me at the main gate.'

Seconds later the long, wailing sound of the siren rolled over the peninsula. It was heard in field and barn, shed and orchard, kitchen garden and pigsty.

Everyone out there raised their head from

what they were doing to stare towards the main gate. When their undivided attention had been secured, the voice of the radio operator in the basement beneath the mansion was heard.

'All guards to main gate. Repeat, all guards to main gate. On the double.'

There were over sixty on day shift and the rest on lay-over in their barracks. From the fields, riding quad-bikes from the farthest reaches, jogging on foot from the barracks a quarter of a mile from the main gate, they converged in response to the emergency.

Van Rensberg took his off-road back through the gate and waited for them, standing on the bonnet, bullhorn in hand.

'We don't have an escape,' he told them when they stood in front of him. 'We have the reverse. We have an intruder. Now, he's masquerading as a labourer. Same clothes, same sandals, same sombrero. He's even got a stolen dog tag. Day shift: round up and bring in every single labourer. No exceptions. Off-duty shift, search every barn, cowshed, stable, workshop. Then seal and mount guard. Use your communicators to stay in touch with squad commanders. Junior leaders, stay in touch with me. Now get to it. Anyone in prisoner uniform seen running away, shoot on sight. Now go.'

The hundred men began to fan out over the estate. They had the mid-section to cover: from the chain-link fence separating the village and airfield from the farmland, up to the mansion wall. A big territory; too big even for a hundred men. And it would take hours.

Van Rensberg had forgotten that McBride was leaving. He ignored the American, busy with his own planning. McBride sat and puzzled.

There was a notice by the church, right next to the door. It said: 'Obsequias por nuestro hermano Pedro Hernandez. Once de la mañana.'

Even with his laboured Spanish, the CIA man could work out that meant: 'Funeral service for our brother Pedro Hernandez. Eleven in the morning.'

Did the manhunter not see it? Could he not work out the sense? It would be reasonable that the priest would not normally visit his vestry until Sunday. But today was different. At exactly ten to eleven he would open his vestry cupboard and see the prisoner.

Why not dump him somewhere else? Why not tape him to his own cot where no one would find him till sundown, or not even then?

He found the major speaking to the airfield mechanics.

'What's wrong with it? Sod the tail rotor. I need it back up in the air. Well, hurry it up.'

He flicked off his machine, listened to McBride, glared and snapped: 'Your fellow countryman simply made a mistake, that is all. An expensive mistake. It's going to cost him his life.'

An hour passed. Even without field glasses McBride could see the first columns of white-cotton-clad workers being force-marched back to the double-gates to their village. Beside the lines of men the uniformed guards were shouting them on. Midday. The heat was a

387

hammer on the back of the head.

The milling crowd of men in front of the gates grew even bigger. The chitchat on the radio never stopped, as sector after sector of estate was cleared of workers, its buildings searched, declared clear, sealed and manned from inside.

At half past one the number-checking began. Van Rensberg insisted on the five checkers resuming their places behind the tables and passing the workers through, one after another, two hundred per column.

The men normally worked in the cool of the dawn or the evening. They were baking alive in the heat. Two or three peons fainted and were helped through by friends. Every tag was checked until its number matched one passed through that same morning. When the last white-bloused figure stumbled towards the village, rest, shade and water, the senior checker nodded.

'One missing,' he called. Van Rensberg walked to his desk to peer over his shoulder.

'Number five-three-one-oh-eight.'

'Name?'

'Ramon Gutierrez.'

'Release the dogs.'

Van Rensberg strolled across to McBride.

'Every single technician must by now be inside, locked in and guarded. The dogs will never touch my men, you know. They recognize the uniform. That leaves one man out there. A stranger, white cotton pants and floppy shirt, wrong smell. It's like a lunch bell to the Dobermanns. Up a tree? In a pond? They'll still find him. Then they will surround him and bay until the handlers come. I give this mercenary half an hour to get up a tree and surrender, or die.'

The man he sought was in the middle of the estate, running lightly between rows of maize higher than his own head. He judged by the sun and crests of the sierra the direction of his run.

It had taken two hours of steady jogging earlier in the morning to bring him from his allotted work patch to the base of the mansion's protective wall. Not that the distance was a problem for a man accustomed to half a marathon, but he had to dodge the other work parties and the guards. He was still dodging.

He came to a track across the maize field, dropped to his belly and peered out. Down the track, two guards on a quad-bike roared away in the direction of the main gate. He waited till they were round a corner, then sprinted across the track and was lost in a peach orchard. His study of the layout of the estate from above had given him a route that would take him from where he had started near the mansion wall to where he wanted to be, without ever crossing a knee-high crop.

The equipment he had brought in that morning, either in his supposed lunch bag or inside the tight Y-front underpants he wore beneath the boxer shorts, was almost expended. The tough dive-watch was back on his wrist, his belt round his waist and his knife up against the small of the back, out of the way but easy to reach. The bandage, sticky plaster and the rest were in the flat pouch forming part of his belt.

He checked the peaks of the hills again, altered course by a few degrees and stopped, tilting his head until he heard the gurgle of the flowing water ahead. He came to the stream's edge, backtracked fifteen yards, then stripped to the buff, retaining only belt, knife and Y-fronts.

Across the crops, in the dull, numbing heat, he heard the first baying of the hounds pounding towards him. What little off-sea breeze there was would take his odour to the muzzles of the hounds in a few more minutes.

He worked carefully but fast, until he was satisfied, then tip-toed away towards the stream, slipped into the cool water and began to let the current take him, slanting across the estate towards the airfield and the cliff.

Despite his assertion that the killer dogs would never touch him, van Rensberg had wound all the windows up as he drove slowly down one of the main avenues from the gate into the heartland.

Behind him came the deputy dog-handler at the wheel of a truck with a completely enclosed rear made of steel-wire mesh. The senior handler was beside him in the Land Rover, head stuck out on the passenger side. It was he who heard the sudden change in pitch of his hounds' baying, from deep-throated bark to excited yelping.

'They have found something,' he shouted.

Van Rensberg grinned.

'Where, man, where?'

'Over there.'

McBride crouched in the rear, glad of the walls and windows of the Land Rover Defender. He did not like savage dogs, and for him twelve was a dozen too much.

The dogs had found something all right, but their yelping was more from pain than excitement. The South African came upon the entire pack after swerving round the corner of a peach orchard. They were milling around the centre of the track. A bundle of bloody clothes was the object of their attention.

'Get them into the truck,' shouted van Rensberg. The senior handler got down, closed the door and whistled his pack to order. Without protest, still yelping, they bounded into the rear of the dog-lorry and were locked in. Only then did van Rensberg and McBride descend.

'So, this is where they caught him,' said van Rensberg.

The handler, still puzzled by the behaviour of his pack, scooped up the bloodstained cotton blouse and held it to his nose. Then he jerked his face away.

'Bloody man,' he screamed. 'Chilli powder, fine-ground green chilli powder. It's stiff with the stuff. No wonder the poor bastards are screaming. That's not excitement. They're in pain.'

'When will their muzzles work again?'

'Well, not today, boss, maybe not tomorrow.'

They found the cotton pants, also impregnated with chilli powder, and the straw hat, even the canvas espadrilles. But no body, no bones, nothing but the stains on the shirt.

'What did he do here?' van Rensberg asked the handler.

'He cut himself, that's what the swine did. He cut himself with a knife, then bled over the shirt. He knew that would drive the dogs crazy. Man-blood always does when they're on a kill patrol. So they would smell the blood, worry the fabric and inhale the chilli. We have no tracker dogs until tomorrow.'

Van Rensberg counted up the items of clothing.

'He also stripped off,' he said. 'We're looking for someone stark naked.'

'Maybe not,' said McBride.

The South African had kitted out his force along military lines. They all wore the same uniform. Into canvas mid-calf combat boots they tucked khaki drill trousers. Each had a broad leather belt with a buckle.

Above the waist each man had a shirt in the pale African-bush camouflage known as 'leopard'. Sleeves were cut at the mid-forearm, then rolled up to the bicep and ironed flat.

One or two inverted chevrons indicated corporal or sergeant, while the four junior officers had cloth 'pips' on the epaulettes of their shirts.

What McBride had discovered, snagged on a thorn near the path where evidently a struggle must have taken place, was an epaulette, ripped off a shirt. It had no pips.

'I don't think our man is naked at all,' said McBride. 'I think he's wearing a camouflage shirt, minus one epaulette, khaki drill pants and combat boots. Not to mention a bush hat like yours, major.'

Van Rensberg was the colour of raw terracotta. But the evidence told its own story. Two scars along the grit showed where a pair of heels had apparently been dragged through the long grass. At the end of the trail was the stream.

'Throw a body in there,' muttered the major, 'it'll be over the cliff edge by now.'

And we all know how you love your sharks, thought McBride, but said nothing.

The full enormity of his predicament sank into van Rensberg's mind. Somewhere, on a six-thousand-acre estate, with access to weapons and a quad-bike, face shaded by a broad-brimmed bush hat, was a professional mercenary contracted, so he presumed, to blow his employer's head off. He said something in Afrikaans and it was not nice. Then he got on the radio.

'I want twenty extra and fresh guards to the mansion. Other than them, let no one in but me. I want them fully armed, scattered immediately throughout the grounds around the house. And I want it now.'

They drove back, cross country, to the walled mansion on the foreland.

It was quarter to four.

# 31

# The Sting

After the searing heat of the sun on bare skin, the water of the stream was like balm. But it was dangerous water, for its speed was slowly increasing as it rushed between concrete banks to the sea.

At the point where he entered the water it would still have been possible for Dexter to climb out the other side. But he was too far from the point he needed to be and he heard the dogs far away. Also, he had seen the tree from his mountain-top, and even earlier in the aerial photographs.

His last piece of unused equipment was a small folding grapnel and a twenty-foot twine lanyard. As he swept between the banks, along a twisting course, he unfolded the three prongs, locked them rigid and slipped the loop of the lanyard round his right wrist.

He came round a corner in the torrent and saw the tree ahead. It grew on the bank, at the airfield side of the water, and two heavy branches leaned over the stream. As he approached, he reared out of the water, swung his arm, and hurled the grapnel high above him.

He heard the crash as the metal slammed into the tangle of branches, swept under the tree, felt the pain in his right arm socket as the hooks caught and the rush down-river stopped abruptly.

Hauling himself back on the twine, he crabbed his way to the bank and pulled his torso out. The water pressure eased, confined to his legs. With his free hand digging into the earth and grass, he dragged the rest of his body onto terra firma.

The grapnel was lost in the branches. He simply reached as high as he could, sliced the lanyard with his knife and let it flutter above the water. He knew he was a hundred yards from the airfield wire that he had cut forty hours earlier. There was nothing for it but to crawl. He put the nearest hounds at still a mile away and across the stream. They would find the bridges, but not just yet.

When he was lying in the darkness by the airfield's chain-link fence two nights earlier, he had cut a vertical and horizontal slice, to create two sides of a triangle, but left one thread intact to maintain the tension. The bolt-cutters he had pushed under the wire into the long grass, and that was where he found them.

The two cuts had been re-tied with thin, green plastic-coated gardener's wire. It took not a minute to unlace the cuts; he heard a dull twang as the tension wire was sliced, and he crawled through. Still on his belly, he turned and laced it up again. From only ten yards the cuts became invisible.

On the farmland side, the peons cut hay for forage on spare tracts of grassland, but each side of the runway it grew a foot long. Dexter found the bicycle and the other things he had stolen, dressed himself so as not to burn in the sun, and lay motionless to wait. A mile away, through the wire, he heard the hounds find the blooded clothes.

By the time Major van Rensberg, at the wheel of his Land Rover, reached the mansion gate, the fresh guards he had ordered were already there. A truck was stopped outside and the men jumped down, heavily armed and clutching M-16 assault carbines. The young officer lined them up in columns as the oaken gates swung apart. The column of men jogged through and quickly dispersed across the parkland. Van Rensberg followed and the gates closed.

The steps McBride had mounted to the pool terrace when he arrived were ahead of them, but the South African pulled to the right, round the terrace to the side. McBride saw doorways at the lower level and the electrically operated gates of three underground garages.

The butler was waiting. He ushered them inside and they followed him down a passage, past doors leading to the garages, up a flight of stairs and into the main living area.

The Serb was in the library. Although the late afternoon was balmy, he had chosen discretion over valour. He sat at a conference table with a cup of black coffee and gestured his two guests to sit down. His bodyguard, Kulac, loomed in the background, back against a wall of unread first editions, watchful.

'Report,' said Zilic, without ceremony. Van Rensberg had to make his humiliating confession that someone, acting alone, had slipped into his fortress, gained access to farmland by posing as a Latino labourer and escaped death by the dogs by killing a guard, dressing in his uniform and tossing the body into the fast-flowing stream.

'So where is he now?'

'Between the wall round this park and the chain-link protecting the village and airfield, sir.'

'And what do you intend to do?'

'Every single man under my command, every man who wears that uniform, will be called up by radio and checked for identity.'

'*Quis custodiet ipsos custodes?*' asked McBride. The other two looked at him blankly. 'Sorry. Who guards the guardians themselves? In other words, who checks the checkers? How do you know the voice on the radio isn't lying?'

There was silence.

'Right,' said van Rensberg. 'They will have to be recalled to barracks and checked on sight by their squad commanders. May I go to the radio shack and issue the orders?'

Zilic nodded dismissively.

It took an hour. Outside the windows the sun set across the chain of crests. The tropical plunge to darkness began. Van Rensberg came back.

'Every one accounted for at the barracks. All eighty attested to by their junior officers. And he's still out there somewhere.'

'Or inside the wall,' suggested McBride. 'Your fifth squad is the one patrolling this mansion.'

Zilic turned to his security chief.

'You ordered twenty of them in here without identity checks?' he asked icily.

'Certainly not, sir. They are the elite squad. They are commanded by Janni Duplessis. One strange face and he would have seen immediately.'

'Have him report here,' ordered the Serb.

The young South African appeared at the library door several minutes later, smartly to attention.

'Lieutenant Duplessis, in response to my order you chose twenty men including yourself, and brought them here by truck two hours ago?'

'Yes, sir.'

'You know every one of them by sight?'

'Yes, sir.'

'Forgive me, but when you jogged through the gate, what was your formation of march?' asked McBride.

'I was at the head. Sergeant Gray behind me. Then the men, three abreast, six per column. Eighteen men.'

'Nineteen,' said McBride. 'You forgot the tail ender.'

In the silence the mantelpiece clock seemed intrusively loud.

'What tail ender?' whispered van Rensberg.

'Hey, don't get me wrong, guys. I could have been mistaken. I thought a nineteenth man came round the corner of the truck and jogged through at the rear. Same uniform. I thought nothing of it.'

At that moment the clock struck six and the first bomb went off.

They were no bigger than golf balls and completely harmless, more like bird scarers than

398

weapons of war. They had eight-hour-delay timers and the Avenger had hurled all ten of them over the wall around 10 a.m. He knew exactly where the thickest shrubbery dotted the parkland round the house, from the aerial photographs, and in his teenage years he had been quite a good pitcher. The crackers did nevertheless make a sound on detonation remarkably similar to the whack-whump of a high-powered rifle shot.

In the library someone shouted, 'Cover,' and all five veterans hit the floor. Kulac, rolled, came up and stood over his master with his gun out. Then the first guard outside, believing he had spotted the gunman, fired back.

Two more bomblets detonated and the exchange of rifle fire intensified. A window shattered. Kulac fired back towards the darkness outside.

The Serb had had enough. He ran at a crouch through the door at the back of the library, along the corridor and down the steps to the basement. McBride followed suit, with Kulac bringing up the rear, facing backwards.

The radio room was off the lower corridor. The duty operator, when his employer burst in, was white-faced in the neon light, trying to cope with a welter of shouts and yells on the waveband of the guards' breast-pocket communicators.

'Speaker, identify. Where are you? What is going on?' he shouted. No one listened as the firefight in the darkness intensified. Zilic reached forward to his console and threw a switch. Silence descended.

'Raise the airfield. All pilots, all ground staff. I want my helicopter and I want it now.'

'It's not serviceable, sir. Ready tomorrow. They've been working on it for two days.'

'Then the Hawker. I want it airworthy.'

'Now, sir?'

'Now. Not tomorrow, not in an hour. Now.'

The crackle of fire in the far distance brought the man in the long grass to his knees. It was the deepest dusk before complete darkness, the hour when the eyes play tricks and shadows become threats. He lifted the bicycle to its wheels, put the toolbox in the front basket, pedalled across the runway to the escarpment side and began to cycle the mile and a half to the hangars at the far end. The mechanic's coveralls with the 'Z' logo of the Zeta Corporation on the back were unnoticeable in the dusk, and with a panic about to be launched, no one would remark on them for the next thirty minutes either.

The Serb turned on McBride.

'This is where we part company, Mr McBride. I fear you will have to return to Washington by your own means. The problem here will be sorted, and I shall be getting a new head of security. You can tell Mr Devereaux I shall not renege on our deal, but for the moment I intend to kill the intervening days enjoying the hospitality of friends of mine in the Emirates.'

The garage was at the end of the basement corridor and the Mercedes was armoured. Kulac drove, his employer seated in the rear. McBride stood helplessly in the garage as the door rolled up and back, the limousine slid under it, across

400

the gravel and out of the still opening gates in the wall.

By the time the Mercedes had rolled up to it, the hangar was ablaze with light. The small tractor was hitched to the nose-wheel assembly of the Hawker 1000 to tow it out onto the apron.

The last mechanic fastened down the last hatch on the engines, clattered down the gantry and pulled the structure away from the airframe. In the illuminated cockpit Captain Stepanovic, with his young French co-pilot beside him, was checking instruments, gauges and systems on the strength of the auxiliary power unit.

Zilic and Kulac watched from the shelter of the car. When the Hawker was out on the apron, the door opened, the steps hissed down, and the co-pilot could be seen in the opening.

Kulac left the car alone, jogged the few yards of concrete and ran up the steps into the sumptuous cabin. He glanced to his left towards the closed door of the flight deck. Two strides took him to the lavatory at the rear. He flung the door open. Empty. Returning to the top of the steps, he beckoned to his employer. The Serb left the car and ran to the steps. When he was inside, the door closed, locking them in to comfort and safety.

Outside, two men donned ear defenders. One plugged in the trolley accumulator and Captain Stepanovic started his engines. The two Pratt and Whitney 305s began to turn, then whine, then howl.

The second man stood way out front where the pilot could see him, a neon-lit bar in each hand. He guided the Hawker clear of the hangars and out to the edge of the apron.

Captain Stepanovic lined her up, tested brakes one last time, released them and powered both throttles.

The Hawker began to roll, faster and faster. To one side, miles away, the floodlights around the mansion flickered out, adding to the chaos. The nose lifted towards the sea and the north. To the left the escarpment raced by. The twinjet eased off the tarmac, the faint rumbling stopped, the cliff-edge villas went under the nose and she was out over the moonlit sea.

Captain Stepanovic brought up his undercarriage, handed over to the Frenchman and began to work out flight plan and track for a first fuel stop in the Azores. He had flown to the UAE several times, but never at thirty minutes' notice. The Hawker tilted to starboard, moving from her northwest take-off heading towards northeast, and passed through ten thousand feet.

Like most executive jets, the Hawker 1000 has a small but luxurious lavatory, right at the back, occupying the whole hull from side to side. And like some, the rear wall is a movable partition giving access to an even smaller cubbyhole for light luggage. Kulac had checked the lavatory, but not the luggage bay.

Five minutes into the flight, the crouching man in the mechanic's coveralls eased the partition aside and stepped into the washroom. He removed the Sig Sauer 9mm automatic from the toolbox, checked the mechanism yet again, eased off the safety catch and walked into the salon. The two men in the rawhide club chairs facing each other stared at him in silence.

'You'll never dare use it,' said the Serb. 'It will penetrate the hull and blow us all away.'

'The slugs have been doctored,' said Avenger evenly. 'One quarter charge. Enough to punch a hole in you, stay inside and kill you, but never go through the hull. Tell your boy I want his piece out, finger and thumb, on the carpet.'

There was a short exchange in Serbo-Croat. His face dark with rage, the bodyguard eased out his Glock from the left armpit holster and dropped it.

'Kick it toward me,' said Dexter. Zilic complied.

'And the ankle gun.'

Kulac wore a smaller back-up gun taped round his left ankle, under the sock. This was also kicked out of range. Avenger produced a pair of handcuffs and tossed them to the carpet.

'Your pal's left ankle. Do it yourself. In vision all the time or you lose a kneecap. And yes, I am that good.'

'A million dollars,' said the Serb.

'Get on with it,' said the American.

'Cash, any bank you like.'

'I'm losing patience.'

The handcuff went on.

'Tighter.'

Kulac winced as the metal bit.

'Round the seat stanchion. And to the right wrist.'

'Ten million. You're a fool to say no.'

The answer was a second pair of cuffs . . .

'Left wrist, through your friend's chain, then right wrist. Back up. Stay in my vision or you're the one saying adios to the kneecap.'

The two men crouched, side by side, on the floor, tethered to each other and the assembly holding the seat to the floor, which Dexter hoped would be stronger even than the giant bodyguard.

Avoiding their grip he stepped round them and walked to the cabin door. The captain presumed the opening door was his owner coming forward to ask for progress. The barrel of the gun nudged his temple.

'It is Captain Stepanovic, isn't it?' said a voice. Washington Lee, who had intercepted the email from Wichita, had told him.

'I have nothing against you,' said the hijacker. 'You and your friend here are simply professionals. So am I. Let's keep it that way. Professionals do not do stupid things if they can be avoided. Agreed?'

The captain nodded. He tried to glance behind him, into the cabin.

'Your owner and his bodyguard are disarmed and chained to the fuselage. There will be no help coming. Please do just as I say.'

'What do you want?'

'Alter course.' Avenger glanced at the Electronic Flight Instrument System just above the throttles. 'I suggest Three-One-Five degrees, compass true, should be about right. Skirt the eastern tip of Cuba, as we have no flight plan.'

'Final destination?'

'Key West, Florida.'

'The USA?'

'Land of my fathers,' said the man with the gun.

# 32

## The Rendition

Dexter had memorized the route from San Martin to Key West, but there was no need. The avionics on the Hawker are so clear that even a non-flier can follow the liquid crystal display showing intended course and line of track.

Forty minutes out from the coast he saw the blur of Grenada's lights slip under the starboard wing. Then came the two hours of over-water haul to make landfall on the south coast of the Dominican Republic.

After two more, between the coast of Cuba and the Bahamas' biggest island, Andros, he leaned forward and touched the Frenchman's ear with the tip of the automatic.

'Disconnect the transponder now.'

The co-pilot looked across at the Yugoslav who shrugged and nodded. The co-pilot switched it off. With the transponder, designed to pulse out an endlessly repeated identification signal, disconnected, the Hawker was reduced simply to a speck on the radar screen of someone looking very closely indeed. To anyone not looking that closely, it had ceased to exist. But it had also announced it was a suspect intruder.

405

South of Florida, reaching far out over the sea, is the Air Defence Identification Zone, designed to protect the south-eastern flank of the USA from the continuous war of the drug smugglers. Anyone entering ADIZ without a flight plan was playing hide and seek with some very sophisticated metal.

'Drop to four hundred feet above the sea,' said Dexter. 'Dive and dive now. All nav and cabin lights off.'

'That is very low,' said the pilot as the nose dropped through thirty thousand feet. The aircraft went dark.

'Pretend it's the Adriatic. You've done it before.'

It was true. As a fighter pilot in the Yugoslav Air Force, Colonel Stepanovic had led dummy attacks against the Croatian coast at well below four hundred feet to slip under the radar. Still, he was right.

The moonlit sea at night is mesmeric. It can lure the low-flying pilot down and down until he flips the surface of the waves, rolls in and dies. Altimeters under five hundred feet have to be spot-on accurate and constantly checked. Ninety miles southeast of Islamorada the Hawker levelled at four hundred feet and raced over the Santaren Channel towards the Florida Keys. Coming in at sea level those last ninety miles almost fooled the radar.

'Key West Airport, runway Two-Seven,' said Dexter. He had studied the layout of his chosen landfall. Key West Airport faces east-west, with one runway along that axis. All the passenger

406

and ops buildings are at the eastern end. To land heading west would put the entire length of the runway between the Hawker and the vehicles racing towards it. Runway Two-Seven means point to compass heading 270, or due west.

At fifty miles from touchdown they were spotted. Twenty miles north of Key West is Cudjoe Key, home to a huge balloon tethered to a cable and riding twenty thousand feet in the sky. Where most coastal radars look outwards and up, the Cudjoe eye-in-the-sky looks down. Its radars can see any aeroplane trying to slip in under the net.

Even balloons need occasional maintenance, and the one at Cudjoe is brought down at random intervals which are never announced. It had been down that evening by chance and was heading back up. At ten thousand feet it saw the Hawker coming out of the black sea, transponder off, no flight plan. Within seconds two F-16s on duty alert at Pensacola Air Force Base were barrelling down the runway, going straight to afterburn once they cleared the deck.

Climbing and breaking the sound barrier, the Fighting Falcons formated then headed south for the last of the Keys. Thirty miles out, Captain Stepanovic was down to two hundred knots and lining up. The lights of Cudjoe and Sugarloaf Keys twinkled to starboard. The fighters' look-down radars picked up the intruder and the pilots altered course a tad to come in from behind. Against the Hawker's two hundred knots the Falcons were moving at over a thousand.

As it happened George Tanner was duty

controller at Key West that night and was within minutes of closing the airport down when the alarm was raised. The position of the intruder indicated it was actually trying to land, which was the smart thing to do. Darkened intruders with lights and transponder switched off are given, after fighter interception, one warning to do as they are told and land where they are told. There are no second warnings: the war against the drug smugglers is too serious for games.

Still and all, a plane can have an on-board emergency and deserves a chance to land. The light stayed on. Twenty miles out the crew of the Hawker could see the lights of the runway glowing ahead of them. Above and behind, the F-16s began to drop and air-brake. For them two hundred knots was almost landing speed.

Ten miles from touchdown the Falcons found the darkened Hawker by the red glow from the jet efflux each side of its tail. The first the aircrew in the cabin knew, the deadly fighters were formating with each wing tip.

'Unidentified twin jet, look ahead and land. I say look ahead and land,' said a voice in the captain's ear.

Undercarriage came down, with one-third flap. The Hawker adopted its landing posture. Chica Key Naval Air Station swept past to the right. The Hawker's main wheels felt for the touch-down markings, found the concrete and it was down on US territory.

For the last hour Dexter had had the spare earphones over his head and the mike in front of his mouth. As the wheels hit the tarmac he keyed the transmit button.

'Unidentified Hawker jet to Key West Tower, do you read?'

The voice of George Tanner came clearly into his ears.

'Read you five.'

'Tower, this airplane contains a mass murderer and a killer of an American in the Balkans. He is manacled to his seat. Please inform your police chief to exercise close custody and await the federal marshals.'

Before waiting for a reply, he disconnected and turned to Captain Stepanovic.

'Go right to the far end, stop there and I'll leave you,' said the hijacker. He rose and pocketed his gun. Behind the Hawker the Crash/Fire/Rescue trucks left the airport buildings and came after them.

'Door open please,' said Dexter.

He left the flight deck and walked back through the cabin as the lights came on. The two prisoners blinked in the glare. Through the open door Dexter could see the trucks racing towards them. Flashing red/blues indicated police cars. The wailing sirens were faint but getting closer.

'Where are we?' shouted Zoran Zilic.

'Key West,' said Dexter.

'Why?'

'Remember a meadow? In Bosnia? Spring of ninety-five? An American kid pleading for his life? Well, pal, all this' — he waved his hand outside — 'is a present from the boy's grandpa.'

He walked down the steps and strode to the

nose-wheel assembly. Two bullets blew out the tyres. The boundary fence was twenty yards away. The dark coveralls were soon lost in the blackness as he vaulted the chain-link and walked away through the mangrove.

The airport lights behind him dimmed through the trees but he began to make out the flashes of car and truck headlights on the highway beyond the swamp. He pulled out a cellphone and dialled by the glow of the tiny screen. Far away in Windsor, Ontario, a man answered.

'Mr Edmond?'

'This is he.'

'The package from Belgrade that you asked for has landed at Key West airport, Florida.'

He said no more and barely heard the yell at the other end before disconnecting. Just to be sure, the cellphone spun away into the brackish swamp water beside the track to be lost for ever.

Ten minutes later a senator in Washington was roused from his dinner and within an hour two marshals from the Federal Marshal Service Bureau in Miami were speeding south.

Before the marshals were through Islamorada, a teamster driving north, just out of Key West, on the US1, saw a lone figure by the roadside. Thinking the coveralls meant a stranded trucker, he stopped.

'I'm going up as far as Marathon,' he called down. 'Any use?'

'Marathon will do just fine,' said the man. It was twenty before midnight.

It took Kevin McBride the whole of the 9th to

410

find his way home. Major van Rensberg, still trying to find the missing impostor, consoling himself that at least his employer was safe, despatched the CIA man as far as the capital city. Colonel Moreno fixed him a passage from the airport to Paramaribo. A KLM flight ferried him to Curaçao Island. There was a connector to Miami International and thence a shuttle to Washington. He landed very late and very tired. On the Monday morning he was early when he walked into Paul Devereaux's office but his chief was already there.

He looked ashen. He seemed to have aged. He gestured McBride to a seat and wearily pushed a sheet across the desk.

All good reporters go out of their way to maintain an excellent contact with the police forces of their area. They would be crazy not to. The Key West correspondent of the *Miami Herald* was no exception. The events of the Saturday night were leaked to him by friends on the Key West force by Sunday noon and his report filed well in time for the Monday edition. It was a synopsis of the story that Devereaux found on his desk that Monday morning.

The tale of a Serbian warlord and suspected mass murderer detained in his own jet after an emergency landing at Key West International had made the third lead on the front page.

'Good Lord,' whispered McBride as he read. 'We thought he had escaped.'

'No. It seems he was hijacked,' said Devereaux. 'You know what this means, Kevin? No, of course you don't. My fault. I should have explained to you. Project Peregrine is dead. Two years of work down the Swanee. It cannot go forward without him.'

Line by line, the intellectual explained the conspiracy he had devised to accomplish the greatest anti-terrorist strike of the century.

'When was he due to fly to Karachi and on to the Peshawar meeting?'

'The twentieth. I just needed that extra ten days.'

He rose and walked to the window, gazing out at the trees, his back to McBride.

'I have been here since dawn, when a phone call woke me with the news. Asking myself: how did he do it, this damnable, bloody man Avenger?'

McBride was silent, mute in his sympathy.

'Not a stupid man, Kevin. I will not have it that I was bested by a stupid man. Clever, more than I could have thought. Always just one step ahead of me . . . He must have known he was up against me. Only one man could have told him. And you know who that was, Kevin?'

'No idea, Paul.'

'That sanctimonious bastard in the FBI called Colin Fleming. But even tipped off, how did he beat me? He must have guessed we would engage the cooperation of the Surinam embassy here. So he invented Professor Medvers Watson, butterfly hunter extraordinaire. And fictional. And a decoy. I should have spotted it, Kevin. The professor was a phoney and he was meant to be discovered. Two days ago I got news from our people in Surinam. Know what they told me?'

'No, Paul.'

'That the real cover-name, the Englishman Henry Nash, got his visa in Amsterdam. We never thought of Amsterdam. Clever, clever bastard. So Medvers Watson went in and died in the jungle. As intended. And it bought the man six days while we proved it was a sting. By then he was inside and watching the estate from the mountaintop. Then you went in.'

'But I missed him too, Paul.'

'Only because that idiot South African refused to listen to you. Of course the chloroformed peon had to be discovered in the mid-morning. Of course the alarm had to be raised. To bring the dogs in. To permit the third sting, the presumption that he had murdered a guard and taken his place.'

'But I was at fault as well, Paul. I honestly thought I saw an extra guard trotting into the mansion grounds in the dusk. Apparently there wasn't one. By dawn they were all accounted for.'

'By then it was too late. He had hijacked the aircraft.'

Devereaux turned from the window and walked over to his deputy. He held out his hand.

'Kevin, we all slipped up. He won, I lost. But I appreciate everything you did and tried to do. As for Colin Fleming, the moralizing bastard who tipped him off, I'll deal with him in my own time. For the moment, we have to start again. UBL is still out there. Still planning. Still plotting. I want the whole team in here tomorrow at eight. Coffee and Danish. We'll catch the CNN news, then go into a major session. Autopsy and forward planning. Where we go from here.'

McBride turned to go.

'You know,' said Devereaux as he reached the door, 'if there's one thing that thirty years in this agency has taught me, it's this. There are some levels of loyalty that command us beyond even the call of duty.'

# EPILOGUE
## The Loyalty

Kevin McBride walked down the hall and turned into the executive washroom. He felt drained; days of travelling, worrying, not sleeping, had left him exhausted.

He stared at his tired face in the mirror above the hand basins and wondered at Devereaux's last Delphic remark. Would Project Peregrine have worked? Would the Saudi master-terrorist have fallen for it? Would his acolytes have showed up in Peshawar in ten days? Would they have made the vital phone call for the listening NSA to intercept?

Too late now. Zilic would never travel again, save to a US courtroom and thence to a maximum security jail. What was done was done.

He dunked his face a dozen times and stared at the man in the mirror. Fifty-six, going on fifty-seven. A thirty-year man, due to take his pension at the end of December.

In the spring, he and Molly would do what he had long promised. Their son and daughter were through college and making their own careers. He wanted his daughter and her husband to make him a grandchild whom he could spoil rotten. While waiting, they would buy the big motorhome he had promised Molly and go see the Rockies. He knew he had a rendezvous with some serious cut-throat trout up in Montana.

A much younger agent, a newly joined GS12, came out of a cubicle and began to wash his hands two basins down. One of the team. They nodded and smiled. McBride took paper towels and dabbed his face dry.

'Kevin,' said the youngster.

'Yep.'

'Mind if I ask you a question?'

'Ask away.'

'It's kind of personal.'

'Then maybe I won't answer it.'

'The tattoo on your left arm. The grinning rat with his pants down. What does it mean?'

McBride was still looking in the mirror, but he seemed to see two young GIs, rat-assed on beer and wine, laughing in the warm Saigon night, and a white petromax lamp hissing, and a Chinese tattooist at work. Two young Americans who would part company, but be bound by a bond that nothing could ever break. And he saw a slim file a few weeks earlier, which mentioned a tattoo of a grinning rat on the left forearm. And he heard the order to find the man, and have him killed.

He slipped his bracelet watch back on his wrist and flipped his sleeve back down. He checked the day-date window. Tenth September, 2001.

'It's quite a story, son,' said the Badger, 'and it all happened long ago and far away.'